"*Hot Girl* is a must-read. . . . Kate is a young girl struggling to stay positive in the midst of the notorious foster care system. Her wit and perception as she narrates this tale will make readers laugh, cry, and cheer her on. This is a no-holds-barred, tell-it-like-it-is tale that every young person can learn from. Dream Jordan has burst on the scene in a big way!"

—Tracy Brown, *Essence* bestselling author of *White Lines*

"Readers will fall in love with Jordan's triumphant heroine as she navigates the foster care system with wisdom, wit, endurance, and hope. . . . A refreshing and touching read."

—Kalisha Buckhanon, Alex Award–winning author of *Upstate* and *Conception*

"Teen readers will relate to the smart, strong-willed protagonist, Kate. . . . Jordan's thoughtfully rendered characterizations and explanations for Kate's behavior are refreshingly authentic. This novel has the makings of a YA classic, and every YA collection should have a copy. Readers will hope for a sequel." —Vanessa J. Irvin Morris, Drexel University, for *Library Journal*

"Dream Jordan's *Hot Girl* is a fantastic first novel . . . the content reflects the struggles and choices facing a young girl wanting to belong with her peers and also within a family. My students have showered accolades on *Hot Girl*." —Amy Cheney for *School Library Journal*

"Characterizations are strong, and voices realistic. . . . Jordan sends a message about doing the right thing. . . . The outcome of Kate's story is positive, and those looking for soft street-lit titles will find the book appealing." —Emily Anne Valente, New York Public Library, for *School Library Journal*

LOVE ME
OR
MISS ME

Dream Jordan

LOVE ME OR MISS ME

WEDNESDAY BOOKS
NEW YORK

LOVE ME OR MISS ME: HOT GIRL. Copyright © 2008 by Dream Jordan. BAD BOY. Copyright © 2012 by Dream Jordan. All rights reserved. Printed in the United States of America. For information, address St. Martin's Press, 175 Fifth Avenue, New York, N.Y. 10010.

www.wednesdaybooks.com
www.stmartins.com

The Library of Congress Cataloging-in-Publication Data is available upon request.

ISBN 978-1-250-30821-4 (trade paperback)

Our books may be purchased in bulk for promotional, educational, or business use. Please contact your local bookseller or the Macmillan Corporate and Premium Sales Department at 1-800-221-7945, extension 5442, or by email at MacmillanSpecialMarkets@macmillan.com.

First Edition: January 2019

10 9 8 7 6 5 4 3 2 1

This book is dedicated to all children in foster care.

Acknowledgments

I am blessed in my Dream Team: Daniel Lazar, a brilliant and fearless agent; Kia DuPree, the most supportive and knowledgeable editor I've ever met; Eliani Torres, my astute copy editor; and the whole St. Martin's team.

Special thanks to the key players in my YA publishing pursuit: Monique Patterson, Sue Shapiro, Sean Eve, Faith, Rebecca, and Courtney.

I am indebted to P.S. 41's seventh and eighth graders who were my first readers and cheerleaders when I began my novel's journey in 2005. Many thanks to my other youthful inspirers: Jasmine, Stacey, Miyls, Jaime, and the young ladies from Elizabeth NAACP Youth Council.

I appreciate and will always remember New Youth Connections for giving me my first byline. Also, good looking out to the early believers in my writing ability, including members of the Tom Joyner message board, my circle of Law School angels, and former classmates of NYU.

A big shout-out to my unknown readers on MySpace who took the time to critique my first chapter and pushed me to complete the work. Many thanks to all who assisted in my research.

And finally, this novel would not have been possible had it not been for the love and encouragement from my closest friends and family. You know who you are. Thank you for being there through trying and doubtful times. Your unwavering support means the world to me. I am forever grateful.

Chapter 1

The hot July sun beamed down on me, but I was in no mood to beam back. The scorching heat had baked the bleachers to a hundred degrees, and my backside was on *fire*. Talk about having a hot booty for all the wrong reasons. If I could afford a pair of breezy capris, I'd be sporting them instead of these shabby short-shorts; right about now, my big old thighs were getting fried like chicken. Not cool. Not cool at all.

It was bad enough this basketball game already had me heated. Instead of popping my collar with pride, I was asking, Why? What was the matter with Charles's game? See, in the beginning, I sat cozy in my front-row seat watching my baby put Crown Heights to shame. Again and again, he glided effortlessly across the concrete, danced his way to the baseline, jumped up to the sky, and then *swishhhh*, the ball was in there. In there every time. Then all of a sudden—*blip*—Charles started losing steam, missing shots galore.

Where, oh where, did my baby's skills go?

But hold up. Wait a minute. Let me keep it real. Charles is not my baby. He's just my homeboy, my dream boy, someone I've known since the second grade and started secretly crushing on in the eighth. And to be honest, I wouldn't know what to do with Charles if he fell into my lap. . . . I never even had a boyfriend before.

Still, Charles was the main reason I stayed glued to my seat. He's a picture of loveliness you just can't turn away from. Soaring six feet tall, covered in the creamiest dark brown skin—how could I *not* stay benched in order to make goo-goo eyes at him?

But the problem with his game remained. Charles was now hogging the ball without making a single hoop. I was so disappointed, I was tempted to leap from my seat, snatch the rock, and land a couple of wicked jump shots my dang self. This was one of the hottest games of the summer, seemed like everybody from the Stuy was present, and I wanted Charles to handle the court like I knew he could. Around the way, Charles is known as the shot-blocker, always ready, never scared, commanding the court like a king. But today, he was playing like a court jester, straight-up clowning himself.

Finally, I couldn't take it anymore. I yelled between cupped hands, "Yo, Charlie, what are you waiting for? Don't hold the ball. Dunk it like a doughnut!"

I was alone at this game, and yelling crazy with the rest of the crowd. That's how I get down when it comes to basketball. I get amped and rowdy, yes sir.

As Charles dribbled up to the net, I leaned forward in anticipation, counting on him to score. Instead, he passed the ball to a clumsy teammate who ended up missing the shot. I was ready to yell at him again, when a girl sitting one row behind me suddenly shouted to her friend, "Yo, check out this *trick* coming our way."

"Good *lawd*, she's lookin' mighty stink in pink!"

"Yeah, homegirl must shop at Sluts-Are-Us." They busted into a fit of loud laughter, sounding like a pair of goofy hyenas.

Tired of watching Charles foul and fumble, I twisted around to sneak a peek at these girls. Both broads were light-skinned, their heads done up in braids, and their necks twisted to the far right. I looked to my right, and—*boom!*—I spotted their target: a golden-brown model-thin bombshell cutting across the basketball court. She was decked to the nines in a super-tight pink terry cloth jumpsuit, and her long shiny hair was flowing in the wind. A pair of black dazzling sunglasses hid half her face, and to complete her luxurious look, a deluxe tan Gucci tote bag hung from her right shoulder, although it looked kinda flat, like she wasn't carrying anything inside. Ms. Thing resembled a hoochied-up high-fashion model, so I decided to give her the nick-name Gucci Girl.

I'm quick to give somebody a nickname; it's just something I do. Like, my real name's Kate, but I secretly call myself Diamond. Why? First of all, because I'm hard as a rock, my skin dark as coal, and I'm as cool as ice. . . . Well, at least I try to be cool. Most of all, I dig the name Diamond because my real name is straight-up corny for a girl from the hood. . . . But it's the name I was given by my deadbeat parents, so oh well, whatever, just call me Kate.

Gucci Girl slowly made her way across the court, tossing her long hair, switching her booty so hard, I thought her hip bones would break. The bounce in her step was determined, like she was trying to prove something to somebody. What did she have to prove? Fly as can be? Don't ask me. Shucks, if I dared walk next to her wearing my shabby gear, onlookers would've sworn I was a bum begging homegirl for a handout.

I was in a sorry state. And the sad thing? No matter how many times I try to come across like a million bucks, I come rolling out the house looking like a million wooden nickels. But what could I do? I'd landed on the Johnsons' doorstep resembling a rag doll, and based on my first shopping spree with my foster mother, Lynn, it seemed like I would stay looking raggedy.

From the jump, my clothing situation was all jacked up. After being removed from yet another nightmarish foster home, I wound up in a temporary group home, where most of my clothes had gotten stolen.

As soon as Lynn and Ted received me, Lynn pounced on my emergency clothing allowance. "We're going shopping," she had announced in a loud official voice. Now I thought I was grown enough to take myself shopping. But oh well, I guess I thought wrong.

On shopping day, however, my head was all gassed up. After Lynn's big production over my clothing predicament, I just knew we'd swagger through Macy's, with me picking out this fly shirt and those fabulous jeans. But nope, as soon as we got off the A train in downtown Brooklyn, I found myself stomping through a no-name store filled with no-name clothes, and the clothes were so tacky and cheap-looking,

I wanted to cry. Lynn aimed straight for all the clearance sections, racking up three pairs of blah-blah baggy jeans, two pairs of nameless shorts, five plain-Jane T-shirts, and a bag of white giant grandma underwear. I almost got me a new pair of sneakers—until I made the mistake of opening my big fat mouth. "But these are rejects," I said, frowning at the wannabe-leather white frights. (Reject sneakers are way more obvious than reject clothing, feel me?)

Lynn stared at me with her big bubble eyes and said, "Okay, they're rejects, and?"

"And they're not cute," I explained. "I'll get clowned on."

"By who?" Lynn demanded.

"Kids around the way . . . kids at school—"

"Do these kids put any food in your mouth?"

"No."

"Do these kids put a roof over your head?"

"No."

"Okay, now do you see my point?"

"Yes," I lied. But no, I did not see her point. All I could *see* were kids pointing and laughing at me if I rocked those cornball sneakers on my feet. Lynn must've sensed I was lying, because she raised one eyebrow and glared at me for what felt like an hour. Without saying a word, she yanked the sneakers from my shopping basket and placed them back on the shelf.

"What happened?" I asked in disbelief.

"How about you get *no* new sneakers and keep the raggedy pair you have on," Lynn explained. "Bet that'll teach you not to worry about what other people say. See, you're going to learn to think differently while living in my home."

"I'm sorry," I said, hoping she'd change her mind and buy me a different pair.

Lynn just looked at me with one raised eyebrow and shrugged. "It's too late for sorry."

It took all of my might not to roll my eyes at her. Instead, I looked off into the distance, dreaming of a better day.

Man, I was pissed—but I wasn't surprised. First of all, Lynn was decked out in rejects, too, looking like corn on the cob in her long drabby yellow skirt, and her whack-as-ever hairstyle—I'm saying, who wears a part in the middle of their head in the twenty-first century? So I could see how she felt justified considering her lack of fashion taste.

Second of all, I had already been warned about how Lynn gets down by my social worker, Ms. Tisha Adams, best lady in my life. Before I stepped foot inside the Johnson household, Tisha had prepped me like I was about to go into the ring. "Don't let Lynn scare you," Tisha warned. "She's really soft on the inside, but comes off hard, and comes out fighting. You just have to get used to her."

Well . . . it's been close to six months now in the Johnson household, and so far, I've been okay. Ted is crazy cool. I'm getting used to crazy Lynn. And I just have to make the best out of my situation. My parents voluntarily terminated their parental rights when I was one years old; they aren't coming back for me. I don't know who, what, when, where they are . . . and I don't have any other family members coming forward. So all I can do now is lay low in the Johnson household. At least here I get fed. Got a roof over my head. I don't get hit. Guess I really don't need to be dolled up in order to survive.

Clearly, Gucci Girl's heart was beating solely for fashion. Seemed like she couldn't live without radiating style and flash. Her fierce sexy strut was killing all the boys sitting in my row, and the females were gasping for breath too, examining homegirl harder than an algebra test. I swear the game almost came to a complete stop upon Gucci Girl's grand arrival.

"*Charles, don't look!*" That's what I wanted to scream. Nevertheless, Gucci Girl was gangster enough to hijack everybody's attention—including Charles's. So what could I do? I couldn't blame her; I couldn't hate. If you have it like that, you need to rock it like that. Trust, if I had it like that, I would be rocking it fierce and lovely too.

Of all places to sit, Gucci Girl chose to squeeze in right next to me. Who needed this extra body heat? And the minute she sat down, the jealous broads behind us huffed an extra loud, "Oh buh-rutha!"

Gucci Girl wisely played deaf.

I watched her from the side of my eye. She slowly removed her sunglasses, stuffed them inside her bag, and daintily dug for something else, but came up empty-handed. A split-second later, she caught me off guard by leaning over and jabbing me with her elbow. "Excuse me, you got a loosey?" she asked, staring at me wide-eyed. She had the hazel eyes of a black cat. They glowed in the sun.

Hmm, this girl had a lot of nerve jabbing me like she knew me. You don't know me. Don't touch me. I have trust issues, okay? But I remained cool.

Poor Ms. Gucci's right leg was moving a mile a minute, like she was having a serious nicotine fit. I felt kinda bad for her. "Sorry, don't smoke anymore," I explained.

Between me and you, I'm so glad I quit smoking. Never did like the taste of it. I *did* like the coolness I felt, though, lighting up with the older girls from my old group home. We used to sit in the park, smoking and joking till curfew. These girls rode around in fancy whips, rocked fabulous clothes, smoked weed, and got drunk. I used to feel so privileged smoking with them. . . . Well, not exactly smoking. As everybody inhaled and exhaled every few seconds, I took one or two puffs, then held the cig in my hand, trying to look smooth as I let it burn down to the butt. When I left that group home, I left my bad habit there too. Saved me some money and the threat of yellow teeth.

Gucci Girl rolled her eyes to the blue sky. "Got gum?"

I shook my head, and again she ho-hummed.

As I sat, wondering why this chick was treating me like a convenience store, she hit me up with another request. "The time?"

I extended my bare wrists to show her—no watch. That's when she exploded into singsong laughter, showing off two rows of perfect white teeth.

I politely chuckled with her. Then I got to wondering how on earth a desperate smoker could have such perfectly white teeth. As a matter of fact, everything about this girl was practically perfect: her perfect jewel-like teeth, her perfect pretty-in-pink jumpsuit, and her perfect sparkling-white Air Jordans, twinkling and glistening, like they'd just been pulled out of the box. How could she dress all fresh and act a hot mess? I mean really, stop begging!

"My bad, I should've come prepared," Gucci Girl suddenly said, as if reading my thoughts. Then she covered her mouth, "I just hope my breath ain't kicking. You know I need fresh breath for my boo."

Boo who? Gucci Girl was acting so familiar with me, as if we had met ten years ago instead of ten minutes. I wasn't used to girls (especially girls who looked like her) coming at me so strong. Look, I'm hard. She's soft. I had on dry clothes. She had on fizzy-fly clothes. I mean, I felt flattered by her attention, but I was still confused.

I had to find out where this girl's head was at. I waited a few seconds, and then asked, "Who are you rooting for?"

"Okay, see the dude in the blue T-shirt?" Gucci Girl pointed a long pink fingernail in Charles's direction. My stomach dipped down to my raggedy sneakers. I wanted to cry. Of all the guys! "Um, Charles invited you here?" I asked.

"Oh . . . you know Charles too?" asked Gucci Girl.

"Who *doesn't* know Charles?"

"Yeah, that's true, he *is* the man." Gucci Girl smiled, more to herself than me. Then she explained, "But I'm talking about the dude in the light-blue tee, behind Charles. . . . See him?"

"Okay, I see him," I said with a sigh of relief.

"Yeah, that's my boo, Finesse. He practically begged me to come to this game. Ain't he fine?"

"Indeed," I agreed. Finesse did look good. He was super-tall, had velvety dark brown skin, and wore his shorts down low, just like my baby. I never noticed this cutie pie before. Matter of fact, I was just getting started with this boy-watching business, and Charles was my main focus right now.

Out of the blue, Gucci Girl patted my leg. "Girl, let me tell you, if I wasn't here for Finesse? I'd surely be trying to holler at Charles, okay?"

"Oh, for real?" I said, hoping she couldn't feel me trembling beside her.

"Mm, Charles could definitely get it." Gucci Girl greedily licked her lips. "He's looking good enough to eat, okay?"

"You better back up, broad!" Well, that's what I wanted to say. Instead, I said, "Yeah, Charles is cute." There was *no* way I was going to let Gucci Girl know about my crush. Revealing crushes has a way of backfiring. Usually, once you like a dude, he suddenly becomes very interesting to your homegirl. I mean, I never had to worry about my best friend, Felicia. But this flamboyant chick? Couldn't trust her at all.

Suddenly, she playfully pushed my arm and said, "I don't even believe you think Charles is just cute. That boy is not cute—he's fine! Matter of fact, I was in his class, but he—"

"Say what?" I interrupted in disbelief. "You went to P.S. 342?"

Gucci Girl ran her fingers through her shiny hair like a movie star and said, "Yeah . . . but I came in at the end of February. I just moved here from Maryland and got thrown straight into Charles's class. Let me tell you, *all* the girls were on his jock. He had a different girl in his face every week. I didn't even try to compete."

I tilted my head and stared at Ms. Gucci for a full minute, then said, "I swear you had to be hiding in a locker somewhere, 'cause I surely don't remember seeing you." *Surely* I would've noticed a fabulous chick like Gucci Girl switching her butt around my junior high school.

"Well, I remember seeing you . . . skipping in the hallways with this tall doofy-looking chick."

"Don't dis," I said. "My homegirl ain't doofy."

Seeing the sudden scowl on my face, Gucci Girl flipped the script back to Charles. "Well, Charles never paid me no mind in class. He didn't even know I existed. But I changed a whole lot since the summer started. Bet he'll notice me now." Gucci Girl winked at me.

I didn't appreciate the wink. Didn't appreciate her sly grin. I had to change the subject before I got myself all worked up. "Anyway, I was asking which team you want to win."

"Oh, I'm rooting for Finesse . . . whatever team he's on."

"Okay," I said, disappointed. Gucci Girl was rooting for the wrong team: Crown Heights. And now I knew exactly where her head was at: up Finesse's butt. True enough, I was mainly here for Charles and sweating him just as hard—but dang, at least I cared about my baby's team!

Then again, I couldn't expect every girl to be crazy about basketball. Can't be pushing balls into a prissy princess's court. And that's exactly why I didn't bother bringing any friends with me to the game in the first place. . . . Um . . . not that I had any to bring. See, my best and only friend, Felicia, had gotten accepted into this once-in-a-lifetime summer program in South Africa. And I had chosen not to go. So basically, I was stuck in Brooklyn for the rest of the summer, with no one to talk to, no one to hang with. Just stuck.

I guess that's why my defenses were down when it came to Gucci Girl. Who else could I hang with until Felicia got back?

Well . . . I could've tried to hang with some new girls. But the thing is, I'm not crazy. New girls are way too choosy for me to try to be chummy-chummy with. You know how they do. Flash them a smile, and they just look you up and down like, *Who the heck is you?* Around my way, it seems like there's nothing but fly girls or gangsters to choose from. And fly girls put the peer pressure on you just as bad as gangsters—only difference is they're packing lipstick instead of heat. Bottom line: I wasn't about to do flips in order to belong to *any* cliques. Feel me?

So with Gucci Girl by my side, I just went with the flow. Now that I had company, I was shouting at the players even louder. I was like, "What are you doing, man? Yoke the ball! *Yoke it!*" And Gucci Girl was like, "What do you mean, 'yoke it'?" When the excitement died down, I turned to Gucci Girl and explained, "Hey, a yoke is like a thunderous dunk. You know—*bam*—in the net. . . ." I used my hands to show her what I meant. But my voice trailed off once I realized she was paying me no mind.

In a flash, she had whipped out her pocket mirror, and her eyes were now glued to her image. Hmm, okay. So even when it came down to her looks, Gucci Girl was clueless. She didn't seem to know she was already fabulous. Flawless. She ogled her reflection with the deepest concentration, redoing her glossy pink lips, fluffing out her long and shiny hair. . . . Meanwhile I was wishing I had hair like hers.

Finally, she clicked her mirror shut. "By the way, my name's Naleejah." She moved her Gucci bag over and stretched out her hand to shake mine. In awe of her crazy long pink glittery nails, I was almost afraid to grab hold.

"Hello? What's your name?" Naleejah laughed.

Oh. I wanted to say *Diamond*, but too late, I blurted out, "Kate."

Kate?

If I ever did meet my parents again in this lifetime, I'd have to ask why the heck they couldn't dump me off with a creative, exotic name with some flavor. Naleejah's name rang in my head like a million bells. *Bong! Bong! Ding dong!*

"How old are you?" asked Naleejah.

"Fourteen."

"Wow," Naleejah exclaimed. "Fourteen and built like a brick house? Girl, if I had your body, I'd be killing the boys even more than I do now!"

Embarrassed, I skipped over her comment and asked, "Well, how old are you?" I was just curious because she wore makeup and was dressed like a twenty-year-old but had a baby face just like mine. (I have those squeeze-me chubby cheeks, and she has that wide-eyed innocent look.) Since she had been in Charles's class, I knew she couldn't have been that much older than me—unless she got left back a couple of times.

"I turn fifteen in August," said Naleejah.

"Oh snap, me too." Finally, we had something in common!

Then out of nowhere, Naleejah started eyeballing my face like a curious cat. "When did you get that?" she asked, pointing at my face. She was referring to the small C-shaped scar over my right eye. But why was she being so nosy?

"I been had this," I explained. "Four years ago . . . my gang—"

"You're in a gang!" Naleejah cried out.

"I *used* to be," I corrected.

I joined the Lady Killers at age eleven, and I was the youngest of the gang. It was easy for me to get in because of my bad-girl rep around the way, but hard for me to get out because I had pledged gangster fo' life.

I lasted only two months. True, I liked to fight, but the Lady Killers went for blood. There were five of us: Crash, Icy, Killah, Menace, and me—Rocky. But I was the softest out the crew. These girls thought nothing of robbing chicks for their jewels and slicing the faces of those who resisted. I witnessed plenty of lock-in-the-sock and swing-on-somebody moments. Though I never swung a sock myself, I watched girls get swung on and bashed in the face for no reason. I just stood back and laughed like it was nothing. But I really didn't feel like laughing. My heart wasn't in this.

After a while, I could no longer fake it. When I told Icy, the gang leader, that I wanted to leave, no words were spoken. She just frowned and walked away from me. I thought I was free and clear to bounce. But the next day, Crash and Icy cornered me after school, in front of Fulton Street Park. Wearing her famous screw-face, Icy said, "You think you can leave us just like that?" I knew I was about to be jumped, but I wasn't about to run. As soon as the first punch landed on my jaw, I started swinging wildly. I fought like a ferocious animal, kicking like crazy so no one could get at me. And they couldn't. It was embarrassing for them. So Crash whipped out her box-cutter and nicked me in my face just before a crossing guard and two random men broke things up. That explains my scar . . . but I wasn't about to explain any of this to Naleejah; I was lucky enough to get out of that gang alive, and I didn't feel like reliving the experience for her nosy behind.

Naleejah was still staring at me wide-eyed when she asked, "Do you have any tattoos from your gang?"

"Nah . . . but, um, I really don't feel like talking about this right now. My past stays where it is. Feel me?"

"Yeah, I feel you," said Naleejah, staring at her nails. "We all have crap in our past. I know I do."

This was getting a bit too personal, so I turned my attention back to the game. By this time, my baby, Charles, was back in control. I wasn't sure if this new swagger had anything to do with Naleejah's captivating presence. Or could it be me catching a case of green-eyed paranoia? Whatever the case, I was just happy to see my baby ballin' beautifully again.

"What high school are you headed to?" asked Naleejah.

"SOES," I answered hastily.

Naleejah jerked her head back. "What kind of school is that?"

"Stands for School of Environmental Studies."

"Sounds special," said Naleejah with a shrug.

"Yeah, I know," I replied in a smug tone. Why so cocky? Well, because Naleejah seemed to be blowing off my school, and my school is hot, the first of its kind; so she needed to be blowing kisses instead of disses. I went from Special Ed, to 7-3, to 8-1, and now I was headed to a specialized high school with nothing but A's and praise lacing up my record. Now if that's not gangster, I don't know what is. Nobody can touch my school grind, okay?

Naleejah tapped my leg and asked, "So is this game almost over?"

I left her question dangling because the score was now tied. I couldn't afford to miss a single play. In protest, Naleejah tapped my leg again, and that's when I jumped up as if stung by a bee. Charles had just made a bee-you-tee-full shot (three points!) and finally won the game for his team.

"Yeah, Fulton Street Park represent!" I yelled as I bobbed my head to an imaginary beat. Then I started singing, *We fly high—no lie—you know this.* I was feeling so hyped, so proud, as if I had played the game myself. "Balllling!" I continued singing and bobbing my head. I happily looked over at Naleejah, expecting her to rock with me. But she leaped from her seat, brushed off her butt, and said, "Well, I gotta go catch Finesse. Nice meeting you. Bye."

Just like that. Not even a "Can I get your phone number?" Or "Hope to see you again." Until then, Naleejah was cheesing and grinning all up in my face, begging for conversation. Now that she didn't need me anymore, she was ghost? Wow.

But I didn't sweat her flagrantly foul move for long. I was used to people disappointing me anyway. Listen, if my own flesh and blood parents could walk out on me, what could I expect from a total stranger? Whatever.

The Bed-Stuy boys were now shouting and high-fiving each other, as the Crown Heights cats stood on the sidelines looking dumb and defeated. The two loud girls who'd sat behind me were now standing two feet away, looking just as dumb and defeated. Their faces screwed up tight once they spotted Naleejah on the verge of diving into the throng of boys.

Then a nasty coincidence occurred. Finesse stepped to Charles as soon as Naleejah sashayed up to Finesse. Why did Finesse have to ask for his ball back at this very moment? I was so mad at coincidence! Now what if Naleejah suddenly decided to lose interest in Finesse and work her sexy magic on Charles? Listen, my fantasy bubble was about to be popped if I didn't take action.

I must admit, it was so weird for me to be feeling this way. So anxious? So catty? So not like your girl Kate. I knew full well Charles didn't like me like *that*. I was practically a boy in his eyes; even with my big old butt and boobies, Charles never *once* tried to holler at me. He even called me *son*, for goodness' sakes.

Still, that didn't stop me from hallucinating. In my dreams, I called Charles my baby, and pictured red roses, candles, and hot and steamy kisses that ended with us snuggled under the covers. (Hey, you can't get pregnant off a fantasy, okay?)

But back in the real world, I had to deal with the straight-up facts. Naleejah might be checking for my man. So before she could even bat an eyelash at Charles, I had to cut her off at the pass.

I hopped up from the bleacher higher than a bunny on crack and rushed up to the trio. As soon as I got within earshot, I heard Finesse making introductions. ". . . And this is my boy, Charlie."

"Hey, what's up, shorty," said Charles, his eyes all big and happy.

"Hey," said Naleejah, trying to sound sexy. *Oh brother.*

Charles stared at Naleejah for a full minute, then said, "Don't I know you?"

"No," said Naleejah with a straight face.

Charles kept staring at her with knitted eyebrows. Then he shook his head and said, "I *swear* I met you somewhere before."

"Nope, wasn't me," said Naleejah. She didn't even blink.

Wow, what a good liar; *I* almost believed her.

Charles relaxed his eyebrows, flashed Naleejah his bright white grin, and said, "Well, I definitely saw you cutting across the court, interrupting our game and whatnot."

"And I definitely saw you hit that winning shot," said Naleejah, tossing her hair dramatically. "Congratulations are definitely in order."

Finesse butted in. "So I don't get no congratulations?"

Naleejah playfully pushed Finesse in the arm. "Oh, stop being silly. You know I'll get to you later." Then she turned back to Charles and said, "I really dug the way you yoked it on those boys!"

I couldn't believe my ears. What the heck did Naleejah know about a yoke? This fake flirty bird had my man's head so juiced up, and his eyes so locked down, that he didn't even notice me standing there with my mouth wide open.

Finesse, who was definitely feeling the same jealous jitters, poked Charles in the shoulder and pointed at me. "Yo, I think she wants you."

Yeah, if only Charles knew how much.

"Oh, hey, shorty," said Charles. "Finesse, you know my homegirl, Kate?"

"Nah." Finesse shook his head, not interested.

"Well, I know Kate," Naleejah volunteered. She flashed me a plastic grin.

I strained a smile at her, then turned to Charles and said, "When you have a second, I have something to tell you."

Okay, I was lying through my teeth, but so what?

Finesse took my words as his cue to turn to Naleejah and say, "I'm out. I got some things to handle. I'll call you later."

"Okay," said Naleejah. Meanwhile, her face read, *You mean I sat through this boring game just to be dismissed?* I guessed Naleejah had no idea that it's not okay to flirt with your man's friend *in front* of your man. The girl really needed a clue.

Finesse snatched his basketball from off the ground and gave Charles a good-bye pound. As soon as Finesse walked away from us, the two braided girls flew up to him, and the taller one looked over her shoulder and flashed a malicious smirk at Naleejah.

Dumbfounded, Naleejah stood frozen in her spot for a couple of seconds. Then she thawed out and said good-bye to us. She sailed across the basketball court, looking wrecked and lost at sea. I exhaled a sigh of relief.

Bon voyage, flirty broad!

I seized Charles by the arm and guided him to the bleachers, as if my news was so big, he had to sit down to hear it. I had no idea what I was going to tell him, but I knew I had to figure out something before he went running after Naleejah. Hey, it was possible. I had to get my man's attention back where it belonged. All eyes on me, see? No time to lose.

Charles sat close to me, staring at me with his radiant brown eyes . . . waiting for me to say something. I was on the spot. I had nothing to say. Now I understood how heart attacks can happen.

Think, Kate. Think!

I fidgeted on the bleacher and looked up at the sky, hoping to find an answer there.

"So, what's good?" Charles asked, cocking his head to the side.

My lips parted as if about to speak, but nothing came out.

"Eh, girl, are you with me?"

When I didn't answer, Charles busted into chuckles. "Oh, you must be still in shock over that monster three-pointer I made, son."

When Charles laughed, his eyes squinted into slits. He looked so dang cute when he laughed. But no. I had to stay focused. I had to think of something "important" to tell him, or else I'd look like a desperate little fool, dragging him away from his boys—for what?

And then it hit me: the game. "Nice three-pointer," I began, "but I just wanted to ask what was up with you earlier? Tell me why you kept passing the ball to butterfingers."

Charles dismissed my question with a wave of his hand. "Yeah, but I won the game for my team, didn't I?"

"True," I said.

"You know I got it going on."

Mm, so true.

Charles lifted the top of his jersey like he was popping his collar. *Mm, so sexy.*

Then to torture me, he lifted the bottom of his jersey way up, and with it, he wiped the beads of sweat from his sweet chocolate face. I even caught a glimpse of his beautiful brown hairless chest, and I was tempted to reach out and touch him. But before things could get steamy, here comes Charles's newest homeboy busting up my peep show. I don't know the dude by name, but he's got a really big nose.

"Yo, Charlie, what's the holdup?" Big Nose asked, all out of breath, like he had just been chased by dogs or cops.

Hmm, I thought angrily, wasn't the "holdup" *obvious*? Wasn't I sitting *right here*, next to Charles?

But then I realized Big Nose was probably confused. Charles is seen only with the flyest chicks, Naleejah-like chicks with fabulous clothes, hair done, and fingernails decked in flawless tips. Big Nose was probably thinking, Why is Charles wasting time on this broke-down pigeon?

Well, if Big Nose had asked me directly, I could've easily answered him. See, Charles and I went way back, so I had it like that. And up until last year, Charles used to roll out the house looking just as flat broke and bummy as me. He even served some time in foster care, and that's when we really became cool. I'll never forget the day Charles came up to me while I was chilling in the school playground by myself. School was over, but I didn't want to go home; I was living in yet another jacked-up foster home at the time.

Charles sat beside me on a swing without saying a word. He was acting strange. "What's up?" I asked.

"They putting me in foster care," he blurted out. It seemed like he was trying to fight the water building up in his eyes, so I looked away from him to make him feel more comfortable. At age ten, I already felt like I had mothering skills. Don't know how or why, but I just felt that way. Charles must've felt the same way, because he had come to little old me for advice.

He held his head down and said, "I can't believe somebody called ACS on my moms."

I didn't have to ask why. Charles's mother was forever hitting and screaming on him—even out in the street. Everybody knew it. I just didn't know why it took forever for someone to save him from her madness.

"You'll be okay," I said, getting up from my swing. I walked over to Charles, put my hand on his shoulder, and said, "They'll get your mother some help, and you probably won't have to stay in foster care for too long."

"But I don't want to live in nobody else's crib," said Charles. He bit his lower lip and shook his head.

"Don't worry," I said, "there's some really nice foster parents out there." This was half-true. I didn't bother mentioning the other half, the meaner side of foster care. I couldn't bring myself to tell Charles about the foster parents who treated me like the family pet, making me eat from separate utensils like I had some nasty disease. I couldn't tell Charles about the many times I've been told, "We didn't have to take you in, so you better be grateful." Didn't mention the times I've been hit for no reason, or sent to bed with no food. Wouldn't dare tell Charles that if his mother didn't get her act together, he'd be a ward of the state just like me, floating from foster home to foster home with no happy end in sight. So, to put Charles's mind at ease, I just focused on the bright side.

We talked until the park got dark. I felt so much closer to Charles that night, like he was my little brother even though he's two months older than me. When I got home, I was in trouble with my foster mother, but I didn't care. I had helped Charles in his time of need, and I felt really good about that.

Lucky for Charles, he had to stay in care for only six months. And check my baby out now. Back with his birth mother and looking mighty fine, rocking the hot new Jordans, the butter-fly haircut, the sparkling diamond stud in his left earlobe. Don't ask me how Charles got this sudden upgrade; I just hoped he wasn't selling drugs to get his. Charles didn't need to be risking his neck for anybody. Who did he need to impress? Listen, he could rock a jacked-up Afro and holes in his sneakers, and I'd still be crazy about the boy.

"How long you gonna be?" Big Nose asked Charles. He didn't look my way not once, as if he resented my raggedy presence.

"Eh, what's the rush, man?" Charles spread his arms wide, like *What?*

Big Nose reached into his saggy shorts and pulled out a fat cigar. "We about to spark this Dutch!"

Charles suddenly changed his tune. "Oh, um, Kate, you want to get down?" He jerked his chin toward the future blunt. A part of me felt flattered that Charles was asking me to join him. The other part had to keep myself in check.

"Nah, I'm straight."

"Why not?" Charles asked.

"Maybe next time," I said, hoping this would be enough.

I wasn't trying to preach about why I don't smoke weed; I didn't want to turn my baby off. Besides, who was I to preach? At one point, I even tried to sell the stuff.

"So you coming to Saturday's game?" asked Charles.

"Yeah, I'll be there."

"Oh . . . and let me get your phone number," said Charles. "I keep forgetting to ask you. Last Saturday this chick came to the Stuy Court trying to show off. She was mad whack. Couldn't even dribble the ball proper. I know you could've rocked her, but I had no way of contacting you."

"Yeah, I would've rocked her, for sure." I pictured myself hooping it up, straight-up embarrassing that wannabe baller on the court. The Stuy Court is *my* court, okay?

"Your number, please—hello?" Charles asked, snatching me from my ego trip.

Then I remembered. *Oh man.* Can't give Charles my number. One word: Lynn. Lynn said no boys calling the crib. Period.

Reluctantly, I explained this to Charles.

"No cell phone?"

"Nope." Then I added, "Not yet," as if I expected to get a celly any minute.

"Well, jot down my digits then," he said. "You got a pen?"

I feverishly searched my backpack. But all I had inside was an extra T-shirt and house keys.

"That big old bag and no pen?" Charles chuckled.

"True." I giggled.

I guess my backpack is like my security blanket . . . bounced from place to place. I like having something to carry around with me at all times. In fact, as soon as I turned ten, I started running away, and my trusty knapsack stayed with me on the run. At every foster home I lived in, I'd wait until nighttime to pack my knapsack with a T-shirt, a sweater, a pair of jeans, and an emergency ten-dollar bill. Always ready. Never scared. I felt the need to be prepared if some drama went down. I'd stash my knapsack under my bed, and in the middle of the night, I'd lean over my mattress just to make sure it was still there. Six months of living with the Johnsons, and I'm finally getting more comfortable. Now, the knapsack stays by my closet door—unpacked. I'm trying to be optimistic for a change.

Charles turned to Big Nose. "You got a pen, my man?"

"No, but I got this." He waved the fat cigar in the air.

"Yo, *chillll*. I'm coming," said Charles. "Go buy yourself a Popsicle, or something."

As if on cue, an ice cream truck suddenly came rolling up the block, blaring ring-a-ding carnival music. I would've busted out laughing at the hilarious timing if I wasn't so pissed at Big Nose. Why did he have to interrupt our flow? Why couldn't he stick his big nose somewhere else?

Charles got up and stretched. I got up too. I was about to give him a good-bye pound with my fist, but he reached out for a hug with his strong beautiful arms. Baffled, all I could do was walk straight into them. Charles held me close for a hot minute. And can I tell you? I almost OD'd from ecstasy; even his sweat smelled sweet.

However, I was a bit confused. Charles was sending me mixed signals all of a sudden. Hugging me since when? But let me tell you, mixed signals never felt so good.

"Don't forget Saturday," said Charles over his shoulder. "Game starts at two."

"No doubt."

Charles bebopped off the court. Slow and sexy, side to side. Mm, I loved the way he walked. Everything Charles did with his body was absolutely breathtaking.

I collapsed back down on the bleacher. I needed a minute to pull myself together. Whoa, what a guy. I don't know how long I sat there before I heard my name. "Yo, Kate! Yo, Kate!"

Charles was outside of the gate, hanging on to the crisscross metal. He nodded toward the washed-out white truck parked ten feet away. "Want an ice cream cone?"

"Nah, that's okay," I said, grinning and waving at him.

"All right," he called out.

All I could do was smile. Mm, how sweet and thoughtful of Charles. I felt so good right now. The warm sunshine on my back made me feel even better. I dreamily looked up at the sky and stared at the clouds. If you stare at the clouds long enough, they become things. *Oh look, there's a puffy heart!* Man, I was in such a happy daze.

I got up and floated off the Stuy Court. Lost in a dream. My stomach was flipping and dipping at the thought of Charles.

But soon the butterflies in my belly turned into hunger pangs. My stomach was on E. Time to fill up.

First, I planned to get a bag of sunflower seeds—my snack for later. Then, I'd head to the pizza shop and grab a cheese slice for now.

I drifted into my favorite corner store.

"Eh, *mami*," the short guy behind the counter greeted me.

"Hey," I said, smiling.

Without having to ask, Shorty slid a bag of seeds on the counter. I paid for them, waved good-bye, and was about to leave. Then suddenly, I felt a light grip on my right arm. Slowly, I turned to find Naleejah grinning at me. She had come out of nowhere.

Of all the girls, in all the world, why did I have to bump into this silly broad?

"Hey," I said flatly.

"Hey, girl!"

I swear Naleejah seemed soooo happy to see me. And I was just toooo confused. How could she be cheesing at me so hard after dissing me so hard less than ten minutes ago?

Man, this girl had me straight tripping; she was shadier than a tree. I couldn't decide whether to return her cheesy smile, or karate-chop her grubby little hand off me. Torn and confused, I allowed Naleejah to lead me out the store.

Chapter 3

As soon as we rounded the corner, I struggled to free my arm.

"Oh, my bad," Naleejah exclaimed, finally letting go. "I'm just so happy to see you!"

"Same here," I said, lying through my teeth.

"What are the chances," Naleejah began, "bumping into you in this neck of the hood?"

"Um, isn't the basketball court just four blocks away?" *Duh?*

"Oh, true!" Naleejah giggled. "Well, I'm just glad I bumped into you before I went berserk. Girl, I've been walking around in circles for the past few minutes." She shook her head dramatically, obviously waiting for me to ask her why.

When I didn't bother to ask, she volunteered. "I swear Finesse is playing himself right now. He's not answering his phone. Not returning my text messages. I had to buy me a pack of cigarettes just to calm my freaking nerves! Now I'd be wrong if I flatten his tires, right?"

My tongue stayed stuck to the roof of my mouth.

"Kate, is something wrong?" Naleejah asked, then stuck a cigarette in her mouth and lit up.

"Nah, I'm okay," I lied.

Naleejah had fallen into step with me, and there was nothing I could do to shake her off. When I tried to quicken my pace, her long legs caught up with me. When I gave her the silent treatment, she just kept right on talking. Naleejah was two heads taller than me, but surely not smarter. Shucks, if I were her, and she were me, I would've *been* taken the hint and gotten ghost.

"Man, I'm so glad I bumped into you," Naleejah exclaimed. "It's so hard meeting cool girls around here."

Now on this, I could agree. Naleejah was far from cool: *Nice meeting you. Bye?* Nah, I'd never forget that.

We were about to cross Lewis Avenue when Naleejah had the nerve to ask, "So where are we headed?"

We?

I hesitated. Shifted from foot to foot, trying to stall for time. I was in the middle of deciding whether I was that desperate for company, or should I flat-out tell Naleejah she was too fake for my taste?

Before I could make a firm decision, my mind played a trick on me, and I blurted out, "Pizza shop."

"Oh, good, I like pizza too," cried out Naleejah. "Let's go get our grub on!"

"Okay," I muttered.

"How far is the shop?"

"Not far," I said. "About four more blocks."

As we walked, I listened without really listening to Naleejah's long, drawn-out story about Finesse. He's got mad money, a Mercedes-Benz, and a whole lot of balls. She ended her story with a claim that Finesse would never get another piece of her pie after the foul episode he pulled today. Then she heaved a noisy, long, drawn-out sigh.

All I said was, "oh" and "yeah" after every one of her long, drawn-out sentences. My mind was focused on more important matters: pizza, Charles, and how to ditch this chick after gobbling down my slice.

"You know, the boys be lookin' good around here," Naleejah began out of the blue.

"True," I said.

"But Charles is a *serious* dime piece, okay?"

This was getting ridiculous. True, Finesse had dissed Naleejah, but couldn't she find somebody else to sweat?

"So why'd you flat-out lie to Charles?" I suddenly thought to ask.

"Lie about what?"

"Oh, you forgot already?" I asked with raised eyebrows. "You acted like you never met Charles before, but you were in his class. I'm saying, why lie about it?"

Naleejah shrugged. "Well, the *old* me was in his class. The new me doesn't want to think about the old me, okay?"

"Wow . . . can't believe you lied to my boy with such a straight face."

Naleejah shrugged again. "Well, a girl's got to have some mystery about her."

Hm, whatever.

Naleejah must've seen the disgusted look on my face because she suddenly changed the subject. "Listen, I don't know about you, but these silly chickenheads out here be getting on my nerves!" She threw up her hands in exasperation, almost dropping her Gucci bag. "Why they got to be so mad at me? I can't help it that I'm fly. . . . Do jealous females around here try to test you too?"

"Nah, not really," I said.

From the corner of my eye, I noticed Naleejah looking me up and down. She probably figured my raggedy gear saved me from jealous drama. She threw down her half-smoked cigarette and stomped on it with her sparkling Air Jordan sole. "Did you hear those crazy bees at the court trying to start some sting with me?"

"Yeah, I heard them."

"They don't even know me," Naleejah said, shaking her head. "I will go straight *ballistic* on those broads."

"Well, just try to keep a low profile," I explained. "Ignore the haters. Take the high road."

"But they always be trying to mess—"

I cut her off. "If a girl wants to fight you, why give her what she wants? Don't fall into her trap. Fall back."

"Seems like these chicks are out to get me no matter what," Naleejah whined. She paused for a minute: "See . . . when I was looking plain and corny, nobody wanted to be my friend. But now that I'm fly, I still can't make friends—that's why I only hang with dudes."

I knew exactly what Naleejah was talking about. Back in the day, I used to target prissy girls like her. Yeah, I can admit it. I especially liked to pop junk with the chicks who held their heads too high. See, when when you feel like every girl in the world thinks she's better than you, you feel the need to take her down a notch, whether by staring her down or beating her down, anything to make yourself feel bigger and better.

"Hey, Kate, you look like you're in another world," said Naleejah, chuckling lightly.

"Nah, I'm here." Next thing I knew, I was actually encouraging Naleejah to chitchat. I guess I was feeling guilty about the memory of my messy past. "So, was Finesse supposed to take you out somewhere after the game?" I asked. "Is that why you're all dressed up?"

This question caused Naleejah to stop dead in the middle of the sidewalk. "You call this dressed up?" she exclaimed. "Oh my gosh, this is just my hang-out gear! I can't *believe* you call this dressed up."

Oh brother, I thought, *just answer my freaking question already!* Finally, she did. "No, we didn't have anything special planned. Getting me a piece from Finesse, then you know, maybe a bite to eat—" Naleejah cut off her explanation and broke out into a fit of giggles.

"What?" I asked.

"I still can't believe you call this dressed up," Naleejah said, shaking her head. "Don't worry, girl. Stick with me, and I'll have a dude lacing you in no time."

"No thanks, I can lace myself."

"Um . . . not really," said Naleejah, reaching down to lift the no-name tag of my white tee. Then she busted into another fit of hearty laughter—well, at least it was friendly laughter. Besides, letting things go was something I had to learn anyway.

Choose your battles, Tisha always tells me. So lately, the shrug has been my new best friend. Somebody says something foul to me, and I just shrug. Lift my shoulders, let the chip fall off, no more weight on my mind, and I'm good. It doesn't work for me all the time, but just enough to keep Naleejah's teeth safe inside her mouth.

Suddenly, my best friend's face loomed large in front of me. Felicia never made fun of me. She only tried to encourage me—first girl to believe in my brains instead of my fists.

In junior high school, nobody liked Felicia, including me. She was too tall, too strange, too skinny and quiet, always walking alone in the hallways with her slumped shoulders, baggy jeans ripped at the knees, rocking neon bright yellow sneakers on her big old feet. She was forever being laughed at and hated on, and I can't lie, I used to join in. But I secretly felt sorry for Felicia . . . though not enough to hang with her.

When Felicia became my math tutor in the seventh grade, I was too embarrassed to be associated with her. I gave her a slight head nod in the hallways, and after school, I'd walk five paces behind her on our way to the Macon Library. But it was there inside that library that I got to know Felicia, and like it or not, I realized she was the kind of friend I'd been searching for all of my life.

To begin with, I had it all twisted about Felicia; there was no need for me to be feeling sorry for her. Unlike me, she had her *whole* act together. She was just "doing her" and didn't give a dang about what kids thought about her. As it turned out, this was *exactly* what I needed help with. Math was not my issue.

The day Felicia called me out, we were two weeks into our tutoring sessions. She had given me a practice sheet filled with geometric problems, and I rocked every answer with no hesitation.

Felicia handed back my sheet and said, "You obviously know this. Why did you let your teacher put you in this tutoring program?"

"Because I failed math last year," I snapped. I didn't appreciate the "teacher" tone Felicia was taking with me.

"But you *know* this," Felicia repeated. "Why act dumb?"

Her question shocked the crap out of me. Felicia might've been taller, but I was way rougher, and she knew my bad-girl rep in school. I couldn't *believe* she was brave enough to come at me like this. We were sitting in the library, so I couldn't scream on her just yet. I quietly packed up my books and waited until we got outside.

My first thought was to ask Felicia if she wanted her butt beat. But a month of anger-management class helped me tone down my question. Instead, I asked, "Why did you come out your face calling me dumb? Who do you think you talking to?"

Felicia's brown eyes widened, and she backed up against the bricks of the library. "Kate, I did not call you dumb," she stuttered. "I was trying to say that you're smart—I just don't understand why you don't want your teachers to know that."

Okay, she had a point.

Around this time, I didn't really care what my teachers thought about me. I didn't care about much. I was living in a group home, unhappy, feeling like whatever. I was just trying to satisfy Tisha by not cutting class and doing my homework for a change.

I didn't know how to come back at Felicia, since she was basically trying to compliment me. So I just stood there looking stupid for a minute.

Felicia spoke up first. "I didn't mean to disrespect you. I just see a lot in you, that's all."

Felicia's words sounded like grown-up words, and I didn't know how to take them from a chick my age. So I just stood there still looking dumb in the face. I couldn't admit to Felicia that she was right, that I hid my brain from other kids, never raising my hand in class, that I loved to read and write stories, couldn't get enough of science class. Basically, I was afraid of being teased for being smart. Having girls scared of me made me feel more powerful than having A's lace up my report card.

During my next tutoring session, I made mistakes on purpose just to avoid being questioned by Felicia. I wanted to keep her as my tutor. I really liked her. I wasn't sure if she was catching on to my scheme, but I didn't care at the time. This charade went on for a whole month. Felicia would crack corny jokes during our sessions. She even got me to smile a couple of times. At my group home, I had to play hard 24-7, so my time with Felicia felt fresh and new. Felicia was the first girl I could just be myself with—to study with, to laugh with. I felt like I was still young when I hung around her.

I remember being lonely ever since I was little. Even when I had friends, I felt lonely. Surrounded by other kids in foster care, I couldn't cry or clown around like I wanted to. We all tried to act hard, because we *had* to. It's called protecting ourselves.

So finally, one day, I said, *Bump it, Kate!! Keep it real.* I invited Felicia to the park to watch a basketball game with me. She said yes. And it was a wrap. From then on, we started sticking together like Krazy Glue. I tried not to care about what kids said about our "goofy" friendship, and tried to stay focused on the brand-new me. I started raising my hand in class, got more A's and praise from teachers. I was finally opening up to a girl my own age for the first time in my entire life. . . . Felicia and I became so tight, people outside of school swore we were sisters even though we looked nothing alike.

Listen, I got ninety-nine problems, but my homegirl, Felicia, has never been one. Man, I missed her so much.

"Felicia never tries to clown me," I said under my breath. I guess *not* under my breath, because Naleejah heard me.

"Who's Felicia?"

"That 'doofy' girl you were dissing earlier . . . my best friend."

"Oh, my bad!" exclaimed Naleejah. "I didn't know it was that deep. Y'all don't look like crew to me."

"We're more than crew," I corrected. "She's like a sister to me."

"Well, where is she now?"

"South Africa—for the summer."

"Oh man, she's way across the globe!" Naleejah smiled and linked her arm through mine. "Shoot, I'm your sister now."

Uh, I don't think so.

We stepped inside the brightly lit pizza shop. White and red tiles covered the walls, and tall fake trees stood in every corner. Five tables were filled with older men playing dominoes and talking Spanish. A red countertop was situated by the window, and two stools were sitting underneath. I claimed the stools, pushed them together, and threw my knapsack on top.

Our spot.

I walked up to the counter where Naleejah was standing, sticking her butt out. For who? I didn't know. Not a single cutie in the shop.

"What are you getting?" Naleejah asked, as if my answer would determine hers.

"A cheese slice," I said.

"That's it?" Naleejah looked at me like I had three heads.

"Yep, that's it."

"Don't want any chicken or pepperoni on your pizza? Just plain old cheese?"

"I'm straight," I insisted. I couldn't tell this jiggy-jive female that I had only enough money for a cheese slice and tap water. It was none of her dang business I was flat broke.

Naleejah studied me for a minute and suddenly said, "Listen, I got you." Before I could blink, she ordered four pepperoni slices and two bottles of Snapple Raspberry Iced Tea. I was tongue-tied for two seconds, grateful and embarrassed.

I muttered, "Thanks."

The pizza slices were smoking on our paper plates. I couldn't wait to dig in. But just as I was about to wolf down a slice, I noticed Naleejah digging into her Gucci bag. She pulled out a silver cell phone decorated with a thousand glittering crystals.

"I swear dude better pick up his phone," said Naleejah. "This is my last time trying, for real." She frantically pushed a couple of buttons.

Well, I didn't want to look greedy. So I decided to wait for Naleejah to complete her call. But her call was complete before it got started. She angrily clicked her celly shut and made a big huffy sound. "Freak him, for real! There's plenty other dudes out here way better-looking than him."

"True," I said, divided between courtesy and hunger. But my stomach could wait no longer. I picked up my first slice, hoping Naleejah would follow my lead. She finally stashed her phone away and turned to face her food.

I peeped Naleejah's eating style from the side of my eye. She was daintily dabbing off the extra grease on the pizza with her napkin.

Then she dribbled a mountain of hot pepper all over both slices. (My mouth burned just glancing at her plate.)

Then I stared in disbelief as she daintily picked up a plastic knife and fork, like we're having dinner at the table. She proceeded to eat her pizza, nibbling like a dainty mouse. Watching her eat made me feel like a savage as I held my greasy slice with my bare hands. I immediately eased up on my slice and took much smaller bites.

Ten minutes passed with us eating in clumsy silence. It was no surprise that I had finished dogging my food five minutes before Naleejah. It felt kinda embarrassing. I had to twiddle my thumbs until she finished.

"Those slices were slamming!" said Naleejah, gracefully patting her lips with a napkin. Then she whipped out her mirror, her lip gloss, and carefully reapplied some shine. Well, the grease from the pizza had done *my* lips just fine, thank you very much.

"Hey, good looking out," I said, hoping I didn't sound too pitiful.

"No problem," she replied. "You seem mad cool."

"You too," I said, half-believing myself.

"What did you say?"

"I said, you too!" I shouted. I had to shout now because the owner of the shop had suddenly decided to pump loud Spanish music. I could barely hear myself talk.

"I wish I would've met you a week earlier!" Naleejah cried out.

"Why? What happened?" I yelled.

"The Fourth of July. We could've gone to Coney Island. I haven't been there yet. I bet there were crazy cuties roaming around that night."

"True, true," I said, now back in my regular voice. The owner finally had enough sense to lower the music a bit.

"Well, what did you do on the Fourth?" Naleejah asked. "Picnic with the family?"

This was not the time to get into my home-life situation, so I simply said, "Nah, I chilled at the crib." Then I stared blankly at my empty paper plate. The mention of family always gets me down.

"Well, I didn't get to see any fireworks either," Naleejah explained.

"I was bored out of my freaking mind! My parents forced me to go to this boring-behind barbecue way out in Queens. There was no music. No honeys. Just my parents showing me off to every long-lost aunt and uncle, like they were so proud of me. Any other time, they barely pay attention to me. I couldn't even—"

I glanced up to see who, or what, had suddenly arrested Naleejah's speech. She was looking out the window now, her mouth shaped like a terrified O.

Boom! I spotted them. The two loud girls at the Stuy Court were now standing outside, leaning against a red car, staring at us with their arms folded tight. Oh man, they must've followed us here! Not cool. Not cool at all.

Two seconds later, the menacing pair decided to step inside. From the look on their faces, I could tell they weren't hungry for pizza; they were hungry for blood. These girls looked much tougher and rougher under the pizza shop's bright lights. One girl wore scruffy bright blond box-braids, and the other wore frizzy burgundy cornrolls. They both wore the same nasty scowl. I knew something dirty was about to go down.

Blondie took one step forward and stood over Naleejah like a shadow. "Can I holler at you for a second?"

"About what?" asked Naleejah.

"You talk to Finesse?"

"I talked to him after the game, and that's it."

"Well, I talk to him now," explained Blondie. "You understand what I'm saying?"

Naleejah shrugged.

"What? Cat got your tongue?" asked Blondie, and then she smirked at her friend.

As if on cue, Burgundy stepped up, looking like a pit bull ready to bite. "Must be the case, cat got her tongue." She shook her frizzy head and laughed.

Naleejah sat silent like a marble statue. I joined her in this moment of silence, all the while wondering when she was planning to go "ballistic" on these broads, you know, back up all that big talk she was spitting at me a minute ago. If I didn't feel so sorry for Naleejah, I would've laughed—ha, ha, ha—right in her big-talking phony face.

Don't get me wrong. I didn't want to see Naleejah hurt. However, I couldn't see myself jumping in. This wasn't my beef, and my fighting days were supposed to be over—only when necessary from now on.

"What? Nothing to say?" asked Blondie, moving closer to Naleejah's terrified face. Poor girl looked about ready to fall off her stool or hide under it. Any minute now, and I expected her to cry out for help. But I guess she figured, why bother? The men in the shop were too busy jamming to their music and slamming down their dominoes to be paying us any old mind.

Naleejah stole a glance at me; she was shaking like a cold wet kitten. I tried to dodge the beam of fear shooting from her eyes. But oops—*zap*—she caught me. I got sucked into the drama.

Blondie poked Naleejah in the forehead and said, "Get your own man, understand?"

Suddenly, I jumped up from my stool and squeezed between her and Naleejah. "I'm saying can we squash this beef already?"

Blondie stared me down, long and hard. Her pupils were pitch black and cold, trying to put my guts on freeze. Oh, so she wanted to take it there? Well, I returned her wicked stare. Now we were standing toe-to-toe. I was in her face, and she was up in mine. Everything around us seemed to disappear.

"Go sit down somewhere," said Blondie.

"Make me," I said, getting all up in her face.

See, it's bad when you know you can fight. You walk around with this S on your chest like you're Superwoman, thinking you can beat any and everybody down. Right now, there was so much bass in my voice, so much courage in my heart, so much adrenaline pumping through my veins that you couldn't tell me nothing. "So, what's up?" I demanded.

Blondie laughed, suddenly taking me for a joke. She placed her hands on her hips and asked, "Who are *you* supposed to be?"

"The wrong chick to be messing with," I snapped.

Blondie slowly leaned her head to the side and said, "Seriously, go sit down somewhere before you get yourself hurt."

"Yeah," Burgundy chimed in. "You can't save a ho, and you ain't got nothing to *do* with this situation."

"Well, this is my friend, and I'm *in* the situation," I explained, surprising myself with these words. Friend? Since when?

"Oh, she just stupid," said Burgundy, shaking her head at me.

"Let's see how stupid," I snapped back. "Why don't you come test me?"

The old Kate was back in full force, ready to rumble and snap some necks. Listen, I don't scratch. I punch. It was going to be downright ugly. I felt wild surges of rage coursing through my blood. I clenched my fists. Ready and set.

"Let's take this outside then," suggested Blondie.

"Bet," I said, courageously leading the way. Once outside, I scanned my surroundings. Not a soul in sight. No passersby. Not even a stray dog. Just Blondie and Burgundy circling me like underfed wolves.

"So, where's your friend now?" Blondie teased, laughing and pointing at me.

"Yeah, where's your friend now?" Burgundy chimed in.

Good question.

I looked to my left, then to my right.

Naleejah was nowhere to be found.

Blondie stepped up to me, rammed her face close to mine, and said, "So swing, or get swung on, *punk.*"

"Punk?" I said, backing up a bit. "Please, you're not even ready for me."

To tell you the truth, I wasn't ready either. Two against one is never fun. Where in the world was Naleejah?

"See, you had all that mouth in there," began Blondie, jutting her chin toward the shop. "Why you standing out here all stiff and quiet? Scared?"

"Scared? Please. I will knock you out."

"Knock me out?" repeated Blondie. "I wish you would."

Her wish was my command. I punched her dead in the face. Blondie staggered back. And then it was on. We went off like a bomb. Fists flying. Hair pulling. I fought that girl with all my Brooklyn heart. When I started getting the best of Blondie, her homegirl, Burgundy, jumped in. Now I had two pairs of hands and feet hitting and kicking on me at one time. Next thing I knew, somebody hooked a foot around my ankle, and—*bam*—I hit the sidewalk hard. Before I could scramble to my feet, I heard loud voices yelling in Spanish, and then I felt a man's hands seizing me by the waist. He held on to me with a vise grip. I kicked and flailed, trying to break free, but no matter how hard I struggled, he held on to me.

Two other potbellied men came running outside, bumping into each other like sumo wrestlers and cursing in loud Spanish. They dragged Blondie and Burgundy down the block by the collars of their T-shirts.

"You better sleep with your eyes open!" Blondie yelled from down the block.

"Yeah, punk," Burgundy chimed in. "This ain't over."

"What? You threatening me?" I yelled back, still kicking and flailing, dying to return to battle. I didn't give a snap. I was ready to kill somebody.

"*Mamí*, no, no," the men chorused. It took both men to haul me inside the pizza shop. Once inside, I collapsed on the nearest chair and put my head in my hands. I was shaking all over with anger.

"Are you all right?" asked the owner of the shop. He slid a cup of grape juice in front of me. I nodded, thanked him, and took three sips of punch.

Two minutes later, I felt someone else standing over me. I looked up to see Naleejah's stupid face. She put her hand on my shoulder, and I flinched as if about to get hit again. "Don't touch me," I said, giving her the stink eye.

"Are you okay?" she stuttered.

"What do you think?" I snapped. "Where *were* you?"

Najeelah pretended she didn't hear my last question. "Do you need me to get you a Band-Aid or something?" she asked.

"Why? Do you see a scratch on my face?" *Better not be a scratch on my face*, I thought angrily. The scar over my eye was supposed to be my last souvenir of my wildin'-out days.

"Let me see your mirror," I demanded.

Naleejah hastily rummaged through her bag, then handed me her pocket mirror with a shaky hand.

I snatched the mirror and peered into it. Not a scratch on my face. Good. But the hair on my head? Bad. Really bad. During the fight, my baseball cap had gotten snatched off my head, and now chunks of hair were sticking out here, there, and everywhere. I looked a hot mess.

I jumped up from my seat and raced outside. Naleejah came running after me.

"Kate, where are you going?" she yelled.

I spun around to face her and said, "Oh, *now* you come outside?"

"But where are you running to?"

"Oh, *now* you act concerned?" I said. "Well, I'm looking for my baseball cap. Can you *at least* help me with that?"

Naleejah joined my search. But all we saw were Blondie's braids scattered all over the sidewalk like worms after the rain.

My hat had disappeared. Man, I was twisted. Naleejah saw the madness written all over my face. "Kate, will you please listen to me?" she begged.

"Listen to what?" I boomed. Without waiting for an answer, I stormed back inside the shop.

Naleejah followed me inside and finished copping her plea. "Kate, please listen to me. I swear I didn't want you fighting for me. But everything happened so fast. . . . You flew out that door, and I was trying to get help, but nobody in here speaks English . . . only the man behind the counter . . . but he was in the bathroom. . . . You should've seen me punching the air and pointing at the door. I know I had to be looking crazy."

I almost busted out laughing imagining the scene, but no, I had to keep my screw-face on. Naleejah had to be made to understand that it's not okay to desert your friends, no matter what. I'm saying, my goodness, have my *back* at least—even if you can't fight, get your butt beat down with me.

Naleejah sighed. "I guess that's what I get for not paying attention in Spanish class—"

I cut her off. "What do you mean that's what *you* get?" I asked. "I'm the one who got jumped."

"And I'm really sorry for that," said Naleejah. Now she put on a pitiful face. I wanted to rip the mask off and slap some realness into her. But I kept my hands to myself and said, "Whatever."

"Oh no, there's a hole in your T-shirt," Naleejah suddenly decided to point out.

Did she really think that pointing out the hole near my armpit was supposed to make me feel better? What a chickenhead!

Then she ventured to ask, "Um, do you mind if I fix your hair a little bit?" Without waiting for my answer, she dipped into her bag and started spreading out bobby pins, scrunchies, a mini-brush, and a comb on the table.

"Go ahead and fix it," I said. "Knock yourself out."

My hair's medium length, and so thick, it breaks the teeth out of combs. I had no idea how she was planning to tame it.

Naleejah began the struggle, trying to pull pieces of my hair together into a ponytail. "You need a perm," she advised.

"Don't *need* a perm," I corrected. "But I do *want* one. . . . I'll get one—one day."

"One day soon, I hope," Naleejah dared to say. Then she put the finishing touches on my ponytail. I could tell my hair looked really jacked up by the grimace she wore. "See, if you had a perm—"

"Can you stop talking about a perm?" I broke. "Do you even know if I have the *money* to get a perm?" (You know I had to be heated for me to mention my financial situation.)

Naleejah ignored my angry outburst and said, "Kate, don't trip. I can do your hair free of charge."

Free of charge?

My hard-boiled face suddenly turned sunny-side up.

Okay . . . it's my birthday!

Of course, I was still pissed at Naleejah, but the streets didn't raise no fool. Hey, if I wanted my hair done, I had to push my pride aside. Push this little incident *wayyy* in the back of my mind; I'm good at blocking things out anyway.

Besides, fighting was first nature to me. Getting jumped, nothing new. The fight was over, and in my past already. So why harp on old news? Feel me? (And if you don't feel me, your hair is probably already banging, so you can't even relate to me.)

"Are you free on Friday?" asked Naleejah.

"Yeah, Friday's good."

Naleejah threw her mini beauty parlor back inside her bag and said, "Come to my crib around ten o'clock. Cool?"

"No doubt."

"And don't worry about buying the perm," Naleejah added. "I got you."

I got you. I got you. This theme was getting so freaking old. But that didn't mean I wasn't getting brand-new! Yes sir, on Friday, Naleejah would perm my hair free of charge, and on Saturday, I'd strut my butt to the Stuy Court with my hair bouncing and behaving beautifully. Charles would take one look at me and flip the freak out, okay?

"What's your cell number?" asked Naleejah, breaking into my delicious thoughts.

"Don't have a cell phone."

"You don't have a cell phone?" Naleejah repeated, her eyes twice their size.

"Is there an echo in the room?" I snapped.

Naleejah raised her pencil-thin eyebrows and shook her head. "Well, I don't know how you do it. I couldn't survive without my phone."

The nasty look I shot Naleejah shut her up real quick. She jotted her number and address down on a napkin, and slid it to me. I stuffed it inside my knapsack.

"Well, can I get your home number at least?"

I gave her my digits and warned her not to ever call me past nine o'clock or else she'd be reading about me in the papers. She chuckled at this, and then suddenly grew serious. "Do you think it's safe for us to leave now?" Worry lines ran across her forehead.

"I don't know about you, but I'm leaving," I said. "Can't sit here all night. I have a curfew. Don't you?"

"Curfew?" Naleejah cracked up laughing. "Too bad for you. I come and go as I please."

"Lucky for you."

"Yeah, I know."

"Okay then, I'm out. See ya."

"Hold up," said Naleejah as she pulled out her cell phone. "I'm about to call my homeboy, Maxwell. Maybe he can drive us home."

"No, no, that's okay," I blurted out.

"Are you sure?"

"Yes, I'm sure."

No, I didn't want Maxwell driving me home. I didn't want anybody driving me home. The front of my house looks like it's about to fall down. Crumbling brown stones. Rickety brown steps. Outside gate chipping black paint. The Johnsons owned the entire brownstone, but they couldn't seem to keep any tenants upstairs. So the third floor looks abandoned: no curtains in the windows, dark and depressing. Nobody can tell the inside of the house looks better, much cleaner anyway, furniture always shining thanks to my own elbow grease.

"Call me when you get to your crib," Naleejah cried out.

"Yeah, I'll holler at you," I said as I trooped out the door.

The last drop of sun had already dipped below the rooftops. The sky had gone from blue to black in one snap. I heaved a deep sigh. Time sure flies even when you're *not* having fun. Would I be late for curfew? I really hoped not. One word: Lynn. And there was another is-sue to worry about. Four words: the Raggedy-Braided Twins.

On my way home, you should've seen me walking down the block, twisting my neck to the left and right like a paranoid fool. I couldn't help but wonder whether this buckwild duo would come out of nowhere, jump down from a tree, and bum-rush me.

Sleep with your eyes open.

As much as I tried to put Blondie's menacing words in the back of my mind, the threat of payback kept ringing in my head like a million bells. And what if the Twins showed up at Saturday's game? Of course, Charles would have my back, but why should I have to worry about that? My heart sunk at the thought of having to look over my shoulder like a gangster once again.

When I made it to Bainbridge Street safe and sound, I wanted to jump up and kiss the street sign. And when I finally made it to my front door, I was ready to kiss the doorknob. I was so grateful to be home. Now I only had to worry about Lynn. If she detected any signs of battle, I'd be in trouble. "Absolutely *no* fighting" was her unbend-able rule. So how could I explain my holey T-shirt? My missing hat?

It was time for Operation Innocent. I plopped down on the front steps, pulled out my fresh white T-shirt, and threw it on over my holey one. I smoothed down my crazy ponytail as best I could. Then I got up, took a deep breath, twisted the doorknob, and hoped for the best.

Chapter 5

I slipped through the front door, skated down the long hallway, and when I heard water running and pots and pans clanging, I was relieved. This meant dinner was over, and Lynn would be going to sleep soon. On weeknights, I loved her schedule: come home from her volunteer job, eat, wash dishes (if I wasn't around to do them), and take her strict old butt to bed. On the other hand, Ted, I never had to worry about. He was too cool to hound me.

I didn't bother to say hello to Lynn. I just ran up the stairs two at a time. I thought I was home free when I made it into my bedroom. . . .

Well, to be exact, my bedroom is not my bedroom. It's Lynn's office (aka my spot).

And actually, my spot is like a shoe box, but it could be cozy if Lynn would let me jazz things up a bit. Too bad she won't budge on the subject, and neither will the furniture. So a futon, a file cabinet, and a computer atop a creaky wooden desk stay crammed in one row. Lynn won't let me use her computer, so I can't even holler at Felicia on My-Space. Can't paint these bland white walls, can't hang up a poster or a picture, can't replace these corny white curtains with some Hello Kitty flavor. Basically, my room is mad boring, bare as a jail cell; all that's missing are bars on the window.

There is a bright side, though.

My room is *my* room.

Not another group home's room.

Not another foster home's room shared with a bunch of other kids. My room.

The last group home I stayed at before moving here tried hard to make the rooms feel like ours. The walls were painted pink, lacy white curtains on the window, but I was never fooled. I never got comfortable. Got shifted around way too much, having to change rooms when we didn't get along with our roommates, or maybe there's another leak that needs to be fixed, there was always some kind of drama going on to displace us.

So like I said: *my* room. Not to mention, I have a fire escape. And on nights like tonight, I grab my bag of sunflower seeds, my extra-large pillow, and I climb outside, lean back and relax, taking in that warm summer night's breeze.

Well, I was lounging outside for a minute, leaning back, cracking salty sunflower seeds, and you know, really feeling that warm summer night's breeze. Then all of a sudden, *boom.* Here comes Lynn, howling my name.

I was tempted to jump down into the backyard jungle just to get away from her. What in the world did that lady want from me?

Lynn tore open my curtains and stuck her big head out of the window. "Kate, didn't I tell you *no* phone calls past nine o'clock?"

"Yes, ma'am," I muttered.

"Then why do you have your little friends calling here this late? It's almost ten o'clock, and I have to be to work early tomorrow!"

"Sorry."

"Please come back inside," Lynn ordered.

I climbed back inside my bedroom, fuming, knowing it had to be Naleejah who had called me. Now, I *told* her not to call me past nine o'clock. Why was she so clueless? Okay . . . true . . . I had forgotten to call *her* to let her know I got home safe, but still.

I stood in front of Lynn, my head bent low, avoiding those big bubble eyes of hers. "And what time is your curfew, Kate?"

This unexpected question took me off guard. "Nine o'clock," I mumbled.

"So, I guess you think I didn't hear you coming in here at fifteen minutes past, huh?"

"But—"

"There's no buts about it," interrupted Lynn.

I'm so glad she interrupted me. I didn't have an excuse ready.

"Kate, I have rules in this house for a reason. If I didn't care about you, I wouldn't care about what time you come in. Do you understand me?"

"Yes, ma'am."

But no, I didn't understand her. If she cared about me, she wouldn't be stressing me for no freaking reason. Fifteen minutes wasn't a big dang deal.

Lynn turned to leave my room. *Finally*. But then she double-backed and stood over my threshold and said, "I need you to help me with the backyard on Friday."

"Friday?" I asked in disbelief.

"That's what I said," Lynn replied.

I wondered if she could see the steam coming from my head. Why Friday, of all days? My hair plans were heading down the drain . . . or maybe not. "Um, Lynn . . . can I work on the backyard tomorrow, or Thursday? I promise to do a good job by myself—"

Lynn chased away my request with laughter. "Listen, you can't be negotiating with me."

"But—"

"No need for the sorry face. This is not a punishment. You're just helping me pull a few weeds. End of story."

A sad story at that. Must be a conspiracy. It *had* to be.

"Kate, did you just roll your eyes at me?"

"No," I lied. (Sometimes I can't control my eyeballs, and I'm always getting caught rolling them.)

Lynn wagged her pointer finger at me. "There's no need for you to be giving me attitude. Do I give you any attitude? Don't I treat you with respect?"

I shrugged in place of an answer. Apparently, Lynn took this as being rude because she placed her hands on her hips and said, "Okay, I'll give you something to roll your eyes about. You can help me with the laundry too. Friday is going to be a very busy day for you."

Now I quickly realized I had better cool it. Any more attitude from me, and Lynn would have me painting her whole freaking house.

Lynn relaxed the scowl on her face and said, "Listen, Kate, I respect you, and I'm only asking for the same in return. Do you understand me?"

"Yes, ma'am," I muttered.

Lynn made her way to my door and added, "I don't want things to get to the point where I have to call Tisha, okay?"

"Yes, ma'am."

Finally, Lynn left my room.

Whatever, witch.

Lynn was forever threatening to call Tisha for every little thing. But on that matter, who cared? Tisha always had my back. I couldn't ask for a better social worker. In fact, if it wasn't for Tisha's earlier coaching, I would've *been* cursing Lynn's crazy butt out. Back in the day, it didn't take much for me to pop off. I don't think I was *born* angry. But having bad experience piled on top of bad experience drove me down a long and rough angry path.

At age two, I was placed with Ms. Richards, a mean-as-could-be foster mother who treated her biological daughter, Brittany, with love—and me with pure disgust. Why did she bother taking me in? The money. Period.

Ms. Richards always smelled like baby powder, and her kitchen always smelled like baking cookies, but there was nothing sweet and loving about living in her home. I remember the first time I tried to give her a hug, she pushed me away, said she was having a bad day. I remember the last time I tried to be nice by drawing her a picture of a flower: I had carefully colored the flower in red, orange, and yellow; then I put a big green tree in the background. I was so proud of my picture. When I gave it to Ms. Richards, she screwed up her face and asked, "What's this?" then put it to the side. Later that day, I found my picture crumpled in the trash.

I would call Ms. Richards "Mom" just like her biological daughter did. But the day I turned five, she flat-out said, "Listen, I'm not your mother." It took me a long time to get over that—and there was so much more to get over. If I didn't do something quick enough, she'd hit me. Not hard enough for me to bruise, but enough to hurt my feelings. I never told on her. I was too young and too scared to tell anybody what I was going through.

But I ended up getting kicked out her house anyway—thanks to Brittany. Ms. Richards always bought Brittany dolls, and didn't buy me any. So one day, I snuck one of Brittany's dolls and Brittany caught me playing with it. When she tried to take the doll away, I yoked her. Kept her in a headlock for a minute. Her tears meant nothing to me. When I finally let her go, she yelled, "That's why both your parents are drug addicts."

"You're lying!" I screamed. "Shut up."

"No, I'm not!" she screamed back. "Go ask my mother."

I jumped up and kicked her butt up and down the living room. I was only six years old, while she was eight, and I *whooped* her tail until her mother came screaming for me to stop. Brittany's face was badly bruised when I got through. Mess with me and get *wrecked*.

Normally, it takes ten days to be removed from a foster home—but I was taken away two days later. Ms. Richards lied on me, said I was a troublemaker and she could no longer handle me. I guessed hurting her precious little Brittany was a deal-breaker; I was considered a threat to the household. But actually, I was a threat to myself, feeling suicidal and wondering why I was brought into this world only to be abandoned by drug-addicted parents. I felt so ashamed. Hopeless. Helpless.

For the next four years, I never lived in a foster home longer than six months. I spent most of my days sitting in lobbies and offices waiting for my next foster home placement. Every school year I had a different "parent" picking me up. The words *mother* and *father* never meant anything to me. I always wanted a family of my own, but I had nobody to raise me but the system. Sometimes I thought about my parents with nothing but hate in my heart. Sometimes I wished they had loved me enough to keep me.

By the time I turned ten, I was out of control. Frustrated. Bitter.

Fighting in school every day, cursing out my teachers, my foster parents, and whoever else dared get in my face. One day, after a big fight and another whole day in the principal's office, my social worker at the time, Mrs. Lawrence, came up to my school and threatened to send me to a residential treatment center. A huge threat to me. If I thought a group home was strict, *please*, an RTC was even worse. She called it "structured living." I called it "jail."

Mrs. Lawrence stared at me through her thick bifocals and said, "Fighting all the time and talking back to teachers. . . . If you don't like being told what to do, then do the right thing! What's wrong with you?"

I shrugged. "Apparently everything is wrong with me. I'm a foster child, right?" The facts were clear to me. I was at risk, hard to place, and basically unwanted.

Mrs. Lawrence drew her chair closer to mine and said, "Listen, Kate, there's nothing wrong with you, and it's not your fault you're in care. You don't have to carry around the 'foster child' label for the rest of your life. But if you end up in a crazy house for acting up all the time, it will be your own fault. You *know* better than this."

I sucked my teeth, a bad habit of mine.

Mrs. Lawrence poked me in the shoulder. "You better let that anger go. It's not getting you anywhere, little girl."

I rolled my eyes at her. Another bad habit.

"Keep acting up if you want to," said Mrs. Lawrence, shaking her head so hard, I thought her wig would fall off. "They'll put your wild behind on medication. Do you want to be put on medication?"

This question sounded mad funny to me, so I busted out laughing.

Mrs. Lawrence banged her desk to get my attention. "It's not funny!" she snapped. "It's real out here. They'll put you away and forget about you. You think this is a game?" Mrs. Lawrence stared at me for a while. "Listen, I see something in you, Kate. . . . You don't even realize the gifts you have. But keep acting up this way, and you give me no choice. I'll put you away in a heartbeat."

Her voice was so cold when she said this, I shivered. And at the drop of this threat, I sobered up. Even started behaving for a little while.

Unfortunately, a year later, I was bored with behaving and joined the Lady Killers. Beating up broads and stealing from stores gave me such a rush, like, *Yeah, what? I'm bad.* And even after I left the gang, I kept their "I don't give a f—" swagger. It wasn't until Tisha came into my life that I finally started to come around.

But on the day I met Tisha, I gave her nothing but attitude and my behind to kiss. As soon as she stepped inside the commons room of my old group home, I greeted her with a scowl. She wore a serious face and a serious black suit; she was two heads taller than me. Seemed kinda snobby, like she came from the sunny suburbs and couldn't relate to me.

I slouched in my chair with my arms folded tight against my chest, my eyes rolling up to the ceiling every other minute.

"Kate, why you keep giving me the screw-face?" Tisha suddenly asked in a "hood" voice. Then she clapped her hands twice, as if about to throw down. "Listen, best believe we can get it cracking up in here!" she said, then rolled up her sleeves, pretending like she was ready to fight me. This was so random, all I could do was bust out laughing.

Tisha looked about thirty years old, and didn't look hood, so I couldn't believe she was coming at me hard-core. I was so caught off guard, I didn't know how to fix my face after that. Before leaving me that day, Tisha confided, "Listen, I used to run the streets too, boo. So you ain't showing me nothing new."

Tisha had my whole card, and she was far from impressed. Even when I told her that I quit my gang—on my own—all she said was, "What do you want, a medal? I expect so much more. I see something in you."

Wow, I thought, *Mrs. Lawrence said the same thing.*

In our next meeting, Tisha harassed me about my falling grades. She knew I didn't belong in sixth grade Special Ed, and so did I. So she warned that I needed to "get my grades up," or else she'd really "push my wig back." Tisha was still talking my language and joking with me, so I was all ears. Unlike other social workers I've had, she wasn't yelling at me (like Mrs. Lawrence), or looking down on me (like a whole lot of other people), and I really appreciated that.

On our third visit, Tisha gave me my first good-bye hug, and her personal cell number. She said I was her favorite girl, and I was going to keep things that way. So, yeah, Lynn could threaten to call Tisha until her light-skinned face turned blue. No biggie. No problem. She could dial Tisha until her freaking fingers fell off.

It was too early to go to sleep, but I was too pissed to stay up and think about Lynn. So I got ready for bed. As a rule, I usually keep my bedroom door cracked open. I don't like being swallowed up in the dark by myself. But tonight, forget about being scared—I was too pissed to be scared. Lynn had overreacted, OD'd on some ill drug, making me pull some dang weeds on Friday. Now my beauty agenda had to be put on hold because of her mess.

Aggravated beyond words, I shut myself inside my bedroom. But then all of a sudden, knock, knock, knock on my dang door. Before I could say, "Come in," Lynn pushed open my door, flicked on my light, and walked up to my bed carrying a FedEx envelope. "I forgot to give you this," she said, wearing an emotionless face. I thanked her, and thanked goodness that she left my room without saying another stupid word.

I blinked a couple of times to adjust my eyes. Then my eyes lit up when I recognized Felicia's perfect curvy penmanship on the envelope. *Felicia!* I ripped open the envelope as if it were a present. Well, this was a present. Hearing from my homegirl was the perfect gift.

> Dear Kate,
> I've been thinking about you ever since I got here. I miss you so much!

(Yeah Felicia, I miss you too . . . more than you know.)

> You were right about the girls in this group, they really suck. But I've been sticking by Sekou and making the best out of the situation.

(Keep your head up, Felicia.)

> As soon as our plane touched land, I haven't had a second to think too hard about them anyway. Sekou has been

taking us all over the place! Yesterday, we visited Victoria Falls, the largest waterfall in the world! It's absolutely breathtaking. And the week before, we took a cruise to Seal Island. But we couldn't stop there because the whole island is overflowing with seals. You wouldn't believe how many!

(*Wow. Must be amazing.*)

There are mountains on top of mountains in South Africa, and roads carved into the mountains. It's surreal. It's also hot as blazes, but the landscape is so beautiful and breathtaking, you hardly notice the heat. Seriously, Kate, this trip would be so much better with you. And I can't wait for us to travel together. I'm trying to do Paris, Italy, and Spain before we turn eighteen.

(*Yeah, easy for you to say. You keep forgetting our situations are different.*)

Sekou has been working our butts off. We have to study trees, wildlife, like we're still in school. I don't mind learning, but dang! Well, I hope you're keeping yourself busy over there too. Sorry you didn't get that summer job you wanted at the Brooklyn Museum.

(*Next time I'll apply earlier.*)

How's Ted?

(*Cool as always.*)

Is Lynn acting any nicer?

(*Please.*)

Is Charles in town for the summer? Did you marry him yet?

(*No, not married yet—still working on my first kiss.*)

Well, I met this fine African honey named Umar at a ceremonial dance. We hit it off instantly, and we were tonguing

down behind a tree before the night was through. But don't
worry, girl, he's not getting any drawers!!

(*He better not.*)

Did you meet any new friends yet? Don't have me replaced
when I get back.

(*Never that.*)

Girl, let me stop here. I don't know why I'm asking you all
of these silly questions, since you can't write me back.
We're traveling from village to village, so I don't have a permanent address. And by the way, I e-mailed you a couple of
times from my Treo, but I haven't heard back. I guess Lynn
must be still acting funny with the computer.

(*Yep.*)

Anyway, I hope you like my picture and your birthday pres-
ent. I know I'm crazy early, but I didn't want to be late!
Love ya like a sister,
Felicia

(*A birthday present? For me?*)
I rechecked the FedEx pack, and sure enough, I found a small
golden envelope, and enclosed, Felicia's picture and a fifty-dollar
American Express gift certificate. First of all, Felicia looked gorgeous! I
could see the sun had gotten to her. She was standing up against a lone
tree, wearing a flowing orange sundress and a white wrap around her
head; she looked like an African queen. And, she was throwing money
at me like royalty too! Fifty dollars? Whoa. Way too much for me. I appreciated the thought, but my goodness, what was my broke old butt
going to do when Felicia's birthday rolled around?

Well, I had five more months to worry about that. Besides, there
was another issue weighing heavy on my mind. But I'd have to wait
until tomorrow to handle that. I was too beat to deal.

Next morning, I dialed up Naleejah. I didn't care if it was too early. I had to give her a piece of my mind. Just a little piece, though. After all, I knew she didn't *mean* to get me into trouble last night. But since she *did* and my hair plans were ruined, she had to be *told* about it—in a sweet voice, of course. Call me a chump if you want. But I still needed my hair done, okay?

Naleejah answered her cell phone sounding groggy and out of it.

"Hey, girl," I began, all nice and sugary, "um . . . just wanted to let you know, please don't call my house after nine o'clock again."

"Why, what happened?" she asked, now wide awake.

"I got in trouble last night."

"Oh my gosh!" Naleejah exclaimed. "It wasn't even past ten o'clock when I called!"

"Yeah, well, I got in trouble anyway."

"Dang, your mother is mad strict."

I didn't bother to correct her. She'd find out soon enough. Right now, we just needed to get down to business. "Turns out I can't come over to get my hair done on Friday, so can you—?"

"Oh my gosh!" interrupted Naleejah. "You got on punishment over a stupid little phone call?"

"Kind of . . . I'm stuck doing yard work and laundry on Friday."

"All day?"

"Looks that way."

"Dang, that's messed up."

"Yeah, tell me about it," I said. "So, um, can you do my hair today?"

"Can't," said Naleejah. "Maxwell told me to leave the whole day open for him. He's supposed to be surprising me with something."

From the giggle in her voice, I could tell that something was juicy.

Still, I was confused. "But I thought Maxwell is just your homeboy. Why are you letting homeboy dictate your whole day?"

"Maxwell *is* my homeboy," said Naleejah. "Haven't you heard of friends with *benefits?*"

"Well, what about Thursday?" I didn't mean to press, but I have an iron will, and besides, Naleejah still owed me for fighting *her* fight yesterday.

"Can't do it," said Naleejah. "Maxwell told me to leave both days open. Last week he surprised me with this banging gold link chain, so I'm not trying to be perming your hair when he calls. Shoot, he might have something bigger and better for me! He even mentioned taking me to Atlantic City on the spur one of these days. Sorry, I just can't take the risk."

"See, that's messed up—" I began, and then I immediately cut myself off. I don't like sounding desperate, and that's where I was headed. I decided to play it off. "I mean . . . that *would* be messed up if you missed Maxwell's call. I hear you, girl."

"No doubt," chirped Naleejah. "When Maxwell says be ready, he means be ready."

"Ready at the jump," I said, hoping she didn't detect the sarcasm in my voice.

"Maxwell's more than worth it," added Naleejah. "He's got way more cheddar than that cheesy chump Finesse."

"Mm, I heard that."

"I mean . . . I know I'm just a booty call to Maxwell, but at least we keep it real. I'm not his only one, and he *thinks* he's my only one. He gets his. I get mine. Works out just fine. And if Maxwell ever wants to take things to the next level—hey, I'm totally with that, okay?"

"Okay." That's all I could say. I was glad this chat was taking place over the telephone and not in the flesh. This way, Naleejah couldn't see me frowning. It makes me sad to hear a girl planning her life around a dude just because he says so. Nothing wrong with allocating time for your honey, but don't let a dude control your entire *life* schedule.

Well . . . yeah, I can admit it. A part of me was tripping for selfish reasons (my hair), but the other part really doesn't like to see a girl play herself. Trust, I can tell you so many stories about the dog in some boys (some boys, not all boys, though it seems like all boys). Yeah, let some boy think he's got you on lockdown, and next thing you know: Woof! Woof! Here he comes barking orders at you. Now you're on lockdown, waiting by the phone like a jailbird; meanwhile homeboy is busy on the prowl for the next chick. I've watched so many older group homegirls go through it, watched so many younger chicks clucking in the same direction. And that's why I got news for any controlling dude who comes my way. Money or not: I am *not* the one.

But in other news, my hair plans were starting to look hopeless. I heaved a dramatic sigh and said, "Listen, I guess we can do this some other time."

"Wait!" Naleejah exclaimed. "I can perm your hair on Saturday."

"Can you do it early in the morning?"

"How early?"

"Is ten o'clock okay?"

"Dang, why so early?"

"I have to be somewhere afterwards," I blurted out. I didn't want to go into details about my sweet little rendezvous with Charles. I didn't want my flirty little friend souring up my game plan.

Naleejah huffed in my ear. "Okay, since you're my girl, I'll wake up early for you. See you on Saturday."

"I appreciate it."

Click.

Mission #1: Accomplished.

Mission #2: Run to the library and check for e-mails from Felicia.

I quickly got dressed and headed for the Macon Library.

To my disappointment, the library was already crowded with other kids. And there was a long irritating wait for a free computer. I grumbled at Lynn for being so stingy with hers. When my turn finally came, I leaped into my seat, swiped my library card to sign in, and logged on to Yahoo.com. Then I sat staring blankly at the screen for five whole minutes. I couldn't remember my username or password for nothing in the world. Back in June, my old e-mail address had gotten spammed, so I created a whole new address. But I didn't bother to enter my correct name and birthday, so now I had no way of retrieving my information.

Kate@yahoo?

I had no freaking clue.

I had planned to write a whole novel to Felicia.

Oh well: The End.

So I decided to Google images of South Africa and beyond. I thought it would be fun to imagine where my girl was at, and pretend I was right there with her. The first image I searched was "Victoria Falls." The instant I clicked on the image of the falls, my face fell flat. Just as Felicia had claimed, the falls were absolutely breathtaking. I stared in awe at the powerful surges of water cascading down massive green mountains, the downward force of the water so powerful that the mist looked like smoke rising up to the royal blue sky. From this mist, I could make out a rainbow, the colors yellow, red, and violet jumping out at me. To think that I could've witnessed this awe-inspiring sight in person instead of at the local library . . . to think that I had let some petty little females keep me from this once-in-a-lifetime experience was enough to drive me mad. Although Felicia had admitted in her letter that I was right about those girls, the fact remained, Felicia was *there* feeling South Africa, and I was sitting *here*, staring at a dusty computer screen.

My South African adventure began (and ended) back in March, on a Saturday afternoon right after orientation. Orientation had taken place inside of a big redbrick church on Fulton Street. Sekou, the group leader, led the discussion by giving out pamphlets and photos from his last trip. Throughout the entire two hours, he used his hands, spreading them wide to describe the landscape, and he kept popping open his eyes to express all of the amazing things we would see: wild lions and hippos and zebras—oh my! Felicia and I were bursting with excitement, especially me. While Felicia has been out of the country before, I barely got the chance to leave Brooklyn.

Besides, with me being a straight-A student and "disadvantaged," I'd be eligible to go on the trip for free. Yes, free. Tisha was the one who told me about the program, and I had planned to thank her a million times when I saw her.

But my plans quickly changed.

Felicia and I were standing outside of the church, talking giddily about the trip, when it all went down.

"I can't wait to go on the elephant-back safari," Felicia exclaimed.

"Well, I don't know about that," I said. "Promise not to laugh?"

"What? You can trust me."

"I'm deathly afraid of elephants . . . can't even picture myself riding on some elephant's back. Not!"

"Girl, it's all in your mind," said Felicia. "And you *know* I got your back."

"Well . . . I'll take the ride, only because it's with you."

"Now, that's what I'm talking about!"

I flipped through the pamphlet. "But see, the hot-air ballooning sounds cool. I'm amped about that."

"Listen, I'm amped about everything!" said Felicia.

Suddenly, in the middle of our conversation, here comes three of the girls from orientation, stepping to me, all wearing scowls. The shortest out the group moved forward. All throughout our session, I had noticed this shorty eyeballing me, but I had made a special effort to pay her *no* mind. And even when this silly broad leaned over to whisper something to her friends and then jerked her chin in my direction, I still tried to stay focused. Kept my eyes on Sekou.

But my focus began to waver when Sekou mentioned that we'd need plenty spending money because there'd be so much jewelry and souvenirs to choose from. When I asked, "how much" spending money, I heard Shorty snicker. All ten of us had been sitting in a circle, so it was easy for me to see and hear every dumb thing this broad did—easy for me to see, but hard for me to understand. The girl was far from gangster, too thin and frail to even think about testing me, yet here she was, itching for me to scratch back?

Like I told you before, I don't scratch. I *punch.* So when Shorty stepped to me outside, I was leaning up against the church's gate, gripping the bars behind me to keep from swinging on her.

"Wow, I'm surprised to see *you* here," Shorty said, looking down her nose at me. Sekou was standing five feet away from us, talking to the other kids, so maybe that's why this chick felt safe getting in my face.

"Do I know you from somewhere? I'm Kate, and *you* are?"

"Gwen . . . Weren't you listening to the introductions in there?" she asked in a condescending tone. "Anyway, you attended P.S. 342, correct?"

"Yeah, and?"

"Well, I guess you don't remember me," Gwen said. "I used to go there too. You beat up my friend back in the sixth grade. I'm the one who had to take her to the nurse."

Small world when you don't want it to be.

Gwen pointed to the mousy girl standing behind her. "Here she is. Remember her?"

I didn't recognize this girl at all. So many fights. So many faces.

I tried to make eye contact with Mousy to say sorry—if that's what this was all about. But Mousy was busy staring at the sidewalk.

I looked over at Felicia for answers. She shrugged. So we were both confused. Was this supposed to be a confrontation? I wasn't being threatened, but I felt threatened. Not physically. Gwen was messing with my mental.

I craned my neck to make eye contact with Mousy again and said, "Listen, I'm really sorry I fought with you . . . but that was two years ago. People change."

I used to like having girls scared of me. Made me feel powerful. But right now, I felt weak, wishing this girl would get out of my face so I could keep my cool and stay on the right track.

"Yeah, we ended up changing schools because of girls like you," Gwen cut in, and then she started laughing in a high-pitched cackle.

Mousy and her other friend tittered behind her. When Gwen's laughter finally died down, she said, "Thank goodness for private school."

In disbelief, I looked over at Felicia, who motioned for me to come on. Just as I started walking away, I overheard Gwen say, "If she's coming on this trip, I hope they give her a clothing stipend."

That's when I lost it. Snapped into action. I was up in Gwen's face in under sixty seconds. "I heard what you just said," I spat. "Now say it to my face. Go 'head, say it."

Felicia ran up to me and started pulling at my arm. "Kate, let's go," she pleaded.

I yanked my arm away from Felicia and started putting my hands in Gwen's face. "You got all that mouth!" I shouted. "Now let's see you do something . . . worried about my gear, for what? You ain't my mother!"

Sekou came running up to us. He pushed me away from Gwen before I wrecked her world.

"No, no, no!" Sekou shouted at me. "We're not going to have this kind of conduct on our trip."

"Won't be none," I spat. "Because I'm not going."

"What do you mean?" he asked.

"I'm not going," I repeated.

When my mind is made up, it's closed for questioning.

I stormed away from Sekou before he could press me further. He called after me, "You'll change your mind."

Yeah, that's what you think.

Felicia and I walked down Lewis Avenue in silence. Then finally, she spoke up. "Kate . . . are you sure about this?"

Felicia has big brown eyes the color and size of walnuts. She stared at me for a long time, breaking my heart. But I stiffened my lip and said, "Listen, you can count me out—those snobby chicks left a nasty taste in my mouth."

Gwen. The kind of girl black like me but can't relate to me. I could already tell that she came from money by the stiffness in her voice and the way she held her nose high. She reminded me of so many other snobs. And to think this crab and her cronies would be going on this trip? Oh no. I couldn't go. I might just black out and punch somebody. May seem extreme to you, but have you ever been forced to live with strangers all of your life, going from house to house, feeling like you've got nobody and no clout? Try dealing with kids who have both parents and want to know why you don't. Point blank, it's hard. You have to put up fronts and cover up facts in order to feel normal around other kids. But you never feel normal. You never fit in. Two months was *way* too long for me to be dealing with that kind of bull. Sorry.

But Felicia wasn't giving up on me. She paused before she spoke, and then said, "Listen, I understand where you're coming from. I don't like dealing with girls like that either. . . . But I'm not about to let them stop me from experiencing South Africa."

"Well, good for you," I said. "But I'm staying right here. Besides, Sekou kept harping on spending money—I don't have it like that."

"Don't worry, you know I got you."

"Nah, that's okay," I said, "Thanks, anyway . . . I'll just make my own adventure in Brooklyn."

"Well—you still have time to think about it."

I stopped dead in the middle of the sidewalk, leaned against the ONE WAY sign pole, and said, "Listen, I already thought about it. . . . The answer is still no."

Felicia's eyes cracked into the saddest expression I ever saw. "Kate, please, I don't want to go without you . . . and you're going to regret it."

I was feeling so bad right now, so torn, watching my friend beg me like this. But I had to stay strong.

"Can you leave it alone?" I snapped. "It's bad enough I'm going to hear Tisha's mouth, so I really don't need to hear yours right now, okay?"

"But I don't understand."

"Yeah, I know."

I didn't expect Felicia to understand. Sorry to say, but Felicia was raised by the Coldwells, who are big-time snobs. Big-time lawyers who hold their noses higher than the project towers they were raised in. Their world is so much more different from mine. Uncomfortable too.

Every time I visit Felicia's house and the Coldwells are present, I feel stiff in the jaws. Careful not to use *ain't* in a sentence. Don't even want to laugh too hard or loud. I just can't be myself around them. I'll never forget the first time I ate dinner over there. The Coldwells were so cold, hawking me as if I was going to steal the silverware, asking me a million questions like I was on an interview. It was my first time having steak, but I couldn't even enjoy the moment because of their stuck-up nonsense.

Between me and you, I truly believe if I wasn't rocking the hot grades, the Coldwells would've sent our friendship to an early grave. I'm surprised they even let my girl go to public school.

Anyway.

When Felicia and I reached Lewis Avenue and were about to part ways, I told her: "Have fun for me, okay?"

Before the words even rolled off my tongue, I was already regretting them.

When I told Tisha what had happened, just as expected, she was extremely disappointed in me. She didn't think I should let those girls stop me from going either. She said I would live to regret my decision. Surprisingly, she didn't go on and on like I thought she would. She just said her piece, and then left it alone—

Suddenly, a tap on my shoulder: "Your time is up," said the librarian, pointing at a sulky kid standing behind me.

"Oh, I'm sorry," I told him.

Yeah, I was sorrier than ever.

Felicia was *there*. And I was *here*.

Chapter 7

On Friday, I was up to my knees in weeds. Every single weed I pulled, I imagined Lynn's greasy hair in my grip. I took all of my frustration out on the weeds. Yank. Pull. Yank. The sun was beating down on my back. I was bent over, sweating bullets, pulling these doggone weeds taller than me. And I was thirsty—so thirsty, I was tempted to drink the sweat dripping down my forehead. This was some bull.

Even though Lynn was pulling weeds besides me, I didn't give a snap. Her help was no help, and this punishment was no fair. Lynn claimed this wasn't punishment, but whatever, I felt punished.

When Lynn ordered me to take an hour break, I wanted to scream, "Witch, no!" I didn't want to hear about no one-hour break! I wanted to get this gardening garbage over and done with as quickly as possible.

During the break, Lynn laid out two bologna-and-cheese sandwiches and a tall pitcher of ice-cold lemonade. She made me eat with her out on the patio. And as I sat, munching my sandwich in silence, Lynn asked out of the blue, "Read any good books lately?"

Oh, now she done lost her mind!

Lynn was actually trying to make small talk with me? Please, she would get nothing but sign language. I shook my head.

Lynn got up and went back into the house. She came back carrying a book in her hand. "I want you to read this before the end of the summer."

So now she was giving me homework?

I mumbled, "Thanks," and rolled my eyes at the back of her head.

After the break, I went back to work.

When I pulled my last weed and Lynn finally dismissed me, I didn't dare forget to bring inside the book just to avoid hearing her mouth.

I stepped inside the house with my shirt full of dirt. Dirt caked on kneecaps, my sneakers. What a dirty trick Lynn had pulled on me today! And to think she wasn't through. We still had a whole stinking pile of laundry to do.

I ripped off my grimy clothes, showered, and came out smelling soapy clean, but still feeling dirty and disgusted with my situation.

On our way to the Laundromat, Lynn marched in front of me like a dictator. I dragged the laundry cart behind her, avoiding any possible body contact. I took deep breaths to keep my cool. Dirt was still stuck between my nails. Mosquito bites itching the freak out of me.

We passed four girls playing double Dutch on the sidewalk. I wanted to borrow their rope to whip Lynn's big old butt with it. But no. Lynn's butt was safe from me. After today? My lesson was learned. From now on, it would be all fake friendly smiles. No more attitude from me. Matter of fact, I was even smart enough to bring that book she had given me: *Manchild in the Promised Land*. And while our clothes dried, I cracked the book open. Honestly, I didn't expect to get into it, but I have to admit, the book caught my attention from the jump: Shot! Expelled! Court date! Drama!

I'd never been shot at before, but I could relate to everything else. Although I'm a fast reader, I didn't make it past the first chapter because of Lynn. Oh brother, she wanted to chitchat again.

"So are you excited about going to high school?" Lynn asked.

"Yes."

"What's your favorite subject?"

"Math."

And two plus two equals leave me alone.

"Do you know what you want to do with your life?"

"Yes."

Lynn creased her eyebrows and said, "Well?"

"Social work," I began, "I want to help kids in care . . ." I wanted to add, *deal with witches like you.* But of course I didn't say that.

"Social work?" Lynn repeated. "Then why go to a school that spe-cializes in environmental studies?"

Because Felicia was going there, that's why. Period. I didn't need no stupid lecture from Lynn about being a leader and holding my own. Feels like I've been holding my own ever since I was born. So, if I wanted to stay close and follow my best friend around, that was my business. Lynn needed to mind hers. But instead of getting defensive, I just kept faking smiles at Lynn and nodding at every dumb thing she said. Oh no. I wasn't about to let her block me from my beauty agenda again. Operation Get Fly was about to be in full effect.

On Saturday morning, I bolted out of bed before the sun could climb high in the sky. One step ahead of Lynn, I rolled up my sleeves and cleaned the bathroom, did my dusting, mopped the kitchen floor. Now she couldn't say one word to me about chores.

At twenty past nine, I shot into the shower, shot out, got dressed, and threw a scarf over my head. Then I paused, thinking about break-fast. Should I? Oh yes, I should. I didn't want my stomach grumbling in front of Naleejah. If she had to feed me too, I'd *really* be feeling like a charity case.

As I stood over the kitchen sink, gobbling down a bowl of corn flakes, Ted walked in on me. I gulped down the last drop of milk and smiled. Always glad to see him. Too bad he was barely ever around.

"Hey, Katie, what's up?" Ted asked, all smiles, as usual.

"Nothing much."

"Now, where's my thermos?" he asked absentmindedly.

Ted was getting ready for work at the garage. He worked six days a week, and it showed. His eyes were always red, most of the hair on his head was sprouting gray, and he walked with a slight limp. Poor guy.

"Where did I put that thing?" Ted grumbled more to himself than to me.

I helped him look for his thermos. I found it on a random shelf. He flashed me a grateful smile and said, "I can always count on you, huh?"

"No doubt."

"So where you running to?" asked Ted, eyeing my gotta-go-gear.

"My friend's house."

"What friend?" Ted asked. "Felicia back already?"

"No, this new girl I met named Naleejah," I explained, ready to leave the kitchen before any more questions were asked.

"Oh yeah? Where'd you guys meet?"

"At a basketball game."

"Paying her a visit so early in the morning?"

"Yeah . . . well . . . she wants me to come as soon as possible. We have a lot of stuff to do," I explained vaguely. No, I couldn't explain any further. I couldn't risk Ted asking me if I had permission to get my hair permed.

"Want a lift?" asked Ted.

"Sure, thanks."

It turned out that Naleejah lived only about eight blocks away, but any time spent with Ted is time well spent. He always has a funny story to tell, always has some knowledge to drop, and I was always all ears with him. Never told him so, but I wished with all my heart he was my father. Before Ted, I never trusted grown men, especially not after a grimy ex–foster father touched my breasts. Once. Once, because the second time he tried to go there, I slapped his big grubby hands away from me and threatened to tell his wife.

"Who do you think my wife is going to believe? You prancing around here like you want me, chest all hanging out." That's what he told me. But I knew that was bull. I'd worn nothing but baggy T-shirts and never once gave this creepy man any ideas. *His* fault for being a pervert. Not mine.

I told on him and was instantly removed from that home. . . . But I don't know why I just brought that up. I don't even like thinking about it.

"Kate, give me a few minutes," Ted called over his back.

I decided to wait for him outside. One word: Lynn. I wanted to be out of the house before she could pounce on me for something silly.

Five minutes later, Ted came outside, and we hopped inside his battered blue station wagon.

I gave him Naleejah's address, and we zipped off into the morning sun. On the way there, we laughed and chitchatted. At a stoplight, Ted turned to me and said, "So, Kate, tell me why did the chicken cross the park?"

"The park?" I asked, "Don't you mean 'the road'?"

"The park," Ted insisted.

"Okay, why?" I asked, already giggling.

"To get to the other slide! Get it? Park? Slide?"

(I didn't say all of Ted's jokes are funny.)

Ted was about to tell me another joke when his cell phone rang. Forget the chicken joke, I busted into giggles at the sound of his silly ring tone. Ted had some old-school singers crooning some shoo-wop mess on his phone—straight-up hilarious. Ted was always complaining about gangster rap, so he stayed stuck in the old school; he knew nothing about Nas, Talib Kweli, and Common doing it real big and mostly positive in hip-hop. (Nas is my favorite, my biggest crush next to Charles.)

I couldn't tell Ted a thing about his music. As for his phone call, I could tell that Lynn was on the other line, flapping her lips. Clearly, she had to be complaining about me. Why else would Ted be glancing at me with one raised eyebrow?

Finally, Ted clicked his cell phone shut and, at the next red light, turned to me and said, "Lynn tells me you're always leaving the house without saying good-bye to her. Is that true?"

"Um . . . yeah."

"Why?"

"Because."

"Because is not an answer."

"Well . . . I used to say bye all the time, and she'd just nod at me, no smile, no nothing—felt like she didn't want to speak to me, so I'm figuring, why bother?"

"To be fair, *you* weren't so nice to Lynn when you first came to us." Ted squinted his eyes like he always did when trying to make a point. "You weren't nice to me either, but I knew how to get past that."

Embarrassed, I stayed quiet. Ted wasn't lying. I always wear a scowl instead of a smile when I first meet grown-ups, a bad habit of mine. I tend to expect rejection from them, so I do the rejecting first.

And it was true, when I first came into the home, Lynn had asked me what I liked to do for fun. I immediately shut her down with, "Nothing much." And whenever she invited me to come out to cultural events with her, I always said, "No thanks." And when Lynn told me that if I ever had any problems, I was welcome to come to her. I never came.

I had my reasons. But if Lynn hadn't come on to me so strong, and gave me time to get used to her, I would've eventually come around.

Ted patted my shoulder and said, "Just try to be nice to Lynn, okay? Remember that high road I'm always talking to you about?"

"Yeah, I remember." Meanwhile I was thinking I wished Lynn would take that high road with me. True, she tried in the beginning, but she should'nt have given up on me so quick.

Of course, I didn't debate this with Ted. I just nodded and agreed with his little lecture until he pulled up in front of Naleejah's house.

Wait . . . could this be Naleejah's house?

I double-checked the address. Yep, right address. Wrong first impression. I couldn't believe Naleejah, the Fabulous One, actually lived in this hot mess of a house sitting slumped on the corner of Quincy Street. The house was gray, faded, and crumbly, just like the crib I lived in. The gate was swinging off the hinges, and the busted garbage cans outside were overflowing with beer bottles and junk in general.

Now, please don't get me wrong. I don't go around judging people's cribs. But boy, did Ms. Gucci have me fooled! Dressing like a diva and living in this dump? I've stayed in a bunch of private foster homes in and around Bed-Stuy, and I'm sorry to say, but Naleejah's house was the worst I'd ever seen.

Ted saw me hesitating, and called out, "What are you waiting for, Kate? Everything all right?"

I was still swearing up and down that I was at the wrong house. But Ted wouldn't leave the scene without seeing who answered the door. (Maybe he thought I was sneaking to visit some boy.) To ease his mind, I finally pressed the bell.

One minute later, the black metal door creaked open and out popped Naleejah, crying, "Kate!" like I was her long-lost friend and she hadn't seen me in years. Satisfied at seeing a female, Ted beeped twice and pulled off.

Naleejah's head was tied up in a black silk scarf, and she had on a pink pajama set. She looked so cute, even rocking sleepwear. She ushered me inside and led me down a long dark hallway that smelled like fish. Two shadows were standing at the entrance. Naleejah introduced them as her parents. Her father, Mr. Mackie, was a super-tall dude full of bright white teeth. (I could see where Naleejah got her flashy smile from.) And Mrs. Mackie was short and had less flash. She had small brown eyes and a mean expression in them. She gave me a limp hand-shake and a wave good-bye like she wasn't interested in getting to know me. *Okay, forget you too.*

"I was just headed out," Mr. Mackie explained. "Nice meeting you, Kate."

"Same here," I said, smiling sweetly.

Mrs. Mackie turned to Naleejah and said, "You should've cleaned up if you knew your friend was coming. What's wrong with you?" Then she walked away from us down the long dark hallway.

Naleejah pulled me into her bedroom, the biggest bedroom I've ever been in. But it looked like a hurricane hit it. Clothes blown all over the wooden floor, jeans and things draped over her desk, and a mountain of unidentified stuff piled up on her king-sized bed.

"Ready to get fierce?" asked Naleejah.

I cracked a smile. "No doubt."

Naleejah pulled a random white T-shirt from her dresser drawer and told me to put it on over my top.

"Don't want to be burning holes through your clothes!" Naleejah exclaimed. Then she started mixing the creamy concoction with a wooden stick like the one the doctor puts in your mouth during a checkup. The smell of the perm was so strong, it felt like my nose hairs were scorched. But I needed a strong mix. Shucks, as thick as my hair was? The cream would probably scream when it touched my head. "I want my hair to look just like yours," I said. "Straight and shiny."

"Well, it can't," began Naleejah, "unless you feel like running to the Chinese store and buying two packs of human hair and some glue."

My bottom lip hit the floor. "Say what?"

Naleejah chuckled and said, "You so crazy. *Girls* can usually tell I rock a weave."

"I wasn't studying your head that close," I said testily.

"Well, if it makes you feel any better, I do manage to fool a lot of people."

"Anyway, can we get started, please?"

"As soon as you take that scarf off your head."

I removed my scarf, thinking a scream would come next at the sight of my wild bush. But no. Naleejah calmly pulled on a pair of plastic gloves and got ready to operate. "When I get through with you, you're going to be a *whole* different person."

"Now, that's what's up," I said. "Do your thing."

But as soon as Naleejah began sectioning my hair, my mind suddenly divided in two. Should I be getting this perm without permission? I wondered. Or should I go ahead and get fly? Tisha's voice rang in my head like a million bells. "Treat every new foster home like a new beginning," she had warned. "Don't sabotage yourself, Kate. Don't repeat the same mistakes."

Yeah, I can admit it. Whenever I had it good—or at least okay—with a new pair of foster parents, for some reason I'd always manage to sabotage my situation. I'll never forget the nicest foster family I'd ever stayed with: the Gordons. They used to take me to amusement parks with their own kids, called me their daughter instead of *foster* daughter, and always complimented me for little things, like washing the dishes without being told, and making up my bed. Seemed like a dream that wouldn't last. So what did I do? Joined the Lady Killers. As soon as the Gordons found out, I was removed. They had smaller children and couldn't risk keeping me. I didn't last longer than three months with them. And I wasn't surprised.

I wasn't used to foster folks remaining nice to me, so maybe a part of me preferred to act up before they could flip the script and get rid of me.

But I wanted the Johnson household to be different.

I wanted to stay with them for as long as possible.

"Hey, girl," I began slowly, "I think I should call home first . . . to get permission."

Naleejah jerked her head back. "Permission to do *what?*"

"To get my hair done," I said.

"Wow."

"Wow, what?" I asked. "Why are you looking at me like that?"

"Like what?"

"Like I'm crazy."

Naleejah started chuckling.

"What's so funny?"

"Well you *are* crazy," said Naleejah. "You must be. It's *your* hair. Why would you need permission to look *decent* for a change?"

Okay, rude of her, but true. My hair was in desperate need of a change. And it was *my* hair, on *my* head, so what harm could I cause with *my* perm? So, bump it. Case closed. I sat back, relaxed, and let Naleejah do her thing.

When she started smearing the smelly white cream all over my head, she exclaimed, "I can't believe you went around with this bush for so long!"

"And?"

"And your hair is fighting with the perm! It doesn't want to get straight!" She shuffled and sighed, running around all sides of my head, smoothing down the cream from root to ends. Twenty minutes later, my scalp was on fire! I squirmed in my seat.

"Okay, okay!" said Naleejah, rushing me to the kitchen. She put me under the sink and let the warm water cascade down my burning scalp. I felt so relieved when she washed that fiery cream out my head. Whew.

After the burning drama, we went back into Naleejah's bedroom. She sat me down on a crooked chair and set my hair in big pink rollers. Then she threw me under a tabletop dryer. Forty-five minutes later, I was finally freed from the heat. My hair rollers were removed and— *bam*—my hair was banging!

I almost cried when I saw myself in Naleejah's mirrored closet door.

My hair was actually flowing, touching my neck for the first time ever. I swung my head from side to side, and my hair moved with every swing. I couldn't believe how fabulous I looked with a bootleg perm. I was so impressed.

Naleejah fluffed out my hair, then stood back and admired her work. "Kate, are you proud of me?" she asked, raising her pencil-thin eyebrows expectantly.

"How could I not be? You got skills to pay the bills!"

"You are so pretty right now."

"Thanks." I beamed.

"Now, you know we have to go out and celebrate this makeover, right?"

We? Uh-oh.

No offense, but Naleejah couldn't roll with me. I felt foul and all, but before I could cop a plea, she pulled me to her closet and flung her mirrored doors open. I looked on in amazement at the rows and rows of clothes and shoes cramming her rod and shelves, like a department store.

"I've never seen so many clothes in my entire life!"

"Girl, I don't play."

"Man, your parents go all *out* for you," I said, shaking my head in awe.

"Parents?" Naleejah jerked her head back. "Please, girl, my parents don't hit me off like this. I get money from dudes, and I take *myself* shopping."

"Say word?"

"Word," replied Naleejah, clapping her hands to emphasize her point. "When it comes to getting mine, I got mad game, okay?" Naleejah crossed the room to lift her Gucci tote off the floor. "Do you think my busted old parents would pay over a thousand dollars for this bag?"

I shrugged.

"Or this?" Naleejah grabbed the thick gold link lying on the edge of her dresser. "Maxwell paid mad money for this chain. Believe that."

I creased my eyebrows in confusion. "So Mom and Pop don't be grilling you about where you get yours?"

"Please, they don't sweat me," said Naleejah with a dismissive wave. "As long as I don't ask them to buy me nothing, they couldn't care less what I do."

"Mm, lucky for you."

"Yeah, I know," said Naleejah. "And I hit the jackpot right before summer vacation. Met this dude named Chase who was dealing out of Breevort. As soon as I gave homeboy some booty, he started lacing me up like crazy . . . and I'd *still* be getting money if he didn't get locked up." Naleejah shook her head and added, "Ever since I got a taste of that cream, I can't *ever* go back to being thirsty. It's so messed up Chase let himself get locked up."

"True, that's messed up," I said. But in my head I was thinking, *Whoa, that's messed up to be sleeping with dudes for money.* But nowadays, I try hard to keep my opinions to myself. I get tired of being called "old lady" whenever I say something moral-like to chicks my age. So let me shut up. Let Naleejah do her thing.

"Girl, I'm ready to get *fierce*," said Naleejah. She sashayed back to her closet and started searching for an outfit. She pulled out a red stretch halter top and asked me what I thought. I said it was *fire*. Then she pulled out a super-short black Guess? skirt. I nodded, *tight*. Then she unearthed a pair of high-heeled black sandals. *Hot.*

"Man, you got it all," I said, fighting off the jealous jitters.

"Please, you got the same goodies I got," said Naleejah. "Ain't no reason for you to be dressing like *that*."

Naleejah's eyes dropped down to my sneakers. "Tell me why your tennis shoes are leaning to one side?" Naleejah did a couple of leans and started singing, "Lean back, Lean back." Then she busted out into a fit of laughter.

I rolled my eyes. "First of all, you're not in Maryland anymore. They're called *sneakers*, not *tennis shoes*. Duh?"

I thought I had dissed Naleejah into silence. But she busted out laughing even harder and said, "Well, your sneakers need to *sneak* off your feet because they're straight up busted. . . . You need a man in your life."

I flipped up my middle finger. "Laugh if you want to, but I'll get mine regardless."

"Get yours how?" asked Naleejah, looking me up and down again, wiping the tears of laughter from her eyes.

I pointed to my head. "I got brains, okay? I don't need no dude to lace me. And when I get out the system, I'll be completely—"

"The system?" Naleejah interrupted.

"Yeah, I'm in foster care."

"Oh," said Naleejah, her mouth shaped like an amazed O.

"So, yeah, when I get out of the system, I'm emancipated. I'll go to college, graduate, get myself a good job. Then I promise you, I'll stay laced with my own money. Feel me?"

"Wow," said Naleejah.

"Wow, what?" I asked, thinking she was impressed with my little speech.

"I didn't know you were a foster child," said Naleejah. "You really don't look like one."

"Well what does a foster child look like?" I demanded. "And by the way, I'm not a foster *child*. I'm in foster *care*, okay?"

In a huff, I plopped down on her bed and folded my arms across my chest.

"Dang, sorry!" exclaimed Naleejah. "Don't bite my head off."

"Well, no need to be labeling me," I said. "I don't like labels."

"Yeah, I can see that," said Naleejah, lifting the tag inside my no-name T-shirt.

"Okay, it's not funny anymore," I snapped. "Now if you're finished clowning on me, I have somewhere to be." I jumped up, grabbed my knapsack, and headed out of her bedroom.

"Kate, wait up," Naleejah called at my back. "Please?"

I swiveled around and barked, "*What?*"

"Don't go yet. . . . I have something to give you."

Chapter **8**

I'll be back in a second," said Naleejah with an odd look in her eyes. Sulkily, I sat down on her bed with a heavy plop. For five minutes, I was left wondering what Naleejah had to give me. More humiliation?

When she came back into her room lugging a giant plastic bag brimming with clothes, I tried to hide my cheesy grin.

"My sister, Tammy's, stuff," said Naleejah in a low tone. She dumped the bag's contents beside me. "We're going to find you something nice to wear, okay?"

I stared at the mountain of clothes and said, "Wow, your sister doesn't want these anymore?"

Naleejah didn't answer me. She sifted through the bag and didn't look my way once. Her weird behavior was making me feel bad, like she wasn't really happy to be hooking me up. Of course, I wanted to be made over. But not like *this*. "Listen, you don't have to give me anything, if you don't want to—"

"It's not that."

"Well, what's wrong, then?"

"It's nothing," said Naleejah.

"Are you sure?" I didn't mean to press her, but she had just changed moods on me fast and crazy, like she was on medication.

Then in a flash, she was all smiles. Felt like a false rebound to me. But, I was about to be laced from head to toe, so I didn't have time to be worrying about what was really on Naleejah's mind. Call me shallow if you want. I don't give a snap. I haven't been fly since the day I was born.

"What about this?" Naleejah asked, holding up a skanky purple tank top.

"Nah, too glittery," I lied.

Then she pulled out a pair of Daisy Duke shorts. "Um, no," I said. "I don't like the flowers on the back pocket." But on the real, I didn't think my big butt could be contained in those things. Honestly, the stuff Naleejah was pulling out looked like straight-up stripper gear.

Finally, Naleejah dug up a pair of sky-blue skintight jeans, size 8, perfect size. "These will look hot on you."

"True," I said, holding them up to me.

Then Naleejah passed me a red stretch tank top to wear. I turned my back to her, tried it on, but it was too tight. My boobies were busting out of it. I turned back to show her: "No."

"But what's wrong with it?"

"Hello? Don't you see my boobies busting out?"

"Don't you know how many chicks would *pay* to have those?" Naleejah pointed at my twins. "Shoot, when I get enough money, I'm buying a pair just as big and bouncy as yours."

I started laughing, but quickly sobered up once I realized she was dead serious. Naleejah gave me a lavender T-shirt to try on. Perfect.

When I tried on the jeans, Naleejah started cracking up. She had caught a glimpse of my white granny panties.

She shook her pointer finger at me. "No you *didn't* walk out the house in those big old drawers."

"Yes, I did, and my big old butt feels just fine in them."

"You so silly," said Naleejah, laughing and shaking her head at me.

"Yeah, I'm silly fly," I said, primping in the mirror. I couldn't believe a bona fide *girl* was staring back at me. . . . First time loving what I saw.

Naleejah came up behind me and grabbed the bottom of my T-shirt and tied it up into a ball so that a bit of my back was showing.

"My sister used to wear it like this," she said in a faraway voice. "Looks better that way."

"Oh yeah," I exclaimed, twisting to the left and right. "Much better . . . so does your sister live with you?"

"No," said Naleejah, suddenly looking away from me. Since she left it at that, I left it alone too. I recognized the need to mind my business.

Naleejah picked up a towel flung over her radiator and said, "Let me take a quick shower, and then we're out of here, cool?"

Oh no.

Not cool.

I mean . . . I was truly grateful for my makeover and all, but it was time to tell Naleejah that she couldn't roll with me. I couldn't risk her eclipsing my moment with Charles. This was *my* time to shine.

Of course, I felt bad about being this way. And I understood Naleejah would feel dissed and pissed when I told her to sit her butt back down.

But what could she do? Nothing. She wasn't brave enough to snatch the clothes off my back, or snatch me baldheaded. I was dolled up, ready to go, and I'd catch up with her later. Period.

"Hold up, Naleejah," I began. "I have to go somewhere first, and then I'll come back for you. Okay?"

"What time will you be back?" she asked with raised eyebrows.

"Um, around four or five o'clock? Cool?"

"Hell *no*, that ain't cool," Naleejah exclaimed. "I'm not staying stuck in this house all day. . . . Where are you going anyway?"

I didn't expect to be questioned like this. And I wasn't able to think fast on my feet. I blurted out, "There's a game at the Stuy Court."

"Wow, you didn't even ask me to go with you," said Naleejah in a hurt voice.

Think, Kate, think!

"Oh nah . . . see," I began, "um . . . I was afraid that those girls might come after you again."

A puzzled look registered on Naleejah's face. "But why aren't *you* worried about them? *You're* the one who had the fight."

"Well . . . if anything goes down again, Charles will have my back."

"But won't Charles have *my* back too?"

"Yeah . . . I'm just saying—"

"What *are* you saying?" Naleejah butted in. "You don't want me to come? You get your hair done and run?"

"No, no, it's not like that," I said, feeling like a butthead. "I mean—you can roll with me, I just didn't think you'd be interested in the game, that's all."

"If Finesse is going to be there, I'm definitely interested. I'm interested in showing him what he's missing out on." Naleejah pointed to her outfit lying on the bed. "When he sees me in *that,* oh trust, he'll come running back. I'll give that boy a heart attack. So let me hurry up and get ready."

"No rush," I said. "We have about two hours to kill."

"Dang, two hours?" exclaimed Naleejah. "Well, I'll take my shower now anyway. I'm feeling sticky."

Fifteen minutes later, Naleejah came back into her bedroom wearing a short orange towel, only covering up her upper parts. I saw nothing but long brown legs and a bright pink thong, and wondered why she didn't get a bigger towel; I didn't need to see all that. Finally, she threw on a pink robe with a big old hole in it.

She pushed off all of the clothes on her bed. We plopped down on it and talked about nothing special. By the time twenty minutes to two o'clock rolled around, I was all talked out. I urged Naleejah to get ready. She slipped into her tight outfit looking hotter than hot. I would've been proud of her fierceness if she wasn't a potential threat.

Naleejah twirled in front of me. "Now *this* is what you call dressed up, feel me?"

"Yeah, okay," I said curtly. "Are you ready to go now?"

"Well, I am." Naleejah pointed at my feet. "But you're not."

I looked down at my feet and sighed. Oh well. I could no longer deny it. My sneakers used to be white, and now they were dingy beige, and the rubber soles had a serious gangster lean.

"What size do you wear?" asked Naleejah.

"Eight."

"I wear a seven and a half," said Naleejah. "But hold up."

She dropped to her knees and started pulling out shoes from underneath her bed. She unearthed a fierce pair of cute brown leather wedges and stuck them out at me. "They're a little too big for me, and they might be too high for you. But if you can walk in them, you can have them."

"To keep?" I asked. "Are you sure?"

"Of course I'm sure," said Naleejah. "I told you I get mine, didn't I? I can get me another pair"—Naleejah snapped her fingers—"just like that."

I tried the wedges on. Then I wobbled across the floor. They were mad tight in the painful sense of the word, but they looked blazing hot on my feet. In pain or not, I was ready to twirl my pretty little self outside. I grabbed my knapsack from off the floor and said, "Okay, let's hit the road!"

Naleejah stopped dead in her tracks and scrunched up her nose as if she smelt a dead rat. "Where are you going with that?" she asked, pointing to my knapsack like *it* was the dead rat.

"What?" I asked, knitting my brows into a blanket of confusion. "I'm saying, what's the problem now?"

"You're a diva now. You can't be rocking no hobo bag. Get your mind right, Kate."

Naleejah crossed the room to attack her closet again. She yanked out tan purses, blue purses, red purses, black.

"Okay, I'll take the black one," I said.

"Yeah, good choice."

I stuffed my keys, headscarf, and a pen inside the purse.

"Ready to rock?" asked Naleejah.

"Let's roll."

We bounced out the house.

Outside on the pavement, I tried to copy Naleejah's *get him girl* walk. But I never wore shoes so dang high before. Felt like I was switching my booty on stilts. Three blocks later, I finally got the hang of it. Bang, bang, bang, watch your girl Kate go. My feet hurt like hell, but I was looking mad good while in pain.

As soon as we rounded the next corner, we came across a posse of guys. They were standing in front of a Chinese food spot, looking like they were waiting for a bus, only there wasn't a bus stop for blocks. As soon as they spotted us, a chorus of "Yo, shorty! Yo, shorty!" rang in the air. I braced myself for the ambush. Let the games begin.

Chapter 9

Out of the posse, a light-skinned guy wearing cornrows in his hair and a bright smile on his face stepped to us.

He stared at Naleejah specifically and asked, "Can I get your name, sweetheart?" He had a deep voice and a sharply trimmed goatee. He had to be at least twenty years old, and he was definitely a hottie—not as hot as Charles, but hot enough for me to want his attention too. *Oh well.* So much for my makeover. I stepped back to give the two some room.

"I'm Tasha, and this is Brandy," said Naleejah with a straight face.

"My name's Daryl . . . so, um, where y'all fly-looking girls headed?"

"To a friend's house," Naleejah lied again. "And we're running late." I could tell she was about to look at her wrist, but she probably remembered—oops—no watch. Then she started shifting her feet back and forth, like she was anxious to leave. But Daryl wasn't taking the hint. He kept on yip-yapping, wasting his pickup lines on Naleejah. She just smiled and nodded, and I just stood there, wondering why she even bothered to stop in the first place. Maybe this was practice for her.

"Yo, is she mute?" asked Daryl, pointing his chin at me.

"Nah, she's just quiet," explained Naleejah.

"Oh, 'cause I was about to call my man over here for her."

"No, no, that's okay. We really have to run, boo," said Naleejah. "I'll catch you later, cool?"

"Well, can I get your phone number?" Daryl called pitifully at our backs.

Naleejah played deaf and pulled me down the block, hot-stepping in high heels.

At the next corner, I had to ask: "Why didn't you talk to him? He was a cutie!"

"Yeah, he was definitely a cutie," Naleejah agreed. "But he was standing on the corner doing nothing . . . not to mention he's broke."

"How do you know that?"

"I could tell by his gear. Didn't you see that dingy T-shirt he had on, and that wannabe diamond in his ear?"

"But that doesn't mean he's broke," I butted in. "My homegirl dresses like a bum, and she's got more cheddar than you and me put together."

Naleejah shrugged. "Well, that's your homegirl—I don't know what her problem is—but I'm talking about homeboy standing on the corner. If a dude can't show me cheddar, then Naleejah can't say cheese." She busted out laughing at her own joke, and then suddenly grew serious. "Listen, Kate, I know you're new to the game. But if you stick with me, I can teach you how to play it. See, you have to be picky when it comes to your men, okay? You don't need to be messing with some dude holding up the wall with his back. You're better than that."

And blah blah blah.

I blocked out the rest of Naleejah's rant during the walk to the Stuy Court. All I could think about was Charles's reaction when he saw me looking beautiful. And if things went my way, Charles could actually be The One to plant the first kiss on my lips. Yes, I said first kiss. Crazy late for me, I know. Growing up a tomboy and forever being vexed about where I'm going to live next, romance had been the last thing on my mind—besides, the few times I felt my heart flip for Charles, I stopped it cold flat. With the way I used to look and feel about myself, I never thought I had a chance with him.

As we neared the court, I saw many of the same heads from the last game present. And I was grateful to see that Blondie and Burgundy's frizzy heads were out of sight.

The game had already started. Unfortunately, my favorite front-row bleacher was filled to the brim. I was pissed. We had to climb all the way to tier number five thanks to Naleejah yapping and taking her sweet time getting ready. . . . Then again, thanks to her, I was now an official hot girl.

My eyes instantly landed on Charles. He was decked out in royal blue shorts and a white tank top. Right now, he was rocking Crown Heights on the basketball court. Finesse was *trying* to ball, but his game was weak.

It felt like the game was over before it even got started. Just as expected, Fulton Street Park won. Yeah! *Bed-Stuy, do or die!* I started yelling crazy with the rest of the crowd.

"Come on, let's get our men," said Naleejah, pulling at my arm.

As she led me toward the players, my stomach dipped down to my wedges. This was it. My moment to shine. Oddly, Finesse seemed to see us coming, but he started walking off. Naleejah released my arm and ran off to catch up with him. I coolly stayed in my spot, waiting for Charles to spot me.

I exploded into smiles when he finally looked my way. And I would pay a million dollars to see the double take he gave me.

When he came swaggering up to me, a mob of butterflies flew straight into my stomach and stayed there, fluttering wild.

"Kate?" Charles squinted like he couldn't see me clearly—like he couldn't believe it was me. "Wow . . . *look* at you, girl!"

"What's up, homey!" I said, grinning, knowing I was too cute for words.

"Wow, you just made my day!" Charles exclaimed. "Turn around and let me see you."

No, I didn't think so. I was no mannequin to be grinning and spinning around for Charles. I wanted my baby to take in my new look, slowly. Let him revolve around me, see? As he stared, I was feeling like a beautiful ebony princess on display.

Suddenly Charles reached out to touch my hair and asked, "So who laced you?"

I jerked my head back. "Okay, Mr. Nosy, did I ask who laced *you?*"

"No."

"All right then," I said. "Mind yours."

"I'm minding mine right now," said Charles, winking at me.

"Since when am I yours?" I asked.

"Since you're looking like a *lady*, for a change."

"Ohhh snap, that was cold," I said, poking my lips into a playful pout.

"Well, I can warm you up, baby," said Charles, staring at my mouth with lowered eyelids. "So when you gonna let me taste those juicy lips?"

Ever see a dark-skinned girl blush? My heart was pounding in my chest; my feet were pounding in Naleejah's hurting shoes. I didn't know what to do with myself. I put the capital A in Awkward. Charles was the first guy I was allowing myself to like, like *that*, and I just didn't know how to act. So I started making jokes. Well, at least I *tried* to make jokes. "You probably can't even kiss, though," I said, grinning like a doofus.

"Baby, kissing is for first-graders," said Charles. "There are so many other things I can teach you."

"Teach me?" I said. "*Please*, you need to let *me* teach *you* how to play ball. You did *all right* this game, but you were slipping in the last, and I'm saying shame, shame, shame!" Hey, I had to switch the subject and talk some smack in order to keep cool under Charles's steady mack.

Charles stared at me wearing an odd, faraway expression.

So I blurted out, "I just blew up your spot, huh? Oops, catch your face!"

Charles snapped out of it and said, "I don't know all about *that*."

"Well, what *do* you know?"

"I know how to *ball* . . . and I can teach you if you want me to." Charles was wearing a sly grin now, making my stomach flip. "I'm good at what I do, baby," he added. "Trust me, I can teach you some things you won't forget."

"So, let's see who can make three shots in a row. How much you want to bet?"

Charles creased his eyebrows in confusion. He ran the palm of his hand across his wavy hair and said, "Okay, why are you acting so random right now?"

"I guess you're too scared to bet me, then," I continued. "Three shots in a row. So, what's up?"

"Come on now, girl, you already know," said Charles, wearing a bored expression.

"I'll show you what's up," I said. "Wait right here." Before Charles could protest, I snatched off my heels and ran up behind Finesse. I was about to ask to borrow his ball when I overheard him telling Naleejah, ". . . but don't be blowing up my cell phone like that."

I timidly tapped his shoulder. He swiveled around, wearing a screwface.

"Um, can I see your ball for a second?" I asked.

Naleejah was already frowning at me, but when I took the ball from Finesse, she looked even more troubled. But really? She needed to mind her own business.

As I walked up to Charles, my feet were screaming *ouch* with every step. The asphalt was hot and hard. What a stupid idea this was. But I already had the ball in my hands, so it was time to get busy. I dribbled the ball with one hand and pushed Charles off with the other. "Defense, baby," I said. "Watch me work."

Snatch. The ball was in Charles's hands within a split second. Then he fended me off by sticking out his butt (I was in my glory) and circling around me, making my head spin. And *swishhh*, he made the hoop.

"Where you at?" asked Charles as he made his third and last hoop.

Where was I at? In heaven. I couldn't care less about Charles winning.

When I went back to give Finesse his ball, I overheard him telling Naleejah, ". . . but you're not even my girl, though."

Oops, sounded personal. Better get back to my baby.

I rushed up to Charles like I was afraid he'd disappear.

Charles tilted his head to the side and asked, "Tell me why you're sounding like you just ran a marathon?"

"True," I said, laughing.

"Come sit down with me," he said. When I bent down to pick up my shoes and put them back on, Charles craned his neck to watch my backside. Since the ice had been broken by us balling, I relaxed a bit more under his steady stare.

As soon as we sat down on the bleacher, Charles reached over to rub my thigh. And can I tell you? His warm hand felt so good even through my jeans. But I quickly brushed him off. "Stop," I said.

Of course, I wanted Charles to continue. But I felt the need to play hard to get . . . for a little bit. The more you hold back, the more they want you. Tisha taught me that.

Unfortunately, before Charles could try me again, I heard yelling from across the court. The voice belonged to Finesse. I looked over to see Naleejah and Finesse standing in the middle of the basketball court in each other's faces. "You need to back up off me!" roared Finesse.

But Naleejah was steady getting closer to his face.

"I said back up off me!" Finesse yelled again.

At these words, Naleejah jumped up as if to say, *You're not going to ignore me this time!* And the next thing I knew, Finesse shoved Naleejah so hard, she fell back—boom—flat on her butt.

"Ohhh snap!" I said.

Before I could turn to Charles to ask, *Did that just happen?* Charles was already on his feet, sprinting up to Naleejah. He helped her up off the ground, and then he called out to Finesse, "Yo, man, you were wrong for that!"

Finesse flipped Charles a whatever-wave and stormed off the court, bouncing his ball like he was trying to shatter the cement.

I snapped out of my shock and ran by Naleejah's side.

Tears were rolling down her cheeks. She looked confused.

"Are you okay?" I asked, brushing off the back of her skirt.

"Yeah, I guess so," she said slowly.

Then Charles suddenly felt the need to throw his arm around Naleejah's shoulder and guide her toward the bleachers. What was his deal? Why was Charles being so attentive, like some play-play doctor on call? The girl was okay. No broken bones. It wasn't even that serious.

I followed behind them, simmering like an unwatched pot. The minute Naleejah's butt hit the ground, *pop* goes my fantasy? Shoot, maybe I needed to fall down on my behind so I could get Charles's attention back where it belonged.

Now that Naleejah was in our picture, I didn't *dare* go back to our juicy conversation. I'd have to quench my thirst for Charles some other time.

I turned to Naleejah and said, "Well, I better get you home."

"Want me to walk with y'all?" asked Charles.

"No, we're fine."

"Are you sure?"

"Yes, we're sure," I snapped. "Later, bye."

Charles took one last look at me with knitted eyebrows. Then he shook his head and bebopped off the court, slow and sexy, side to side. I hated to see him leave. But I had to let him go. Bad enough he already had unnecessary body contact with Naleejah. If we stuck around this court any longer, he'd have his tongue down her freaking throat.

I took Naleejah by the hand and dragged her off into the opposite direction.

Chapter 10

We headed down Lewis Avenue in silence. Naleejah had nothing to say. I didn't know what to say. I was too upset and frustrated. Charles and I seemed to be finally getting somewhere, only to be interrupted by Naleejah's drama. No disrespect to her, but dang, would Charles and I *ever* get to first base?

Six blocks away from Naleejah's house, she stopped short, leaned against a nearby telephone pole, and blurted out, "I don't want to go home."

"Well where do you want to go?" I asked, trying to hide my irritation. I had to keep reminding myself that if it wasn't for Naleejah, I wouldn't have come this far with Charles; she had turned me into a certified hottie. I had to be grateful and patient with her.

Naleejah dug into her bag for a cigarette, stuck it in her mouth, and lit up. "Don't know where I want to go—I just don't want to go home right now."

"Okay, then, we can take a walk," I said. "You need to walk off what just happened to you anyway."

"Yeah, good idea."

"Finesse is a total punk," I offered. "He shouldn't have put his hands on you like that."

"Yeah, I know," said Naleejah.

"And you don't *need* no crazy dude like that in your life, feel me?"

"Yeah, for sure." Naleejah took one puff, exhaled a circle of smoke, and then threw down her cigarette and squashed it with her heel.

"And you know if he put his hands on you once, it's bound to happen again, because—"

"Okay, okay, enough about me," said Naleejah, throwing up the stop signal. "Now let's get to *you*."

"Why? What did *I* do?"

Naleejah tugged at my shirt. "Tell me why you were playing basketball in your diva clothes . . . like you crazy?"

I jerked my head back. "What's crazy about me and my homeboy shooting a couple of hoops?"

Naleejah stopped dead in her tracks. "Okay, Kate, let's stop it with the 'homeboy' crap. It's easy to see you like Charles. I'm not blind."

I was about to deny it, but my eyes couldn't lie. I paused then said, "Okay, I *do* like Charles. You got me."

"Well, if you want to *get* him, you can't be looking a hot mess. Peep your underarm pits."

I lifted up my arms and checked underneath. Then I wanted to sink into the sidewalk. I had two sloppy wet circles blotching up my beautiful lavender T-shirt. Oh no. Did Charles notice? Was I stinking?

"*Never* let him see you sweat," said Naleejah, wagging her finger at me. "And you need to start acting like a *lady* for a change," she said. "Have some mystery about you."

"But Charles and I go way back," I explained. "There's nothing mysterious about me."

Naleejah didn't understand. Charles and I had history. He had already witnessed me at my worst, had already seen me growing up in the system, sometimes dirty, sometimes clean, shirts too big for me, sleeves hanging off my fingertips—he's even been there for me through rough times. Once, I lived with a foster mother named Ms. Phillips, a nasty old bag who was cheap with her food. She used to put a lock on her fridge and dared me to ask for seconds at the table; she had me feeling like a roach wanting to sneak food in the dark. I was only nine years old and not yet the outspoken bad-butt I was to become, so I let her get away with this mess.

One day, she told me I wasn't getting any dinner because I didn't move fast enough when she called me into the dining room. I was the only kid she picked on like this. Late that night, I snuck out the house, which was easy to do since Ms. Phillips had four other kids in care she didn't care about. I sat by myself, five stoops away, crying from hunger pains. I was starving like Marvin. Charles happened to be passing by with his older brother Jermaine. When I didn't return his "What's up?" greeting, he stopped short and asked, "What's wrong?"

"Nothing," I said. He heard the crackle in my voice and told his brother to wait up.

"Kate, what's wrong?" Charles repeated. I looked away from him. Embarrassed. I was starting to feel like a problem child.

I didn't want to tell him what was going on, but my stomach did the talking, the growling, sounding like a monster inside my belly. I let out a nervous chuckle to play it off. But somehow Charles understood my situation. Next thing I knew, he went over to his brother, whispered something in his ear, then pulled me from the porch and announced that we were headed to his building three blocks away. Charles waited with me outside while Jermaine snuck out a paper plate filled with warm rice, beans, and delicious fried fish. I'll never forget that night—never forget what Charles did for me, and there was no way I could act brand-new with my dude from way back.

Naleejah was still looking at me, shaking her head.

"Listen, I'll get it together," I said. "I just have to get used to my new look, okay?"

"Well, how long is it going to take for you to feel fabulous?" Naleejah asked. "Can't you see the dudes are already checking for you?"

"I *said*, I'll get it together, okay?"

"Yeah, I hope you get it together," she replied. "Because if *you* don't know what to do with Charles, *I'll* surely handle him for you."

"Oh, it's like that?" I asked with an attitude.

"You know I'm only kidding." She laughed.

Ha, ha, whatever. I wasn't laughing with her.

As we were about to cross Malcom X Boulevard, a sparkling emerald-green Range Rover pulled up on the opposite side of the street. The driver honked at us three times. Naleejah's eyes popped out of her head, and she almost broke her neck trying to peep at the brothers inside. They waved at us. Naleejah grabbed my arm and made me wave back like I was her puppet. Next thing I knew, the driver made a zany U-turn and slid so close to the curb, he almost ran over a fire hydrant.

Naleejah zipped over to the truck, and I stood right where I was, trying to look cool and blend in with the background. Five minutes were filled with Naleejah's flirty chatter. Her head was all up inside the ride.

"Who's your friend?" I heard the passenger ask. "She lookin' mad shady standing way back there."

"Kate, come over here."

I trudged up to the Rover.

"This is Sting and Jason."

"Hi," I muttered.

I hung back, waiting for Naleejah, the giraffe, to pull her long neck out of the truck. Five minutes passed. Next thing I knew, Naleejah was motioning for me to come even closer. I shook my head in protest, growing impatient, thinking she needed to get the digits and get gone already. But no. Next thing I knew, Naleejah was jerking open the back door. In disbelief, I watched her hop inside the truck. She held the door open, motioning for me to follow her lead.

I knew Naleejah was crazy enough to roll with these dudes whether I came with her or not. For some reason, I felt the need to protect her. However, before I leaped inside headfirst, I walked up to the front of the truck's grille and made sure these dudes saw me checking the license plate. I moved my lips as if memorizing the letters and numbers. I stood mumbling for a minute. I wanted to look smart about it.

"Yo, your girl is mad scared," said the passenger, laughing his head off.

"Kate, get in!" shouted Naleejah.

I finally hopped inside. The driver had a shiny bald head. He looked like a roughneck and at least ten years older than us. He wasn't cute to me, but I guessed his Range Rover was fine enough to take Naleejah's mind off funky old Finesse. On the other hand, Jason was a dark-skinned cutie with the waviest hair I've ever seen on a dude; he must've worn his do-rag for years to get that special effect.

The Rover rolled through the streets bumping old-school Jay-Z, a chorus of children singing "Hard Knock Life"—and you know that's my song because I can surely relate. I tried to get lost in the song and not to worry about being trapped inside of a stranger's ride. But it was hard to chill. My body shook from the bass of the music, and my ears were ringing from the earsplitting treble pumping out of the speakers. All I heard was *boom, boom, boom,* my head pounded with every beat. And Naleejah's perfume wasn't helping my headache; the smell of strawberries invaded my nose and flooded up to my head.

Sting, the driver, was coasting two miles an hour, so everyone standing on every corner could get a good look at him. He had all of the windows rolled down, and half his body leaning out the truck. Either the truck was brand-spankin'-new, or he had just gotten it detailed, because the shiny flyness was catching mad attention, and this seemed to be Sting's sole purpose for driving.

"Ohhh snap, check that out!" Naleejah said in an excited whisper. I glanced up and saw what she was so keyed up about. A mini television hung up in the front, but it didn't need to be turned on for my entertainment, I was too busy watching Naleejah act the fool, like she wasn't used to anything. I'm not used to anything either, but I try not to show it. Dudes love a giddy wide-eyed chick, and I'm not the one.

At a red light, Naleejah scooted up in her seat and tapped Sting's shoulder. "How much did you pay for this?"

Right then and there, I wished the seats were made of quicksand instead of butter-soft leather. How embarrassing! But Sting just laughed off her tacky question.

"I paid *money* for my Rover."

"I know you paid money." Naleejah giggled. "I'm just asking you how much."

"Too much," piped in Jason.

"But you always riding with me, right?" Sting cracked back.

"Anyway, did y'all eat already?" asked Jason. "Our original plan was to cop some KFC, but Sting got sidetracked by you." His chin pointed toward Naleejah.

"No, that's okay, we're fine."

"I know that's right," said Sting. "Mm, *mighty* fine!"

"Thank you," said Naleejah, giggling.

I was pissed. How did Naleejah know "we" were fine? What if I wanted some food? I didn't push the issue, though. I didn't want to seem like a pig.

Sting slid into a spot in the KFC parking lot. Jason hopped out, and ten minutes later came back, carrying a bag full of sweet-smelling chicken. The mouthwatering aroma caused my stomach to grumble and cuss out Naleejah with me. But as we coasted out of Bed-Stuy and into Crown Heights, my hunger pangs turned into fretful flips. Man, I was nervous! This was just not right! We didn't know diddlysquat about these dudes. I had done this kind of thing before with my older group homegirls, but back then, I was too young to think about consequences.

We parked in front of a four-story apartment building, and I was the first to jump out the truck, still on edge. Naleejah hopped out, looking happy and proud to have just been riding in style. Sting slid out his truck and walked around it three times before leaving its side, like this shiny piece of metal was a newborn baby. And Jason was busy glancing over at me, grinning, like he just knew I was going to be his baby for the night. *Not.*

Naleejah tapped Sting's arm. "So, is this *your* crib we're headed to?"

"Of course," said Sting. "Don't you know I'm the *man?*"

Sting's apartment was on the third floor. We climbed up, up, up the stairs, and on the third landing I was out of breath, and still feeling wrong about this whole situation. But I couldn't leave Naleejah flat. Nope, no way.

"Enter my castle, ladies," said Sting, smiling mischievously as he ushered us inside.

We entered the dim apartment, passed by a tiny kitchen, the bathroom, and then we were led into a boxlike living room that smelled like Sex on the Beach incense. (I know that scent anywhere. One of my ex-foster mothers used to burn it all the time, trying to hide the weed smell in her bedroom.) Sting flipped the light switch on. A single yellow bulb barely lit up the living room. Dull navy-blue carpet covered the floor, and pictures of brown naked women covered the four white walls. A droopy blue couch sat up against a bare window, and a matching love seat sat on the opposite side. A tiny spot. No room for anything else, not even a bar of sunshine could come through the apartment. The dullness of the crib couldn't compare to the shiny flyness of Sting's ride . . . but at least he had his own apartment, so let me shut up.

"Cozy, ain't it?" said Sting, searching for praise.

"Yeah, your crib is nice," offered Naleejah in a fake voice.

"It's cool," I said.

Naleejah and I dropped into the love seat. We didn't say one word to each other. I was too busy being uncomfortable, and she was too busy checking herself in her pocket mirror. But when Sting went into the kitchen and Jason into the bathroom, Naleejah got close to my ear. "I want Sting," she whispered.

"Okay," I said with a shrug.

"Do you think Jason is cute?"

"Yeah, he's cute, but not my type."

"Well, I hope you know Charles isn't the only guy in the world."

"Yeah, I know that already," I snapped.

"Well, if you want Charles, you better get with it. Guys like a girl with experience—and in order to please a guy, you *need* experience. So if I were you, I'd practice on Jason."

Before I could reply, Sting and Jason entered the living room, carrying their delicious fried chicken on plates. They sat down on the opposite couch so I could smell it. My mouth watered resentfully.

"Are you sure you don't want anything?" asked Sting, in between bites.

"Yes, we're sure," Naleejah answered for me once again. "But can we get some music up in here?"

"Hey, pop in a CD," Sting ordered Jason. Jason licked his fingers, jumped up, and did as he was told, like he was the butler.

A slow jam flooded the room.

Hmm, I thought, they were really setting moods up in this piece. But I wasn't in the mood. As Naleejah wriggled seductively to the music, I was busy wondering when we were going home. Hungry, hot, bothered, and bored, I continued to watch Sting and Jason polish off their plates.

After the meal, Sting hopped up from the couch, swaggered to the kitchen, and came back carrying a big bottle of wine and four glasses on a tray. "See, I'm a classy kind of guy," he said, winking at Naleejah.

Sting poured Naleejah the first glass. He was about to pour me a glass, but I quickly said no thanks. I act straight stupid when I drink, so I don't drink anymore.

I used to drink to forget my life. Started at age ten and would still be tapping forty ounces if it wasn't for Tisha and Felicia changing my world. I used to get drunk and *reckless*. Ready to fight at the drop of a wrong look, but add liquor to my mix and I'd get *buckwild*. Pick up a garbage can and throw it at you in a heartbeat. On special occasions, the older girls from my group home used to let me get twisted with them in the park. "Shorty drinking vodka like it's nothing," they'd say, laughing their heads off. I always wanted to show how big and bad I was. But I always went too far. Throwing up my guts. Stinking like vomit. Mad awful for me. . . . Thank goodness for Felicia. As soon as she came into my life, I never had to prove a thing to her. The realest friend. For real.

"Not even a sip of some Moët?" whispered Naleejah. "Why you such a cornball?"

And why you such a gold-diggin' slut? Well, of course, I didn't say that, but I wanted to. What did Naleejah care if I turned down a drink? Funny how knuckleheads like her always pressuring me to be down, but when I get my butt in trouble, they ain't never around.

Jason and Sting gulped down two glasses each. Naleejah sipped down three—guess she was also drinking for me. Sting and Jason started making small talk with us. I gave one-word answers. Naleejah sputtered paragraphs. Then it became clear that she could no longer contribute to the conversation. Her head was all twisted up. She was saying stupid stuff— then again, she's always saying stupid stuff—but adding to that she was giggling uncontrollably, wriggling on the couch to the music, and big-time flirting with Sting, playing with her hair, licking her lips, acting the straight fool.

Next thing I knew, Sting and Naleejah shot up from the couch and headed to the back.

Now Jason was ogling me in anticipation. I looked away from him and stared at the navy-blue carpet, wishing it were an ocean I could dive into.

I mean, yes, Jason was cute, but he had to be more than cute to get my attention. He had to be Charles.

Uninvited, Jason got up and plopped down next to me. "Why are you so quiet?" he asked.

"I'm just a quiet person."

Jason slipped an uninvited arm around my shoulder, and said, "Well, you can talk to me. I don't bite."

To escape his arm, I bent down to take off my wedges. Perfect timing. My feet were hurting for real.

"Tight shoes?" asked Jason with a smile.

"Yeah, Naleejah talked me into buying them," I lied. Wasn't any of Jason's business the shoes were hand-me-downs.

"Want me to rub your feet for you?"

"No," I said flat-out, far from amused.

"Well, can I suck your toes, then?" He chuckled.

About twenty minutes of this creepy nonsense dragged by like a year. I was so pissed at the situation. And by the freaking way, what was Naleejah doing back there? I wanted to be out of here already.

Jason kept trying to pull conversation out of a magic hat. But, *poof*! There was nothing there. My mind was gone. I just nodded and smiled, nodded and smiled. His desperation was making me want to throw up.

"I think I better go soon," I said, wishing I had a wristwatch to stare at to help me act like I had somewhere important to be. This desperate dude was getting on my last nerves!

Jason raised his thick eyebrows at me and said, "I'm saying, what's the rush, ma? Your friend *surely* ain't ready to go. I bet the panties are on the knob right now."

I jerked my head back. "Panties on the knob? What do you mean by that?"

"The Do Not Enter sign," Jason explained. "You ain't up on that? I mean, you look kinda young, but you ain't that young."

"I'm sixteen," I lied, for no reason. I guess Naleejah was rubbing off on me.

"You got a nice body for sixteen."

"Thanks," I said blandly.

"Well, can I at least get a kiss on the cheek?" Jason asked. "I mean, your friend is taking care of my boy, so why can't you take care of me?"

I stared straight ahead like a zombie.

"Please?" Jason begged. "Just one kiss?"

Believe it or not, just to shut him up, I leaned over and pecked him like a bird, and then I flew over to my side of the love seat.

"Okay, now my turn," he said, grinning. He scooted over to me, kissed me on the cheek, and waited for my reaction. I have to admit, his lips were warm on my skin. Then Naleejah's voice started ringing in my head:

You need experience.

Practice on Jason.

I didn't want Jason to be my first kiss. Then again, I didn't want to be awkward when my lips finally met Charles. I guessed I had to start somewhere.

Jason realized I was suddenly with the program, so he wasted no time going for my lips. Only problem was, his lips were crazy wet and his breath smelled like chicken.

Then he started trying to shove his tongue in my mouth. Reluctantly, I opened my mouth and let him inside. Our tongues went round and round each other, but I felt no desire in my belly. I was just going through the motions.

Then Jason laid me down on the couch and climbed on top of me. He started grinding against my leg like a horny puppy. He was going too far. I wiggled, trying to get from underneath him, but he assumed I was getting into it, grinding to match his movements.

"No, let's stop," I whispered. "That's enough."

"No, baby, we're just getting started," said Jason in a hoarse voice. In one swift motion, he unzipped his shorts and whipped it out.

I stared down at it, horrified. "Put that thing away!"

"Don't be scared of it, baby."

He tried to grab my hand. I snatched my hand away.

"Please?" he asked in a pitiful voice. "Touch it, just once?"

"No!" I pushed at his chest to get him off of me. He wouldn't budge.

Next thing I knew, he was groping me like a demented octopus. He squeezed my boobies, grabbed my butt. He was all over me.

"Are you serious?" I yelled, "Stop it! Get off of me!" I struggled under his groping hands.

"Trick-tease, stop fronting," growled Jason.

Finally, I got out from under him. When he tried to climb on top of me again, my kneecap met his groin. Jason yelped like the horny toad that he was.

"Word to my mother, you lucky I'm on probation!" he yelled.

Probation? Oh, hell no! Jason probably hadn't had a piece of pie in a minute. Well, he wasn't getting a slice of me. I was out!

While Jason doubled over in pain, rocking and cursing me under his breath, I snatched up my shoes and raced down the hallway barefoot, ready to snatch up Naleejah and get the heck out of this apartment.

My bottom lip hit the floor when I laid eyes on the pink thong hanging on the bedroom doorknob. Jason hadn't lied. It was just too crazy for words. Just a few hours ago, Naleejah was lecturing me about being *selective* with guys, and now she was sleeping with a guy she *just* met? I was too confused, too upset for words. I almost lost it when I came closer to the door and heard a bedpost rhythmically knocking up against the wall, and springs squeaking, and Naleejah moaning like a porn star.

Oh my goodness.

I quickly pulled myself together. Right now I couldn't worry about what Naleejah was in the middle of: We had to be *out*. I pounded on the door. "Naleejah, let's go!" I yelled.

Two minutes later, Sting cracked the door open wearing nothing but boxers. I peeped inside at Naleejah, who was lying on the bed with the covers pulled up to her neck. I swiveled my eyes back to Sting and said, "You better tell your man something—he's acting like he wants to rape me."

"Aw, he don't mean no harm, baby," said Sting, chuckling and crinkling his eyes at me like this was funny.

"But I'm not joking," I said.

"He just likes you, that's all."

"Well, I don't like him. And I promise you, I'll send his butt *back* to jail if he tries anything else. You better tell him something, for real."

Shaking his head, Sting shut the bedroom door behind him and moseyed on down the hallway, I guess to talk some sense into Jason, if that was possible.

I shoved the bedroom door open to find Naleejah still under the sheets, sprawled out in Sting's bed. "Come on," I demanded. "We got to go."

From the doorway, I monitored Naleejah to make sure she was getting ready. I didn't wince when she climbed out of bed butt-booty-naked. After living in group homes, you've seen it all. But I couldn't believe Naleejah's crazy calm composure. No concern. No shame in her game. No rush, no rush at all. At her own lazy pace, she slipped into her top, her skirt, twisting this way and that, acting like we had all the time in the world for her to get dressed.

"Hurry up," I cried. "We have to go!"

Finally, Naleejah emerged from the bedroom. Her hair rumpled, her skirt twisted to the side. She walked past me without a glance and started for the bathroom. She was walking mad funny. I ran up behind her and yanked her drunken butt away from the bathroom. "We don't have time for you to be primping!"

I dragged Naleejah out of the apartment before Sting or Jason could block us.

But Sting had already got what he wanted from Naleejah, so he didn't even try to stop us.

The minute we hit the streets, Naleejah plopped down on the stoop, pulled out her cell phone and a business card. "Call a cab for us, please?" she slurred. "I can't talk. My head hurts."

"Do you have cab money?" I asked.

"Check my wallet for me?"

I dug in her purse and pulled out her wallet, and thank goodness she had a twenty-dollar bill on her. But could we even catch a cab with Naleejah looking so tore up, like she was ready to throw up any minute?

I was still half-wondering if Sting would eventually come downstairs and offer us a ride. Then I had to remind myself again: This was a hit-and-run situation. Sting couldn't care less how we got home.

Well, I'd been through this drunken drama plenty times before, been twisted personally and with friends, so I knew the drill: I had to walk Naleejah around in the fresh air before we hopped into any cars. Naleejah beefed about having to walk, but I didn't care. She needed to sober up—and possibly throw up—and then we could think about a cab.

Besides, I needed to clear my head too. The sight of Jason's stuff was enough to give me nightmares. I had never seen one that up-close before. Shudder.

We walked downhill on Kingston Street. Five minutes into the walk, Naleejah stumbled toward a parked car, bent over, held on to the car door, and a rainbow glob gushed onto the curb. Then she started retching.

I sat her down on a random porch, and then ran across the street to the store and bought her a bottle of water. Finally, I called the cab. The cab took less than ten minutes to arrive, thank goodness.

We rode home in silence. Naleejah's head was leaning way to the side, like she was about to doze off on my shoulder. She kept her mouth shut for most of the ride. But then she started talking—well, more like gibbering. "Is my hair okay, Kate?" she asked.

"Yeah, it's fine," I said without looking at her.

"You got a light?" she asked groggily.

"I don't smoke, remember?"

"Aw, dang—I need me a smoke!" she cried.

"We'll be home soon," I said, trying not to gag because her breath smelled like vomit. Forget water—I should've brought this chick a pack of peppermints.

When the cabbie pulled up in front of Naleejah's house, I was so grateful to see lights off in every window. That meant Naleejah's parents were most likely not home, or getting their freak on behind closed doors. Who knows? Who cares? As long as they weren't around to interrogate me. Shhhooot, I could already imagine them asking me twenty questions about their smashed-up daughter—and I would have no answers to give.

I fumbled with Naleejah's keys, found the right ones, got her all the way inside, and shoved her purse into her hands.

"Get some sleep," I whispered, and slipped out the door.

During the long walk home, I received compliments left and right, like "Hey there, beautiful" instead of "Nice big booty." Felt kinda good being appreciated for being cute; this took my mind off the grimy drama I had just gone through.

But I wasn't stupid enough to stop for any of my admirers. No cutie in the world was worth me being late for curfew.

I made it home at eight o'clock on the dot, with a whole hour to spare, and thank goodness for that. After the day's crazy turn of events—Naleejah the Drunken Sexpot and Jason the Ex-Con Groper—I didn't need any more stress in my life.

I stepped inside the house. Lynn was in the living room, watching television. I suddenly remembered Ted's "high road" speech, and stuck my head inside to say hello; I even flashed a fake smile. Instead of Lynn returning my hello, she just stared at me funny style and nodded coldly in place of a greeting.

Jealous of my new look? I wanted to ask. Instead, I simply shrugged. Hey, at least I tried. I sprinted up to my room, hopped into my house clothes, carefully wrapped my hair the way Naleejah had showed me, and covered up my tresses with the silk scarf she gave me. Then my stomach started rumbling.

I went back downstairs to raid the kitchen. (That's one thing I liked about the Johnsons'. Unlike in other homes, I could go into the fridge anytime without a problem.) But before I could start opening cabinets and whatnot, I felt Lynn's eyes blazing on my back. There's a clear view from the living room to the kitchen. So to confirm my funny feeling, I stole a peek at her. Sure enough, Lynn was still staring at me hard. Why?

"Leftover steak is in the fridge," she offered. "Rice and green beans too. Leave enough for Ted."

"Oh, okay, thanks," I said, still feeling funny. Something weird was going on. But I couldn't figure out what. As I pulled out pots and pans to warm up my food, Lynn suddenly raced up the stairs. Five minutes later, Ted came through the door, red-eyed and hungry. I offered to warm up his food too, and asked if he wanted to play a game of checkers in the meanwhile.

"Lynn upstairs?"

"Yeah."

"Well, let me go say hello to Lynn first," Ted said. "You know she'll have a fit if I forget." Ted headed upstairs.

Next thing I knew, Ted was having a fit upstairs. I heard him yelling about something (and Ted never yells), so I wondered what he could be howling and huffing about.

I soon found out.

From the top of the staircase, Ted ordered me to come up.

My bottom lip hit the floor when I laid eyes on my room. Ransacked. Clothes all over my bed, papers all over the floor—my room was a total wreck.

Lynn did this.

I looked at Ted for answers, but he looked too angry for words.

Lynn flailed her hands in my direction. "Ask her if she's dealing drugs, Ted. Go ahead, ask her!"

Wearing a sad expression, Ted turned to me and asked, "Kate, where'd you get money for your new clothes . . . your new hair?"

Okay, now I understood.

Brokenhearted, I had to pause for a second. Guilty without a trial, huh? A lump formed in my throat and almost choked me to death. I was hurting so much right now.

"Well?" demanded Lynn.

"Lynn, calm down, will you?" Ted shot her a nasty look.

Lynn flashed her big bubble eyes at Ted and said, "We shouldn't have to wait this long for a simple answer."

I stared directly at Ted and said, "Remember the girl's house you drove me to?"

"Yes."

"Well, she did my hair—"

"But what about the clothes, Kate?" Lynn cut in. "What about the clothes?" Lynn's voice was stupid loud, and she had her hands on both hips like she was trying to scare somebody. Instead of giving Lynn an answer, I stared directly at Ted again and explained, "Naleejah gave me her sister's clothes."

"Oh, I don't believe that!" She waved her hand in the air as if swatting flies.

"Lynn, what did I tell you? You need to calm down—you went about this all wrong in the first place."

My eyes started filling up. I couldn't believe this was happening. Was this really happening? "Ted, I'm not lying to you," I said in a shaky voice. "I swear, I'm not lying to you."

The crease in Ted's forehead disappeared. "I know, Kate. I believe you."

"You believe anything, don't you?" butted in Lynn.

Then suddenly, the smoke alarm in the kitchen started going off. I ran downstairs to turn off the pots and escape this terrible scene.

I got to the kitchen too late. My food was crispy burnt. Didn't matter, though. I'd lost my appetite. Instead, I drank a glass of cold water just to cool my nerves.

Lynn and Ted were still upstairs arguing, and I was still shaking, shaken. I had to call Tisha. Hearing her voice would calm me down. It was Saturday, true, and I knew Tisha was off, but she'd told me I could call her anytime, and this was the time I needed to call. I needed to talk to her right now. I needed Tisha to answer her phone. But no. No answer. I got voice mail. I left Tisha a desperate message: "Please, please call me as soon as possible."

I dragged myself into the living room and flung myself on the couch, ready to cry. But no. Oh no. Not here. Before I dropped a tear, I wanted to be shut inside my bedroom, away from everybody.

But when you got to flow, you got to flow, and years of pain suddenly poured out of me. I was crying so hard, I hoped nobody heard me upstairs. I felt so bad and alone. I had given up trying to be loved by a family a long time ago. All I wanted was to stay somewhere stable—stay in one place, graduate, and be gone from the system for good. But now look at *this* bull. Seemed like I wouldn't last a year staying here. Might as well live in a U-Haul truck—this way I'd never have to unpack.

In my head, I went back and forth over the whole jacked-up situation. Okay, okay—yes, I knew my record follows me wherever I go. I understood that Lynn had already peeped my file. Plain as day, it reads: possession. A past offense. I'm guilty as charged. But could I move on, please? I'm saying, wasn't my sparkling report card proof enough that I had changed?

The echo of footsteps on the stairs interrupted my thoughts and tears. I quickly dammed up my eyes.

It was Ted. Thank goodness. He wanted to know if I was okay. No, I was not okay, and no, I would not go back upstairs if that stupid witch was still lurking around.

"Lynn really means well," said Ted, sitting down next to me.

"Yeah, okay," I said, rolling my eyes—not at Ted, but at the thought of Lynn meaning well. Ha, now that's a laugh.

"Listen, Kate, I understand how you feel, and I'm sorry this happened."

"Not your fault," I said. "*Her* fault."

Ted hesitated and said, "Believe it or not, my wife really thinks a lot of you."

"Yeah, okay . . . she thinks a lot of me, so she treats me like a suspect? I can see how that makes sense."

I shifted my weight on the couch, growing uncomfortable with myself, feeling fidgety and foul. I was snapping at Ted, and I didn't mean to be snapping, but I couldn't help myself: I was heated.

"Tonight was unfortunate. But I promise you, things will get better. Just give Lynn another chance."

I started rocking back and forth, trying to calm down. "Well, she should've given me a chance," I spat. "Ransacking my room like she's some crazy B—"

I stopped myself in midrant. When my sadness turns into anger, there's no telling what I am capable of. A part of me was tempted to ask for my removal from this house. But no . . . I wasn't in the mood to be shipped to a new family, learning new rules and feeling new discomforts—not to mention what if there were no other foster homes available? It might be back to a group home, sharing everything with a bunch of girls again. No. I had already gotten used to having my own room for the first time in my entire life. I'd rather stick things out here. At least I knew Ted had my back; he was definitely showing and proving tonight.

Finally, I was ready to go back upstairs, get in my bed, close my eyes, and calm the heck down—but not before asking, "Is *she* still in my room?"

"No," said Ted. "And I promise she won't bother you again."

Ted's word is bond, so I went back upstairs to my bedroom. He followed. I was surprised to see everything put neatly back in its place. Ted stood in my doorway, smiling. "Did I do a good job?" he asked.

"Thanks," was all I could say. Between me and you, why was *he* the one cleaning up my room and checking to see if I was okay? Why wasn't *Lynn* the one cleaning up and apologizing to me? Oh boy, I was getting myself worked up all over again. Thank goodness Ted intercepted my thoughts with a random question. "Hey, why is your life book so bare?"

"What life book?" I asked absentmindedly.

Ted walked over to my closet and reached up to pull out my beat-up life book. *Oh, that.* I was only keeping it just to be keeping it. I'm a pack rat.

"This life book," said Ted as he opened the shabby brown book to the first page featuring my latest honor roll certificate. I said to myself: *Don't remember putting that in there.*

Ted explained, "See, I'm starting you off. You should be filling this book up yourself. Why haven't you?"

Hmm, don't ask me.

A life book is like a scrapbook for us kids in foster care. We're supposed to put the things that matter to us in our books. But I've never been interested. Didn't have much mattering in my life when I first received it, and don't have much mattering now.

I shared my thoughts with Ted.

He disagreed. He placed the book on my dresser and said, "Listen, Kate, you need to capture all of your life's moments. Big things, little things, good times and bad. Whatever happens to you is important—and I promise you, when you fill up all of the pages in your book, we're going to commemorate the moment, celebrate your life."

I didn't like when Ted said things like this—"when you fill up all the pages"—like he's hinting at a long-term future of me living here when there's really no guarantee. I mean, look at what happened to-night.

But I just nodded at Ted and smiled at him, and tried to make a joke to keep myself from crying again. "Celebrate my life?" I began, "Ted, you mad funny—got me feeling like I'm in some after-school special."

Ted chuckled at this and said, "Well, that's because you are special, and I'm schooling you. Now go to bed, missy."

"Sorry I burnt your dinner."

"Not your fault." Ted patted me on the shoulder and left my room.

I went to bed feeling a whole lot better, calmer, cooler, and com-posed. But the next morning I woke up anxious and uptight, still dying to settle the score with Lynn.

On Sunday morning, at ten o'clock on the dot, I cracked my bedroom door open. All was quiet on the home front. Lynn was still asleep, and Ted had gone out to take his usual Sunday stroll for the newspaper. Cool. I blazed down the stairs to call Naleejah. She was going to help me make Lynn feel stupid. Real stupid. One phone call, and Lynn would find out that yes, Naleejah did my hair, and yes she gave me her sister's clothes, and yes, her parents could back up my story. *Bam*, take that!

But before I could pick up the telephone, it rang. It was Tisha. Telling me to sit tight; she'd be over before twelve o'clock. Whoa, I didn't expect her to make a special trip over here, especially not on her day off! But she had already said bye-bye before I could protest.

Then I called Naleejah, who answered in a groggy voice.

"Listen, I need you to speak to Lynn for me," I blurted out.

Oops, I didn't even ask her how she was feeling, whether she was still hungover or not. Sometimes I have a one-track mind when I'm stressing. Pardon me.

"You need me to speak to Lynn about what?" asked Naleejah, still out of it.

"The stupid witch I live with got me dealing drugs—"

"Oh my gosh!" Naleejah cried, now wide awoke. "She got you dealing drugs? But that's crazy! How can she make you—?"

"No, no, I don't mean she got me dealing. I'm saying—the new clothes you gave me, the new hair—she thinks I sold drugs to get mine."

"Oh no, Kate!" exclaimed Naleejah. "You got in trouble over that? Man, you *stay* in trouble."

"No, I'm not in trouble this time. I just want to make Lynn feel stupid for accusing me. So it would be really cool if your mother, or father, could speak to her, because I—"

"Oh, girl—I can do better than that," Naleejah interrupted. She told me to hold on, and next thing I knew she was like, "I'll be over in about a half hour. What's your address?"

"Dang, you don't have to come over," I said. "A simple telephone conversation would do."

"Hush, girl. My father's going to drive me to your crib. We were supposed to be headed out of here anyway, but I fell back asleep. I got five freaking bags of laundry to do."

"Whoa, five bags?"

"Yeah, my mother is too damn lazy, and my father don't do jack around the house, so I'm stuck doing the laundry when I could be in my bed."

"That's messed up," I said. "Five bags?"

"By the way—I wanted to bring over the rest of Tammy's clothes."

"More gear for me?" I exclaimed, "Thanks!" *I stay fly . . . no lie . . . and you know this—*

"Hello, Kate?"

"Oh yeah, I'm here . . . just in another zone."

"Shoot, I'm the one who should be out of it after last night."

Well . . . since you brought it up.

"Hey, are you okay with the way things went down with Sting?"

"Girl, I stay okay," said Naleejah. "Don't nobody stop my stride. I keeps it moving, feel me?"

"Now that's what's up."

"I'm too fly to cry," said Naleejah. "No dude is worth my tears."

"I hear that," I agreed. "Let it roll off your back—oh hey, could you do me a favor and bring my backpack with you?" I suddenly thought to ask.

"Girl, I threw that piece of junk away."

It took me a full minute to process what Naleejah had just said.

"You did what?"

"I threw that sorry knapsack away, what?"

"You mean in the garbage can?"

"Where else is it going to go, silly?"

"But who told you to throw my bag away?" I asked in disbelief.

"Calm down, calm down, there was nothing inside of it. I checked it twice."

I was speechless.

"Dang, Kate, I'm letting you *keep* the pocketbook I gave you!"

"But why didn't you ask me first?" I demanded, anger rising up to my throat. "How could you throw away my bag?"

"I thought I was doing you a favor. The thing looked like it was ready for the trash can. Now you have a *better* bag on your shoulders, what?"

"Well did the trash get taken out yet?" I asked in desperation.

"Oh my gosh!" Naleejah exclaimed. "Is it really that serious?"

I grew quiet. I had to. I was holding back a storm. It wouldn't be pretty if I opened my mouth.

"Listen, Kate, I promise to buy you a new knapsack, okay? Please don't trip over this."

I was tripping inside. Twisted inside. Felt like I'd just lost my best friend. I'd had that knapsack for as long as I can remember. I was so angry, hurt, shocked at Naleejah's nerves. But as hard as it was, I had to calm myself down and count to ten. I still needed Naleejah to clear things up with Lynn. If I said what was really on my mind, Naleejah would never speak to me again.

"Kate, I'm really sorry, all right? I'll be there soon . . . okay?"

"Yeah, yeah, okay." I gave her my address. Click. Hung up the phone, and exhaled a mouthful of fire.

Lynn was already downstairs when Naleejah rang the bell. Before I could reach the bottom step, Lynn bum-rushed the door. I hung back and watched.

"Hi!" Naleejah chirped to Lynn.

"I'm sorry, young lady, but Kate didn't ask me if she could have company."

"Oh, I'm just here to drop off clothes," said Naleejah, wearing her famous smile. I inched toward the door and waved at her.

"Hey, Kate!" Naleejah busted into a goofy smile.

Lynn swiveled around to face me, and then turned back around to face Naleejah's father, who was now carrying a garbage bag jam-packed with clothes up the porch steps.

Full of smiles, Mr. Mackie introduced himself and then said, "So I hear there's been a bit of confusion about Kate's makeover."

"No, no confusion at all," said Lynn, creasing her eyebrows.

I wanted to slap the lie out of her mouth.

"Well, I would invite you in," Lynn continued, "but I wasn't expecting company—"

Mr. Mackie interrupted Lynn with a careless wave of his hand. "Don't worry about it," he said. "I'm just here to drop off these clothes."

At that moment, Ted rolled up and introduced himself.

"You mind taking these off my hands?" asked Mr. Mackie, holding up the giant bag to Ted.

"No, not at all." Ted handed me his newspaper, and then he grabbed the bag.

"More clothes for me," I explained, beaming.

Ted flashed me an *I believed you all along* wink, and then he said his good-byes, and dragged the bag inside. Lynn followed his lead, looking all stupid in the face.

Bam! Take that, Lynn.

Mission accomplished.

I thanked Naleejah and her father. Her father hopped inside their little red hoopty. Naleejah stayed behind and started tugging at my arm. "Can you come with me to the laundry?" she asked. "I could use some help."

"Sorry, I—"

"I don't expect you to touch the dirty clothes—just help me do some folding, please?"

"I can't," I said. "I have to stay here. Tisha's coming over . . . don't you have your father to help you out?"

Naleejah jerked her head back. "Please, picture him helping me out with *anything*. My dad is just dropping me off, then he goes off to do whatever the hell he does and comes back for me when I'm done—but it's okay, I'll handle it. I always handle it."

"Oh, all right," I said, feeling bad for her. "See you later, then—maybe around five o'clock?"

"Will you be done with your *friend* by then?" asked Naleejah in a jealous tone.

"What friend?"

"Tisha."

I chuckled. "Tisha is my social worker, silly."

"Social worker?" Naleejah repeated. "What's *that* all about?"

"I'll explain it later." But no, I wouldn't.

"Mm, that's a relief," said Naleejah, smiling. "I thought you were having me replaced as your homegirl already. . . . So, what time will you be through with Tisha?"

"Don't know, she said she'll be here around—"

"BERTHA, COME ON!" Naleejah's father interrupted. His head was stuck out the car, his hand motioning wildly for her to hurry up. But wait. Did he just call my homegirl Bertha—or was I just hearing things?

I didn't have time to ask Naleejah, because at the sound of her father's booming voice, she had already sprinted to the car, hopped inside, and waved good-bye.

Oh well. I'd ask her later.

I plopped down on my front steps, closed my eyes, and leaned my head against the railing, waiting for Tisha.

Tisha pulled up in her adorable white Volkswagen. She looked so fly inside of it; I wanted a car just like hers. She hopped out, radiating fabulousness. Had her hair cut in a short bob, and she was rocking a stunning yellow summer dress and gold strappy sandals. She sashayed up to the porch, knowing she was all of that.

"Work it out," I said, smiling. "Rip the runway."

Tisha spun around like a model and said, "Watch out, now!" Then she gave me a hug and asked if I wanted to talk outside or in. She should've known *out*. This didn't need to be a group discussion. I ran back inside to get a cushion for her to sit on the porch steps.

But after I told Tisha everything, a group discussion it was going to be. It had to be, Tisha claimed, because there's two sides to every story. Oh well. I went back inside and told Ted that Tisha wanted to speak to them. Then I escorted Tisha into the living room and made her sit next to me on the love seat. I grabbed a random throw pillow just to hold on to. Two minutes later, Ted and Lynn walked in. They sat side by side on the opposite couch.

First thing out of Lynn's mouth: "Kate, I don't understand. Why did you have to get Tisha involved? I thought we settled this already."

"But I didn't *ask* her to come over," I protested, making sure my eyeballs were under control.

Lynn acted like she didn't hear me, then turned to Ted and said, "Do you see this? She's getting everybody involved. First she has her friend's father come over, and now she's got Tisha coming here—on her day off!"

Ted reached over to pat Lynn's hand and said, "Baby, please calm down."

Yeah, Lynn, get back in your cage.

Tisha raised her index finger. "Listen, I chose to come here on my own. Let's not make this a big deal. Now can we move on?"

The discussion began. But we didn't get far. Lynn suddenly went off on a detour, hyperventilating like she always does. "I try so hard with these kids. So, what am I to do? You act too nice to them, and they take advantage of you. You give them tough love, and they call their social workers on you. Do you know how many children I had to have removed because they couldn't handle the freedom I gave them? I mean . . . my fault for knowingly taking in an at-risk child."

Tisha broke in again, this time in a much sterner voice. "Now why would you say that in front of her?" She jutted her chin toward me. "Kate, do me a favor and go upstairs. I'll call you back down in a second."

Gladly.

When I was called back into the living room, Lynn avoided eye contact with me. Tisha must've ripped Lynn a new one, Brooklyn-style. Go, Tisha, represent!

Tisha said a few more choice words, and then the drama was finally over. I walked Tisha to her car and thanked her for coming through.

"Kate, get in the car."

I was confused. Tisha was wearing the same stern face she had reserved for Lynn. Why?

I hopped inside her ride.

Tisha tilted her head and stared at me for a second, then said, "You know you're not a hundred percent innocent. You have some responsibility for this. Lynn told me that you didn't ask for permission to get your hair done and bring new clothes into the house."

"Well . . . I didn't think I had to," I said. "It's my hair . . . and to me the clothes were just hand-me-downs."

"Even so, you could've told her."

"Okay, true."

"Always take responsibility for your actions," said Tisha. "You know you owe Lynn an apology, right?"

"Why?" I whined. "Do I have to?"

Tisha gave me one look, and I knew the answer was yes. "Okay, I feel you, but still, she didn't have to ransack my room like a crazy crackhead."

"Don't worry," said Tisha. "I already lit into her about that."

"Yeah, I could tell." I wanted to giggle, but Tisha was still looking serious in the face.

"See, Kate, you have to make sure you're always on point," explained Tisha. "Don't give Lynn any reason to come at you. You've been doing so well so far."

"Yeah, if it wasn't for you—"

Tisha cut me off. "Stop saying that, 'if it wasn't for me' crap. I don't want to hear that."

"Well . . . nobody else cared about what I did until you came along."

"But you have to care about yourself," said Tisha. "What if I never came along?"

I had no answer for this.

"Kate, remember the day you told me you wish you were never born?"

I paused. The memory was painful. "Yes . . . I remember."

"And what did I tell you?"

I muttered, "That I'm here now, so I might as well do something worthwhile."

"And what else?"

"Always go for greatness."

I bent my head low, pretending to be preoccupied with my stubby nails. I didn't want to cry. Not in front of Tisha. I had to be strong.

"Life's hard enough already," Tisha began, "don't make it harder for yourself. It's not your fault you're in foster care. You didn't do anything wrong. But it *will* be your fault if you don't do anything *right* with your life. Understand?"

Tisha was right. I mean, why hit the rock and become a crackhead when I could hit the books and become a CEO instead? But still, I felt sad and uninspired at the moment.

I turned my head to look out the window. Now I really wanted to cry. There's always been a part of me missing—times I wished I didn't have to wake up in a stranger's house every single year, times I wished I didn't have to wake up ever again. It's hard to feel like you don't belong anywhere, or to anybody, and—well—it's just hard, and I wasn't sure if Tisha fully understood my pain.

But of all people, I didn't want to disappoint Tisha. She's always telling me that I'm strong, and that I shouldn't dwell on my past, and that I should live for my future. It sounds good in a speech, but it's really not that simple.

Tisha tapped my knee. "Listen, girl, I'm not trying to sit here all day and watch you feel sorry for yourself. I got me a hot date, and you're blocking."

A smile crept across my lips. I turned around to face Tisha. She reached over to rub my shoulder. "Kate, I deal with twenty kids at one time, and you're the one I'm checking for . . . on my weekend, at that? Come on, now, what does that tell you?"

I shrugged, feeling all shy, and suddenly . . . kinda special.

"So, I'll see you at my office on Tuesday?" Tisha asked.

"For sure." Tuesday was the day I was to meet my new law guardian. I didn't even know I had a lawyer until Tisha told me. Nice to know

I had someone to protect my legal rights, even though I didn't feel like dealing with anything that had to do with court right now. If I could help it, the next time I planned to be in court was when I was being emancipated from the system.

But I *was* looking forward to spending more time with Tisha. She always took me to Baskin-Robbins after our business was complete, and I loved that part. I knew she wasn't supposed to be bonding with me so deep, but that's just how Tisha rolled. She says I'm special, and I accept that.

"You better be on time," Tisha warned.

"No doubt. . . . So is my lecture over?"

Tisha playfully pushed my arm and said, "Don't make me put you in a headlock."

"Nah, you look too fly to be fighting." We laughed. I hugged Tisha good-bye and hopped out of her car. She sped down the block like she had a hot date—well, that's because she did. I'm sorry, but I still have to say: If it wasn't for Tisha, where would I be? Listen, she had a hot date, and she was still checking for me? How could I *not* be touched? Quite a few social workers I'd dealt with treated me like I was just a paycheck and a pain in the butt, like they couldn't be so bothered with me—leaving me to wonder why they chose to work with kids in the first place. Why not work with adults whose hopes and dreams are probably already dead? But whatever.

I went back inside the house. First things first. Apologize to Lynn. I didn't want to do it, but it had to be done. I found Lynn in the living room with Ted. Perfect, now he could witness me taking the high road.

"Excuse me," I began.

They both looked up at me.

"Lynn, I'm sorry I disrespected you," I said. "I should've told you that my friend hooked me up with hair and clothes."

Lynn gave me an odd look, and then relaxed her face. She paused for a long time and then said, "Well . . . I should have asked you first."

I guess that was Lynn's way of apologizing. I'll take it.

Chapter 14

The next afternoon, Naleejah called to see if I wanted to hang out. *Hell yeah.* I needed to get out of the house, especially after what had happened yesterday. Lynn's crack actions were forgiven, but not forgotten. It was best to stay out of her crazy way.

"So, what you wanna do?" I asked.

"Girl, it's hot outside. I want to get wet. . . . I heard there's a pool somewhere around here. You down?"

"Nah, we can't," I said. "Marcy Pool is closed. But we can get wet on Chauncey Street. They always have a fire hydrant going."

"Fire hydrant? Is you crazy?" Naleejah exclaimed. "That's mad bootleg! What would I look like playing in water out in the street?"

"Like you were getting *wet*," I snapped. Naleejah was forever worrying about what she looked like to other people, and she was getting on my nerves with that—not to mention rubbing off on me.

I sighed. "Forget it. We can find something else to do."

"Oh, maybe we can—"

Suddenly I heard Mrs. Mackie's muffled yelling in the background. Her and Naleejah went back and forth for a long minute. I thought Naleejah had forgotten I was still on the phone. I was about to hang up, but then she got back to me in a huff. She called her mother the B-word then asked me if I could come with her to Restoration Plaza.

"Why, what's happening there?"

"I have to pay the stupid electric bill—if I don't, we'll be in the dark. Don't ask me how many times we've been in the dark before."

"Yeah, I'll come with you," I said. "What time?"

"Soon as possible. . . . Are you dressed?"

"I can get dressed," I said.

"Well, call me when you're ready."

I got ready. Hopped into Tammy's clothes, hooked up my hair, threw on my hurting wedges, and wobbled out the house . . . wobbled back into the house because my feet were in serious pain. I could no longer fake it. Raggedy sneakers, back on my feet.

Naleejah and I met up on Malcom X Boulevard. As soon as she saw me, she looked me up and down and said, "Oh no, girl, what happened to the shoes I gave you?"

"They hurt . . . bad."

Naleejah scowled. "And you don't own another decent pair?"

"Yeah, I have another pair at home," I snapped. "I just didn't feel like wearing them today." I wouldn't call the penny loafers Lynn bought me "decent," but I didn't like the way Naleejah had just come out of her face, like I was so freaking pitiful and poor. So I had to play it off.

"But what if we bump into some cuties?" Naleejah asked worriedly.

"Then we'll just have to bump," I said. "Anyway, can we go now? It's too hot out here to be messing around."

As we neared Fulton Street, I wondered if I would see Charles hanging out in front of Boys & Girls High, his favorite spot. I didn't share my curiosity with Naleejah. She was on my nerves right now, talking about my leaning sneakers nonstop.

Then again, I had to keep reminding myself that Naleejah was only trying to help me be the best that I could be.

We walked on. No sight of Charles on Fulton Street. Oh well. Naleejah paid her bill. On our way back from Restoration Plaza, I peeped a shoe store's window and saw a beautiful sight that made my heart flutter: a pair of black leather strappy sandals sitting regally on a perch, waiting to be worn by me.

I pointed them out to Naleejah.

"Oh yeah, now those are banging." Naleejah said, "If you don't buy them, I will. . . . But nah, I have enough shoes as it is. So *you* better cop those bangers, girl! Don't front."

Cop them, how? I was saving my fifty-dollar gift certificate from Felicia to help out with my school clothes. And Lynn had already spent all she was willing to spend on my summer gear. I wasn't about to ask Ted for anything. He was mad cool, but his wife was in control of his wallet. So, what could I do? Nothing but bypass the store. As we passed by the window, the sandals seemed to call at my back: *Kate, please don't leave me here.*

Disappointed and mulling over my financial situation, I was in another zone when Naleejah tapped me. "There's your boy," she said, jutting her chin forward.

Before I realized it, we were already in front of Charles's building, and Charles was ten feet away, sitting on the island of cement near the parking lot, talking to a quartet of dudes.

Next thing I knew, Naleejah grabbed my arm and started pulling me in the opposite direction. "Yo, what are you doing?" I protested, tugging my arm away from her.

"Time to make a U-turn!" Naleejah exclaimed.

"What?"

"I just remembered," she began, "you can't be rocking those raggedy sneakers in front of Charles. He'll think you fell off the fashion wagon and hurt yourself."

I jerked my head back in confusion. "But don't I look good enough from the ankles up?"

"Far from good, girl," said Naleejah, shaking her head at me. "Your sneakers are tragic. You need to go home and change. We'll come back this way when you got your act together. Ain't no half-stepping when it comes to Charles, okay?"

Naleejah's face looked so serious and so concerned that I believed every word she said. Okay, true. Last time I saw Charles I was rocking sweaty armpits and acting the fool. This time, I had to come correct from head to toe, or I might lose his interest for good.

Naleejah came with me to my house. But I asked her to wait on the stoop while I went inside to change into her tight-as-can-be shoes. Didn't feel *all that* welcome in the Johnson household to be inviting my friends in.

I zipped to the bathroom, smeared on a ton of deodorant under my arms, and helped myself to a squirt of Lynn's flowery perfume from the bathroom cabinet. *Boom,* now I was smelling good, looking good, ready to get my man.

As I wobbled down the porch steps, Naleejah eyed my feet approvingly and said, "Now, that's much better."

By the time we made it to the corner of Fulton Street, my feet were killing me. We spotted Charles sitting on the island, and his homeboy-count had whittled down to one.

Charles smiled as soon as he saw me. "What's up, baby?"

"Nothing much," I said.

"*Heyyy,* Charles," said Naleejah, smiling harder than necessary.

"What's the deal, ma?" he asked. Then he turned to his friend and introduced him as Divine. He *was* divine, fine as ever. Not that tall, though, but he was oh-so-dipped in beautiful cinnamon-brown skin. Nice white smile. Cool baggy clothes. He looked good enough to grab Naleejah's attention, thank goodness.

Naleejah stayed in Divine's face, and Charles guided me over to somebody's red car. He sat on the trunk and pulled me toward him. "Get closer, Kate. . . . Why you acting all jittery?"

"I'm not acting jittery," I lied.

Charles cocked his head to the side and said, "Matter of fact, the last time I saw you, you were acting mad nervous. You practically ran away from me. What's up with you, girl? You changing on me?"

I tried to pull myself together. I had to get rid of the goofball actions once and for all. So I decided to turn on my sexy charm (if I had any to offer). "I'm not changing on you," I said, smiling seductively (I hoped). "So, why don't *you* tell me how you want me to be." Then I winked for special effect.

"Stop teasing a brother," muttered Charles.

"I'm not teasing you."

"Yes, you are, and you're silly too."

"I'm not silly."

"Yes, you are."

I puckered my lips, and in a baby voice, I said, "Aww, him mad at me?"

"Sweetheart, you need to grow up and get some," Charles said. "Even your nerdy little friend is getting hers."

"Shut up," I said. I punched Charles in the arm for teasing my home-girl. It was a shame how word had whizzed around P.S. 342 so fast about Felicia. She had trusted a bigmouthed liver-lipped boy with her heart, gave up her golden treasure, and Liver Lips went around our school shouting out the news.

"So, you're just going to stand here looking like a pretty statue?" asked Charles. "You're usually running your mouth."

"Well, *you* have a mouth too," I said, even though I knew Charles was right. Before this beauty business, I had a whole lot of mouth—couldn't shut me up for nothing. But now I was being careful. Didn't want to say anything stupid. I wanted to take things to the next level, but I didn't know how. I was expecting Charles to lead the way to romance.

Out of nowhere, a trio of boys on BMX bikes rode up on us. "What's up, Charlie? What it do?"

"Nothing new," said Charles. "Catch y'all later on tonight, a'ight?"

One of the boys winked at me for whatever reason, and they rode off.

Then another interruption.

"*Heyyy*, Charles," a voiced called over my back. I swiveled around to face a short honey-brown girl rocking a burgundy weave and a skintight leopard-print dress.

"What's up, Imani?" said Charles, looking over my head to greet her.

"Is your brother upstairs?" Imani asked, now standing two inches away from me, but not bothering to look my way.

"Yeah, he's home."

"All right, Charlie, thanks."

As soon as Imani walked away, here comes another girl around my age rocking a black weave with blond tips, and a red dress that barely covered up her butt.

"What's up, *Charlie?*" she asked in a squeaky voice.

"What's up, Tyesha?"

"When you planning to give me back my DVDs?" she asked, playfully tapping his leg. She acted like I wasn't standing there, didn't even say hi to me.

Charles cocked his head to the side and said, "Come on, now—I live two doors down from you, where am I going?"

"But I want them back *now*," she squeaked. "I'm headed to a friend's house, and I promised I'd bring them." Tyesha glanced over at me. She was smiling, but the smile was not friendly. Charles jumped off the car, gently pushed me to the side, and said, "I'll be back."

"Okay, Mr. Popular," I joked.

I worriedly watched Tyesha and Charles disappear into their building. Naleejah must've been watching the whole scene from the corner of her eye, because I suddenly heard her call out, "Bye, sweetie," to Divine, and she was by my side in a flash.

"What was that all about?" Naleejah exclaimed. "No he *didn't* just leave you for that broad!"

I explained the DVD situation, and Naleejah shook her head. "Still, the chick saw that Charles was busy with you—she could've waited."

"True."

"She did that mess for spite."

"Well, he's coming back out," I said. "No big deal."

Five minutes later, I didn't expect Charles to come back out *with* Tyesha still by his side. Big dang deal!

Twenty feet away from us, Tyesha grabbed Charles's arm, and they stopped short. She told him whatever she had to tell him, he nodded, and she laughed. I wished I had bionic ears.

When Charles tried to walk away, Tyesha pulled him back again.

I remained calm, although don't get it twisted. When Charles and I got serious, these chickenheads had better go clucking somewhere else. Trust and believe, I wouldn't be so patient when he was officially my man.

Naleejah stared at Tyesha, shaking her head. "Now she's *really* violating."

"Violating, for real," I said, wishing I could read lips. What did Tyesha have to say that was so freaking important? To get my mind off of what was going on in front of me, I turned my attention to Naleejah. "So did you get the digits from Divine? He's a cutie."

"Did I get the digits?" Naleejah repeated, then whipped out a piece of paper. "Oh yeah, I got the digits. You know I'm always on my grind."

I laughed, a little louder than usual, just to let Teyasha know I wasn't fazed by her—even though I was.

"I swear, I *hate* a jealous chickenhead," Naleejah continued harping. "She *knows* she's disrespecting you, and she's loving every minute of it."

"Well, if Charles doesn't come over here soon, I'm about to be out. It's too hot out here for this bull."

"Yeah, I don't blame you."

Then suddenly, from wayyy down the block, I heard Charles's name being called. By his mother. Mrs. King. Putting my baby on blast out in the streets like she always did. She was carrying a gang of grocery bags in both hands. "Come over here and help me with these, *boy*!" she shouted.

Mrs. King may have stopped beating on Charles, but she surely hadn't changed her loud ways. The only thing I was grateful to her for was getting Tyesha out my man's face.

Charles sprinted up to his mother and grabbed the bags. As he walked past Naleejah and me, he called out, "Wait for me, Kate. I'll be back down."

Mrs. King butted in. "I don't *think* so. Not until you put *all* these groceries away."

By now, my feet were killing me; I was sweating from the heat, tight about Tyesha, ready to go home.

"Hey, I'll catch you later," I said.

"A'ight, ma," Charles called over his back.

Then I turned to Naleejah and said, "Let's go."

But Naleejah stood her ground, wearing a scowl.

"What's wrong with you?" I asked, perplexed.

She jutted her chin toward Tyesha, who was now standing in front of a nearby fish and chips joint, talking loud into her cell phone.

"What about her?" I asked.

"You need to go find out what's going on with her and Charles," said Naleejah in a stern tone.

"Nah, that's okay," I said. "I don't fight over dudes—not even Charles."

"I'm not asking you to *fight*. I'm asking you to find out if something's up between him and her."

"Like she's really going to tell me the truth," I said.

"Well, you can play blind if you want to. But that wasn't right what she did. She straight-up *violated*."

Before I knew what I was doing, I was standing in front of Tyesha. Naleejah was close behind me. I waited for Tyesha to click shut her phone, then said, "Excuse me, can I ask you a question?"

"Why, what happened?" Tyesha staggered back a step. The sight of two girls in her face must've frightened her. So I made sure to soften my tone when I asked, "Do you talk to Charles?"

"No," said Tyesha. "Why?"

"I was just wondering . . . that's all."

" 'Cause *she* talks to him," piped in Naleejah, folding her arms across her chest.

"Well, she can have him," said Tyesha with a shrug.

"Listen, it's really not that serious," I said, staring at the sidewalk.

"Well, do you need to know anything else?" asked Tyesha sarcastically. Before I could say no, Tyesha walked away from us, shaking her head.

When I parted ways with Naleejah, I was shaking my head too.

The entire day was a bust.

On Tuesday, I was getting ready to head to Tisha's office when Naleejah called. It was nine o'clock in the morning, so I wondered why she was calling me so early . . . and why was she sniffling over the phone? I went from confused to worried in under sixty seconds. "What's wrong?" I asked. "What happened?"

"Kate . . . I think I caught something."

"Oh no, are you—?"

"And I'm scared."

"Man, I'm sorry to hear—"

"And the messed up thing is . . . I don't even *know* who gave this to me."

"Well, do you know if—?"

"I can't tell my mom, definitely not my pops. . . . I can't even go to our family doctor, because I'm afraid my parents will find out."

Finally I jumped in. "Listen, you can go to the free clinic around our way. Those doctors won't tell your parents anything."

"Yeah?" she sniffed. "Well, where is it?"

I ran down the address and gave Naleejah directions to a T. I've escorted so many group homegirls to the cootie clinic (don't laugh, that's what we called it), I could get to that grimy old building with my eyes closed.

"Can you come with me?" asked Naleejah.

I paused, and then reluctantly said, "Sorry, I can't."

Man, I felt so bad for having to say no. But Tisha is no-nonsense when it comes to me keeping appointments. Tisha was meeting me on her own time, something she didn't have to do. If I fronted on Tisha, she would be furious with me. I told Naleejah this.

"But can't you meet her tomorrow, or some other time?"

"No," I said flatly. "I really can't."

"But what time is your appointment?"

"Eleven."

"And it's only nine o'clock."

"Yeah, but trust me, there's always a long wait at the cootie—um, I mean, clinic."

Silence on the other end.

"Naleejah, I'm really sorry that I can't come with you."

Next thing I knew, *click*, bam in my ear.

Okay.

Foul of her, but whatever, I had to go.

Turned out to be a nice day. I met my new law guardian, Mrs. Morrison. Sweet older black lady. She had short curly gray hair and a friendly smile. Tisha made sure I understood everything Mrs. Morrison could do for me as my lawyer, and after that meeting, I was feeling more protected than before.

As soon as I got home, I was still feeling positive. So I decided to call Naleejah. I was reaching out to her because I'd had the chance to step back, relax, and put myself in her shoes. I imagined how scared she must be. If I were her, and she were me, I'd want my friend to check up on me too—even if I had acted like a butthead, hanging up phones and whatnot.

But Naleejah wasn't home, nor was she picking up her cell phone. All day, I left messages, but Naleejah returned none of my calls. Was she still upset with me? I wondered. Of course, I understood why she'd be upset—at first. She probably felt let down and dissed. But dang, time has passed, don't overdo it. Can we move on, please?

Then again, maybe Naleejah needed some time to herself. Maybe she was too embarrassed to talk about it—or maybe she was still crying in her bed and *couldn't* talk about it. I had no clue.

All I knew was that I'd wait two more days, and then I'd try her one more time. And if she didn't pick up her phone, or call me back, I'd have to count her as another homegirl lost. Like I told you before, I don't jump through hoops for nobody. Bump that. Naleejah had no right to be mad at me. Wasn't my fault I couldn't go with her to the clinic. I didn't *choose* to be in my situation—having courts decide what happens with my life. Some people only have to see courts on TV; meanwhile, I have to experience the real deal even when I've done nothing wrong.

On Friday, Naleejah's deadline, I prepared to make my final call. Since I'm only allowed to use the phone in the kitchen, and have no privacy to speak of, I waited until Lynn and Ted were fast asleep before dialing her up.

Finally, I reached her on the celly at eleven o'clock on the dot. She answered in a cheery voice, so things couldn't have been that bad.

"Girl, I've been calling you off the hook!" I said. "Are you okay?"

"Of course I'm okay," Naleejah replied. "We don't have to speak every day. I'm a busy woman, you know."

"Don't get it twisted," I said half-jokingly. "I was only checking up on you."

"Well, I'm fine."

"Glad to hear it."

"Not as much as me," exclaimed Naleejah. "It was nothing. Nothing a little cream can't fix."

"Oh," I said, wondering what she had to fix.

"Yeast infection," Naleejah volunteered. "Doctor said no more tight jeans, but he must be crazy. I don't do baggy clothes, feel me?"

"Yeah, true—not you."

"Girl, I'm so happy! Now I can keep my date with Finesse."

Naleejah suddenly broke out into song. "I'm getting me some tonight. I'm getting me some tonight."

"You still messing with Finesse?" I asked in disbelief.

"Yeah, and?"

"After he put his hands on you?" I said, not believing this forgetful chick. "I thought you were through with him."

"Well, minds are meant to be changed . . . like panties." Naleejah giggled.

"But . . . don't you think you should slow down?" I asked. I didn't mean to ask her this, but the words just fell out of my mouth. I couldn't believe Naleejah had recovered so quickly from an itchy STD scare.

"Slow down?" Naleejah repeated. "Don't you think you should catch up? Besides, did I say anything about us having sex? Shoot, a little oral never hurt nobody, you feel me?"

"Naleejah, hate to tell you, but oral sex *is* sex." *Duh?*

"No, it isn't. Calm down."

"Yes, it is. You better ask somebody."

"Girl, you're just paranoid," said Naleejah with a chuckle.

"Well, would you drink after a dude who has AIDS?"

"Hell no, is you crazy?" Naleejah exclaimed. "I ain't putting my lips on nobody's AIDS cup!"

"Okay, then."

"Okay, then—what?"

"You can't even catch AIDS from drinking after someone—but you can from having oral sex. How do you know if Finesse has AIDS or not? Did he show you results from a test, or are you just hoping for the best?"

"Kate?"

"What?"

"You really want to be a teacher when you grow up, don't you?"

"See, you always got jokes—too bad I'm not laughing."

"Too bad you're not getting any either," said Naleejah. "You need a man in your life, for real."

"Are you done yet?" I snapped.

"All I got to say is, you don't know what you're missing. I mean really, you should try the lollipop—matter of fact, you should try to put it on Charles. Bet you won't have any problems keeping his attention after you go down on him. He'll love you for life. I promise you that much."

Well, promises are made to be broken, just like phones are made to be hung up. Me? Go down on Charles? *Please*. Not until he was officially my man. Maybe not even then. But I could see this conversation was going nowhere fast, so it was time for me to go.

I wanted so badly to tell Naleejah that she didn't have to let guys use her up like that, that she was worth more than that. I mean, I could understand where she was coming from. I've been wanting to be loved forever too, but I know I can't get no love from a horny dude who just wants to get some. What's love got to do with a quick hit? Nothing. I'd be his freak for the week and that's it.

I didn't bother to share my thoughts. I knew my words would just go through one of Naleejah's ears and come out her mouth as laughter—mocking me—and I would only get mad, so forget it.

"All right," I said, faking a yawn. "Let me go catch up on some sleep. Holler at you later."

Chapter 16

I was in the kitchen making a tuna sandwich when Naleejah called. She wanted to know if I was ready to try my luck again with Charles.

"You already know," I said, smiling to myself. "What time you talking?"

"Don't know yet. I have to run some errands for my dad first. I'll call you . . . probably no later than five o'clock."

"All right, then, cool."

"Wait! Hello?"

"Yeah, I'm here," I said.

"Make sure you're looking fabulous, okay?"

"For sure," I said, feeling unsure. I hung up the phone with an uneasy feeling in my stomach. Wasn't hunger pains. More like anxiety mixed with frustration. I had a huge selection of Tammy's clothes to choose from, but no fly shoes to complete the fly look. I couldn't dare wear Naleejah's painful wedges another single day, so what could I do?

I ate half of my sandwich at the kitchen table. The other half got thrown away. Feeling too queasy to eat, I fretted over my footwear dilemma for a whole hour before I finally made my decision: Operation Five-Finger Discount.

Once an idea gets into my head, it's hard to shake out. I knew what I was about to do was wrong, risky and stupid, but I found myself not caring. Bad thing about me, depending on where my head is at, I can do grimy things without blinking. There's times when I feel like the world owes me something, and this was just one of those times.

I hopped on the A train, headed to downtown Brooklyn. Walked up and down Fulton Street, looking for the busiest shoe store. Bingo. Found one. The store was small, dark, and crowded. One harried clerk was scurrying from the cash register to the back of the store. She didn't know which way was up. Perfect. This setting allowed me the opportunity to do my thing. Of course, I thought about juvie, and being locked up in a box over some bull—but the shoes in this store were banging, and I could already see myself singin' to Naleejah: Yeah, girl, you can't clown me now, 'cause I don't need your hand-me-downs!

"May I help you?" asked the store clerk in a sweet voice. Now why did her voice have to be sweet? It would've helped if she was nasty. Oh well.

"Yes, thank you," I replied in a soft tone. I pointed to three pairs of sandals I wanted to see. She took more than a minute to bring them out.

I wore my innocent face as I tried on pair after pair. The ones I fell in love with were black and sexy high-heeled killers.

With the three shoe boxes surrounding my feet, I waited for the clerk to disappear. As soon as she turned her back, I looked to my left and right. Nobody paying me any mind. I snatched the strappy sandals up, stuffed them under my arm, and dashed out the store.

I knew I looked the fool carrying sandals out in the street, so I dipped into a corner grocery store, flashed a sweet smile, and asked for a free plastic bag. Bagged my new shoes up, and I was headed home with a smile on my face.

But as I waited on the platform for the A train, the smile faded. I started feeling like a donkey, like I was stepping back into time—doing petty crime to get mine.

I got off at Utica Station, still feeling bad. As hard as I tried to convince myself that the sandals wouldn't be missed, I couldn't stop thinking about that store clerk. Poor lady. What if her paycheck got docked because of me?

I walked down the block feeling worse than a jerk. My head was still under storm clouds when suddenly, I felt a tap from behind. I spun around to face Tyesha, joined by two other friends. The friend with the long hair and silver piercing under her bottom lip turned out to be my homegirl, Sheri. We were in the same fifth-grade class together, and she was my road dog until she got pregnant at age twelve.

"Hey, Sheri, what's up?"

"Oh snap, Kate!"

We hugged.

"You know her?" asked Tyesha in disbelief.

"This is *homegirl*, right here," said Sheri. "And you don't want none of Kate. *Trust* me on that."

Tyesha trusted Sheri, because her face suddenly relaxed into a grin when she said, "Well, shorty, you got a lot of heart stepping to me in *my* territory."

"But I wasn't stepping to you," I explained. "I had no beef with you."

"Didn't seem that way," squeaked Tyesha. "Ready to fight for Charles, huh?"

"No . . . well, my bad . . . I let my homegirl get into my head," I said.

Sheri playfully tapped me on the arm. "Kate, since when you let anybody get into your head?"

Tyesha piped in, "It's a good thing you know Sheri. Normally, I don't let no females pop off in my face and get away with it."

Tyesha was smiling the whole time she said this, so I didn't feel threatened . . . but I didn't feel at ease either.

Sheri wore a serious expression when she grabbed my arm and said, "Kate, don't even tell me you're slipping. You don't need no thug friends in your life anymore."

"Oh . . . Naleejah's not a thug," I corrected. "She's more like a diva."

"And that diva chick almost made you get your butt kicked," said Sheri. "We were fitting to jump you and ask questions later."

I paused in thought, and then said, "Well . . . good looking out. I owe you one."

"You don't owe me anything. You used to always have my back—you think I forgot? I'm just returning the favor."

"Well, good seeing you again," I said.

"All right girl, take care of yourself."

As the trio walked away from me, I exhaled a heavy sigh of relief. That was close.

Naleejah called me at five o'clock. She was ready to hang. Cool. I anxiously changed into my new shoes. Admired how the straps around my ankles brought the sexy to my sandals, loved how the height from my heels made me feel model-like. I stepped out the house feeling six feet tall.

Naleejah and I met up on Malcom X Boulevard. First thing she said: "Oh my gosh, Kate, you look so pretty!"

"Thanks," I said, beaming.

"And your hair is still banging."

"Yes sir, I wrapped it up just like you showed me."

Then she looked down at my feet. "Oh snap, you got some new kicks too! Those sandals are crazy blazing."

"Aren't they, though?"

When Naleejah calmed down, she said, "But I thought you didn't have any cash flow?" She eyed my feet suspiciously.

"My foster father gave me some money," I explained with a straight face. Then I quickly took the attention off me by complimenting Naleejah. "So you're always doing it real big, huh, girl? Look at *you*."

"Yeah, well . . . you know how I do," said Naleejah with a smile.

She had on a pair of tight white stretch pants, a sky-blue T-shirt tied up in a knot to show off her rhinestone belly-button piercing, and a pair of white high-heel sandals, showing off her toes, painted hot pink.

"Ready?" I asked.

"Always ready. Let's go."

The minute we hit the next block, an old man riding a creaky red stretch Cadillac stopped in the middle of the street and honked at Naleejah. "Eh, lady in the blue," he called out.

Naleejah spun around to see who was honking. When she saw it was a crusty old man in an ancient car, she swiveled back around, wearing a scowl. "What makes that old clown think he can get some of this? He done lost his mind!"

"Can I smell you?" shouted the old man. "Just one sniff, baby?"

"Ill, yuck, stop!" Naleejah cried out, flipping her middle finger at him. Shucks, if that old man jumped out the car and came after her, she'd be on her own. No more fighting Naleejah's battles.

When we made it to Fulton Street Park Building, no sign of Charles. Thank goodness no sign of Tyesha either. We waited in the park for a half hour. Still no sign of Charles. Naleejah wanted to wait around even longer, but I said no. There was no need to starve.

So we got up and let our feet take us wherever. We got wolf whistles from every other corner, and catty chicks sucking their teeth as we walked by. Clearly, looking good in the hood brings you nothing but hate and hollering. And this was getting old fast. I guess Naleejah was getting tired too, because she started complaining. "Psst, psst, that's all they do. I don't answer to *that*. Do I *look* like a cat?"

Well, actually, you do . . . your eyes.

". . . And all these broke dudes can say to me is baby this and baby that. Shoot, my *name* ain't Baby. If you ain't a baller getting money, you have no right to be calling me out my name. Feel me?"

"Yeah, I feel you," I said. "Oh, hey . . . the other day . . . why'd your father call you Bertha? Is that your middle name or something?"

Naleejah took a long time to answer me. Finally, she did. "Well . . . since you're my best friend . . . I guess I can tell you. . . . Bertha is my *real* name. I was named after my grandmother." Naleejah raised her pointer finger and aimed it at me. "But only family is allowed to call me Bertha. So don't be putting my name on blast, okay?"

"Oh, trust me, I won't," I said, and quickly turned my head away, pretending to stare at a random tree. *Bertha?* It took all my might not to bust out laughing. As we walked on in silence, my stomach was bursting at the seams.

Finally, on Patchen Avenue, Naleejah came to a halt in front of a squat building with a red-and-white awning. "Let me stop at this store," she said.

Hmm, didn't look like a store to me. The minute I stepped inside, the smell of stankin' kitty litter hit me—*bam*—in the nose. There was bulletproof glass everywhere and barely anything on the shelves. Never been to this store before, I thought warily. And that's when it suddenly hit me.

No she didn't.

I decided to wait outside.

When Naleejah emerged from the spot, no paper bag in hand, that's when I knew: Oh yes, she did.

"Don't tell me you had me up in a weed spot," I said through gritted teeth.

"Okay, so I won't tell you," Naleejah replied with a shrug.

"Don't get smart," I snapped. "Why would you do that to me?"

"Do *what* to you?" Naleejah asked. "I thought you knew what time it was. You don't look soft."

"Seriously, it's taking all of my strength not to snuff you," I said. "How you gonna have me in a funky weed spot without telling me?"

Naleejah raised one eyebrow and chuckled. "Um, Kate? I think you might be watching too many cop shows. Bodegas don't get raided, boo. The feds ain't coming for you." She laughed, trying to make merry about the situation, but ha ha ha, whatever. I was mad tight.

"You always got jokes," I said. "But you ain't even funny."

Weed is no laughing matter to me. Three years ago, I got locked up in juvie for possession of four bags. All because I was hanging with a tricky chick named Latoya. I had *just* met her. She was new to my group home, and just as sneaky as Naleejah. She didn't dress fly, though, never flashed her money, so it came as a surprise when I found out about her side hustle. One night, we were chilling in the park, when Craig, a thuggish dude from around our way, rolled up on Latoya. "You ready to count?" he asked.

"Yeah," she said coolly.

"Wait right here," Latoya told me. Then she followed Craig into a crumbling brownstone across the street. She left me waiting for more than a minute, and I was heated when she got back. I didn't want her to know I was mad, though, since I was grateful for her company. She was four years older than me, and I felt really flattered that she was trying to hang with me.

Next thing I knew, two weeks later, on a Friday night, we were in the same park, and out of nowhere, Latoya convinced me to "hold" the bags for her. Said she had to go find Craig real quick. "If people come up, don't give them any problems," she explained. "Soon as you see their money, give them what they need. Ten bills each."

She handed me four bags. Without hesitation, I stuffed them in the pocket of my baggy red sweatpants. Latoya bounced. Five minutes later, two customers rolled up. "What you want?" I asked. The tallest of the two asked "What you got?" Me not knowing what to do, I just pulled out a bag and said, "Ten dollars." The tall guy pulled out a shield and says, "You're under arrest." Bagged up on the spot. Latoya long gone. I was taken to the local precinct. Then off I went to Family Court, where I already had a file on me just for being a foster child. My case was pending because of the Memorial Day holiday. So I had to stay locked up in a cell on Friday, Saturday, Sunday, and Monday, being told when to eat, sleep, shower, talk—it was one of the worst experiences of my life, locked up with eighty other girls on some stupid random decision I made. Lucky for me, I wasn't carrying too much weight. So I got off on probation. But a weekend and a day in jail was more than enough for me to stay far away from weed—for good.

"I can't believe you tripping so hard," exclaimed Naleejah, as we stood on the corner of Malcom X. "You act like I just copped a kilo of cocaine!"

I didn't bother to snap back. At the moment, I was too busy thinking about this new friendship . . . or was this friendship? I'm saying, would Naleejah have something new and dirty up her sleeve every time we hung out? I actually believed her when she said *store*. The silly broad shouldn't say *store* when she really meant *spot*—why not give me the chance to decide whether I want to be down or not? It's called common courtesy. I was so tired of her surprises, and of her treating me like I'm some soft chick with no clue.

I stared hard at Naleejah and said, "I thought I was your homegirl. Why couldn't you just *tell* me you were going to cop weed?"

"I'm sorry," said Naleejah uncaringly. She didn't even look at me when she said it.

I was pissed. Tempted to go home, but too bored to go home. So I mentally shrugged and carried on with Ms. Liar.

"Oooh, I got the munchies," Naleejah suddenly exclaimed.

"The munchies already?" I said sarcastically. "But you didn't even puff yet."

"Shut up!" Naleejah laughed. "Anyway, what do you want from the store?"

"Sunflower seeds," I said, quickly whipping out my own dollar bill. I didn't want to hear those three awful words—*I got you*—ever again.

"Okay, I'm getting me some peanut chews and a cherry Blow Pop."

We entered a bona fide store and copped our candy. And when we came back outside, I suddenly decided to call it a night, even though the sun was still shining high in the sky.

Naleejah hiked up her eyebrows. "But we were just getting started!"

"Yeah, but—"

"Are you mad at me or something?"

"No," I said. I didn't have the heart to tell Naleejah that yeah, I was mad, that she had gotten on my last nerve, that her walks-to-nowhere honestly sucked, and that her weed-spot scam was really foul—not to mention, less than a few hours ago, I almost got my butt beat down by Tyesha *partly* because of her, and I had on shoes that were stolen *partly* because of her. Listen, I was ready to part ways with this girl. Quick!

"Are we still friends?" Naleejah asked, suddenly looking pitiful.

"Girl, stop tripping," I said. "It's not that serious."

"You don't even want to go back and see about Charles?"

"Some other time," I said. "My head hurts." And this wasn't a complete lie. Naleejah had given me a headache.

Besides, as much as I wanted to see Charles, there's a difference between desire and *desperation*. You should *never* want a guy more than he wants you. Now, that's the law.

"Okay, Kate . . . hope you feel better."

"Thanks. I'll call you tomorrow." But no. I wasn't planning to call Naleejah tomorrow. Yeah, I got tricks up my sleeves too. I can lie through my teeth too. Besides, *she* was the main one talking about, "We don't have to speak every day." Well, guess what, I couldn't agree more. I'd call her when I *felt* like it, and not a minute before.

Chapter 17

When I came home, I found the surprise of my life lying on my bed: a brand-new life book . . . from Lynn? She had left a Post-it note that read: "Ted told me you needed a new book. Make sure you fill it up." She even drew a smiley face.

I frowned. This wasn't the best time to be receiving a peace offering. How could I feel good about myself, when I was feeling so shady and foul? I had just stolen a pair of shoes, and Lynn was finally deciding to be nice to me? Terrible timing, right?

Hard as it was, I pushed the shoe incident to the back of my mind. Brushed my shoulders off and concentrated on the book in front of me. It was beautiful with its pink cover and white satin ribbons decorating the spine. Inside, there were stickers, stamps, and black felt letters of the alphabet for putting captions underneath pictures. I went into my closet to grab my dusty old life book. I removed my honor roll certificate and carefully placed it in the plastic sleeve of my spanking new book. STAR STUDENT. Now it was official. I wondered if I should keep my old crappy book for old times' sake. After a quick debate, I said nah, no use hanging on to a book that stayed empty. I dumped it in the trash. A new beginning.

When I went to thank Lynn, I felt weird, and awkward. She received me with a nod and a smile. "Just make sure you use it," she said.

The next day, I wanted to keep the good times rolling, so I initiated a conversation with Lynn. She was sitting at the kitchen table going over paperwork for her volunteer job at her school. During the school year, she works as a guidance counselor, and she could have the whole summer off if she wanted to. But she chose to counsel the summer school kids three times a week. I admired the fact that Lynn worked so hard for free. Couldn't be me.

I inched up by her side. "Um, can I ask you a quick question?"

Lynn looked up from her papers. "Sure, what is it?"

"Just wanted to know how you think I should I start out with my life book."

Lynn cracked a rare smile. "Well, you can start anywhere, and any way, you want. It's yours. You can write a journal, sketch, take pictures—whatever you want to do."

Take pictures . . . hmm, not a bad idea.

"Do you think Ted will let me borrow his camera?" I asked timidly.

"Doesn't hurt to ask," Lynn said with a shrug. Then she went back to scanning over her papers, as if to dismiss me. I wasn't offended. I could tell she was busy. The fact that she smiled at me was a serious breakthrough.

I thanked Lynn and left the kitchen feeling satisfied. Ever since the air had been cleared by Tisha, things seemed to be sailing smooth in the Johnson household. True, I almost risked everything by stealing a pair of sandals, but I was slick with mine, and got away with it, didn't I?

Now if only I had somewhere to go.

I sat in my bedroom, looking out the window, drifting in deep thought. I thought about shooting some hoops, but then again, my hair. I wanted Charles to see me looking good 24-7, and the only activity worth sweating out my hair was a hot and steamy kissing session with my baby.

So in the meanwhile, what to do?

Then, *boom*! It hit me.

Why not go to Prospect Park? At the park, I could chill out, walk around taking pictures of the trees, the lake, the swans in the lake, whatever. This would be something new for me to do.

I have Felicia to thank for making me want to try new things outside the box of Bed-Stuy. She was the first friend to appeal to my defiant side—on the positive tip. I'll never forget the day we were sitting bored on Felicia's porch and she popped up and asked me to go bird-watching in Central Park. I looked at her like, *What?* Then I laughed at her and said, "Are we senior citizens now?"

"Why does it have to be all that?" Felicia asked. "You're the one always talking about how cute the sparrows are, but now you're trying to act brand-new?"

"What sparrows?"

Felicia pointed toward the curb at a brown little bird. "That sparrow."

"Oh, I didn't know that was a sparrow."

"My point exactly," said Felicia.

We debated back and forth for a minute. Then finally, I sighed and said, "Sounds mad boring, but let's do it."

Next thing I knew, Felicia and I were in Central Park, laughing, bugging the heck out, and having a crazy good time. The park let us borrow binoculars for free, and we threw them around our necks and got busy tramping across the trails looking up through the trees for different species of birds. I saw my first woodpecker. My first robin redbreast. The experience was too cool. During the train ride home, I turned to Felicia and said, "My bad, that was really fun."

"No doubt," Felicia replied. "I'm just glad you came through."

Since then, I vowed to keep myself open. Go outside the box. Be defiant. Be adventurous. Be the opposite of what people imagined I should be. Think I will fail? Then watch me succeed.

So, yeah, I'd go to Prospect Park. Be a photographer for the day. After that, I'd lounge on a bench in the shade, breathe in the trees, then come back home and figure out which pictures should make it into my life book. Sounded like a plan.

My program for the day was hot, and I was all keyed up about it. As soon as Ted came back from his stroll, I pounced. "Hey, Ted!"

"Hey, Kate!" he exclaimed, imitating my animated voice.

I chuckled, waited a few moments, and then asked, "Can I borrow your digital camera?"

He raised his eyebrows. "For where? Here?"

"No, Prospect Park," I said. "I want to start lacing up my life book, like you told me to." I beamed, thinking he'd be thrilled over my initiative.

But Ted's eyes bugged out of his head like I had just asked for his firstborn child. "Oh no, sorry, Kate," he began, "but I can't let you take my digital out this house."

My face fell flat. I didn't know it was like that. I thought Ted trusted me.

"Kate, what's the sad face for?"

(I need to learn how to control my face. I don't like folks reading my mind all the time.)

"I'm not sad," I lied. "Just trying to figure out what I'm going to do at the park . . . that's all."

"Who are you going with?" Ted asked. "Your new friend?"

"No. Going solo."

"Really?" Ted said with raised eyebrows. "Well, you be careful out there. No strolling in deserted areas, always stay out in the open where there's other people around, understand me?"

"Of course I understand you," I said. "I know how to handle myself."

(I guess I need to control my tone of voice too, because Ted could hear I was still upset.)

"Listen, it's nothing personal. I just don't want you dropping or losing my three-hundred-dollar camera. . . . Shoot, I don't even trust myself with the digital in Prospect Park. But you wait right here. I got something else for you."

Ted went upstairs and came back carrying a clunky black camera, big as a TV. Oh no. I didn't think so. Ted must've snapped pictures of cavemen with that prehistoric-looking contraption!

"Don't screw up your face like that," said Ted, laughing. "It still works. I even have some film left for you."

"No offense, but nah, no thanks."

"Why?"

"That thing looks mad heavy, and I'm carrying a small purse."

"Since when do you carry a purse?" Ted chuckled.

I shrugged.

Ted stroked his chin and asked, "Well, what happened to your trusty ol' knapsack? Maybe you can carry that."

It hurt my feelings to think about my knapsack sitting in a dump somewhere. I quickly said, "Oh, it's somewhere around here," and then I quickly changed the subject. Ted looked at me funny, but he didn't press me further.

"Oh well, thanks for trying to look out," I said.

I was about to leave the living room, but Ted called me back. He leaned forward to see if Lynn was still busy with her papers before reaching into his shorts pocket, and pulling out his favorite (and my favorite) tan leather wallet. He pulled out a twenty, and my eyes lit up. Ted slipped it in my palm so slick, I felt like I was pushing dime bags on the streets. This is how we had to get down, since Lynn didn't believe in allowance.

Okay, so no camera. No problem. I had a twenty-dollar bill in my purse. I was set. Now maybe I could check out the petting zoo, or go for a boat ride, or do whatever I wanted to do. Hey, I was free to do me. It would be strange going to Prospect Park without Felicia, but even stranger to stay stuck indoors. Nah, I wasn't trying to stay stuck. I needed to be out!

I got dressed. Kept my outfit simple. An old yellow T-shirt, a pair of baggy blue shorts, and my hair hooked up into a ponytail with bangs swished to the side. My bangs kept falling into my eyes, but that was okay, I loved the feeling of flicking my hair out of my face—like I'm a diva, because I am.

I grabbed my keys, my purse, said my good-byes, and headed out for the sun. But the split second I stepped outside, Ted whipped open the front door and called me back in. I had a phone call. It was Naleejah. Her "hello" sounded shaky, like she had been crying. What was up *this* time?

Chapter 18

"Hey, girl," I said. "What's wrong?"

"Listen, my parents are fighting. I need to get out of this house. Can I come over, please?"

"Well . . . um . . . I was headed to Prospect Park—"

"With who?" Naleejah blurted out like a jealous boyfriend.

"By myself."

"By yourself? Are you crazy? This is Brooklyn!"

"Why crazy?" I asked. "I'm not walking through the forest butt-naked. It's no big deal."

"But . . . why didn't you ask me if I wanted to come?" Naleejah sniffed.

"I didn't think you'd be down."

"Well, I'm down," said Naleejah. "What are you trying to do there?"

"I'm open to whatever."

I was shifting my feet, itching to bounce, but I tried to consider Naleejah's possible state. I know it's nerve-racking to hear grown folks yelling at each other in the house, and it's worse when you have no place to go to escape the madness. So I sighed, hoping Naleejah didn't hear me sigh, and said, "Listen, if you want to come with me to the park, I'll wait for you, okay?"

"Hey, we should go to Coney Island!"

"Nah," I said firmly. "Prospect Park." We needed to do something *I* wanted to do, for a change. I had let Naleejah lead me around like a brainless puppy on a leash for far too long. It was *my* turn to call the shots.

Finally, Naleejah said, "Okay, I'll come with you."

We met up at the B46 bus stop on Macon Street. Naleejah was dressed for a pool party. She had on a hot pink halter top, dark green Daisy Duke shorts, and silver flip-flops decorated with rhinestones. She looked mighty pretty, but mighty silly for the park. I wondered how she was going to sit comfortably on dirty buses and trains and wooden park benches in those coochie-cutting shorts of hers.

Naleejah gave me a stiff quick hug, and the first thing out her mouth was: "Girl, I gave you all those clothes, and *this* is what you wear?"

"Hello to you too," I grunted. "No need to wear a ball gown to the park."

Two seconds later, she said, "Honestly, it's burning up out here! We should be headed to the beach, not some dang park."

Okay, be nice. She's going through some things.

When we got off the bus and headed to the Utica Avenue number 3 train, Naleejah tapped me on the shoulder and said, "Oh my gosh, I can't believe we have to take a bus *and* a train just to get to some park! See, that's why I need me a full-time man with a hot whip to chauffeur us around, feel me?"

I nodded and flashed a fake smile.

When we entered Prospect Park, I didn't have a solid plan. I just wanted to chill out, bug out, see where our feet took us. But no, not Naleejah. The queen of walks-to-nowhere had the nerve to be beefing with my idea. She couldn't appreciate the silky blue sky or the beautiful green trees surrounding us. . . . The cute kids wobbling on their first bikes didn't amuse her, and the old folks trembling on Rollerblades didn't make her laugh. So, everybody was outside having fun—except for us. I tried to be patient with her at first, because Felicia had to point these same things out to me once. But ten minutes into our walk, Naleejah jerked her chin up at me and asked, "Are we there yet?" Then she rolled her eyes.

Between me and you, I was ready to chin-check her. But I took a deep breath instead. "Do you want to go to the zoo? Six dollars to get in."

"The zoo!" Naleejah exclaimed. "I'm not trying to pay six bills to see nobody's animals. We got enough mice in our house as it is. You sound crazy."

Wow, this was some bull.

Listen, the first time Felicia invited me to Shakespeare in the Park, I thought it would be mad boring, and I was correct, but I went along with the program anyway. I didn't clown my homegirl or complain. If Felicia could roll with me to watch a basketball game, then I could roll with her to watch Romeo and Juliet commit suicide. It's called give and take. But right now, all I wanted to do was give Naleejah a black eye and take my black butt home.

"Where to now?" asked Naleejah.

"Let's sit down for a minute," I said, pointing to a bench under a weeping willow tree. "I'll think of something we can do."

"Hope you can," said Naleejah, shaking her head as we sat down.

I put my hand to my cheek. "Uh, do *you* have any suggestions, Ms. Thing?"

"No," Naleejah said. "But you're the one who dragged us here—remember? Got me taking buses, trains, and planes to get here to do what?"

I clenched my fists, then unclenched them, leaned back on the bench and counted to ten. Naleejah suddenly leaned forward and looked to her left and right. "I can't believe not a single hottie in this whole park! Nothing but bratty kids and grown folks. I wasted my dang outfit."

Okay. Last try.

"Hey, there's an electric boat tour we can go on," I suggested. "Me and Felicia had crazy fun on it last summer—my treat, okay?"

The boat ride would be ten dollars for the both of us. Ten dollars was worth spending to shut this chick up and save my day; it was too sunny outside to let this cloud named Naleejah rain on my parade.

"Well, where's the boat?"

"On the other side of the park—closer to Ocean Avenue, I think. We'll find it."

"No, *you'll* find it, because I'm not trying to walk across no damn park."

I pressed my lips together and shook my head in anger.

"Naleejah, you could at least *try* to have fun," I said, rubbing the back of my neck; she had me feeling mad tense in the neck bone!

Naleejah didn't reply. She just whipped out a cigarette, stuck it in her mouth, and lit up.

I jumped up.

"Where you going?" Naleejah asked.

"Don't want your smoke blowing all up in my face."

"You mad at me?"

"Do you really care?" I asked. "I'm saying, you don't want to do anything I want to do. You ain't open to nothing."

Naleejah blew a circle of smoke and said, "No disrespect, but it seems like you and your homegirl be trying to do white people stuff."

I jerked my head back. "What? Black people can't ride boats now? You didn't get the memo? We're *free*."

"Well, sorry to say, but you and your homegirl be sounding mad nerdy."

"Don't be sorry," I said. "Nerds do it real big. So I'll be getting cake, while you'll be getting crumbs. . . . If you're lucky, I'll save you a slice."

"Please, girl, I had you riding in a shiny fly Range Rover the other day."

"And, what?" I asked. "We didn't go anywhere special, and it wasn't even your truck."

"Yeah, okay, whatever."

"Trust me, Naleejah, I'm going places. So don't sleep on me."

"Okay, so *now* I see," began Naleejah, "you don't think you're *white*, but you do think you're too good for the hood, huh?"

"Girl please, when I get my college degree, I'm still shouting out Brooklyn and keeping it *me*. What?"

"Sure you will." Naleejah blew out another circle of smoke and flashed a smart-aleck smile.

I looked away from her, kicked at the ground, and stared at the tree in front of me. I tried to tell myself to ignore her, but she was taking me back to a bad time, reminding me of a group of girls I had rolled with in the beginning of the seventh grade. Chandra. Melissa. Tina. Rolanda. Bad girls for life. They weren't technically a gang, but they were close, bullying weak broads and acting up in general. They used to cheer me on whenever I yoked somebody up, but scrambled and ran once I started doing good in school and my teachers started sweating me like fans. "You think you too good now?" they'd ask, passing me by in the hallways. I felt so rejected and hurt by them, especially when they swore I was trying to be better than them, when I was only trying to *do* better for myself.

Once, in the lunchroom, Chandra stepped to me as I was sitting quietly with Felicia, minding my own biz. Felicia and I were running partners by then, and Chandra seemed upset about it.

"Yo, Kate," she began in a bass tone. "Don't *think* you can come back to us when you get bored, okay?"

I shrugged in place of an answer.

"You heard me, right?"

"Yeah, I heard you," I said, then turned to face my dry hamburger. After Chandra left the table, my face must've looked pitiful because Felicia patted me on the shoulder and said, "I hope you're not tripping over her. She's mad stupid. That was so random and unnecessary."

"Yeah, I know, but when I was down with her, she was riding my bra strap hard, and now that I'm hanging with you, she got a problem with that? She makes me so sick. None of those other girls talk to me anymore either, and we used to be mad tight—two-faced broads. I don't need them anyway."

Felicia dropped her hamburger on the tray and stared at me for a second, then said, "But why do you sound so bitter?"

"I'm not bitter," I insisted.

"Yes, you are. I can hear it in your voice."

I shrugged whatever, and then started picking at the limp lettuce on my hamburger. Then Felicia began her lecture. I didn't hear anything she said but the last paragraph: "Let those girls laugh at you. And they'll be flipping fries for a living, while you'll be getting paid. Don't even worry about them. You can't be rejected by a group you don't want no parts of. Let it go, girl."

That day, I let it go.

But thinking back to that day, and the way those girls had treated me, had me heated all over again. Naleejah was taking me back. And there was an old Kate deep down inside of me. If Naleejah wasn't careful, I'd introduce her to the side of me she didn't want to meet.

Naleejah stamped out her cigarette, raised her hand as if in class, and said, "Um, professor, can we go home now?"

Naleejah had jokes.

I had enough.

I sat down heavy next to Naleejah, looked her dead in the eye, and asked, "Listen, do you have a problem with me?"

Naleejah jerked her head back, her hazel eyeballs popped wide open. "But . . . why would you ask that?"

"Because you always got something smart to say."

Naleejah started twitching in her seat. "No, I don't have a problem with you. I told you . . . you're my best friend."

"But those are just words," I said. "I have to deal with a *whole* lot in my life. So I don't need to be dealing with my own friend dissing me all the time. If you have a problem with me, just say so, and word is bond, I'll leave you the hell alone."

"Kate, please don't be like that," said Naleejah, grabbing my arm. "You know I'm only playing with you."

I yanked my arm away. "Nah, but the joke is always on me, and I'm getting tired of the bull."

"Dang, girl, I'm sorry."

"But you don't sound sorry."

"What? Do I have to get down on my knees?"

Nah, that would be too easy for a slut like you.

"Listen, I'm ready to go," I said, getting up, and brushing off my backside.

"Me too." Naleejah got up, and I wondered if she had any splinters in her butt. Her shorts were crazy Daisies, and come to think of it, she'd be turning mad heads on our way back home. Honestly, I wasn't in the mood to hear no grimy hollering. I was wishing I had a spaceship to beam me back to Bainbridge Street.

Naleejah tugged at my arm and asked, "Are you going to dump me as soon as your homegirl gets back?"

I purposely left her question dangling in the air.

Chapter 19

Riding any train anywhere in New York City, nine times out of ten—*boom*—the train door bangs opens and a homeless person walks through with the following speech: "Excuse me ladies and gentlemen . . . I'm homeless and I'm hungry. . . ." The situation is so common that I don't even blink twice when it happens. But while Naleejah and I sat on the number 3—not speaking to each other—the train door banged open, and my eyes popped wide open once I looked up and recognized the voice and the face coming through. She recognized me too.

"Kate!"

"Roberta . . ." I hoped she couldn't hear the shock in my voice. "Hey, girl—"

I was about to add, *What's good?* But I already knew the answer to that. Roberta's brown face was ashy, her hair sticking up on all sides, her oversized T-shirt no longer white, and her sneakers were dirty and unlaced; her whole appearance was far from the fly girl I remembered when we had shared a room in my very first group home.

It hurt my heart to see Roberta like this. I had always looked up to her—she was older, always looking fabulous, and always looking out for me. I've had homegirls who've been to jail, even had a couple of distant acquaintances die on me, but the sight of Roberta had me shook.

I scooted over to give Roberta room. She sat down, placed her coffee cup chock-full of change on the dirty floor, and reached over to give me a hug.

I could feel Naleejah's eyes on me; I could feel all the train's passengers' eyes on me, but I paid these people no mind. I introduced Roberta to Naleejah. Naleejah cracked a fake smile, looking all fidgety in the face.

"Kate, so good to see you," said Roberta.

"For sure," I replied, not knowing what else to say. Roberta was probably used to the stunned look I was giving her, so she volunteered her story: She had a baby at seventeen by a dealer named Cisco. He had promised to take care of her forever, but when he found out she was pregnant—poof—he was gone. She didn't get to finish high school, she couldn't find a good job, her baby was taken away, she went a little crazy, lived in a residential home until she turned twenty-one, and on her twenty-first birthday she received a small discharge check and was shown the front door. The group home was a revolving door. I saw younger girls come in who reminded me of me, and older girls who showed me what I could turn out to be. But I never once believed Roberta could turn out like this. It was so scary to see.

Roberta nudged me in the arm and said, "Anyway, how are *you* doing?"

"Oh . . . I'm cool."

"Yeah, I can see that. You look cool too . . . seems like you calmed down a lot." Roberta leaned over to address Naleejah. "Homegirl used to be a wild child for real."

Naleejah flashed . . . was it a smirk or a smile?

"Well, I've been staying out of trouble for a while now," I said. "My homegirl *Felicia* holds me down . . . but she's away right now, so wish me luck in the meanwhile."

Yeah, I said this on purpose. I wanted to hurt Naleejah's feelings, remind her that I had a *real* homegirl who was coming back for me.

Roberta reached out to touch my ponytail. "Kate . . . I didn't know you had *this* much hair! I've never seen you with your hair done. Girl, you're full of surprises!"

"Thanks," I said. "Naleejah gave me a perm."

I knew Naleejah heard her name being called, but she kept her head jacked to the right like she didn't want to be associated with us, like she was too busy caring about the rude people on the train eye-balling us. But if she was a *real* friend, she would've said bump these idiots, and hold me down for once, jump into the conversation and say something, anything. But she couldn't even be bothered to help me keep up appearances. I was trying so hard not to cry.

Naleejah's nonchalance didn't matter for long, though. As soon as we pulled into the next station, Kingston Street, Roberta sighed and said, "Well, let me get back to work." She was about to get up, but I held her arm down. I fumbled for the fifteen dollars I had left in my pocket and tried to stuff the bills in her hand. She hesitated like she didn't want to take the money. She looked about ready to cry.

"Please?" I whispered.

Roberta cleared her throat, about to say something, but I cut her off at the pass. "Remember all those times you snuck some McDonald's in for me? You never asked me for a dime back. Plus, you used to protect me from those chicks always trying to jack me for my fries." I forced a laugh. "Remember that?"

"Yeah . . . I guess."

"And remember how you used to help me with my homework when I actually bothered to do it? Girl, you used to hold me down all the time!" I touched her arm and forced a smile, trying to keep the mood light and unsentimental.

Roberta looked down at the floor for a long time, and then a thin smile formed on her chapped lips. "Man, you just took me back for a minute—yeah, I do remember that."

I held her by the arm. "Listen, I promise you, I'll be straight. Please, take it."

Finally, Roberta stuffed the money in her back pocket and reached over to hug me even tighter than before. "Don't worry, I'll be back on my feet in no time. Watch me."

"No doubt," I said, "I know you will."

Roberta reached down to grab her cup of change. Then she turned to Naleejah and said, "Nice meeting you, bye."

Naleejah cracked a fake smile and flipped her hand up and down, a weak-as-can-be send-off for a girl down on her luck.

Fake broad.

As soon as Roberta left our car, Naleejah turned to me and said, "Wow, I feel so sorry for her."

I raised my eyebrows. "Oh really—well, I'm surprised. You acted like you didn't care to know her."

"Well, y'all share a past. I don't know her like that . . . matter of fact, I'm surprised *you* know her."

"Why would you be?" I snapped. "She was in foster care just like me."

"Okay, okay, you don't have to jump down my throat. Dang, what did I say?"

"I'm saying, *I* could be Roberta . . . foster care is no joke . . . you have no idea . . . look I'm feeling all messed up right now. Let's forget it, okay?"

"But you're *not* Roberta, so you can relax."

"Don't tell me to relax," I blasted. "Didn't I say forget it? You're really starting to piss me off!"

"Seems like I did already—"

"Because you keep saying stupid sh—"

Naleejah cut in. "I mean . . . I was just trying to say that you have foster parents already, and—"

"And they're not guaranteed," I snapped. "And when I turn twenty-one, I'm completely on my own. I don't have anybody, okay?"

"But you have me," said Naleejah.

Not a comforting thought.

Naleejah paused, then said, "Well . . . Roberta is still pretty. I wish I could give her a makeover or something. Did you smell her? She smelt like pee."

I jerked my head back and glared at Naleejah. "Are you out of your freaking mind?" I exploded. "The girl doesn't have a place to live, she got her baby taken away, and that's all you can say? I swear you say the stupidest things. Be quiet. I'm serious. Don't talk to me."

Naleejah was smart enough not to open her mouth for the rest of the train ride, but when we got outside to wait for the bus, she started running her mouth about the oppressive heat.

Finally, I decided, I couldn't take it anymore. I had too much on my mind, mostly Roberta, and I wasn't in the mood for Naleejah's nonsense.

Operation Ditch Chick was about to be in full effect.

Chapter 20

Fortunately, Naleejah was easy to trick. I pretended to be in a sudden mood for a walk in this nice little heat wave. Her reaction was just what I expected.

"Is you out of your mind?" Naleejah exclaimed. "It's burning up out here!"

If I wasn't so bummed out about Roberta, I would've smiled at how clever I can be. "Well, I'm sorry," I said, "but I'm in the mood to walk. You don't have to come with me, though."

"Please, girl, I'm taking a cab," said Naleejah, digging in her wallet to confirm her cash flow. She dug up a twenty spot, and yep, she was good to go. Well, good—then go.

As soon as Naleejah hailed herself a cab and hopped inside, I exhaled a big huffy sigh of relief. Whew, what a day.

I hopped on the next B46 bus and rode home in peace.

I had a terrible dream that night. All I could remember was standing over Naleejah, screaming at her. She was crying like crazy. I was cursing out of control and screaming, "What is your problem, what is your problem?" Then out of nowhere, I hauled back and was about to punch Naleejah dead in her face. But before my fist connected, next thing I knew, Naleejah's face turned into Felicia's—don't ask me how, that's just how dreams do. I woke up in the middle of the night sweating and shaking under my sheets. The nightmare was so real, it was scary; the thought of hurting Felicia made me sick to the pit of my stomach. I'd never dream of hurting Felicia. At least not on purpose.

The only time I ever tried to deliberately hurt Felicia was two days before she was about to leave for South Africa. She had called to tell me how much she would miss me, and all she had said was, "Kate, I really wish you were coming."

And then I broke on her.

"Well, I'm not coming," I said. "So, stop talking about it. Go ahead and have fun without me."

"But, Kate, you're the one who decided—"

"Look, just go ahead and leave," I spat. "People always leave me. No big deal to me." I was trying to take her far away on a guilt trip.

It worked. There was silence on the other line.

And then came the sniffles.

I felt so bad for purposely making my homegirl cry that day. But it was the only way I knew how to deal with the hurt I was feeling. Felicia, my only friend, was leaving me for two whole months, and I just couldn't handle it.

Before I could explain myself, Felicia had hung up on me. I called her right back, but she said she was too busy with last-minute packing. So I asked her if I could come over to help. She said no . . . but I could ride with her to the airport on Saturday. Much as I can't stand Felicia's parents, on Saturday, I rolled with them to see Felicia off. And when it came to saying good-bye, I started crying, not boo-hooing out loud, but the tears were steady rolling down my face.

"Kate, please stop," Felicia said. "Now you're going to make me cry."

I stopped crying, but still felt terrible. When we hugged, I couldn't seem to let go of Felicia. She ended up having to pull herself away from my death grip. I guess she was trying to keep the mood light when she said, "Dang, Kate, you act like I'm dying! I'll be back all right? . . . Are you okay?"

"Of course I'm okay," I said, stiffening my upper lip. But during the ride back home, I sat in the backseat of the Coldwells' icy cold Benz, with my heart broken and my eyes blinking back tears. Felicia and I had a rhythm going, and now that she was leaving me, I felt offbeat. Alone. And look at me now, so desperate for friendship, I was stuck with a chickenhead like Naleejah who was clucking on my last nerves.

Naleejah knew I was upset with her. So I didn't think she'd have the guts to call me anytime soon. But she did. She called me three days later, at two o'clock in the afternoon, when I was alone in the house, studying the PSAT book Lynn had bought for me two months ago. At the time Lynn handed it to me, I said to myself, "Come on, now, lady—I got two more years to sweat this mess." But after my encounter with Roberta, nuh-uh, I was scared straight, realizing my future is not a game. I'd rather be ahead of my class than behind . . . get myself a scholarship, and make big moves before I'm ever forced to move again. My new thing is, wherever I go, I'm going to have my act together.

"Hey, Kate, look outside your window," Naleejah squealed into my ear.

Feeling apprehensive, I put down the phone. I went into the living room, kneeled on the couch, and peered outside.

Naleejah was waving at me with her right hand and holding a big brown Macy's bag with her left. *What the—?*

I hung up the phone and came outside, with my eyebrows knitted. The first thing I said was, "I didn't ask for permission to have company."

"Girl, hush, I just came over to bring you this." Naleejah held up the shopping bag. "I bought you something I know you've been missing for a while."

Is Felicia inside the bag?

Naleejah handed me the shopping bag. I peeked inside and pulled out a black sporty knapsack with silver zippers and pockets everywhere. . . . Whoa, this bag was crazy fly—but—well—it couldn't replace my trusty old knapsack. However, I'd be looking hot and sporty with this sleek backpack on my shoulders.

"Wow, thanks," I said, reaching out to hug Naleejah. "Good looking out."

"No problem."

"So what's popping?" I asked.

"Nothing much," said Naleejah. "What you been up to? What it do?"

"Chilling . . . reading . . . whatever."

But to be exact, on my days off from Naleejah, I'd been reading, journaling in my life book, taking pictures (yes, with Ted's digital camera!) of the flowers Lynn had planted in the backyard. I'd been building up my life book and actually having fun doing it. I'm not a crafty person, so I was surprised at myself. But of course, I wouldn't mention any of this happy la-la-la stuff to Naleejah. She might've tried to clown me again, and I didn't want to go off on her, especially not after she'd come over to give me such a sweet and thoughtful gift.

Don't get me wrong, though. My friendship is not for sale. It just seemed like Naleejah was trying to show me that she was sorry . . . that she was trying to make things right . . . or at least better. I appreciated that.

Naleejah suddenly reached out to feel the top of my head. "New growth," she said, "You'll be needing a touch-up soon."

"Oh, already?" I frowned.

"Yeah, but I got you. Don't worry."

"Oh, okay," I said. But *ugh*. I was in no mood to have that creamy white stuff burning up my head again. How could I prolong needing another perm? Oh snap. What about a new hat? I just got my knapsack replaced, so why not cop a new dome piece too?

But no more baseball caps for me. I was too cute for that. I'd buy myself a fly and sexy hat that I could tip to the side like a true diva. Hide my new growth too. As a matter of fact, just the other day, on Lewis Avenue, I had passed a rainbow assortment of hats displayed in a fancy boutique's window. I had always wanted to check out the store. Now was a good time. Should I invite Naleejah to join me? Sure, why not?

"Hey, you got any plans?" I asked.

"Nah, not lately," said Naleejah. "Guess I better get me a new batch of boys."

I ignored her comment and said, "Well, I want to check out some hats at a store around the way. You down?"

"What?" Naleejah exclaimed. "You know I'm always down to shop!"

"A'ight, I'll be back." I turned around to go get my gift certificate.

"Um—why I gotta' wait outside?" asked Naleejah. "You've seen *my* house already."

"Nothing personal," I said. "I didn't ask to have company, and I don't want Ted or Lynn popping up."

"Dang, they sound crazy!"

"No, it's not like that," I said. "They're okay. . . . I'm just trying to show them some respect, you feel me?"

"Yeah, I feel you, but hurry up. I can't wait to get my shopping on!"

I took my time digging up Tammy's hottest gear. I knew I had to come correct when I stepped inside this classy boutique. When you dress like a bum, store clerks be hopping on your back and riding you all around the store, swearing you're about to steal. I wasn't in the mood for any back riders. I'm no thief—well, then again.

I threw on a low-cut white top and slithered into a pair of formfitting hot pink capri pants. Slipped on my sexy black leather sandals. Then tended to my head. Put a dash of coconut oil on my hair and brushed it down flat on all sides. Now I looked like a bootleg Cleopatra. I must say though, I looked good. I strutted outside.

Naleejah was grinning at me proud, like yeah, *I hooked my homegirl up.*

"Okay, Ms. Thing," Naleejah said. She reached up to smooth down my hair. "Maybe you can go another week, and then I'll perm you."

"Okay, cool," I said. "Ready to rock?"

"Let's roll!"

We walked the six blocks to the boutique, only to find out the store was closed. At random? No gates down? No explanation? Just dark windows and no souls inside.

I was totally pissed. I had always wanted to visit this shop, never had the nerve to go inside, never looked good enough to step in. Now that I was looking hot, the shop was closed. My timing was whack.

"What about Fulton Street?" began Naleejah. "I'm sure there's a hat store somewhere over there."

"Cheap hats though," I said. "Didn't you tell me, I need to step my game up?"

"True," Naleejah agreed.

We spun around in our tracks.

"Hey, we should try Macy's or something," suggested Naleejah. "There's more of a selection there."

"Okay, I'm down with that."

We hopped on the A train at Kingston Avenue and headed to Thirty-fourth Street. Once we got there, a mob of people were already there, pushing and bumping shoulders on every sidewalk. I wasn't used to the crowd, the loud honks of horns and other sounds, and I was ready to go home as soon as we were through with Macy's—a glitzy store—which had no hats I liked or could afford.

We walked down Thirty-fourth Street with me feeling dejected and Naleejah full of energy.

"Well, we didn't come all the way up here for nothing!" exclaimed Naleejah. "So come with me to Victoria's Secret."

The minute we stepped inside the store, Naleejah grabbed my hand and whispered in my ear, "Kate, I didn't forget about those big old drawers I saw you rocking. You better get yourself some sexy thongs—you getting too old for granny panties."

I snatched my hand away. "Here you go again, telling me what I need. You need to calm down and mind your own business, for real."

But I came out of Victoria's Secret carrying a pink-and-white shopping bag filled with two lacy white bras (I couldn't dare pass them up—they were on sale) and three scandalous red, pink, and white thongs.

My whole fifty-dollar certificate was spent. On the train ride home, I was kicking myself as Naleejah chattered about nothing.

As soon as we made it out of the Utica Avenue train station, I spotted five tall guys standing in front of Boys and Girls High. One guy stood out from all the rest. See, when you have a serious crush, you'll spot your sweetheart from a million miles away. I knew all of his moves. The way he dipped forward when he laughed. The dramatic hand clap he just gave the boy standing next to him.

As I watched my baby from afar, my heart lit up like a stick of dynamite. I couldn't wait for Charles to see me, hug me, and make adoring comments about my good looks again. Maybe this time, we could finally get somewhere.

But Naleejah grabbed my arm and said, "Kate, let's walk the other way, please. I see somebody."

"Why, what happened now?" I asked, confused. Just the other day, Naleejah had stopped to talk to the storefront dude, cheesing and grinning, as if getting any male attention was better than no attention at all. But now, she was acting mad shady and crazy over the sight of some boys? Her nervousness reminded me of the pizza shop drama. And after what had happened there—me fighting over some nonsense?—I felt I had a right to know what was up this time. "Naleejah, does some *guy* want to fight you now?"

"Can we just turn back, please?" she said. "It's not about a fight. I don't want to see Divine."

"Why, what happened with y'all?"

"Let's just put it this way, size *does* matter." Naleejah gave the "tiny" measurement with her fingers and added, "And I really don't feel like seeing him again. He can't satisfy me."

"I hear you, but if we turn back, that would be too obvious," I said, lying through my teeth. Of course, I was only concerned about Charles. I wanted to finish what we started.

"Listen, wait for me at the corner," I said. "I just want to say what's up to Charles, okay?"

"Hurry up, Kate," said Naleejah in a big huff.

Now, what was she huffing for?

"I promise I'll only be a minute," I said.

"Well, I'll be sitting in the park."

Naleejah zoomed to Fulton Street Park, and I stood six feet away from the opposite curb, waiting for Charles to spot me from across the street. I didn't want to go up to him. Let him come to me. Finally, I couldn't wait any longer. I made a megaphone out of my hands and yelled, "Yo, Charles!"

Charles saw me and waved. He was about to cross the street on the solo tip, but this annoying dude named Qwan attached himself to Charles's hip.

"Hey, y'all," I said.

"Hey, where you been hiding?" asked Charles.

Qwan stared at me with his tongue wagging out his doofy mouth. "Yo, Charlie, if this ain't yours, can I scoop it?" he asked, wearing a grin. Qwan has a gold grille in his mouth. I wanted to kick all the gold out of his stupid blowhole. Since when did I become an *it* to *scoop* anyway? And why was he blocking me from my baby?

"Qwan, stop playing," I muttered.

"Ohhh snap, what's up, Kate?" he said, recognizing my voice. "Dang, you done changed! You looking good, ma!"

"This is mine, right here," interrupted Charles.

Mine?

At these words, butterflies entered my belly and started flapping wild. Qwan saw the way Charles was staring at me, and he finally took the hint and bounced.

I stood in front of Charles. He leaned up against a nearby telephone pole and kept staring at me. Intensely. Eyes roaming through my soul. I squirmed under his magnetic stare.

He glanced at my Victoria's Secret bag. "For me?"

I put my finger to my chin as if in deep thought. "Hmm, could be." Then I smiled. I was tempted to wink too, but I wasn't overly confident in my flirting abilities yet.

"Don't tease a brother."

"I'm not teasing."

"Yes, you are, and you know it."

I smiled shyly. Since when did I start acting shy around Charles? I guess since things were no longer cool and easy between us . . . more like hot and hard. Listen, the way Charles was staring at my chest right now made me feel like a piece of meat he just wanted to beat. I was starting to wonder: Does Charles like me as a *person*, or just a *booty*? So to get back on familiar terms with him, I tried to make jokes. "Hey, Charlie, my face is up here." I pointed to my face. Then I forced a chuckle—his cue to laugh too, but his eyes were still glued to my chest, not paying the rest of me any mind. Sad to say, I stayed in his face anyway.

"You got a man yet?" Charles asked. "Looking all good . . . I know you got a man."

"Nope, I'm just chilling."

"So . . . when are we going to chill *together*?"

At these words, my heart skipped three beats.

Charles had *never* asked me out on the official tip. Imagine that. No, I couldn't imagine that. I had to be dreaming. My insecurity seeped out. "Since when do you want to take me out?" I asked.

Charles passed his hands over his wavy hair and said, "Don't you know how long I been checking for you? You had my nose wide open since the second grade."

How beautiful, I thought. Sounded like a poem.

"So, Kate, I'm saying, when are you free?"

"Where do you want to go?" I stuttered, hoping he couldn't hear the excitement in my voice. Would he take me out to dinner? The movies? A walk in Prospect Park? What did my dream boy have in mind?

"Well, we can chill at my crib," suggested Charles.

"Oh," I said, as my high hopes dropped down to zero. But that didn't mean I wasn't still open to his program . . . depending on what the program was. "Chill at the crib and do what?" I asked.

"I'm sure we can find something to do." Charles licked his lips with the tip of his tongue, like a sly cat.

"Well, do you have PlayStation?" I asked, trying to keep a shred of my dignity. I didn't want Charles thinking it was *that* kind of party. Repeat after me: R-e-s-p-e-c-t. Okay?

Charles put his finger to his chin as if in deep thought. "Let's see, I think Grand Theft is the only game I got left. My peoples are foul, though; I let them borrow games and I never get them back."

"Oh, you're just making excuses," I joked. "You know I got skills, and you're too afraid to lose."

Charles paused. Then a slick smile spread slowly across his lips. "Mm, I can help you lose something else. But you're the one afraid."

"Oh, best believe, I'm not afraid," I replied. "And I'm keeping that." I rolled my eyes at him.

Between me and you, Charles was the most likely candidate to get my virginity. Making love to Charles would blow both our minds. We had enough electricity to light up Manhattan—man, our first kiss would be so freaking explosive, we'd probably black out the entire city, okay?

"Listen, I want you wearing a skirt when you come through." Charles winked at me. "I never see you in a skirt. Matter of fact, I want you rocking skirts from now on, a'ight?"

I blinked, not because the sun was in my eyes (even though it was), but because I couldn't believe my ears. Bad enough Charles wasn't taking me out on a *real* date. But now he had the nerve to be trying to dictate my gear? I jerked my head back in confusion. "I'm saying, what are you, fashion five-oh?"

"Yeah, and you're under arrest if you don't dress like a girl from now on." Charles threw back his head and laughed.

I bit my lip to avoid biting him. He looked so dang delicious right now.

Charles reached out and touched the back of my neck, trying to tickle me with his light feathery touches. I was going crazy inside.

"So, where were you headed anyway?" asked Charles. "Looking all good, for who?"

"Nowhere special, I said. "Me and my homegirl were—" I suddenly cut myself off, realizing I had left Naleejah waiting for more than the minute I'd promised. And that wasn't right. No matter how much the girl got on my nerves, she was still my friend. Friends before men. Now that's what's up.

I turned to Charles and said, "Hey, can we kick it a little later?"

"Why?" he pressed.

"I left my homegirl hanging."

"Where is she?"

"Sitting in the park."

"I'll walk with you."

"Okay," I said reluctantly.

We found Naleejah slouched on a bench, smoking a cigarette. She looked from me to Charles, and then jumped up wearing a cheesy smile on her face. She flung her cigarette to the ground and stomped it. "Hey, Charles!" she exclaimed, gleaming.

"Yo, what up, shorty?" said Charles . . . gleaming back? Or was this just my paranoia at work?

Naleejah stood between us like a clueless third wheel. And I wanted her to roll the heck away. And at this ill-timed moment, Charles suddenly thought to ask, "Eh, Kate, I'm really trying to hang with you. Let me get your digits so I can get back to my boys."

"Um, can I get your number instead?" I asked.

"Oh, I still can't get yours, huh?" Charles asked absentmindedly.

"Nothing's changed," I said. "I'm still at the same foster home . . . *surprisingly*."

"Yeah, her foster mother's mad strict," Naleejah butted in.

"Man, that's messed up. I forgot about that," said Charles. "And see, my cell phone got turned off because I didn't pay the bill. My house phone is turned off too because we didn't pay that bill either, plus we're moving to a bigger apartment on the third floor of my building next week—"

"Oh," I said, disappointed.

"Yeah, basically, I'm on the move right now. So you can't reach me. I have to reach you. But I got plenty of quarters, see?" Charles jingled the change in his pockets.

I marveled at Charles's unique swagger. Diamond blinging in his ear and he couldn't even pay his phone bill. Nobody but my baby could do it like that! But I was so glad that Charles had just volunteered this broke-as-a-joke confession, thinking now maybe Naleejah would be forever turned off by him. But my hopes crashed louder than the thunder of Naleejah's next words: "Hey, Charles, you can take down *my* number, and I'll call Kate for you."

Naleejah whipped out a pen quicker than lightning, jotted down her number, and slipped it to Charles. Suddenly, I felt sick to my stomach; the butterflies died inside.

"So, Kate, as soon as we get settled in our new crib, I'll holler at Naleejah and she can holler at you. Cool?"

"Yeah, okay," I said vacantly.

"Bye, ladies," Charles called over his shoulder. "Stay beautiful."

Later on that night, instead of dreaming of Charles, I went to bed seeing red.

Bright and early on Saturday morning, I decided to pay the library a visit. I decided to let books be my hangout buddies for a while. Books were safe. They didn't flirt with your crushes, offering their phone numbers and whatnot. No, books don't stress you out, or dis you, or test your patience; they just sit there nice and quiet, waiting for you to open up and read.

As a matter of fact, I had already finished reading *Manchild in the Promised Land*. It was a good book. The day I tried to give the book back to Lynn, she said, "No, keep it."

"Thanks," I said.

"Now do you understand why I gave you that book?"

"Yes."

"Just yes?" Lynn patted the couch, her signal for me to sit down beside her. I sat down and prepared myself for a long, drawn-out talk.

"So, what did you get out of the story?" Lynn asked, flashing me a rare smile.

"I got a lot out of it," I said. "I like the way the character went through so many problems, but he made it in the end. He also made me laugh a lot—even though his life wasn't funny, he was able to look at the funny side of life."

"Good for you," said Lynn. She looked thoughtful for a moment, then said, "Since you love to read so much, why don't you start a summer book club?"

My eyes lit up at the idea—then dimmed. "Well, I don't have anybody to start it with."

Lynn raised one eyebrow. "What about your new friend? You can start with the two of you, and then grow from there."

"Well . . . nah, Naleejah doesn't like to read."

"Mm, that's a shame," said Lynn, shaking her head. "See, you need to widen your circle of friends. I tell my students this all the time. Don't miss out on opportunities just because your friends aren't down— In fact, I'm in contact with a few of my girls from school. They're around your age, and most of them love to read. If you want, I can ask them to join your club."

"No, no, that's okay," I blurted out. What fourteen-year-old needs a friendship hookup from a grown-up? How desperate and doofy could I be?

"Okay," said Lynn with a shrug. "It's your choice." She seemed to be no longer in the talking mood, so I left the living room.

On Monday, Tuesday, Wednesday, and Thursday, you could've found me lounging inside the Macon Library reading and chilling. Copped my little corner in the cut, and skimmed through a pile of books. Picked at least two. Then whipped out my library card like it was made of platinum, and strutted out the door with my books under my arms. Listen, everything was all good. I had my routine down pat: reading, chilling, and laying low in the Johnson household. Trouble couldn't find me, because I was busy hiding in the library—until the day I received that fateful call.

Chapter 22

On Friday afternoon, as soon as Naleejah mentioned the words *big-time party*, I dropped my books—*boom*—flat in one snap. I was ready to get my party on. "Girl, you know I'm down!" I exclaimed.

"Ow, don't bust my eardrums!"

"My bad," I said. "I'm just amped. Haven't done anything hot this whole summer."

"Listen, mad cuties will be there," said Naleejah. "I can't wait!"

I hoped she was right about the cuties. I needed to move on from Mr. Flaky anyway. Charles was flakier than the snow! He hadn't even bothered to leave a single phone message with Naleejah, and every time I asked her if he had called, Naleejah just said, "No, sorry." What could I do but leave it at that? I couldn't see myself sweating him anymore. All I could do was brush my shoulders off and prepare to crush on some fresher meat. Moving on from Charles would be difficult, but absolutely necessary.

"So, who's throwing this party?" I asked.

"You heard about that new gangster rapper T-Money on Death Scope Records?"

"No," I said blankly. Hanging with Felicia for so long, I'd been out of the hardcore hip-hop loop for a minute.

"Well he used to live in Fulton Street Park Building," explained Naleejah. "He got a record deal last year, and he's about to blow up."

"Whoa," I said. "So, who invited you?"

"This dude named Rahiem. I met him last week. Said he wants me to be his 'trophy' for the night." Naleejah giggled at the thought.

"Work it out, girl."

"Yeah, Rahiem is paid," said Naleejah, "but please believe he's not getting any from me any time soon."

"Okay!" I said admiringly. "Now that's what's up."

"Yeah, I'm learning that you get more dollars from dudes if you make them wait at *least* a week or two."

No comment from me, so Naleejah got back to spouting the rest of the party info. "I heard T-Money is like Jay-Z and Fabolous—you know, a dude who keeps in touch with his peoples from the Stuy."

"Now that's hot."

"And listen, if Jay-Z or Fabolous show up at this party? I'll just about die, okay?"

"I feel you on that," I said. "I'll die right along with you. Man, I hope I can go."

"What do you mean *hope?*" boomed Naleejah. "We can't miss out on this *hotness!* Rahiem is already bringing a friend . . . and I told him to make sure his homeboy is a hottie or else don't bother. Girl, you better tell your parents you're spending the weekend over at my house or something. They don't have to know a thing about this party."

"Well, did *you* get permission yet?"

"What? I gave *myself* permission," said Naleejah. "Now, you better get your lie together and call me back. I want you to stay over tonight because I have to fix your hair and stuff."

"Man, I don't know about lying," I said.

"Then you don't know about going to this party."

I paused. "Okay, I'll call you back and let you know."

"Call me before eight."

"Yeah . . . okay."

I hung up the phone and sighed. I was divided into three parts: excitement, confusion, and concern. Everything was going so well in the Johnson household. Why should I ruin it for a little party? Well, no . . . this wasn't exactly a *little* party. This party was a main event, taking place in a swanky crib, probably with a big old pool, and there would be good music too, exciting people all around . . . maybe a Jay-Z sighting? Come on, now. How could I resist?

I couldn't resist.

No, I *had* to resist.

Oh, the temptation was killing me.

For a hot second, I thought about Tisha and her "Give Lynn no reason" speech, but then suddenly—I blacked out. When I came to, I was headed to the living room to find Lynn and Ted. Found them sitting on the couch, arms around each other, watching television—how cute. I drew in a deep breath like I was about to jump into deep water and asked, "May I spend the weekend over Naleejah's house?"

"Kate, why'd you wait till the last minute?" asked Lynn. "You know about the home visit rule."

"Oh yeah," I said, suddenly deflated. All of my friends' homes have to be checked out by my social worker before I can spend the night over there. Oh well.

Abort Mission.

But Ted suddenly leaped to the rescue. "Well, we already met Naleejah's father. He seems like a good guy."

Lynn said nothing. Instead, she shook her head and pinched the bridge of her nose. Did she smell something fishy? I wondered.

Ted turned to me and asked, "Did you feel comfortable when you were at Naleejah's house? Nothing crazy going on, right?"

"No, nothing crazy."

"No other males besides the father living there?"

"No, just Naleejah and her parents."

Ted turned to Lynn. "Seems okay to me. Besides, Kate knows how to handle herself. She's responsible. Hasn't she proven herself to us already?"

Watching Ted fight for me when I didn't deserve it was really breaking my heart. But you know me and my one-track mind. All I could think was: Party. Music. Having something exciting to tell Felicia when she got back. I let Ted fight till the end.

Finally, Lynn folded her arms and said, "Okay, you can spend the night tonight. But I'm not comfortable with the whole weekend until we authorize a home visit." Lynn twisted around to face Ted and said, "You know I like to do things by the book."

Oh no.

The party was on *Saturday*, not Friday! How could I fix this?

I purposely lingered in the living room, looking up at the ceiling as if trying to figure something out. Ted chuckled at me. "Why are you standing there like a statue?"

"Um . . . I was just wondering if *Saturday* would be better because . . . um, well, Naleejah mentioned she might want to go to Prospect Park for a bird-watching tour."

"Now, that sounds like fun," said Ted. "Whatever you decide. Just don't stand there blocking our TV set!"

"Oh, I'm sorry," I said, moving out the way.

Ted had no idea how sorry I was feeling right now.

Lynn piped in, "On Sunday, be back here no later than ten o'clock."

"Ten o'clock *at night?*" I asked incredulously.

"Of course not, silly." Lynn chuckled. "In the morning, bright and early, so we can have breakfast together."

Wow, I thought. This was the first time Lynn was suggesting a Sunday breakfast together. Like a real family. How nice of her. But if Lynn only knew what I was about to do, I'd have some serious egg on my face.

I went into the kitchen and called Naleejah. In a robotic voice, I said, "Okay, I can spend the night on Saturday. Talk to you later." But Naleejah, forever clueless, kept repeating, "Why not spend the night Friday too, why not spend the night Friday too?" She sounded like a demented parrot. Finally, I had to hang up on her. I think she got the hint because she didn't call me back. Later on that night, I snuck downstairs and called her again, explaining everything. All she said was, "Dang, your foster parents are mad strict." All I said was *click*.

On Saturday, late in the afternoon, I packed my overnight clothes and all of my guilt inside my brand-new knapsack. When I got to Naleejah's house, she had already turned her bedroom into a bootleg nightclub.

She had a forty-ounce sitting on her dresser, music pumping loud from a raggedy boom box sitting in the corner, and she was dancing up and down her bedroom.

I put my knapsack down and did a vicious booty shake just to join in the festive mood. Naleejah stopped in mid-wiggle to stare at me. "Wow, you ain't that *stiff* after all! Work it out, girl!"

"See? I keep telling you not to sleep on me." I dipped down low, dropping it like it's hotter than hot, just to emphasize my point. "I gets down, okay?"

"Ohhh, you just ripped it!" exclaimed Naleejah, clapping wildly. "You ain't no joke."

"You already know," I said.

Just then, I heard Naleejah's parents. Front door banged open, then slammed shut.

"Oh brother," said Naleejah. "I didn't think they were coming home so soon. They better not hold us up for no bull."

I expected them to stick their heads into the bedroom to say hello or something, but they didn't bother. This was a relief to me. I didn't want Naleejah getting into it with her parents. I was ready to party like a rock star. No stopping us now.

At nine o'clock, Naleejah and I started getting ready. Naleejah flat-ironed the mess out of my head; I smelt my hair burning. But guess what? My do was *blazing* when she was through. Then I slipped into Tammy's tight fire-engine red tank-top dress, which had straps made of lace, very unique and banging. My hot leather sandals added the sexy touch. Whew, I was looking like *fire*.

After granting approval of my appearance, Naleejah went to take a long shower. Thirty minutes passed, and I started getting antsy. I knocked on the bathroom door. Naleejah fumbled with the knob, and then cracked the door open. "Yeah, what?"

"Are you okay in there?"

Naleejah swung the door open wider and stood in front of me with one brown eye and one hazel. She looked mad scary.

Before I could get out the words, Naleejah said, "Calm down, I wear color contacts. And I just dropped one. I can't find it anywhere."

"You want me to help you find it?" I asked, about to step forward. But Naleejah pushed me back. "No, no!" she exclaimed. "You might step on it. I'll keep looking. Go back in my room, please?"

I went back inside of Naleejah's bedroom. I plopped down on her bed, letting the shock of another bogus first impression wear off. Naleejah had a bag full of tricks, huh? Twenty minutes later, she emerged with a pair of hazel eyes and a stupendous outfit. She wore a sexy jean miniskirt that looked more like a belt, and a bright pink tube top that she constantly had to pull up or else she'd be flashing folks. Her hair was hanging down in picture-perfect spiral curls. And she was stepping lively in open-toe high-heel black sandals. I'm telling you, the girl was fierce.

I raised my hand to give her a high five, but she grabbed my hand in midair and examined my bare and stubby nails. Her own nails were painted hot pink, and her toes were matching too.

"We've got to do something about this," Naleejah said, shaking her head. She dragged me over to her dresser and started fumbling through a tray crammed with lipsticks and nail polishes.

"Pick your color," she said.

I picked up a light pink bottle of polish.

"No, no, that's not right," said Naleejah, taking the bottle away from me.

Okay, so why'd you ask me, then?

"You look better in red," said Naleejah as she picked up a curvy bottle filled with scarlet red polish. She led me out to the kitchen table. As soon as we sat, she grabbed my hand and started painting my nails with expert precision. Homegirl was multitalented. She had it going on in the whole beauty department.

After my nails were done, Naleejah poured us some nice cold ice tea. We were sipping tea and chilling at the table until Mrs. Mackie tottered into the kitchen. Was she drunk? She took one look at me, and her mouth dropped open, like she had just seen a ghost. Then her lips curled into a tight snarl. "Why is she wearing Tammy's dress?" she suddenly demanded, pointing at me.

"She needed something to wear," Naleejah stuttered.

"I thought you gave those clothes away," said Mrs. Mackie with her hands on her hips.

"But you know I wanted to keep them," said Naleejah, her voice shaking like an earthquake.

Mrs. Mackie shook her head. "Just like your sister. Lying and scheming. That's why she's not here today."

Now Naleejah was crying, and I was feeling so confused and uncomfortable. Stuck in the middle. What was going on?

"You do the stupidest things sometimes," said Mrs. Mackie. "I told you to get rid of those damn clothes."

Naleejah jumped up from the table and leaned over it. "But Dad was right there—he said it was okay to keep them. He even brought the rest of the clothes to Kate's house, so what the F are you talking about!" Naleejah swiped the tears from her eyes.

"What did I tell you about cursing at me?"

"Dad said it was okay to keep them," Naleejah cried.

"And did he say it was okay for your friend to be prancing around in your dead sister's clothes?" Mrs. Mackie yelled back. "When are you going to face it, Bertha? Your sister's gone. You can't bring her back."

My bottom lip hit the floor.

Naleejah's fist hit the table. "You're full of it, Ma. You wasn't worried about her when she was here, but now you want to sweat her clothes?"

"Don't make me have to slap you." Mrs. Mackie stepped forward, and Naleejah stepped back, grabbed my hand, and we fled from the kitchen.

"Don't run away from me while I'm talking to you!" Mrs. Mackie yelled at our backs.

My skin began to itch. I felt queasy. Sick.

Naleejah locked the door to her room and said, "I swear my mother is so stupid. I hate her. That's why my dad is always trying to be out this house—to get away from her evil butt. That lady is evil for no reason."

I sat on Naleejah's bed, stunned.

Naleejah must've read the confusion in my face because she sat next to me and in a fast voice said, "Tammy got killed a year ago. She was at the wrong place at the wrong time. . . . One of her friends was in a gang, and she stopped to talk to her at the corner store. . . . They caught Tammy by mistake. . . . She was my oldest sister . . . my *only* sister, and my mother has the nerve to tell me what to with her clothes?"

Naleejah started crying again. I put my arm over her shoulder, not knowing what to say. I felt so bad for her, really. Although I never had a sister, I could relate. If anything happened to Felicia, I would go out of my mind; they would have to take me away to the crazy house. Poor Naleejah. I wished I could do something to make her feel better.

I rubbed Naleejah's shoulder and told her it was going to be okay. She seemed to stiffen at my touch, so I quickly removed my hand.

We sat in silence for what felt like an hour, but really it was only ten minutes. I know because I was staring at her alarm clock the whole time.

Naleejah suddenly jumped up from her creaky bed and began to walk up and down her room, as if she forgot I was still there. Then she sat back down and looked over at me, suddenly flashing a fake smile. "I'm sorry about that," she said.

"No, don't be sorry. . . . Are you okay?"

"Of course I'm okay," chirped Naleejah. "We're still going to have us some fun tonight!"

Well . . .

I was glad Naleejah was back to bubbly, but I was not okay. Now that I knew the real deal, I couldn't happily rock a dead person's clothing—no way. And I wasn't about to go to the party butt-naked, so what could I do?

"Kate, what's wrong?"

"Um, Naleejah . . . I'm sorry, but I don't feel right wearing this dress knowing—"

"It's all right, I understand," Naleejah butted in. "But I don't know if I'll have anything else to fit you."

She went into her closet and started digging. Finally, she came up with a yellow T-shirt that read, I'M SEXY and a super-short white tennis skirt—both stretchable for my thickness. The T-shirt strained against my chest, making me look boobalicious, and the skirt barely reached the bottom of my butt. Yeah, I could definitely work with this. I was bound to gain interest from some beautiful boys while rocking this outfit. *Charles could eat my dust.*

At ten o'clock, we were hooked up and ready to go. Rahiem was supposed to have picked us up by then. Instead, we got a phone call from him at eleven. He was on his way—in fact, two blocks way, but his homeboy wasn't with him. Man, I grumbled, I was going to be the third wheel.

"Don't think I want to go," I said.

"Kate, you can't back out on me now!"

"But I don't want to be the third—"

Before I could finish my sentence, the doorbell rang. Naleejah hosed us down with some fruity strawberry-smelling perfume, and dragged me out the door with her.

Rahiem had double-parked his sleek black Lexus coupe equipped with rims shinier than the stars in the sky. A fat red curly ribbon hung from the rearview mirror as if the car was a gift to himself. He looked mad young, though. So was he a rapper, or a drug dealer? Then again, it was none of my business.

I turned off my worry-meter and crawled into the backseat of the shiny coupe. New-car smell drifted up to my nose as if to say, *Welcome to the good life.* So I leaned back, relaxed, and made myself welcome.

Naleejah made introductions, and Rahiem nodded at me in place of a hello. He couldn't even be bothered to turn his head around to greet me. *Okay, forget you too.* For the rest of the ride, all I saw of him was the outline of a square jaw and the back of his fat cornrowed head.

After an hour on the crowded Belt Parkway, we finally sailed off a narrow exit and cruised into the suburbs of Long Island. We passed by nice houses, tall trees, and quiet dark streets with no people around. Felt like a ghost town.

When we pulled up in front of a huge redbrick two-storied house, my heart filled with anticipation. I'd never been inside a house this big before. I couldn't wait to make my grand entrance. But shiny Range Rovers and Lexus coupes were cramming up the block, so there was nowhere to park. I had to wait.

We circled the block twice, but no dice. So Rahiem told us to wait in front of the house, by the curb. As we waited, four dudes dressed in all black were eyeing us from the front porch like a hungry pack of wolves.

Chapter 23

Five minutes later, Rahiem bebopped up to us. "Y'all ready?"

"You know it, baby," squealed Naleejah.

We followed Rahiem up the walkway made of white rocks. All the while, we were being ogled by the clowns on the porch. They didn't bother to make room for us when we tried to step inside the house. The tallest of the group grabbed Naleejah's arm and dared Rahiem to say something. Naleejah forced a grin and yanked her arm away. Rahiem was smart enough to keep his mouth shut since he was outnumbered. When I walked past, the shortest chump out of the group touched my hand and said, "Yes, you are sexy. Can I get with you?"

My *"Sexy" T-shirt. Ugh.*

I gave him the famous Kate scowl, and he left me alone.

Hip-hop music pounding through the bricks. Once inside the house, the music was even louder, earsplitting. We walked down a long hallway lit by a blue bulb. We passed by a huge kitchen, and I peeked inside and saw a couple of lovebirds cooking up a storm with their lips. The girl was perched atop the kitchen counter with her legs cocked open. And the guy was standing between her legs grinding his butt to the music like a puppy in heat. We stepped inside the living room, and a fog of smoke fell over us. The room glowed yellow light, and bodies were everywhere. On the couch, against the wall, and even sprawled out on the floor. We squeezed into a corner, and all three of us just stood there looking stupid for a while. Then Rahiem and Naleejah started moving to the music, and I stood there looking stupid by my-self. I brushed imaginary lint off my skirt every ten minutes just to look occupied. The night was dragging for me already.

I lied to get here?

Naleejah reached out to tap my arm and said, "Now, this is a real party, ain't it!"

"Yeah, it's okay," I muttered. "But where's Jay-Z?"

I was too pissed for words. I recognized a few peoples from around the way, but I didn't *know* anybody, and I didn't want to. The vibe in the room was unfriendly. Mad shady. Two girls sitting on a black leather recliner were now giving me the stink eye. I had no idea why, and I didn't want to find out. The chicks looked straight out of a rap video, long weaves and tight short skirts included. Matter of fact, all the girls here looked like that. No one was smiling, everyone had come with their own crew, and you just had to do you. So I stood alone and did me.

"This is not cool," I complained to myself. I couldn't complain to Naleejah, because she was too busy up under Rahiem, rump-shaking in front of him, laughing at everything he said, paying me no mind.

A tall skinny girl dressed in all black stood next to me. Was she alone at this party? Or did she have a whack friend like me? I tried to think of an excuse to talk to her, but I quickly chickened out when she looked over at me and rolled her eyes.

Oh well.

I had no idea why Naleejah even bothered to invite me to the freaking party in the first place. If she was going to have her head stuck up Rahiem's butt the whole night, what was my purpose for being here? I was so tight about the whole situation. I had to let her know.

I tapped Naleejah on the arm. "Can I holler at you for a minute?" (Yeah, I really wanted to *holler* at her.)

"What's up?" she asked nonchalantly.

"Um, can we talk in private for a second?"

Naleejah turned to Rahiem and said, "Honey, girl talk. I'll be back, okay?"

"Hurry back, baby," said Rahiem. He licked his big lips, trying to be sexy. Not sexy.

Naleejah and I walked out into the hallway where I could hear myself speak. We stopped in front of the kitchen. Then I got right down to the point. "Listen, I'm not feeling this party, and I—"

Naleejah cut me off. "But you act like it's my fault Rahiem's homeboy didn't show up."

"I didn't say it's your fault. I said I'm not feeling this."

"Well, at least *try* to have fun."

"Yeah, I already tried," I said. "And I'm not having fun. How long are we staying?"

"Dang, but we just got here!" Naleejah exclaimed. "And it's not up to me. Rahiem's our ride, remember?"

Oh yeah.

I was piping-hot pissed. Stuck in faraway Long Island with no way to get home. "Guess you really screwed me this time," I said.

"Please, nobody twisted your arm to come here," Naleejah snapped. Then she sashayed away from me. My feet felt like heavy rocks as I followed behind her.

Once we made it to the living room, T-Pain's song, "Buy U a Drank," came on.

Yeah, I needed a drink.

"Ohhh, this is my song," cried a chubby girl with long box-braids. She was standing in the middle of the room, doing a booty-clap. Then she hiked her jean skirt up to her thighs and started humping the air. Two tall guys, dressed in white jerseys and shorts hanging low, sandwiched her and started grinding away, X-rated style. I had to look away. I stood in the corner, hiding, feeling so out of place.

Finally, a spot opened up on the black leather sofa. I collapsed on it, laid my head back, and sadly gazed at the bare beige walls. About ten minutes later, my song came on, so I started bobbing my head to the music, trying to look cool and laidback. "We fly high . . . no lie," I sung to myself. "Balling."

From the corner of my eye, I peeped a light-skinned baldheaded guy sitting next to me, leaning over the glass coffee table about to prepare a fat blunt. He split the cigar with a knife, shook out the tobacco, poured in the weed, licked the cigar, and stuck it back together with his spit. Then he took a lighter and ran the flame along the seam. "Yo, where's T-Money?" Baldhead called out to no one in particular. "He's supposed to get the first hit. It's his party."

Nobody answered, so Baldhead decided to begin the puff and pass ceremony without the guest of honor. I was the closest one to him, so he handed the blunt to me first. "Nah, I'm straight," I said, and passed the blunt to the girl sitting next to me. She was a dark-skinned, short-haired, short-skirt-wearing chick. She took a few greedy puffs, passed, then waited a few minutes, and out of nowhere, jumped up singing, "What it is! What it is! Get it how you live!" Then she looked my way and started singing, "Bet cha can't do it like me. Yeah, yeah, bet cha can't do it like me!" Then she came up on me and started doing a booty-dance. This girl was out of her mind! Time to vacate. I bounced from the living room.

By now the house was overflowing with people and smelled like weed and strong perfume. Heads in the kitchen, the stairway, the bathroom, against the wall, on the porch—people, people everywhere. Loudness all around me. Now, where could I go for some peace? I wandered around aimlessly.

As soon as I came across a staircase, T-Money was coming down the steps. I knew who he was when a swarm of chicks flew at him, screaming his name, pecking kisses on his cheek and cooing at this five-foot-tall Mohawk-wearing rapper. He looked kinda silly, if you ask me.

I walked past the frenzy, stepped over a few more heads, and slinked further to the back, not knowing where I was going but desperate to be anywhere but here.

Finally, I discovered a back door and cracked it open. My eyes met with a huge backyard. Grass looking like a smooth green blanket. The main highlight was the pool, blue-green water sparkling by moonlight and nobody inside of it. If I had a bathing suit, I swear, I would've said, "Freak it!" and jumped right in.

My situation was not cool, and the night was chilly. My hands were getting cold, my legs too . . . This stupid short skirt, this stupid "big-time" party. Man, I wanted to go home so bad.

"Yo, how you doin', sweetheart?" A deep voice said to my back.

I swiveled around to face a brown-skinned guy wearing a black velour tracksuit in the summer. True it was cool outside, but not *that* cool. He wore sunshades in the dark, and a thick platinum rope chain that was bigger than him. On the spot, I could tell he was a wannabe rapper, or a plain old wannabe, the kind of guy who tried too hard.

"My name's Keith," he said, extending his hand.

I shook his sweaty hand and said, "Diamond."

"Pretty name," said Keith. Then he leaned closer to me and said, "And you is sexy!"

Oh brother. The T-shirt again.

"Mm, you smell like strawberries," Keith said, smiling. "Strawberry shortcake."

"Thanks," I said flatly.

"Do you have a man?" asked Keith.

Okay, he was quick about it. And stupid too! Couldn't he tell that I wasn't interested in him by the way I was looking at everything *but* him?

To get away from him, I used the most reliable lie I could think of. "Um . . . nice meeting you, but I have to use the bathroom," I said, wanting to let him down easy. I was probably the hundredth girl rejecting him that night.

"Do you know where the baffroom is?" he asked. "'Cause I can show you."

"Yeah, I know where it is."

"But I can come with you, if you want," he said, holding my elbow lightly.

"No, no, that's okay." I jerked my elbow away. Did Keith have rocks for brains? Shoo, fly, shoo!

He wouldn't shoo, so I hurried inside the house.

I don't know what came over me, but suddenly, I wanted a drink. I needed a drink to forget where I was. I was miserable at this party. Didn't fit in. Didn't *want* to fit in. I wanted to go home, but I was stuck like Chuck. I headed to the kitchen and asked a random guy to point out the liquor. I hadn't touched alcohol in years, but tonight was the night to take a little sip.

Well, I didn't take a little sip; I took ten big swallows of Alizé. The sky-blue liquid trickled down my throat, and before I knew it, I was light-headed, but feeling *nice*. I was still standing in the kitchen—or should I say, swaying—when I felt a light tap on my shoulder.

I spun around to face Charles, of all people, looking mighty fine and surprised to see me. "Hey, Kate, what's up, baby," he exclaimed. "What are you doing here?"

"What's up," I replied coolly, trying to ignore just how good he looked.

He paused and tilted his head to the side. "Kate, what's wrong? Did I *do* something to you?"

"No, just tired," I lied.

"You twisted?" he asked. "Let me smell your breath." He bent down to get near my mouth. Then he pressed me against the stove and blew his hot breath in my ear. His body felt good, but I was still mad at him.

"Don't worry about what I'm drinking," I said, pushing him away from me.

Three tall guys stormed into the kitchen, talking loud and demanding drinks. Charles bent down again, this time to whisper ear. "Hey, I can hardly hear myself talk. You want to go out to the backyard?"

"But I just came from back there."

"Well, let's go back again." Charles grabbed my arm and led me out the back door.

Two fly girls dressed in identical pink were blocking the doorway. They parted ways to let us through. A trio of guys in do-rags and white tees were standing poolside, but when Charles and I sat in the lounge chairs close by, the trio suddenly decided to go back into the house.

Charles pulled his chair close to mine, and his face lit up like the moon as he stared at me. "I'm really glad to see you here . . . looking all good."

I didn't return the compliment, even though he looked more than good. Shoot, let *me* play nonchalant, for a change.

"Well, who are you here with?" he asked.

"Naleejah."

Charles shifted his eyes away from me and stared at the ground.

"Well, how do you know T-Money?" I asked.

Charles was still staring at the ground when he explained. "T-Money is down with my brother. Everybody knows T-Money. Who doesn't?"

"I don't."

"Well, that's because you're special," said Charles, finally looking back up again.

I shrugged. "Apparently not *that* special."

"What do you mean by that?"

"I thought you were supposed to call me," I said, staring at him accusingly.

Charles paused for what felt like five minutes, and then he spoke. "Well, I did try to holler at you. . . . I had called Nagee—"

"Na-lee-jah," I corrected.

"Whatever her name is—I called her—but um, she wasn't picking up her phone. . . ."

"Well, did you pay your phone bill yet?"

"Oh yeah!" exclaimed Charles. "I finally got a new cell phone—pay as you go." Charles laughed, dug a pen and piece of paper out his pocket, jotted down his number, and gave it to me. "Use it."

"Unlike you, I will," I said.

When Charles noticed I was softening up, he pulled his chair so close, our arms touched. But before he could get romantic, a posse of chicks in skimpy bathing suits came pouring out the back door, laughing and screaming as a gang of guys followed behind in hot pursuit. Next thing you know, *splash*. One by one, the girls were being thrown into the pool.

"Mm, this is a bit *extra*," said Charles. "You want to go back inside?"

"Yeah, okay."

Charles and I went back inside and were met with rap music pumping louder than before. He shook his head in disgust. "Man, I can't even hear myself talk. . . . Let's go upstairs to my man's bedroom where it's quiet."

I shook my head. "No, I don't think so."

Working pretty fast, ain't cha?

"Come on, now," said Charles. "You can trust me. We're not going to do anything—"

"Just to talk?" I asked. Didn't want him thinking I was easy.

"For sure," said Charles. "Just to talk—I promise."

Charles and I did very little talking. Once we made it upstairs and into a large dimly lit bedroom, he sat me down on the king-sized bed and apologized for not trying harder to get in touch with me. Still feeling a nice light-headed buzz, I accepted his apology. No more beef between us. Then Charles grabbed my hand and fiddled with my fingers as if trying to feel every bone. The warmth from his hand set my whole body on fire. I let out a soft moan, hoping he didn't hear me. He heard me, because the next thing I knew, Charles released my hand, got up from the bed, then *click* went the light.

Charles came back to the bed and groped for my face in the darkness. He gently caressed my cheeks, my eyebrows, like I was a precious work of art. He kissed my neck. Behind my ears. I was going crazy inside. I couldn't believe I had the boy of my dreams, someone I thought I could never get next to like this, making sweet music with me.

Charles laid his warm body on top of mine and searched for my lips. *Mmmmm.* Electrifying. When our lips met for the first time, it was a pleasure I'd never felt before in my entire life. Our kiss was so warm and sweet, like chocolate pudding just off the stove, like a blanket on a cold winter day, like red roses in the summer, like champagne and light rain, like anything that makes you feel giddy and alive and all good inside.

On the smooth tip, Charles slowly lifted my shirt over my head and I let him. As he fumbled with my bra strap, he whispered my name like he was in pain. "Kate . . . I been wanting you for so long." He couldn't get the strap undone, so he gave up on it. Then he grabbed the back of my head and crushed his lips to mine. He started tonguing me down like crazy. He was so, so passionate, it felt like we were making love already. "Mm, you smell so good, baby," he whispered.

"I want you so bad." Then his hand started creeping inside the elastic of my thong.

That's when I had to stop him. "No," I said, removing his paw.

"Please?"

"No."

As hot as I was, there were still too many questions crowding in my mind: Should I go all the way with Charles *tonight?* Was he officially my man now? Would it hurt? Would he care about me afterwards? I wanted my first time to be special and romantic. But where were the candles? The roses? Why were we laid up in someone else's bed? I felt my first time should be much more magical than this. But with Charles's every touch, I was growing weaker by the moment. . . . I was about to give in.

I'd always wanted Charles to be my first anyway. We had history. I trusted him. I was deeply attracted to him. Never said I was saving myself for marriage, did I? Um, then again, we were moving kinda fast . . . weren't we?

"Please, Kate?" Charles continued to beg. "Don't you want me too?"

Of course I do. That's what I wanted to say. Instead, I stayed quiet, still thinking should I, or shouldn't I?

Then Charles brushed my lips with his and said, "Baby, I'll be careful. . . . I can control it."

Oh no. Hold up. I didn't think so.

Control it?

Charles must've bumped his head if he thought he was getting some without wearing protection. If he lost control of a single drop, I would be in big belly trouble.

No condom, no coochie, no exceptions to the rule.

I grabbed his hand and said, "If we're going to do something, you have to wrap it up . . . I'm sorry."

Charles kissed my neck, trying to take my mind away, but I was fully alert by now. I wasn't doing it raw. Period. Guys always want the sex, but they never want the baby. So I was steady guarding mine like I had Fort Knox between my legs.

"But I'm clean baby," Charles whispered. "I took a bath."

"It's not about that," I said. "I don't want to get pregnant, and I don't know *who* you been with before me." I didn't mean to be so blunt, but Charles was trying to open a case that was already closed. If I hadn't taken so many trips with homegirls to the abortion and cootie clinic, I might not have been so strong. But I've seen too many girls suffer while the boys be carefree and moving on.

Charles finally realized I wasn't budging, so he got up in a huff and said, "I'll go get a condom. Be back." He closed the door behind him.

I lay waiting in the dark, anxious, nervous. Tonight was the night. A wave of excitement raced down my spine. Oh man. It was about to go *down.*

When Charles opened the bedroom, I saw a crack of light behind him, and then I heard a girl's voice. A familiar voice. Naleejah's voice? Yes, the voice belonged to her.

"Charles, why are you avoiding me?" Naleejah screamed. "You got some booty from me, now you got some other ho up in here? Who is she?"

At first I thought I was hearing things. Then I swallowed Naleejah's words and their meaning. I felt like I had just been punched in the stomach. Quietly, I laid in the dark, staring at the outline of Naleejah's body in the doorway, unsure whether I wanted to get up and bust her stuff, or stay right where I was until I calmed down.

"Get out of here, you're drunk!" Charles yelled, and pushed Naleejah from the doorway. He shut the door and locked it: *bam, click.*

I sat straight up, calmly slipped on my shirt, and waited for Charles to explain himself.

Well, he was taking too long to say something, so I set it off. "You can't even keep it in your pants, huh?"

"No, it's not like that—see I—"

"See you *what?*" I butted in. "First of all, you lied to me. You said the broad wasn't picking up her phone, but you were the one busy picking *her* up."

"Kate, listen to me, please. . . . I *did* call for you, but . . . well, let's just put it this way: She showed up at my house instead of you."

"Wow," I said, shaking my head. "Such a dirty dog."

"But why are you mad at me for?" asked Charles. "You weren't trying to give me any."

"Oh, so now I'm just a *piece* to you?"

"Of course not," said Charles, trying to grab at my hand.

"Get off of me," I snapped.

"Kate, come on, now," pleaded Charles. "I'm sorry."

"Yeah, I'm sorry for you."

"Listen, she meant *nothing* to me. Just a quick hit and that's it. I thought you already knew how she was living."

I felt my eyes narrow into spiteful mean slits when I said, "Yeah, I do know how she's living, so you better get yourself checked. The grimy broad probably got more crabs than Red Lobster . . . and she ain't even all that. Fake hair, fake eyes . . . y'all deserve each other. A couple of fake hos."

"Kate, wait!" Charles called at my back. Too late. I was already up and on my way to settle the score with Naleejah. I was so angry, my head hurt. It was hard to breathe. My anger was in control instead of me.

"Kate, hold up!"

"Don't follow me," I warned Charles. "You better fall back, for real."

I found Naleejah in the living room, drooping drunk on the couch. Rahiem was nowhere to be found. But there was a group of girls and one guy in the living room grinding to reggae. I didn't care who was watching when I stepped to Naleejah and poked her in the forehead with my pointer finger. Her head jerked back. Her mouth shaped like a confused O. "Huh, what happened?" she asked groggily.

"You call yourself a friend?" I shouted over the music.

Naleejah's red eyes could barely focus on my face. Her head dangled this way and that. She was higher than the sky and lower than dirt. Just as I hauled back ready to mush her in the face, Charles came up from behind and grabbed my hand in midair. I yanked my arm away and faced him. "Get off me," I demanded.

The music didn't stop playing, but the people stopped dancing. They crowded around the couch to watch the unruly scene I was creating.

"Kate, please stop, she's not even worth it. Can't you see she's blitzed? She can't understand a word you're saying." Charles didn't wait for a comeback. He forcefully dragged me away from the living room, down the long hallway, and out into the backyard. As we stood on the back porch, I was struggling to set myself free from him. But he was too strong for me. He took me by the shoulders and shook me like a Kate-shake. "Listen to me! I don't want you fighting, okay?"

I jerked my shoulder away. "Who cares what you want? You're not my man."

"Listen, you'll *hurt* that girl. And I don't want you going to juvie over her. Do you understand me? She's not worth it."

True.

Naleejah already had her piece of Charles. She had gotten him nice and easy too, which meant Charles was never mine in the first place; apparently, he was up for grabs. Besides that, since when do I fight over guys? Ain't I too cool to be brawling over boys? So yeah, forget Naleejah . . . forget Charles too. What a horny jerk.

I needed to get away from Charles before I blacked out and tried to fight him too. I faced him and said, "Listen, I'm not trying to beat the girl anymore, so don't follow me around. I don't want to see your face."

"It's like that, Kate?" asked Charles with sad eyes.

"Yeah, it's like that."

I went back inside and bumped into bodies along the way to the bathroom. Locked myself inside the bathroom and sighed. To calm myself down, I threw cold water on my face.

I looked into the mirror. I was horrified by the dark and spiteful look I wore. My lips were twisted into a hateful sneer. My eyebrows were knitted down to my nose. This ugly face was not mine. This was the face of the old me. How angry I *used* to be was coming back to haunt me.

I had to get out of this house. Away from these people. Away from Charles. Far away from Naleejah. She was poison.

But to my dismay, Charles was standing outside of the bathroom, waiting for me.

"Shoo fly. Didn't I tell you to go away?"

"Kate, please?"

Please nothing.

I raced down the hallway and zipped out of the front door. Don't ask me how I was getting home. I had no idea. I passed by the same four guys who were standing on the porch when we first came in. I was tempted to ask one of them for a hitch, then quickly came to my senses and started walking aimlessly down the dark deserted block. I was surrounded by darkness. Unfamiliar houses, cars, and trees felt like they were closing in on me. I was scared.

Suddenly, a blue beat-up pickup truck started following close beside me, and an old white man with only three front teeth yelled out, "Hey, brown sugar, can I take you home?"

Getting hollered at by toothless perverts? Oh no. I had to turn back. It was about two o'clock in the morning. So where was I going?

I went back to the house. Charles was standing on the corner, waiting for me, as if he knew I'd come crawling back. "Kate, you're overdoing it now," he said. "Where did you think you were going?"

Finally, I admitted, "Well . . . I can't go home. I was supposed to be spending the night at Naleejah's house. But after what she did to me, I can't go anywhere near that trifling broad."

"Well, I can sneak you in my house," said Charles. "You can crash there."

I still wanted to crash my fist in Charles's jaw, but I remained calm and quickly came to my senses. At the moment, Charles was my only option. If I came home this late, Lynn and Ted would surely know something was up. And after gaining their trust, this was the wrong time for me to be backsliding.

This whole situation was so jacked up. This sneaking-out-to-party bull had me at the mercy of Charles. The dog. I was so mad at him

right now. So mad at myself . . . but I was no fool. I swallowed my pride
and accepted his offer for a ride.

Unfortunately, we still had to wait until Jermaine was ready to
leave. "I'm going to the backyard," I said in a huff. "Don't leave without me."

"Can I come with you?" asked Charles.

"No."

Thank goodness, he left me alone.

I went into the backyard. Two girls in identical skimpy gold bikinis
were sitting by the poolside, splashing water with their feet. I sat opposite them in a lounge chair and sadly stared at the water.

About twenty minutes passed. Next thing I knew, Naleejah was
standing over me. She had a lit cigarette in her hand and a sorry expression pasted on her face. "Kate, I know why you're mad at me. . . .
Charles told me you found out about what happened . . . and I apologize for what I did. I mean, one thing lead to another and—"

"Yeah, I can imagine how sorry you are," I interrupted.

"But can you forgive me?"

I paused for a whole minute and then said, "I'm over it."

"So . . . does that mean we can be friends again?"

"No," I said. "Hell no."

"But why not?" Naleejah threw down her cigarette and squatted to
be eye level with me. Her eyes were blurry hazel. "I thought we were
best friends."

"Best friends?" I repeated in disbelief. "You don't even know how to
be a friend. And I don't have time to be teaching you."

"But how can I make it up to you?"

Naleejah's persistence was getting on my nerves. Was she freaking
kidding me?

"Listen, forget it. What's done is done. You got what you wanted.
Now leave me alone."

"But you acted like you didn't want to give him any," Naleejah
whined.

"Yeah, but you knew I liked Charles," I spat. "He called looking for *me*. Not *you*. You're living foul, plain and simple. Now can you step to the left, please?"

"But how are you going to stay mad at me?" Naleejah asked, exasperated. "Aren't you sleeping over my house?"

"Please, picture that."

"So where are you going to stay?"

"Don't worry about me," I said. "I'm straight."

Naleejah hovered over me, staring at my blank face. But I had nothing more to express.

Finally she said, "Okay . . . if that's how you want it to be."

"Yeah, that's how it *has* to be."

"Well . . . I'm used to this anyway," said Naleejah. "Nobody ever stays friends with me." She slowly walked away, her head bent low. I almost felt sorry for Naleejah, but not enough to stop her from leaving.

About twenty more minutes passed, and I was sitting in a lounge chair by the pool, feeling antsy. Alone. Tired. Ready to go home. Dying to go home. But Jermaine wasn't ready yet. How long did he plan to stay? I wondered. Shoot, I was tempted to hijack his freaking Jeep and take myself back to Brooklyn—even though I can't drive worth a dang.

I rolled my eyes up to the black night sky. Then I sighed, got up, ready to go back inside the house to look for Charles and Jermaine, maybe hover around to give them the hint that I was itching to bounce. But before I could touch the back door's knob, Naleejah came charging outside, pointing her finger in my face. She took me off guard, so I backed up, quick.

Naleejah stared at me with a hurt look and said, "You know what? You're not even right, Kate. I tried to teach you how to get a man, I did everything to help you get him, and just because you didn't know what to do with him—and I did—now you don't want to be my friend anymore?"

"Naleejah, get out of my face," I said calmly.

"No, because that's not right."

"We're no longer friends. Peace. Get over it."

"Take off my shirt, then!" Naleejah yelled.

People started pouring outside. They seemed to be headed for the pool, but when they heard us yelling, the crowd formed around us, mostly girls, laughing and shouting "Cat fight!"

But there would be no fight. I walked away from Naleejah.

Believe it or not, she followed me. The crowd followed too, still laughing and joking and growing in numbers. Seemed like half the party people were outside watching us beef.

"Take off my shirt," Naleejah repeated.

"Are you stupid?" I asked, holding my chin up. "You better fall back or get wrecked."

"You lucky I was even willing to be seen with you," Naleejah spat. "Look at your hair. I did that. The shirt on your back. I gave you that. I *made* you, baby. You would be *nothing* without me."

Somebody from the crowd yelled, "Ohhh, shorty is wearing hand-me-downs."

I couldn't believe the words that had just come out of Naleejah's mouth. I felt stripped, left in rags. I wanted to cry, but didn't dare. I wanted to punch Naleejah dead in her mouth. But I stepped two feet away, telling myself that Naleejah was not worth fighting. If I fought her, I might kill her. She was not worth doing time for.

"Oh, she just punked you," a girl cried out, obviously talking to me since I was standing there like a mute statue. But whatever, I had nothing to prove to anybody at this party. Everybody sucked at this party, and they could all kiss my big black butt.

Once again, I tried to walk away from Naleejah, but she followed behind me, still popping off at the mouth. I didn't know what she was saying, because my mind had already gone blank.

We were close to the pool's edge now when Naleejah made a huge mistake. She grabbed at the neck of my shirt and shouted, "Take the shirt off, it's not yours!"

Putting her hands on me was not a smart thing to do. She had already embarrassed me in front of all these people, and now she was really pushing her luck by getting physical. I tore my body away from her grip, then in one swift motion, I reached up for her hair and shouted,

"This is not yours either!" I pulled at her weave like the reins on a horse. Giddyup, ho!

Nobody was trying to break things up. We were the main attraction for the night. "Ooohhhhh!" went the crowd as Naleejah fought me off with her head down.

Naleejah was no match for me. Neither was the glue that held her weave together. *Snatch.* I pulled out a huge chunk of weave and started waving it around like my victory flag. Everybody around me started whooping and hollering. I threw the horsehair on the ground and stomped on it. "Now what?" I said. "You want some more? I'll snatch you baldheaded, girl!"

Naleejah called me the B-word, then came charging at me, spinning her arms like windmills. I sidestepped the charge, grabbed her by both arms, and pushed the silly broad in the pool.

Splash!

"Ohhhhhh!" everybody yelled.

Naleejah stood up in three feet of water dripping wet, glaring at me like she was ready to do something. The crowd gathered around me. Some girls were laughing. A guy standing beside me called me cold-blooded.

"What you want to do?" I challenged, spreading my arms wide, like *What?*

Then Charles suddenly emerged from the crowd, pushed past me, and offered his hand to Naleejah. She grabbed hold of him and crawled out of the water like a crab. As she sat shivering wet on the deck, I stared her down, ready to do something else. If Charles wasn't blocking, she might've taken another splash.

"Yo, can somebody get a towel, please?" Charles called over his shoulder.

I couldn't witness this bull anymore. Charles pampering this tricky broad straight to my face? I had to get away from the scene. I stormed inside the house and went looking for Jermaine to ask him when he was planning to roll. But he was busy in the hallway trying to mack two chicks at the same time—now I see where Charles gets it from.

I was so angry. Ready to *go*. I was even tempted to call Ted: Come pick me up, *please*! But then again, I'm not crazy.

The party was still going strong when Charles found me on the front porch—the only place I could be *somewhat* alone.

First thing out of Charles's mouth: "Why'd you push Naleejah in the pool?"

"The grimy broad needed a bath," I spat. "Any more questions?"

"But she could've drowned," said Charles.

"Please, I pushed her in the shallow end—you know all about *shallow*, don't you?"

"Still, that wasn't right," said Charles. "Kate, you're better than that."

"Oh brother, here you are taking up for that slut, after you *dissed* me for that slut. . . . I'm not even surprised."

Charles fixed me with a stern stare. "Look, I just came out here to tell you we're leaving in five minutes."

"It's about time," I said.

Charles left my side, shaking his head.

I stayed on the porch, watching people come and go, arms folded across my chest, looking mean, daring anyone to say anything to me.

Two minutes later, Rahiem's sparkling Lexus coupe pulled up in front of the house. He honked his horn three times. The front door cracked open, and Naleejah stepped out the house wearing an oversized T-shirt, and her weave still wet and stringy. But the second she saw me, she flew back inside. Scared? She *should* be.

Raheim honked again, and Naleejah stuck her head back out, peeking like a frightened little mouse. She looked about ready to cry.

But I had already decided that I was done with Naleejah. I no longer had the desire to mess her up. Naleejah's life was already messed up—a train wreck waiting to happen, and believe it or not, a small part of me felt sorry for her. Never thought I could feel sorry for such a fly girl. I used to think Naleejah was doing *me* a favor by being in my company.

But I had it twisted from the start. Naleejah was the one who didn't deserve to be in *my* world. Before she came into my life, I had left fighting alone, left feeling bad about myself alone . . . dealt with all this chick's bull just to avoid being alone. But like Tisha always says: Birds of a feather flock together, so I'm only hanging with swans like Felicia from now on.

Rahiem honked his horn again. But why was he so lazy? Why didn't he just get his tired butt out the car and go get his girl? Since he had no sense, I had enough for him. I decided to go back inside so that Naleejah could leave freely. I pushed open the front door, and—lo and behold—there she was, standing in the hallway, hugging herself. Her eyes popped out of their sockets when she saw me. But I held my head high and walked straight past her. *You're not even worth my time, baby.*

Chapter 24

Finally, Jermaine was ready to go. Charles opened the back door of the red Cherokee and asked, "Can I sit back here with you?"

Before I could say no, Jermaine interrupted. "I ain't no chauffeur. You're sitting up here with me."

Charles hopped in the front and stayed quiet for most of the ride.

When we cruised onto the Belt Parkway, he twisted around in his seat and said, "Kate, please don't stay mad at me, okay?" The scowl I flashed let him know he needed to turn back around and leave me alone.

Jermaine was the first to walk inside the apartment to check for a clear coast. Coast clear. We followed him inside. Creeping. In the dark. Charles and I groped our way into his bedroom. He quietly locked the door behind him.

"Can you turn on the lights, please?" I whispered. I didn't want him getting any ideas.

"Do you want us to get caught?" Charles whispered back. "My mother is in the next room. We don't need the lights on anyway. We can't do nothing but go to sleep."

All I could see in the small bedroom was Charles's twin bed, two tall speakers flanking the bed, and the rest of the room was still packed up in boxes. Guess he hadn't had a chance to unpack. Too busy humping that nasty ho, Naleejah.

I sighed in despair. This was not how I imagined my first time visiting Charles to be. I didn't want to be in the dark. I didn't want to be upset with him. I wanted to be in ecstasy.

Tired and deflated, I kicked off my shoes and lay in the bed fully clothed. Charles was about to climb in beside me, but I stopped him cold with a hard shove. "I don't think so."

Charles fell back. Then he dropped down on his knees, held on to the edge of the bed, and leaned his face close to mine. "But where am I supposed to sleep?"

"That's your issue," I said.

Yes, I was being hard and cold. But the warmth from his breath in my ear was weakening my mental barricade. So I had to stay strong, or be defeated.

"Guess I'll sleep on the floor, then."

"I guess you're right," I snapped.

Charles creaked opened his closet door, grabbed a blanket, and spread it out on the floor. But it wasn't long before I felt sorry for the lump lying there. I reached down and gestured for him to come to bed. Immediately, Charles hopped in next to me.

I turned my back to him before he could get happy . . . before I could get happy. This was a hazardous situation. I had the man of my dreams lying beside me, and all I could give him was my attitude, because the moment I let down my guard, I would give him something else. His body felt too warm, too good. There was no room in his bed for me to escape his body heat. I was trapped.

"You know she didn't mean anything to me, right?" Charles whispered in my ear.

I remained silent. But my stomach was doing more flips than a little bit.

"You know she didn't mean anything to me, right?" Charles repeated.

I didn't let a syllable escape from my lips.

"I don't want her, Kate. I want you."

"Then why'd you sleep with her?" I finally asked.

"Sweetheart, you confuse me," began Charles. "You don't want to be my girl, but then you're sweating me about some ho who meant nothing to me? Come on, now—a chick who gives it up that quick can't mean anything to me . . . and I wouldn't have done anything with her if you were my girl."

"Yeah, okay."

"I'm serious, Kate," insisted Charles.

"And my name is Joey. Whatever."

"You know what? Forget it."

"Good, it's forgotten," I spat. "Just don't let me oversleep. I have to be home before ten o'clock."

"All right, then, sweetheart, good night."

"Nothing good about this night," I said. "And I'm not your sweetheart."

"You'll always be my sweetheart," said Charles in the softest loving tone.

Whoa. Those words alone melted the icy block of resentment stored inside my chest. *Careful, girl, keep it gangster.*

"Kate," Charles whispered in my ear, my weakest spot on my body.

I turned to him and said, "What?"

He reached out to touch my face. He lightly trailed his fingers on my cheek. "You've got the cutest chubby cheeks, you know that?"

"Thanks," I said flatly.

"I bet you were a cute baby."

"I don't have a single baby picture, so I wouldn't know." I turned my back to Charles again. For ten silent minutes, we lay still. I just wanted to stay like this forever. Yes, I was still upset with him, but I wanted to be close to him. Feel his body heat, his warm breath in my ear. Charles must've sensed my weakening resolve. The next thing I knew, he was caressing me from behind, and I was letting him. He danced his fingers over my neck, my shoulders, and up and down my arms. Then he pulled me closer to him, and the warmth from his body, his breath on my neck, had me going crazy inside.

"I'm sorry, baby," Charles whispered, burying his face in my hair.

"Okay, that's nice," I said, moving my head away from his hot delicious breath. Back to reality.

"Kate, please don't be like this."

"Why do you keep trying so hard? I said *no*."

"Baby, you're lying in my bed, dressed like you want some skins and you expect me not to try again?"

True. My skirt was hella short. Not to mention, guys seem to know when our bodies are calling, even when our minds are telling us no. They keep going for the panties until we surrender. I think we give off some kind of smell . . . like a cat in heat. Still, it wasn't going down like that.

"Sorry, Charles, after what happened, I'm just not feeling you like *that* anymore." This was a bald-faced lie. I still felt for Charles, too much for my taste. Lucky the room was pitch black; Charles couldn't see my nose growing. "Listen, no hard feelings, a'ight?" I added. "You're still my dawg."

"But I don't want to be your dog," Charles said. "I want to be your man."

At these words, I smiled, more to myself than to him, thanking goodness that I still had some self-esteem left in my soul. With guys like Charles, the pie is all the same, and if I let him get a slice—game over—he wouldn't be hungry for me anymore. Like Tisha always tells me, "You can't choose your parents, but you can choose your men and your friends." So, I'd be choosing wisely to leave Charles alone.

Charles fumbled for my hand. "Kate, baby, you know you got that number-one spot."

"Yeah, as your *homegirl*," I interrupted, releasing my hand from his grip. "Now, can we get some sleep, please?"

Early next morning, I woke up fully clothed (thank goodness) and snapped into action. It was already nine o'clock. Luckily, Charles's mother slept in late on Sundays, so we didn't get busted by her.

I didn't want Charles walking me home, not even beyond his building's lobby. I could already picture Ted on a Sunday stroll and bumping into sweet little Kate being escorted by a boy too early in the morning.

"See you later," I said to Charles, standing by the elevator door.

"Can I at least get a good-bye kiss?" asked Charles, bending down for me to reach his lips.

"Nope," I said, wearing a smirk.

"So, it's like that?"

"Yup." I sashayed out of Charles's lobby, feeling powerful in my strut. I knew Charles was still standing there, watching me go. I looked over my shoulder, and sure enough, his eyes were stuck on my back-side. I playfully blew a kiss at him and he pretended to catch it. That's all Mr. Player would be getting from me—ever. Now he'd always be left to wonder what *could've* been; and that's the mystery I needed to keep. I'd be the One Chick Charles couldn't get. Now that's what's up.

Feeling good, I squared my shoulders and kept it moving down the block, pride swelling in my chest with every step.

My head was bloated with ego by the time I made it to Bainbridge Street. I had resisted the man of my most passionate dreams, and I thought nothing in the world could bring me back down to earth.

But I thought wrong.

Dead wrong.

As soon as I neared the house, I saw Ted standing on the stoop.

Why was he standing on the stoop with no Sunday newspaper in his hand and no smile on his face? I had no idea. His arms were folded tight across his chest, and for the first time since knowing him, after I greeted him, he scowled. Before I could make it up the steps, he demanded, "Where were you?"

And before I could answer him, he turned his back on me, shoved the front door open, and ordered me to get inside.

Chapter 25

I followed Ted into the living room, where Lynn was already sitting on the couch, arms folded tight against her chest. She wore a scowl too.

"Now where were you?" Ted asked in a whisper that seemed worse than a shout.

"Um, I spent the night at Naleejah's house," I stuttered.

"So, where's your overnight bag?" asked Lynn. I noticed her eyes were pink, like she'd been crying.

Over me? Oh man.

"Where's your bag?" Lynn repeated.

"Um, I left it at Naleejah's house by mistake."

Ted sat down next to Lynn, paused for a second, and then said, "Come up with a better lie, Kate."

I stood frozen in shock.

Ted cleared things up for me. "Your friend called here three o'clock in the morning looking for you. Now, let me ask you again: Where were you?"

His words hit me like a slap.

Busted. Naleejah was such a spiteful broad. Wow.

Right then and there, I wanted to come clean, start new, and stay true in the Johnson household. But then again, if I had told them what really happened last night, there'd be much bigger problems to deal with in the future. Sleeping overnight with some dude? Oh yeah, they would swear I was sexually active or getting close to it, and I'd be getting hawked harder than usual. So if I was going to lie, I'd better make myself look good in the process.

I took a deep breath and explained that yes, I lied to go to this party, but, when I found out Naleejah had planned to smoke weed and hitch a ride with guys we didn't know, I decided that I didn't want to roll. Naleejah called me a punk about it, I got mad and left the party alone. . . .

As I recounted my tale, I started believing it myself. I even noticed Lynn's face soften after hearing my courageous story.

"But where'd you stay all night?" asked Ted. His face had softened too.

"I slept on the train," I blurted. This perfect little lie didn't just fall from the sky. Back in the day, like I told you, I used to run away from foster homes all the time. I'd ride the train from the first stop to the last. Rode the A, B, C, 1, 2, 3—didn't matter to me as long as I had somewhere to sleep.

"You rode the subway all night?" Lynn shouted. "Are you crazy? You could've gotten yourself raped or killed!"

Or pregnant by Charles.

"Why didn't you just come home?" asked Ted, scratching his head, looking disgusted.

"It was really late, and I didn't want you guys to be upset with me."

I stared at Ted, thinking, *Please believe this lie.* Ted looked in my face. I don't know what he saw, but he seemed to believe me.

Lynn pointed at me. "Ted, do you see the skimpy clothes she has on?"

Ted frowned and nodded. "This is not the Kate I know."

Lynn jumped up from the couch and started pacing the living room with her head down. Then her head popped up, and she began a long lecture about making choices and facing consequences. And as Lynn lectured nonstop, my thoughts drifted into an abyss.

I could already picture Lynn calling Tisha, already heard myself being told that I would have to leave, already saw myself out of the Johnson household, and maybe taken to a diagnostic center to be diagnosed by people who didn't know me like that, already pictured myself in a new group home, getting into new fights for no reason, trying hard to make new friends.

I already imagined myself back where I had started—the nightmare of relocation after relocation flashed before my eyes.

But Lynn's next words suddenly put my mind at ease: punishment. One week. No TV. No telephone. No outside. . . . *No problem.*

I wore a blank face to hide my relief.

"Did you hear me?" Lynn demanded.

"Yes, ma'am."

Of course I heard her. I wasn't getting kicked out, and that's all I heard. But I tried not to look too pleased. So I knitted my eyebrows and frowned deeply.

But Lynn's next words made the frown on my face legit. "Listen, Kate, we care for you, we want the best for you, and we want you to stay here. But you're too old to be making silly mistakes like this, old enough to know right from wrong. We trusted you, Kate. And you destroyed our trust. So it's going to take a long time for you to earn our trust back. Now I'm going to be real with you. I'm not calling Tisha this time. But the next time I have to call Tisha about a behavioral issue, it will be to request your removal. I'm sorry, but that's the way it has to be. Do you understand me?"

"Yes, ma'am." I looked down at the floor and swallowed hard. No. I couldn't face being shipped to a thirteenth foster home. New people, new rules.

I was so used to the Johnsons now. I didn't want to leave them.

But because of what I had done, the number thirteen would be forever hanging over my head for the rest of my stay. Tears welled up in my eyes.

"Crying isn't going to help you now," said Ted. He left the living room shaking his head at me. Lynn followed behind him.

I threw myself on the couch, grabbed a pillow, and rocked back and forth, crying my eyes out, my heart out, my frustration and pain; everything was coming out of me in streams. I cried so hard and so long, I gave myself a headache.

I dragged myself up to my room and changed into bedclothes; just when my day should've been getting started, I was going to sleep. I slept all day long. Didn't even eat dinner. The next day, I tried to avoid leaving my room. Didn't even want to use the bathroom. I was too embarrassed to face the Johnsons. Talk about laying low? I wanted to live in the basement for a while, just to hide my face. My shame.

For the length of my punishment, I mostly stayed in my bedroom, or on my fire escape reading the library books I had taken out earlier. Lynn and Ted talked to me only when necessary. I tried to do extra chores around the house just to get back on their good sides. No dice. Things didn't lighten up until my birthday rolled around.

On my special day, the blue sky was filled with August sunshine, and I was stuck inside my bedroom, listening to the birds tease me by chirping and singing outside my window. When Lynn summoned me downstairs to get the phone, I thought it was Tisha calling about some foster care issue. But when Lynn covered the phone and said "Five minutes—only because it's your birthday," I knew someone special was on the other end.

The line was full of static. But all was clear because I knew my homegirl's voice anywhere—across the globe, it didn't matter. "Felicia!" I cried, breaking out into a happy grin.

"Kate, I miss you so much!"

"Miss you more," I exclaimed. "And you remembered me on my birthday!"

"How could I forget you!" Then she broke out singing "Happy Birthday" to me. I laughed at her crackly voice. But I had to cut the song short. Lynn was in the living room. Lynn said only five minutes, so five minutes it would be. "I appreciate you thinking of me," I said. "But you need to hurry up and be back!"

"I'll be home in seven days. I've been counting."

"Cool, I'll be off punishment by then."

"Punishment? Oh no! What happened?"

"Long story."

"Well can't you tell me half of it?" whined Felicia.

I looked over to see if Lynn was engrossed in her television program.

She was.

I turned my back to Lynn, pretending to look outside the kitchen window. Then I whispered as loudly as I could, "Girl, I finally kissed Charles." I was bursting to tell Felicia this news first.

"Oh my gawd!" exclaimed Felicia. "What happened?"

"Well, I met this new chick, some crazy mess went down, and next thing I knew I ended up in Charles's bed . . . and now I'm on punishment."

"No you didn't!"

"Yeah, girl, I spent the whole night with him."

"Did y'all do it?" Felicia was so excited, it seemed like she was about to jump through the phone.

"No, we didn't do it, but we sure did *something*."

"Oh man, the suspense. This isn't fair!"

"Don't worry, girl, this is only temporary," I said. "We got all the time in the world to talk when you get back."

"Okay, I guess I can wait. . . . Friends for life, right?"

"Come on, now," I said. "You already know."

"Yeah, you can't get rid of me!"

"Wouldn't want to," I said. "But I have to go now."

"Okay, girl, see you in a week! Can't wait to give you a big sloppy kiss on the cheek!" I pictured the goofy grin I knew Felicia had to be wearing, and smiled as I hung up the phone.

"So, who's Charles?"

I spun around to face Lynn, who had come out of nowhere.

She stood two feet away from me, hand on her chin. "So, who's Charles?" she repeated, her eyebrows raised up to her hairline.

My heart was in my throat. I didn't know how much she had already heard, but I knew she heard something. Oh well. Busted. It was now or never. If I was going to start fresh in the Johnson household, I had to tell the whole truth, and nothing but.

When I was through telling it, I braced myself for the attack.

Lynn leaned against the counter, folded her arms across her chest, and stared at me for what felt like hours. Then she said, "Well, I do appreciate your honesty . . . but what you did was risky and plain old ridiculous. Spending the whole night with some boy, Kate?"

"But we didn't have sex," I blurted out.

"I'm glad to hear it, but that doesn't change what you did—I trusted you."

I dropped my gaze and lowered my head in shame.

"I was young once too. I *do* understand . . . but that doesn't mean I'm not adding one more week to your punishment."

Oh no.

Felicia.

I raised my sad eyes to meet Lynn's. She knitted her eyebrows and cocked her head to the side. "Now what's that ridiculous face for? You act like I just sentenced you to prison. You're getting off easy, if you ask me."

I was surprised to see a hint of laughter in Lynn's eyes. And this tiny hint of playfulness caused me to open up a bit. "Well . . . it's just that I wanted to be available when Felicia got back . . . but now I won't be able to." I was hoping my voice sounded pitiful enough for her to make some adjustments to my punishment.

But Lynn only shrugged and said, "Think about that the next time you decide to do something crazy. Hope you had yourself a good time at that party. Hope it was worth it. Do you think it was worth it?"

"No," I muttered.

"Now if you act right, next year you won't be stuck in this house. Ted and I can take you out on your birthday."

Next year?

Just then, Lynn had no idea that she had made my day—my whole year—with those two simple words. Two extra weeks of punishment couldn't even bring me down now. Lynn's words, *next year*, rang in my head, made me feel light and giddy in the head. This was the first time a foster parent was talking in future terms with me . . . like I actually had a natural place in the Johnson household. I felt so good on this day, my birthday. Born again, and starting over. Without a second thought, I walked up to Lynn and hugged her, holding back my tears. She looked baffled when I came at her, but she had enough sense not to ask questions. She just hugged me back.

Three days later, Lynn and I bonded even more. I was in the bathroom, primping for no reason, when I discovered my hair was falling out in small patches. Terrified, I flew to the kitchen, where Lynn was sitting at the table surrounded by paperwork.

"Look," I said, fingering my bald spot. This was my first time coming to Lynn for a problem. She looked just as surprised as I felt.

"I shouldn't have let Naleejah give me that bootleg perm," I muttered.

"Don't worry," said Lynn. "Go sit in the living room."

She got up from the table, went upstairs, and came back down with a comb, brush, and hair grease.

She sat on the couch, I sat between her legs, and she started braiding my hair into tight cornrows straight back. This was the first time I could remember my hair being touched by a grown woman, and it felt strange at first, but good, like I was being cared for—like I'd seen so many other kids get cared for—by a woman, a mother figure . . . maybe.

When I felt the last braid fall into place, I couldn't wait to look in the mirror. Lynn must've felt me trembling because she said, "Go ahead and take a peek."

I ran to the bathroom, eyed myself in the mirror, and my face broke out into a smile. I was so happy with what I saw. Lynn came up behind me and asked, "You like?"

"I love!" I exclaimed. "I didn't know you could get down like this."

"Yeah, and I could've been doing your hair all along . . . as a matter of fact, when you first came to the house, I asked if I could do your hair and you practically barked, *No!*"

"I did?"

"Yes, you did. . . . You're good at blocking stuff out, huh?"

I smiled shyly. Now I remembered. First day at the Johnsons', didn't want Lynn touching my head. I didn't know her, didn't like her; my scarves and hats were my only friends. My bad.

When Ted came home from work, he complimented my hair and asked how much I paid Lynn for her excellent service. Lynn said, "Pay Ted no mind," and we all laughed together—first time ever.

Lynn let me off punishment three days early for good behavior. First thing I did was call Felicia. Before she could say hello, I blurted out, "I'm off punishment. What you doing?"

"Waiting for you to be off punishment!"

I laughed. "Well, hurry up and get ready. I can't wait to see you."

"For sure," said Felicia. "Quick shower and I'm out."

"Okay, what do you want to do?" I asked.

"See *you* first, and then we can think of something to get into."

"Okay, bet."

When I went into my closet, my heart stopped. The memory of Naleejah's sister came flooding back to me. I had a dead girl's clothes cramming up my closet. The more that I thought about it, the more the situation spooked me.

I had to get these clothes out this house . . . then there were my shoes, my beautiful but stolen shoes. They had to go too. If I wanted to get rid of all my ghosts, ain't no half-stepping. I had to come fully correct.

I ran into the kitchen to call Felicia with the sudden change of plans. "Hey, girl, don't rush," I said. "I have to take care of some business first."

"What business?" asked Felicia.

"I have to drop off some clothes at the Salvation Army."

"You need help?"

"Nah, I'm good—but if you want to come."

"Of course I want to come! My dad can even drive us to drop off the clothes."

"No, no, that's okay," I blurted out. (You know I don't dig Felicia's father—at all.)

"Well, my dad can drop me off at your house, then," said Felicia. "Then we can go from there."

"Cool." I hung up the phone and got busy. Took my shower and threw on my old red shorts and a white tee.

I grabbed two large plastic bags from the kitchen and asked Lynn if I could borrow her laundry cart. When I told her why, that I was getting rid of Tammy's clothes, she said she was proud of me, and that I didn't look right wearing them anyway.

I packed up the clothes, threw in the shoes, and Lynn helped me drag the big bags down the stairs.

Fifteen minutes later, the doorbell rang.

I ran to answer it.

"Kate!"

"Felicia!"

Felicia opened her arms wide, and I ran into them, hugging her for a long, long time. "I'm so glad to see you," I said.

"What? I was missing you like crazy," Felicia replied.

She looked so pretty and refreshed. She had a serious tan, which changed her skin tone from brown to cocoa brown. She wore a pink T-shirt, baggy blue shorts, her favorite loud yellow sneakers, and her medium-length hair in a ponytail. Her smile lit up my hallway.

Felicia came inside to say hello to Lynn and Ted. They were sitting in the living room, full of questions. I was itching to leave so that we could swap stories. But Lynn was busy interviewing Felicia and spouting off South Africa trivia—she just couldn't help herself.

On the sly, Felicia slowly backed out of the living room, smiling and nodding at Lynn until she was finally over the threshold.

I grabbed my cart, called out good-bye, and Felicia helped me down the steps with the cart. Before we made it off the porch, Felicia grabbed me and said, "Stick out your arm and close your eyes."

"Huh?"

"Just do it!" Felicia exclaimed.

I closed my eyes and stuck out my arm. Felicia inched cold metal over my hand and onto my wrist. I opened my eyes and saw the most beautiful, sparkling sterling silver bangle I'd ever seen. It was engraved with elephants, and it fit perfectly on my wrist. "Wow, thanks, girl!"

"No problem," said Felicia, smiling.

"I'm never taking this off," I said. "I'm sleeping with it!"

I couldn't stop grinning at my bangle . . . at Felicia. She was finally back in my world.

As Felicia and I trooped up my block, I kept playing with my bangle and raising my arm to admire it in the sunlight.

"Thanks again," I said.

"Okay, you can stop thanking me now," Felicia joked. "By the way, I'm loving your hair. . . . Where'd you get it done?"

"Lynn."

"What!" Felicia's brown eyes widened. "You let *her* put her hands in your head?"

"Yeah . . . well, Lynn's actually cool now—I just had to get to know her."

"Well, I'm glad to hear you guys are finally getting along."

"Not as much as me!"

"So, tell me about Charles. What happened? Don't leave a sister hanging!"

I told Felicia everything. About Charles. About Naleejah. About Naleejah and Charles. Felicia's mouth stayed fixed into a shocked O.

"Wow, that's so foul!" she exclaimed at the end of my tale.

"Yeah, tell me about it," I said. "But enough about me—anything juicy happen on the trip?"

"Hmm, let's see. . . . I almost did it with Umar."

"What!"

"*Almost!* But I remembered your silly song, and it didn't happen."

"What song?" I asked.

Felicia busted out singing, "Hey, lookie, lookie, is he *really* worth the nookie?"

I busted out laughing. "I don't even remember making that one up."

"Girl, you're getting old." Felicia pinched my arm. "And don't think I forgot about your birthday punches."

"Nah, the birthday present you gave me was more than enough—even though I spent it up in one day."

"Why, what did you buy?"

"A couple of bras and some thongs from Victoria's Secret."

"*You?*"

"Yes, me. I let that silly broad Naleejah talk me into it. . . . Well, I guess, *I'm* the silly broad for listening to her."

"Don't beat yourself up," said Felicia. "Every girl needs to own some scandalous lingerie at least once in her lifetime."

"But I wasted my *first* sexy bra on Charles."

"Yeah, well, be glad you didn't waste anything else on him—if you know what I mean."

"True."

And speaking of the devil . . .

We were approaching the corner of Fulton Street when I spotted Charles standing against the concrete island with a tall skinny girl leaning against him. My stomach took a nervous dip. I wasn't quite ready to see him. But I quickly recovered and straightened my back. I wasn't about to slink past Charles without saying anything. I wanted to be strong. To show him he didn't faze me—that we were still friends.

"Felicia, there's Charles," I said. "Be cool."

"No, *you* be cool."

I waited until we were six feet away and then called out, "What's up, Charles?"

"Yo, what's up, Kate!"

Felicia and I had already walked a dozen paces when Charles came running up to us. "Hey, Felicia, welcome back," he said, out of breath.

"What's up, Charles?" asked Felicia, tagging him in the arm.

"So, how was South Africa?"

"It was all good," said Felicia. "I had fun."

"Nice tan."

"Thanks."

"Did you find yourself an African lover?" Charles chuckled.

"No, silly."

"Did you get to see live lions and hippos and whatnot?"

"I'm looking at a hippo right now," joked Felicia. "How you gonna leave the girl standing there? Why not bring her over and introduce?"

Charles looked over at the girl and then turned back to us. "She'll be all right. . . . So, Kate, I haven't seen you in a minute. Where you been hiding? How you been doing?"

"I'm fine."

"I know you're *fine*, but how you doing?" Charles's eyes sparkled as he stared at me. But I tried to keep my cool.

"You're too much," I said, shaking my head.

"Not enough to satisfy you?"

"Boy, you better stop playing."

"If I could get with you, I'd be out the game for good."

"Such a smooth pimp," I said, rolling my eyes.

When Charles realized he wasn't getting anywhere, he glanced at my shopping cart and asked, "Headed to the laundry?"

"Something like that," I said. Then I glanced over at the girl. I started feeling bad for her. "You better get back to your lady friend," I said, jutting my chin in her direction.

I stuck out my fist to give Charles a good-bye pound, but he grabbed my hand, stared at me intensely, and pursed his lips into an air kiss. "I really miss you," he said softly.

Hot shivers raced through me. I looked into Charles's radiant brown eyes, and I almost tripped under a dizzy spell. But I quickly came to and refocused, seeing Charles for what he *is* instead of who I *wanted* him to be. With all I've been through, why would I purposely pick a player to give my heart to? If a guy burns you once, his bad. Twice? my bad. So, sorry, *son*. Game over. Charles could go find some other chick's heart to toy with. I am not the one.

I snatched my hand away from his. "Listen, your girl is waiting for you. I'm out."

"And I *said* she can wait."

"But *I* can't. . . . Me and Felicia got things to do."

Charles shrugged and said, "All right, then, ya'll—peace."

"See ya," said Felicia.

"Bye, Charles," I called over my back.

I grabbed my shopping cart, and we rolled.

As soon as we got out of earshot, Felicia tapped my arm. "Did you see how he left that poor girl hanging just to make goo-goo eyes at you?"

"I know, right," I said, trying to cover my smile. "And I'm looking all bummy too."

Felicia stopped dead in the middle of the sidewalk, twisted her lips to the side, and said, "You *know* you don't even look bummy, so stop it."

"Yes, I do," I said. "Check out my sneakers leaning." I let go of my cart, did a couple of leans, and laughed.

"And?" said Felicia, cocking her head to the side. "You still look good—and it's not even about what you wear."

Okay, I guessed Felicia was right. Let me stop. Doesn't matter what I rock, as long as I'm holding my head high to the sky.

Felicia shook her head at me. "You need to be confident on your own. Stop fishing for compliments."

"I wasn't fishing—but thanks."

"And Charles always liked you anyway."

"Yeah, as a *homegirl*."

"Not even," said Felicia. "I've seen the way he used to look at you. . . . I just never told you. I didn't want you to get your hopes up."

"Really?"

"Yes, really," said Felicia. "But to be honest, I never thought he was good enough for you anyway. Too much of a player."

"True," I said. "But you have to admit, Charles *is* a dime—"

"Whatever," Felicia broke in. "*Players* come a dime a dozen."

"True."

"And if Charles ever plays my girl again, you know I'll have to jack him up! Dissing you for some loosey goosey chick?"

I laughed and squeezed Felicia's arm. "See, you always got my back."

"You already know," said Felicia. "But I can't believe you let that girl make you think something was wrong with you."

"Yeah . . . I know . . . but then again, you have to admit, if it wasn't for Naleejah, I wouldn't have gotten as far as I did with Charles. No matter what you say, Charles sure wasn't checking for me until I got fly."

"And even with you fly, he still dissed you for some used-up booty. He's not even good enough for you, girl."

Oops, she had a point.

I didn't say a word, and Felicia thought I wasn't convinced. So she looked over at me, knitted her eyebrows, and said, "I know you're not second-guessing me. You'll be straight *playing* yourself if you ever go back to Charles. He'll always be the first thing on your mind, and you'll always be the last thing on his. He already disrespected you once, sleeping with your friend behind your back? Come on, now, Kate. Get a hold of yourself!"

"Naleejah wasn't my *friend*," I corrected, trying to make myself look better.

"Whatever," said Felicia, waving her hand. "If you start falling for the okeedoke now, I feel sorry for you when you get older."

"It's not that serious," I said. "Calm down." I playfully tapped Felicia on her arm. We weren't arguing. Just a friendly debate. That's how Felicia and I get down. It was all good.

"You better know *you're* the prize," Felicia continued. She was waving her arms around, getting excited. "There's plenty other guys out here who will like you for *you*."

"Dang, girl," I suddenly broke in. "Be easy! You're starting to sound like me."

"Exactly . . . so what happened to the Kate *I* know?"

"She's right here." I pointed to myself.

"Well, act like it."

"Okay, okay, I hear you. I *am* the prize."

"Thank you," said Felicia, nodding her head in approval.

"And this is why I'm hot," I sang, wiggling my shoulders in a happy dance.

Felicia started smiling and singing, "And Naleejah's mad 'cause she's not." She wiggled her shoulders too.

I pretended to pass on my fabulousness to Felicia with a wave of my hand, and sang, "And this is why *you're* hot."

Felicia clapped her hands. "What? You thought I forgot?" Then she passed her fabulousness back to me. We bent over laughing at how silly we could be. Felt like old times again. So natural and so cool. Standing there at the intersection of Fulton Street and Malcolm X Boulevard, I made a mental note: This is how friendship should feel from now on.

"Girl, I'm so glad you're back."

"Same here," said Felicia. "You already know."

I smiled at her. "You ready to roll?"

"Always ready. . . . We can't let this beautiful day go to waste."

"No doubt." I linked arms with Felicia, grabbed my cart, and we kept it moving down Fulton Street straight into the sunshine.

To all Survivors

Acknowledgments

I'm now two books strong and still blessed in my Dream Team: Daniel Lazar, my sharp and dazzling agent, Sara Goodman, my amazing and extremely perceptive editor, Kia Dupree, an early believer in my work, who has put her editing pencil aside to pen her own novels, and the entire St. Martin's Press staff, who helped bring my book to life.

Many, many thanks to all who gave me invaluable insight and feedback for my work. Big shout-out to those of you who consider yourselves true-blue *Hot Girl* fans. Your encouraging messages are invaluable. You make me blush.

And what would I do without all of the wonderful librarians and teachers who have spread the word about Kate? A toast to you! I'm so happy to have met some of you, too. Special thanks to PEN American Center; it is always a pleasure and an honor to work with your organization.

Finally, I am deeply indebted to all of the special people in my life who have supported me in times of doubt, and cheered me up just by being there throughout my writing journey. You know who you are.

Prologue

This time it wasn't my fault.

On the last day of June, I was leaving the Johnson household and headed to my thirteenth placement. This day I had dreaded for so long. Standing by the front door, baggage by my side, I faced my foster parents, playing my best tough-girl role. "Y'all don't have to wait outside with me," I said.

"Are you sure?" asked Lynn, her light-skinned face red from crying.

"Yeah, I'm good," I lied.

Lynn reached out and hugged me so tight I almost lost my breath. Ted hugged me, too, then hastily let go. I could tell he wanted to cry just as bad as me. His hair was so much grayer than I remembered. Usually jolly as can be, he now looked plain old miserable.

I quickly looked away from Ted. No need to prolong this sad scene. I had rehearsed an unemotional departure in my mind for an entire week. Just needed to say my good-byes and be done with it. "Well, guess I better go," I finally said.

Wearing a fake smile, I flashed them the peace sign, swung open the front door, and stepped outside into the late-afternoon air. As soon as I closed the door, my smile instantly faded, and my heart sank inside my chest like a torpedoed battleship. I felt so defeated, so alone.

As I struggled down the porch steps with my enormous red suitcase on wheels and two black duffel bags hanging from each shoulder, a rusty blue van pulled up to the curb. "Hello there, young lady," the baldheaded driver called out his window.

He received a polite nod instead of hello. I was in no mood for chitchat and he looked like the chitchatty type. He opened his door, about to hop out and help me with my bags. I stopped him cold flat with an outstretched hand. "No thanks," I said, "I got this."

I heaved my bags onto the backseat, climbed inside the van, fastened my seat belt, and stared dead ahead. Didn't dare look back at the Johnsons' house, just in case they had snuck outside to watch me go away. Listen, the sight of my foster parents standing on the stoop waving good-bye would only make my situation sadder, harder. Harder for me to build up my guts in order to face the drama sure to follow. Never thought I'd have to see the inside of a group home ever again. Well, never say never. The Old Kate was supposed to be dead; stomping out chicks in my distant past. But now, there was a good chance I'd have to bring her back to life.

"Nice day outside, isn't it?" asked the driver.

I put my mouth on mute.

"Weatherman threatened rain," he continued, "but look how sunny it is outside . . . that's why you can't believe everything you hear. Gotta go by what you see."

Seriously?

Hoping this dude would get a clue and be quiet, I turned my head away from him, and silently stared out of the window at the sun-drenched streets and people bustling about. "We're headed to the boondocks," the driver said with a chuckle. "Hope we don't get lost. Do you know your way around Brooklyn?"

I shrugged and continued staring out of the window. I wasn't trying to be rude to the guy, but I just couldn't muster up the strength to make fake conversation. Luckily, he finally took the hint and zipped his lips.

The driver smelled like a cheeseburger; I rolled the window all the way down. Warm summer air blew on my face, but I felt so cold and empty inside. The farther we got from Bed-Stuy, the emptier I felt.

As the van rumbled down Ocean Parkway, I took in my surroundings, bland as white bread with no butter. All I saw were tall trees and short houses and barely a soul hanging around town. When we turned off the parkway and headed down a side street, I realized we were getting closer to my dreadful destination. My eyes watered up against my will. Tears began to flow down my face. I furiously swiped at my eyes.

Keep it gangster, Kate.

We're almost there.

Oh, best believe, crying was not an option. Boohooing in front of my new housemates would only bring on their bullying faster. They'd take me for a silly punk and test me till I flunked. I should know. I wrote the script on this.

And as I stood in a huge shabby living room being given the stink-eye by five hard-looking chicks, I realized the script was now flipped. What goes around comes right back, and like a backhanded slap, I was *it*. Three girls were huddled on a sagging plum-colored couch. Two sat on the floor, eyeballing me nonstop. I felt like a juicy steak they couldn't wait to tear up. When Mrs. Cooper, the ancient group home supervisor, pushed me forward to introduce, nobody cracked a smile.

Mrs. Cooper patted my hand. "Kate, I promise you're really going to like it here."

Me, like it here? Please, picture that. My spirits plunged with the evening sun as I took in my surroundings: grim green paint covered the living room walls, cigarette-burned brown carpet covered the floor, and the smell of dirty feet and corn chips swirled up my nose. I'm saying, the Johnsons didn't live in a mansion, but at least they kept their home clean and funk free. This home, way out in Gravesend,

Brooklyn, was not the place to be. I was already plotting an escape in my head. . . . Straight up fantasy though, because I had no place to go. No family to speak of. No power to make my own moves. As a ward of the state, the system has me yoked up by the throat until I turn eighteen.

Mrs. Cooper smoothed down her gray crooked Afro with her bony, wrinkled hands and said, "Now for the rules."

I followed her out of the living room. She walked with her body bent low, slow as a turtle. Behind my back, I heard one of the girls say, "Dang, her cornbraids is mad fuzzy!" Wow, clowning me already, I thought.

Mrs. Cooper had either heard the diss and pretended not to, or she was plain old hard of hearing. Whatever the case, her frail little self probably couldn't discipline a fly.

"Yo, peep her dusty wardrobe," another girl piped in. Then they busted out laughing louder than necessary.

See? The dumbness was really going down. But I swallowed a nasty comeback and kept my dusty butt moving. Who cared that I was rocking a faded black T-shirt, and busted blue jean shorts? Worrying about my gear was so last year. No reason for me to pop off on these broads to gain respect. Been there, done that. Got me nowhere.

I had bigger and better things to worry about. Had to get on my grind before it's too late. In two more years, I had to be college-bound. Four years after that, I had to be on point—or be homeless. Basically, at age eighteen, you have the choice to stay in foster care or get out. But by age twenty-one, the only choice is to let the door hit you where the sun don't shine.

The system is dead serious like that. You could be living in foster care one minute, and in a cardboard box the next. My old room-mate, Roberta, proved this simple fact. Last year I had bumped into her while she was begging on the number 3 train. The saddest sight I'd ever seen: Roberta was ashy and embarrassed, but trying hard to play it off. I tried to play it off, too; meanwhile a lump stayed stuck in my throat. I was staring at my own future if I didn't get it together. So, like I said, bump these silly broads. I had to stay focused on what really mattered.

Mrs. Cooper stopped short in front of a giant white poster hanging on the wall. Rules numbered one through ten were written in gigantic red letters. The rules that stuck out the most involved fifteen-minute phone calls, a crazy early ten o'clock curfew, and no boys calling the crib until you're sixteen years old. Well, I had a month and some change before I could think about a boy calling me.

Then again, I had no boyfriend to think of. Couldn't seem to meet any boys worth my time. All they did was holler at my big butt instead of trying to make love to my mind. Real talk, it was downright hopeless for me in the romance department. I'm saying, could a girl get some love, please? My last kiss had happened last year with a two-timing chump named Charles, who had taken my kindness for weakness, and played me for a fool. So if it wasn't love kicking my behind, it was foster care kicking me to my next location. I couldn't help but wonder if my life would ever change for the better.

"Any questions?" asked Mrs. Cooper, jolting me back to the present. She ran a long bony finger down each rule, to make sure I understood each and every one.

But all I wanted to ask was: "Why am I here? Why can't I *ever* live a normal freaking teenage life? Why was I ripped away from the first foster parents I could ever truly call Mom and Dad? It made no sense to me. I finally had a family to call my own, and then all of a sudden, I had to leave them? Just like that?

Everything had happened so fast. On a cloudy April afternoon we got the sad news: Ted's father was deathly sick in South Carolina. One month later, the Johnsons' roof literally fell apart. Next thing I know, the Johnsons are moving down South at the end of June.

The only upside of this: I found out Ted and Lynn actually wanted to adopt me; it was the first time in my life a family actually wanted to *keep* me.

Unfortunately, the Johnsons were so broke they couldn't afford to pay attention. With all of their backed-up bills and family complications, no amount of pleas or paperwork could convince the state that relocating down South would be a stable move for me. It was decided that I had been through enough disruption in my life already. Bottom line: I had to stay in New York without my family.

I remember the discussion about my future like it was yesterday. I was sitting on the living room couch flanked by Ted and Lynn, with attitude written all over my face. Tisha, my former (and best ever) social worker, was busy trying to convince me that this move was for the best. But all I could do was stare at the floor, my arms folded tightly across my chest.

"You have a ton of resources while in the system," Tisha explained, as worry lines creased her entire forehead. She could tell I was tight.

"Yeah, okay," I muttered. "Tons of resources."

"And staying in the system will help you get money for college—"

"Man, listen," I interrupted, "staying in the system is helping me go insane. . . . I'm tired of this moving-around mess."

"Trust me, I understand," said Tisha.

I knew she meant well, but her understanding didn't help my situation. I shook my head in disgust, feeling hopeless, helpless. "I swear I can't take this anymore," I said.

"What do you mean, you can't take this anymore?" Ted suddenly piped in. "You're a survivor, missy. This world can't stop *my* Kate!"

Ted and his silly self. He was only trying to make me feel better, even though it wasn't working. Lynn, the more serious one, simply said, "We're always going to be your family, Kate. Always remember that."

Comforting words at the time.

But right about now?

I was feeling mad uncomfortable, left to deal with group home staff instead of family. There would be no hugs here. No jokes. No love. Somehow, getting kicked out of people's homes was much easier than growing attached to them. I had only known the Johnsons for a year and a half, but it felt like I had known them my whole entire life . . . and now, *poof*, they were gone. Just like that.

"Kate, you seem so far away," said Mrs. Cooper, bringing me back to the present.

By now my tears were welling up again. But I quickly dammed up my eyes.

"Are you sure you have no questions for me, sweetheart?" she asked, staring at me with what looked like pity in her eyes.

I shook my head no, but wanted to scream, "Please, leave me alone already!" I had no freaking questions. Everything was crystal clear. Ready or not, I had to serve my time at the Common Grounds group home. Keep my head up. Control my temper. Make it out of this hellhole alive.

I don't know what I was expecting, but I wasn't expecting *this*. As soon as Mrs. Cooper left me alone inside my bedroom, I wanted to call her old butt right back, and ask, "Are you serious right now?"

I looked around the shabby room in disbelief. Junky and funky— the first words that came to mind. In other group homes, we were never allowed to leave clothes sprawled on the floor, or food floating around in our rooms. Yet here I was, staring at a mountain of dirty jeans sitting in the middle of a stained gray carpet, and a half-eaten hot dog resting on top of a cheap wooden dresser. Four walls were covered in chipped beige paint, and white dirty blinds hung from the single window in our room. Twin beds sat across from each other. One bed was surprisingly decked in clean white sheets, the other was mad messy.

Earlier in the day, I was told Tracy was to be my roommate. Well, Tracy was a straight-up slob. I unpacked my bags with a serious attitude. Man, I missed my old bedroom so much. Although it was small as a shoebox, at least it was *mine*. Didn't have to share it with *nobody*. And I missed the Johnsons even more.

In the Johnson household, I had no big beef or worries. As soon as I had stopped acting like a knucklehead and learned how to return the love they gave me, it was so easy and breezy living with them.

Once my chores were done, it was all about creating my own program. I could chill by myself and watch the portable TV they'd bought me last Christmas (for getting all As on my report card), or I could sit up in bed and do homework in peace; I could play Spades with Ted, or have girl talks with Lynn; I could lounge on my fire escape, reading good books and cracking sunflower seeds. Real talk, I had it made in the shade while living there.

But here? *Please.* No peace up in this piece. Nobody to talk to. Nowhere to break away from the madness. Even the fire escape connected to our bedroom was located in a weed-filled backyard with a view of a corroded cemetery beyond it. How mournful could things get? I was ready to cry again.

After stashing all of my clothes away, I sat on my bed and leaned my head up against the wall, wondering what to do next. I wasn't trying to go downstairs and beg the girls for friendship. I could hear them from upstairs, talking and laughing loud, bonding nicely without me. Well, my room was disgusting; I needed to bond with a broom.

I jumped up and tried to make my bedroom more livable. Cracked open the window to let in some clean air. Using my foot, I pushed the pile of jeans closer to Tracy's side of the room. Then I kicked her sparkling white Adidas underneath her bed.

And just then.

Boom.

The second my foot connected with Tracy's sneakers, here she comes, sheathed in a tight sky-blue jean jumper and silver gladiator sandals, hands on her hips, scowl on her lips. I had the worst timing in the world.

Tracy is a shorty like me, dark-skinned like me, thick body like me, but she wears a long burgundy weave and has slits for eyes. She was using them to glare at me right now, trying hard to scare me. Not possible, though. I stood my ground.

"Yo, why are you kicking my things around?" Tracy snatched her sneakers out from under the bed and placed them in full view, to spite me, I guessed.

"My bad," I replied. "Sorry."

"Yeah, right, *your* bad," she snapped.

"I *said* I was sorry," I snapped back. Her attitude was so unnecessary. When someone apologizes to you and they really mean it, accept it and move on, silly chick. I had no time for this.

I looked at Tracy like she was minor league, and dared her to say something else. She had nothing more to add. So I marched right past her out of our bedroom, and braced myself for a possible attack from behind. But Tracy just called me the "B" word when I was halfway down the hall. I guessed she was all mouth, no action. Weak witch.

I decided to take a trip to the bathroom, for no other reason than to be alone. I pulled the rickety door closed with its flimsy (pray-nobody-busts-in) hook in the hole lock. Clicked on the light, which was mad bright, revealing all the grime surrounding me. Stray hairs and blue soap scum decorated the sink, a see-through plastic shower curtain revealed scummy tub tiles. No bath rugs in place. No pretty pictures on the wall. The main attraction: a noisy toilet with dirty brown water swirling around inside. Ugh. Straight-up nasty in here.

Thank goodness I didn't need to use the bathroom yet. I just needed to be alone for a few. I pushed the shower curtain aside and sat on the edge of the tub, feeling crazy depressed and out of it. Then someone pounded on the door, bringing me back into it.

I heaved a lungful of air, and stepped out of the bathroom to find Makeba, a pierced-up brown-skinned chick, doing the two-step like she had to go real bad. "It's about time," she huffed in a husky voice.

I flashed her the illest mean-grill and kept it moving. It felt like I had to be in defense mode 24/7. I'm saying, it felt like the whole house was against me for no apparent reason. I just couldn't understand it . . . but then again I could. I had played the same dirty game back when I was all about bullying. The new girl gets clowned on until she proves herself. *Yeah, I get it.* But now that the combat shoe was on my foot, it hurt like hell . . . drafted in a war I wasn't prepared for.

I couldn't complain to Mrs. Cooper about how the girls were treating me. No snitching is my rule—street code in my blood. And the other two grown-ups in the house, Belinda and Gerald, were a big fat joke. They could care less about encouraging us girls to get along. I could already tell they were just there to collect paychecks; chilling around the crib like a couple of stone-faced simpletons.

I had absolutely no one to confide in, to comfort me. I wanted to scream at the top of my lungs, "Get me out of this madhouse!" But if I screamed, who would hear me? Even my new social worker was *ghost*. She never returned my calls. I don't even remember her name.

I had nobody. Absolutely nobody.

When Mrs. Cooper called me down for dinner, I lied about a stomachache. Wasn't in the mood to be sitting at the table flanked by these skanks.

From upstairs, I heard their forks and knives clanging while my stomach was sangin', "Kate, what's going on? I'm starving like Marvin!"

Later that night, I tossed and flipped around in my strange new bed, hungry and restless. I couldn't sleep for nothing. Meanwhile, the whole house was catching zzz's. I had to do something to keep myself busy or I was about to lose my mind. I had left all my novels back in my old bedroom; had no magazines to flip through, no nothing to do.

Just then, I remembered my Lifebook, the book given to me by Lynn, the book Ted had told me to keep all of my experiences in. "Kate, you need to capture all of your life's moments," he had explained. "Big things, little things, good times and bad . . ."

Well, these times were bad and I needed to capture them. Then maybe one day I could look back and release them, saying to myself, "After all of the hardships you've experienced, look how far you've come."

Careful not to wake Tracy, I eased out of my bed and slid my knapsack from underneath it. I crept downstairs, hoping no one would block me. The hallway lights were on, but thank goodness not a soul in sight to stop me. I went into the living room, turned on the end table's lamp, and sank down on the couch. I pulled out my Lifebook, opened it up, and quickly flipped past all of the pictures of me and the Johnsons. Looking at those pictures would precipitate a rainstorm inside of me.

From my knapsack's side pocket, I pulled out my favorite fancy black felt-tip pen Ted had given me, and stared at the blank page staring back at me.

Now how should I begin?

My first day here and I hate this dirty stinking house. These chicks are asking me for problems, but I can't be snapping necks anymore. I have too much to lose. Too much I've already gained by changing my old ways. I know if Tisha were around, she'd tell me to suck it up and be strong. And I know I can be strong. Sometimes I forget that I'm a survivor. Always have been. Always will be. So let me stop tripping. I can do this. I can really do this. Nobody can bring me down, but me.

Seeing these words in print eased my mind. I repeated the last line out loud: *Nobody can bring me down, but me.* I wanted to believe in these words. I needed to believe in these words. I clicked off the light and sat up in the dark, repeating these words over and over again. I felt a little crazy, but what else could I do? I had no one around to put my mind at ease.

Finally, my eyelids got heavy. I made my way upstairs, feeling peaceful, maybe even a little hopeful about the rest of my stay at Common Grounds. From now on, I could write down all of my pain and frustrations, I reasoned. My Lifebook would be my lifeline to sanity. But three days later, bump a freaking journal. I was ready to choke a chick to death.

The drama began brewing in the dining room.

I was sitting at the long wooden table, slumped over my plate, staring sadly at soggy scrambled eggs and cold sausage patties. I had gotten used to Lynn's slammin' feasts; I'm talking hot creamy cheese grits, juicy turkey bacon, and warm flaky biscuits with melted butter on top. And now *this*?

The girls were busy chomping away like this was the best meal they ever had. Meanwhile, all I could think about was how much weight I was going to lose while living here. Hungry as I was, I could only take one last bite out of my sorry sausage before finally giving up and pushing my plate forward.

"New Girl's turn to do the dishes," Makeba suddenly cried out as she jumped up from the table.

The other four girls looked my way, waiting for me to react. I shrugged, and said, "No problem." But I wasn't about to skyrocket out of my seat. I sat still for a minute, just to show them I had some spunk. Kate, a pushover? Please.

"You have to do them *now*," said Ciara, a tall, beady-eyed broad. "We don't let dishes sit in the sink."

It was too early in the morning for some bull. To avoid a scene, I got up, gathered the rest of the plates, and quietly walked into the kitchen. I gently placed the dishes in the sink, soaped them up, and scrubbed them sparkling clean. Before drying the last dish, a random little mouse poked his head out of the nearby stove's burner, as if to say, "Welcome home, Kate!" I wasn't scared of mice, so I didn't drop a plate; I just felt even more disgusted with my world. So this was my new life? Coping with bold rodents and silly broads? Wow, what a way to live.

From the kitchen, I had a clear view into the living room where the girls sat in front of the television, two on the floor, three on the couch. Then I glanced over at the far corner of the room where a large wooden bookcase filled with board games sat. I peeped a box of Checkers and Monopoly from where I stood.

A part of me wished I could bulldoze the barricade between me and these girls and just sit nice and pleasant with them playing games all day—I'm Queen of Monopoly, okay? But I knew I'd never get to reign here. The only game these chicks were interested in playing was: Let's Make Kate Miserable. There was nothing I could do to be cool with them; they clearly had it in for me, no matter what.

To test my theory, I lingered in the kitchen in full view of them. Just chilling. Idling about. Would someone be strong and throw Kate a bone? Ask me a question? Crack a stupid joke? *Something?* Even in my baddest days, I used to interrupt my bullying agenda to make the new girl feel included every once in a while.

So let's see. My kitchen location wasn't working. I inched closer to the living room, leaned against the archway, and looked at the TV from a safe distance.

Still no luck.

The group was busy talking mad loud during the commercial break, paying me absolutely no mind.

"Yeah, the Fourth of July gonna be off the hook in my hood," yelled Venus, a scrawny girl from the Bronx.

"You already know, *ho*," said Makeba, laughing.

"Y'all so stupid," cried out Asia, the flyest girl in the house. She reminded me of my foul-living, ex-friend Naleejah. Both chicks rock fake hazel eyes, silky long weaves, and slutty gear. "I'mma be flossin' in my boyfriend's BMW on the Fourth. Hair done, nails done, everything big!"

"You always bragging, B—" said Venus.

"Yeah, instead of bragging, come pick us up in the Beamer, trick!" cried out Makeba.

Asia laughed like it was a joke. They called each other disrespectful names all the time. Said mean things to each other for no reason. I quickly snapped out of wanting to be cool with them. I wanted to be out. Had to be out. Maybe not today. But at least for the Fourth of July. I hoped it wasn't too late to sign up for the volunteer opportunity I had already turned down.

A week ago, my best and only friend, Felicia, had asked me to volunteer with her for the Bed-Stuy Community Garden's annual July 4th celebration. A fund-raiser for the homeless. Now, I love a good cause, and you know I love The Stuy, so I told her I was in. But the next day, Felicia told me her man, Marlon, would be joining us. Oops, no offense; I'm out.

Not that I had a problem with Marlon. He was mad cool. But whenever I hung around the lovey-dovey couple, I stuck out like a sore loser. So rolling with them as the third wheel had been out of the question. But now? Considering my current chaos? I was ready to roll in third place, fourth place, whatever it took to get me out of *this* place.

I ran upstairs, found the volunteer coordinator's phone number in my backpack, and ran back downstairs to call the office. Our communal phone was located in the hallway, less than fifty feet away from the occupied living room, now under enemy control. No such thing as a private phone call, so I kept my voice low, trying not to call any attention to myself.

"Mr. King at your service!" the coordinator exclaimed. (Yes, this is how he really answered the phone. Mad extra.) And he sounded even jollier when I told him I wanted to volunteer. "Great to have you on board, Kate!" he shouted. Then he gave me a quick rundown of my duties.

"What time do you need me there?" I asked.

Before Mr. King could answer, I felt a tap on my shoulder. I spun around to face Makeba. "How long you gonna be?" she grumbled.

"I *just* got on the phone," I said in my calmest tone.

"Well, I need to use the phone *now*," she replied, clearly cookin' up some beef to boil. But I decided to let the silly chick stew for a minute.

"Be off in a second," I said.

Makeba huffed and sashayed away.

I got back down to business. "Mr. King, sorry for the interruption. What time do you need me there?"

"Ten o'clock sharp."

"No problem. See you then."

I hung up the phone softly so as not to get caught by the phone police. Then I picked it back up to call Felicia. We were allowed fifteen minutes for phone calls and my *full* fifteen minutes I would get.

"Hey, girl, can't talk long," I blurted, before Felicia could say hello. "So I'll see you at the Garden, and—"

"Oh no," Felicia interrupted.

"What do you mean 'oh no'?" I asked.

"I had to give up my position," she explained. "Marlon's performing poetry at the African Street Festival tomorrow. He's a last-minute addition to the show. I'm so excited. This is a big deal for him!"

"Um, okay," I said, feeling deflated, like a stabbed balloon. I was really looking forward to seeing Felicia. Blocked from my best friend. Again. Bad enough our whole school year had already put a wedge between us.

Basically, our new high school is populated with more kids like Felicia, barely anybody like me. Felicia's life is upper crust, while my life is crusty. So when Felicia made friends with this stuck-up duet, Brittany and Janette, I knew I wasn't going to be hanging with my homegirl too tough anymore. I couldn't stand these chicks. Black like me, but couldn't relate to my world. They talked in fake high-pitched voices, shopped exclusively on Fifth Avenue, and bragged about their countless trips around the globe—I'm talking Africa, France, Italy, Japan. Meanwhile, the most exotic place I've ever been to is Staten Island.

Funny, though—aside from world travel, I had no idea what Felicia saw in them. And it was mighty clear these girls were confused about me, too. I could tell by the way they turned up their noses, frowning and sniffing at me like they smelled a hood-rat.

Well, I'm far from a hood-rat. But I couldn't blame them for thinking that, since I got that Brooklyn swagger and I'm stuck with a C-shaped scar over my right eye. No doubt Felicia and I looked like a serious odd couple: nerdy girl and gangster chick prancing down our school's hallway.

But anyway.

I was seeing less of my homegirl because of Brittany and Janette. Now add Marlon to the mix, and you get a drifting friendship.

"Why do you sound so surprised about the festival?" asked Felicia. "I called the house yesterday to invite you."

"Wow," I exclaimed, shaking my head in disgust. "Nobody told me *jack*."

"OMG, you didn't get my message?" asked Felicia. "I called you around two o'clock."

"I swear, I can't stand these spiteful broads," I muttered. "I gotta get out of here, for real."

"See, that's why you need to hang with us," said Felicia. "I'll be helping Marlon's group all day, but you can lounge backstage with me while I work. You won't have to lift a finger, I promise."

"But I'll be the third wheel . . . as usual."

"You're not going to be the third wheel," she assured me. "There's going to be tons of people there. Lots of cute guys in Marlon's group, too. Don't you want to meet some cuties?"

"You know I'm not thirsty like that," I protested.

Meanwhile I was more than thirsty. Matter of fact, dehydrated. I wanted a boyfriend so bad I could drink him in my dreams. Seemed like everybody had a man, but me.

". . . . Come on, Kate. Please? I really miss you."

"Well . . . I already told Mr. King that I'd help him at the Garden. It wouldn't be right for both of us to diss him."

"But you can do the Garden *and* the festival," explained Felicia. "Marlon doesn't perform until five."

Hmm . . . rocking both events wasn't such a bad idea. The longer away from this madhouse, the better.

"Okay, I'll call you around—"

Suddenly, I heard Makeba's voice at the back of my head. "New Girl must think she running things 'round here," she rasped. Next thing I knew, the receiver was snatched from my grip, and the phone was hung up with a bang.

"Your time been up," Makeba snapped.

Oh. No. She. Didn't.

My bottom lip hit the floor. I stood frozen in my spot. Did that really just happen? I was in so much shock, I couldn't move a muscle.

Four years ago, in under sixty seconds, Makeba would've been drop-kicked flat on her back, with every silver piercing snatched from her stupid face. What? The Old Kate used to punch chicks dead in the mouth just for looking at her wrong. But this New Kate needed New Tactics.

So I locked my hands to my sides and mean-grilled Makeba for a minute. As angry as I was, I didn't say a word. This was such a proud (and painful) moment for me. Proud because I was so smooth with my 'tude, the other girls didn't even realize the craziness that had just gone down. Painful because I wanted to bash Makeba over the head with the phone, and I couldn't.

A split second later, the phone rang. I knew it was Felicia calling back to find out what just happened. Makeba snatched up the phone and said, "Check for her later. I gotta make a call."

Click.

I swear . . . if it wasn't for Tisha's voice in my head telling me to walk away, Makeba would've been calling 911.

So yeah, I walked away. Calm. Cool. Collected.

Before I had learned to walk away, I used to get into fights all day, every day. Some fights I would start, some I would not. It was all about maintaining my respect in any given situation. I thought I was the baddest chick in my school. Most kids agreed, and knew to steer clear of me. So imagine my surprise when Tisha called me a punk one day, straight to my face. I was sitting in the principal's office, fresh from a fight, my face all scratched up in zigzags. The principal had nothing to say to me; he needed Tisha to "reach" me.

"So I guess you think you did something," Tisha began. "Look at you!"

"Yeah, but I won the fight," I stated proudly. "These scratches don't hurt. I got the best of her."

"So where's your prize?" asked Tisha, cocking her head to the side. She wore a light brown curly weave that day, and it shook every time she moved her head. I wanted to laugh, but this was no laughing matter. Tisha was not playing with me. "Your face is all scratched up, and you're about to be suspended from school . . . so I'm asking you: Where's your prize for winning the fight?"

"But I bet that B— knows better than to call me out my name again."

"What did I tell you about cursing in front of me?"

"My bad," I said. And I only said, "my bad" to Tisha. No other grown-up had me in check like that. Tisha was the first social worker I had ever met who was *real*. From the hood and proud of it. The first day I met her she told me all about her wilding-out days and explained how she had to overcome a shipload of obstacles. I had much respect for Tisha because she wasn't schooling me from textbooks; she was speaking from real life. And even though she sat opposite me in her rigid navy blue suit, I knew that underneath her business front was a bad chick who could get down with her hands if she had to.

But at that moment, she was getting down with me—verbally— and her ferocity was astonishing. "Dang, calm down," I wanted to say. But I didn't dare.

"Kate, you let that girl play you," continued Tisha, her eyebrows knitted tight in anger. "And that makes you a *punk*. You hear me? A straight-up punk!"

I sat stock-still, staring at Tisha, blank-faced. The office was freezing cold from the air conditioner blowing on my back, and I just wanted to get the heck out of there.

"It takes a real woman to *walk away* from a fight," explained Tisha. "But you're always running *to* one. Are you going to throw up your hands every time somebody says something stupid to you?"

"I gotta do what I gotta do." I shrugged.

"And now you *gotta* get suspended. So like I said, Kate, you're a punk." Tisha pointed at me with her long fingernail to emphasize her point. "So go ahead and get left back in the sixth grade if you want to. You're the smartest girl in your class, yet you act so dumb! Always bragging that you never lost a fight, but there's always somebody out there bigger and badder than you. Remember that."

"Yeah, okay," I said.

"And if you ask me, I'd rather be a *living* punk, than a *dead* hero any day."

"But I *didn't* ask you," I wanted to say. Instead I just said, "Can I go now?"

"Not until you understand what I'm telling you."

"Yeah, I understand what you saying."

At the time, I was lying, I didn't understand jack. But during my weeklong suspension, I had a lot to think about. Tisha's words started ringing in my ears, oh so loud and true. And after reflecting on my countless battles with chicks over nonsense, I realized there were no trophies to show, no medals to wear. Where was my prize? What was my point? I had to face the fact: My life was a vicious cycle of violence for no good reason. It was high time for a change.

"Bawwwaaahhaa!"

The girls' loud guffaws brought me back to the reality that I was a "living punk" right now. Makeba had probably just told her telephone takeover story, and the girls were probably loving every detail of my humiliation. So despite my calming thoughts about Tisha's words, every step I took up the stairs caused my heart to skip three beats in my chest. Hearing their laughter rubbed salt into my wounded pride. I felt so disrespected, clowned on . . . forced to walk away? Oh man, I was tight. Nothing I could do but run upstairs, grab my Lifebook, and write.

I swear on my life, I better keep myself in check because Makeba is itching for me to snap her neck. She may be taller than me, but I've been known to knock down bigger broads flat on their backs. They used to call me "Rocky" for a reason.

And then there's Felicia. I'm happy Felicia wants to include me all the time. I know most girls would get a boyfriend and be like, Kate who? But homegirl needs to really fall back with this third-wheel crap. It's always pitiful, single me, hanging with a couple of lovebirds. Bird-watching just ain't my thing. I'm saying, when will I find a boyfriend to call my own? When will these spiteful group home chicks leave me the hell alone? I can't even lie. I'm feeling so hopeless these days. Every time I turn around, another smackdown comes my way.

Growing tired of my own pitiful words, I stopped my pen in its tracks. If I had continued writing like that, I was sure to start crying, and my Lifebook ain't waterproof.

I stashed my Lifebook in my duffel bag and covered it with a towel to conceal it. Then I sat on my bed and leaned my head against the wall and tried to think good thoughts. First thing that came to mind was the upcoming Fourth of July celebration. Not even a week spent at Common Grounds, and already I couldn't wait to return to my old hood. As sad as it would be, knowing Ted and Lynn were no longer there, I was still dying to return to Bed-Stuy. My present sucked so bad, a little touch of my past couldn't hurt . . . at least that's what I thought at the time.

Chapter 3

On Saturday morning, I jumped out of bed higher than a bunny on crack. I was so excited about getting out of the madhouse. But then I remembered my roommate, and calmed my happy self down. Tracy was knocked out cold with the sheets over her head, and I didn't want to wake her crazy butt up. She was not going to hold me back from hitting up my old hood.

I quietly rummaged through my drawers and pulled out a plain pink V-neck T-shirt, a pair of black baggy jean shorts, and laid the items out on my bed. My gear was corny as could be, but I didn't care; I was getting the freak outta here!

I took a cold shower—not by choice, there was no hot water in the joint—and raced back into my room, shivering cold. I silently got dressed. Finishing touches were my black dollar-store flip-flops, and then I dug up my beautiful silver bracelet from the bottom of my knapsack (carefully hidden from sticky-fingered bandits). Felicia had brought me this bracelet from South Africa and it meant a whole lot to me. The only genuine jewelry I ever rocked. Probably cost more than my entire outfit.

I went downstairs to find Gerald sprawled out on the living room couch, snoring like a pig, instead of watching us. I didn't know where Belinda was hiding. Mrs. Cooper was off for the holiday. So I was free to do me, no questions asked. The rules posted on the wall were mad bogus. This was the most lax group home I'd ever been in. Everything was done backward here; but since this meant my freedom could be achieved with so much ease, their careless sloppy system was just fine with me.

I went into the kitchen. Was about to hook me up a quick bowl of corn flakes. But then I peeped a mousetrap sitting on the stove. *Ugh*. Lost my dang appetite.

I signed myself out of the group home, hit the streets, and exhaled a big sigh of relief. I looked back at the shabby, three-story house wishing I could make it disappear with a magical stare. Two blinks later, nope, it was still there.

Our block was deader than a graveyard. Nothing but small brown houses, perfectly paved sidewalks, and Beamers and Benzes lined up against curbs. Not a soul in sight.

Come to think of it, I kinda liked things quiet and empty. At my other group homes, we had to deal with snoopy neighbors on the block peeping out of windows and doorways, giving us group home girls the side-eye every time we walked out the house. At least here, nobody was around to judge us, to mistrust us, to give us a hard time just for being in foster care.

Anyway.

The morning was cloudless and warm. I felt drama free as I breezed through the open air. The six-block walk to the F train was cool and uneventful. The train took less than five minutes to pull into the Avenue U station. It felt like it was going to be a very smooth day.

The feeling didn't last long.

My whole train ride to Bed-Stuy was jacked up. The "F" train must stand for Foul. First, there was a track fire, and then I was stuck in the tunnel for twenty minutes. Next thing you know, a passenger decided to get sick on the A train. Stalled again. I practically crawled out of the Utica Avenue train station, feeling hot, sticky, and beat.

But when I caught a whiff of the fresh morning air, I felt revived all over again. My emotions were running wild, up, down, and sideways.

The streets were alive in Bed-Stuy. Cars driving by pumping bass in the AM, people roaming around handling their business, firecrackers popping off in the far distance. Gravesend is a ghost town by comparison. Matter of fact, there is no comparison. I'll be reppin' Bed-Stuy till I die.

As I neared the front gate of the garden, tall trees with enormous leaves blocked my view of the inside. Then I stepped through the gate and was hit with a floral wonderland. Sunlight beamed from all different directions as I explored the breathtaking surroundings. Sunflowers and red roses were everywhere. A winding path made of red bricks led me to a cute little wishing well, then a pretty pond full of goldfish surrounded by big rocks, and then a towering willow tree with crazy shade underneath it.

The garden was huge, I marveled. Crazy space to lounge in. There were benches all over the place, and lots of cozy private corners to cuddle with your boo. . . . Too bad I didn't have one.

As I came across each nook, Felicia came to mind. She would have loved it here; and she was the main reason I even know what a "nook" is. Because of her, I could also name the "paper birch tree" situated in front of me, and the "sparrow" that just flew past my eyes. There was so much to learn while hanging with Felicia. So amazing how she went from being my seventh-grade math tutor, to my "life" tutor and best friend in the whole world. Too bad she wasn't here with me now. I really missed her.

A sudden rush of volunteers swirled around me from all sides. Some were carrying food to and fro, others were pulling weeds here and there. Out of the blue, a sweaty, short, stocky man who looked like Humpty Dumpty scurried up to me.

I was the only one not doing anything, and he wanted to change that. He had to be Mr. King. "Kate?" he asked, with his hand extended for a handshake.

He was so frenetic and fidgety I was tempted to deny it. "Yes, Kate," I finally admitted, shaking his clammy hand. *Ugh.*

"I'm Mr. King," he exclaimed. "Glad you're here! We need all the help we can get!" He waved his chubby arm forward. "Follow me."

I brushed past folks, trying to keep up with him. He led me to the back of the garden, and stopped short in front of a long wooden table.

"This will be easy work," he assured me, handing over a potato peeler.

Homeboy had me skinning a giant mountain of potatoes. Next thing you know, he had me shelling a mob of peas. By the time I was through peeling and shelling, I had rusty hands and green crap stuck underneath my stubby nails. I was hot, dumb hungry, tempted to eat some raw peas and potatoes. My day was starting off busted, for real. But when Mr. King gave me my next errand, I was ready to run for my life.

"I need you to pick up some donated paper plates and cups from the Fulton Street Market," he explained.

The Fulton Street Market?

Of all the stores in all the world, why did I have to go *there*?

"You know where the market is, right?" Mr. King asked.

I heard the question, but I didn't answer him. I was still stunned, like I had just gotten sucker-punched.

"Hello?" said Mr. King, twitching his nose like he had something up it.

"Oh, sorry, yes, I know where it is," I stuttered.

I knew the Fulton Street Market all too well. A few years ago, I used to terrorize the store's owner, Mrs. Thomas, with my old gang-banging crew, the Lady Killers. We were terrible with our madness.

I can't say she didn't deserve it, though. The first time I stepped inside her store she had disrespected me for no reason. "Miss, let me get a pack of sunflower seeds," I had said.

Mrs. Thomas stood behind the tall counter with her thick

eyebrows raised and she snapped, "My name is Mrs. Thomas, and it's not 'let me get,' it's 'may I have.' Your mother didn't train you better than that?"

Say what? Oh, your girl Kate was *hot*. This lady had some nerve talking down to me, as if speaking from a throne. She wasn't ruling anybody, especially not me. Time to put a chick in check. I stood on tippy toes, raised my pointer finger as close to her face as I could get, and said, "You don't know me like that, stupid B—"

Then I stormed out the store, making sure to slam the door. I usually don't call grown women the "B" word, but the lady had really gotten to me that day.

The next time I went inside the store was only because no other store had my favorite brand of fifty-cent chocolate chip cookies. I was five deep with my gangster girls this time, so I felt mighty powerful. We, the Lady Killers, wrecked worlds all day, okay? We had money in our pockets and we were ready to buy a grip of cookies and candy, and the oldest of my crew was going to hook us up with five forty ounces of beer. But before we could start picking up stuff, Mrs. Thomas sent her son Percy to follow us through the aisles, making sure we didn't steal anything. When we collectively peeped the dirty game she was playing, we were collectively pissed and wanted to do something about it. Icy set it off by saying, "Bump that, let's give her a reason to treat us grimy."

On the count of three, we spread out and ran through all four aisles, knocking down cans and bottles. Splashing and crashing everywhere. "Rocky, kick the glass in!" Icy yelled. My foot whapped at the glass enclosure in the front of the store, but it didn't break. "Yo, snatch some sour cream chips," yelled Killah. "I got you!" shouted Crash. Menace snatched up three packs of my favorite cookies and one forty-ounce beer, which was all she could carry.

Everything was happening so fast, we had Mrs. Thomas's and Percy's heads spinning. But Percy finally caught his bearings, and yanked me up from behind. Like a karate kid, I spun around and kneed him hard where it hurts. He let go of me, doubling over in pain. Then Icy kicked open the door and we all ran out, screaming and laughing like a wild pack of hyenas.

After that incident, you could find us in front of the Fulton Street Market giving Mrs. Thomas mad problems. Sometimes Percy would chase us away, sometimes Mrs. Thomas would call the cops. All the time, we had so much fun causing mayhem at their expense.

Funny though. Back then, I didn't realize how fine Percy was. In my tomboy days, dudes were the last thing on my mind. But about a month ago, I'd seen Percy outside, sweeping the sidewalk, and let me tell you, brother has it going *on*. From way across the street, I could see his body is *sick*, delicious muscles galore, towering tall, wrapped in beautifully smooth almond vanilla skin. His wife-beater tank top fit him oh so right. His swagger was out of this world. He had to be about eighteen or nineteen years old by now. Maybe a bit too old for me, but a girl can dream, can't she?

During my five-block walk to the market, a million thoughts ran through my mind. Would Percy remember me? Would Mrs. Thomas kick my behind for giving her such a hard time?

The only good thing was: I looked mad different. Back in the day, I used to rock my baseball cap pushed so low over my eyes you couldn't see my face, and my jeans were always extra baggy like a boy's. I was a thuggish ruggish broad back then. But now, at least I look like a female. My big boobies and booty are crazy hard to hide these days.

When I reached the front of the Fulton Street Market, I took a deep breath, and walked inside like an innocent little customer. The store still looked the same. Still smelled the same, like lemons. Bright overhead lights, shelves fully stocked, black-and-red tiled floor spotless because Percy was forever mopping.

Mrs. Thomas was standing behind the counter looking mean as ever. Her flawless brown skin wasted on a mean old face. She wore her usual green sack of a summer smock, and her thick eyebrows were knitted as if she had a 24/7 headache.

I approached her like a timid little kid.

She stared at me for a full minute, as if she had a moment of recognition. "May I help you?"

"Mr. King sent me for the cups and plates," I said in a soft sweet voice, hoping with all my heart she didn't recognize me.

"Percy!" she yelled. "Come out here!"

And that tall fine creamshake of a man emerged from the back room. He swaggered toward the counter, staring at me hard, just like his momma.

Did *he* remember me? I really hoped not.

"Bring me the bag for Mr. King," ordered Mrs. Thomas.

"Where is it, Ma?" he asked, in a deep voice.

"Do you ever *listen* when I talk to you?" asked Mrs. Thomas with her hands on wide hips. "The bag is sitting plain as day by my chair."

Percy rushed into the backroom and came back carrying a giant black plastic bag. He handed me the bag. "Here you go . . . *Rocky*," A slow grin crept over his lips.

My bottom lip hit the floor.

Percy jutted his chin toward me and said, "Ma, you know who she is, right?"

Part of me wanted to flee. The stronger part of me stood my ground. But my knees were made of liquid.

Mrs. Thomas frowned at me for what felt like an hour, and finally said, "Oh yeah . . . I *do* remember you. . . . You used to raise a ruckus in my store."

I lowered my head in shame. If I were light-skinned, I would've been beet red in the face.

She cocked her head to the side and added, "But I guess you've changed . . . hopefully."

I raised my eyes to meet Mrs. Thomas's. She was still staring at me with a deadpan look. Percy was standing next to her, a gleam of amusement pasted on his handsome face.

Mrs. Thomas broke the ice by saying, "Doesn't the party start at twelve? I'm sure Mr. King is waiting for you, young lady."

"Oh, yeah, thanks," I stuttered. "Okay, good-bye." I headed for the door, carrying the giant black bag with both hands.

Percy dashed ahead of me, and blocked the door with his beautiful body, spreading his arms wide. "I'm not letting you get away from me this time," he said, grinning.

"Quit playing around, fool," Mrs. Thomas yelled. "Let the girl go."

Percy flashed me a boyish smile, stared at me for long minute with his light brown eyes, and then held the door wide open for me to make my exit.

"Thank you," I said, without looking at him, still embarrassed as ever.

"My pleasure," said Percy, playfully bowing from the waist. "Come again."

Joking or serious, *heck no*, I wasn't coming again. I had made it out the store in one piece, and I wasn't trying to press my luck.

On the other hand, the fact that Percy said "come again" made me feel like he actually *wanted* to see me again. Really?

I mean . . . putting me on blast in front of his mother was not nice at all . . . but Percy's gorgeousness was so powerfully blinding that all I could do was sweat him in my mind.

Percy was so unique. Usually, super fine guys like him are too busy being fine—not playful. The way Percy had teased me as if he *liked* me or something was so unexpected and appreciated. I loved the way his smile lit up his whole entire face. I never had a guy stare straight into my eyes the way Percy did. Charles came close, but Percy's gaze was mad *intense*.

Point-blank, Percy had revived the girly feelings inside of me. I wanted to see him again. *Had* to see him again. But how? I don't believe in acting thirsty when it comes to boys. So I wasn't about to stalk his store.

What to do? What to do? How could I make my move?

I walked back to the garden with my new crush on my mind. But as it turned out, I had no time to plot on how to make him mine. To my surprise, I had another bombshell waiting for me around the corner: An old flame ready to light up Percy's spot.

Chapter 4

Charles.

My almost-boo, posted up by the garden's front gate, talking on his celly, looking too freaking good for words. I'm saying, why the fine men all up in my mix today? Before Charles noticed me, I took in all of his loveliness. His dark brown skin sweeter than chocolate, his towering six-foot frame posed like a beautiful work of art. He was dipped in his favorite royal-blue jersey and baggy khaki shorts hanging off his sexy behind, not enough to show his drawers, but just enough to show his swagger. No more waves in his hair. Now he rocked a blown-out Afro. I must say, my boy be mighty fly from head to toe.

But every time I see Charles, I try to look straight through him like he's a dirty window. Ignore the fact that he's a dime, and concentrate on the grime. Just when I was ready to give my whole heart to him, he played me for a chump. So why should I make the same mistake twice?

Yet and still, sad to say, Charles can make my stomach flip to this day.

"What's up," I said, as I walked up to him, trying hard to look nonchalant.

Charles looked in my direction and his face broke out into a giant grin, showing off dazzling white teeth, and a large wad of purple bubble gum sticking out between them. He told whomever goodbye and shoved his phone into his back pocket. "Kate, what's really good?" he exclaimed, reaching out to hug me.

I put the plastic bag on the ground and opened my arms wide. He held me for a long minute. His body felt so hot, a deep burning current ran through me. Oh man, I was getting flashbacks of the good old days.

Kate, remember the grime.

I caught my breath, pulled myself away, and said, "So what you been up to?"

"Same old," he replied. "I haven't seen you since what . . . May?"

"Yeah, that's about right." From the beginning of May till the end of June, I had stayed mostly in the house, mad depressed over my upcoming removal from the Johnson household.

"I missed you, Kate," Charles said. "*I really* missed you." He stared at me long and hard.

Whoa now. I didn't want to be catching feelings again. No need for us to go back *there*. Charles already had his chance, and he blew it.

I quickly changed the subject. "So, are you here to support the cause, like the good dude that you are?" I was being sarcastic by stressing the word "good."

"No doubt," he replied. "What about you?"

"I'm volunteering."

"Wow, that's really sweet of you," said Charles. "So where's your partner in crime?"

"Up Marlon's butt," I wanted to say. Instead, I just shrugged.

"Did Felicia tell you I've been asking about you?" Charles asked. "She gave you my number?"

"Yeah."

"Then why didn't you check for me? Too busy for me?"

"Nah, I'm just trying to do something with my life."

Charles smiled. "See, that's why I admire you. You make me want to do something with my life, too . . . we'd be so good together."

"Yeah, okay."

Charles closed his eyes and busted into song. "Baby you're my everything, you're all I ever wanted, we could do it real big—"

"Anyway," I interrupted, "the party doesn't start till twelve. Craving to get in, huh?"

"Craving for you," said Charles, lowering his eyelids seductively.

"Boy, stop playing."

"Playing is for boys," said Charles. "I'm a grown man now."

"Please, you ain't even old enough to drive yet," I teased.

"Seriously, I've *grown* a whole lot."

"You're still the same height if you ask me." Yes, all six luscious feet of him still the same. I loved craning my neck to look up at Charles. So dang fine, mm, what a shame.

"Seriously, Kate, trust me . . . I slowed down a whole lot. . . . It's real out there . . . I mean . . . well . . . you heard about Naleejah, right?"

"No, what happened?" I asked, crazy curious. "What did the hussy do *this* time?"

"I can't talk about that right now," said Charles, looking down at the ground. "It's not a good time. I just assumed you already heard by now."

I hit Charles in the arm. "Man, don't leave me hanging like that!"

"I'll tell you eventually . . . just not now."

"Aw see, you suck!"

"Anyway, I'm early because I needed to get out the house. Our air conditioner broke. I was sweating mad bullets in the crib."

"That's not a good look," I said, careful not to bring up my own home-life situation. No need to be sharing my pitiful business all the time.

Charles rubbed his sexy stomach. "Man, my mom's been bugging me to get this food all morning. She heard the spare ribs go quick. I gotta be the first in line. Feel me?"

"Yeah, I feel you," I said.

Mm, I wanted to feel *him*. Charles's arms wrapped around me again. Oh man, I was so confused about my outlook on him.

Suddenly, Mr. King spotted me through the gate, and frantically waved for me to come inside. I asked if Charles could come, too.

"Only if he's here to help," Mr. King replied hastily. I looked over at Charles. He shrugged and said, "I'll help, if it means I get to hang with you."

With every sweet line Charles laid, he was making it so hard for me to act aloof toward him. Luckily, the beautiful image of Percy kept popping into my brain. Percy's stunner smile and bangin' body was like whoa. It was time for a change anyway. Charles already had his chance.

But when Charles was ordered to pick up stray trash around the garden, and he said he was doing it "just for me," my heart skipped three beats. I watched his swaggerlicious moves around the garden, picking up trash just for me. Why were his legs so freaking sexy? Why did the sweat dripping down his face drive me crazy? I was in seventh heaven watching my boy work it just for me.

Then Mr. King busted my bubble by calling Charles inside a shed to break down boxes. From the look on Charles's face, I could tell he was pissed. I kinda felt bad for dragging him into this.

Ten minutes passed. Now Mr. King had me sitting at another small round table folding garden literature into pamphlets.

Charles suddenly came up from behind and whispered in my ear, "Yo, I swear this dude about to catch a beat down. Tell me why he's ordering me around like he crazy?" I flinched from feeling his delicious warm raspberry bubblegum breath in my ear. OMG.

Recovering my sanity, I said, "Well, help me with these, please?" I pointed to the heap of paper I had to fold. To tell you the truth, I didn't need his help; I just wanted his company a bit longer.

"Nah," said Charles. "Mr. Crazy already told me we can't work together. He thinks we won't get anything done. So I'm out. I'll be back for my food, okay, baby?"

See, why did Charles have to call me "baby" all out of the blue? You know how it gets when it's been a long time since you been somebody's baby. You lose your freaking mind. You conveniently forget the bad times and let the same doggish dude back in your life. My mind was such a murky mess right now.

To clear my head, and to take a break from pamphlet duty, I walked Charles toward the exit. Charles stopped short in front of the pond, dug a quarter out of his pocket, and threw it in before I could stop him.

"That's not a wishing well!" I said, grabbing his arm. "Don't you see the goldfish swimming around?"

"Oh, my bad," said Charles. He quickly bent down, fished his quarter out the water, and wiped his hands dry on his shorts.

"What were you wishing for . . . to choke the fish out?" I joked.

"Nah," Charles said. "I was wishing for your forgiveness . . . your one-hundred-percent forgiveness."

Oh boy. Now where did that come from? It was fine when Charles was joking about "us," but now I could tell he was dead serious. . . . Apparently, he knew I was still hurt. Must have been a case of classic Kate: I think I'm hiding my true feelings, acting like everything's all good, but somehow my innermost feelings always manage to shine through.

"Kate . . . it's not the same between us. I can *feel* it."

"Look, let's drop that already, please? What's done is done. We're good. Okay?"

"I don't believe you."

"Well, you don't have to believe me," I snapped, suddenly thinking how funny it is that dudes who do the dirt always try to act so freaking clean. They be on some *whodunit*, when *they* done it. Shoot, Charles needed to learn the word "accountability," just like I had to.

After beating up so many girls with no apology, Tisha had to drill it in my head that I was wrong; that I needed to accept responsibility for my own actions. Nobody *made* me stomp those girls out; so I fully deserved the trouble I was constantly getting into.

"You know what, Charles," I began, "you really need to stop acting so clueless. It's really annoying."

Charles stood in one spot, staring at me with sad eyes. "But you been on my mind for a long time. . . . I just wish you'd give me another chance."

Growing frustrated, I didn't want to prolong this pointless scene, so I finally said, "Anyway, like I said, we're cool. We'll always be cool. So can we move on, for real this time?"

"Yeah, okay," said Charles, staring at the ground. "We can move on."

"And listen, thanks for helping me out," I said.

"Anything for you, Kate . . . but you already know."

I flashed a smile, and quickly looked away before I got trapped by his hypnotic dark-brown eyes. My crush since the second grade had already crushed me once before. Never again.

"Mr. King is coming our way," Charles blurted. "Catch you later." He left the garden, gliding with that smooth walk of his that no one else can duplicate. I swear, his swagger was so official. Too bad his faithfulness was not.

When Charles returned to the garden, a mob of people were already standing on a long line, anxious to get their grub on. Old-people's soul music was playing. The sun was shining brightly. It was turning out to be a really nice day. Surprisingly, Mr. King let the volunteers eat first, so I was already fed and relaxing in a chair near the front entrance when Charles walked up to me. "Hey, why didn't you save me a spot on line?" he asked.

"Shoot, why didn't you save *me?*" I countered. "Mr. King was riding my bra strap all day!"

"Well, I hope the food is as good as everybody is claiming," said Charles. "That line is way too long for it not to be."

"The food is mad good," I said, rubbing my belly. "Especially the potato salad. Trust."

"Mm, can't wait," said Charles, licking his sexy lips.

I was glad Charles seemed to get over his "forgiveness" question. I wasn't in the mood for rehashing old wounds. At the moment, all I could see were sunbeams spreading throughout the garden, all I could smell were burgers, chicken, and ribs simmering on the grill, and all I could hear was soul music pumping out of a nearby speaker.

"Kate, let's get this party started right," Charles said, grabbing my hand and hauling me out of my chair.

A corny old-school jam song was now playing, and the next thing I knew, we were dancing to it. Charles pulled me close to him, spun me around a few times, and I couldn't stop laughing as he sang off tune, jacking up the words to the song.

A trio of women stopped what they were doing to watch us. I heard one of them say, "Aww, they're so adorable. I remember when I was that age."

I must admit, we *were* adorable, and it was so rare for Charles to show his silly side in front of other people. He had a lot of hard-core friends holding him back from playfulness, just like I did . . . before I met Felicia.

When the song was over, I was out of breath from being whirled around. Charles was busy grinning at me like a schoolboy.

We sat on a long green bench located in the cut. Plenty of space on the bench, but Charles chose to sit so close our legs made delicious contact. Then he touched my hair out of nowhere. "I like your braids."

I laughed at this. "Picture that. These raggedy braids are almost two weeks old!"

"Doesn't matter, I still like them," he said, touching my hair again. My braids reached the middle of my neck. The warmth from Charles's fingers brushing against my neck had me going bananas inside.

"Shoot, I wish I had your hair," I said. "Yours is so much longer than mine."

"And you're so much prettier than me," Charles replied, reaching out to pinch my cheeks.

"Boy, stop!" I said, playfully slapping his hand away.

"I can't help it if I love your chubby cheeks." Then Charles started playing with my braids again. "So who did your hair?" he asked.

"Me," I said proudly. I had mastered doing my own hair two months ago. Before being shipped off to Common Grounds, Lynn had taught me how to be self-sufficient and braid my own hair. Now I could rock cute cornrows without paying a soul. Considering the pitiful allowance the group home gave, this was a really good look.

"So can you hook me up?" asked Charles.

"Of course I can."

"How much you charging?"

"You don't have to pay me, silly."

"Wow," said Charles, shaking his head. "See what I mean about you?"

"What?" I asked.

"You're so sweet."

"Oh, stop," I said, but I wanted him to keep going. I love hearing good things about myself. "So when do you want your hair done?"

"Today?" asked Charles, smoothing down his lovely mane.

It didn't take me long to think about it. The fund-raiser was over at five. I could be in and out of the African Festival before six. I was in no rush to go home. Why should I rush home? I could already picture Charles sitting on the floor in front of me, his luscious arms resting on my lonely little legs.

"Today is good," I said. "Around six o'clock, no later than seven?"

"Cool," replied Charles. "Call me when you're about to come through."

"Okay, let me get your digits."

"How you gonna lose my number, Kate?"

"My bad," I said. "I'm unorganized." But between me and you, I didn't *lose* his number. When Felicia had passed me Charles's new number, I threw it straight in the trash. Hey, I didn't want to be tempted.

But now, don't ask me how, I was kinda open to Charles again, as my make-believe boyfriend: someone I could stare at for hours, drool over secretly, and get my rocks off from a simple touch, or a hug; hey, he was better than nothing. At least I knew not to take the boy seriously anymore. You can never be disappointed when you already know what's up. Basically, I just planned to keep Charles far away from my heart and enjoy him up close and personal.

Charles grabbed a pen from the table, jotted down his cell number on a pamphlet, and pushed it my way.

I threw the pamphlet in my pocket and said, "It shouldn't take me too long to get at you."

"I'll wait for you forever, girl," Charles replied, with a wink.

He joined the long line to get his food, came back fifteen minutes later with two paper plates wrapped in foil, and before walking out the gate, he blew an air kiss at me.

I playfully blew a kiss back, thinking how much I missed "us." I missed us back in the day, how we used to talk for hours sitting on random stoops; I missed us buggin' out on the basketball court shooting hoops, playing defense—my favorite part—when his sweet chocolate body constantly bumped against mine.

Although Charles and I would probably never work out as a couple, he made me feel so good inside—even as my friend. And who knew. . . . Maybe we would end up like Tisha and her new husband, Greg. They were friends since grade school, too. Had their ups and downs. Greg acting like a clown, Tisha constantly turning him down. It took them over twenty years to figure out they were meant for each other. First, a reconnection on Facebook. Now they're married and headed to Paris in August. Such a beautiful love story . . . .

The only sad part: Tisha was on leave and no longer my social worker. She said I could call her anytime, but why would I? This was the happiest time in her life, and the saddest time in mine. If I called Tisha, I knew all of my new group home problems would be spilled, no matter how hard I tried to keep them stuffed inside.

"Kate, I need you to help me finish breaking down boxes," said Mr. King, jolting me out of my thoughts. "Your little boyfriend just abandoned me."

Boyfriend. I wished . . . well, sometimes, I wished.

I begrudgingly helped with the boxes. Then I sat back outside at the table with a heavy plop. With Charles gone, I suddenly started feeling lonely. I looked all around me. Everybody eating, dancing, and merrily chitchatting with each other. Me? By myself. Stuck at the table and bored to death.

Didn't last for long, though. Here comes Mr. King again, forcing a bunch of pamphlets into my hands, nudging me outside the front gate. As crowded as it was, he still wanted more people inside. He was raising money for the homeless and he wanted the world to know it.

I stood out front, doing my thing. Passersby either snatched the pamphlets from me, ignored the pamphlets, or wanted to talk for hours about the pamphlets. Growing tired on my feet, I was relieved when I got down to my last pamphlet; I gladly gave it away and called it a day.

I went back inside the garden and found an empty chair near the front gate. My feet thanked me. Ahhh, what a freaking load off! I hoped Mr. King wouldn't spot me for a while. I needed some time to rest.

A few peaceful minutes passed. I closed my eyes. Then opened them. Instinctively, I glanced toward the front gate.

Then *boom*.

I was hit with my third shock of the day.

Percy. In the flesh. Headed my way. His electrical smile aimed dead at me.

My head was spinning from the sudden pull of two dudes. Percy? Charles? All in one day? Well, let me pop my collar, 'cause I didn't know I had it like *that*. I mean, Charles, I could understand. We had so much history. But Percy? I'm sorry. It just didn't seem possible that I could snag a super fine guy like him. No disrespect to me . . . I'm only keeping it real.

"Hey," Percy said, before grabbing a nearby chair.

"Hey," I replied, quite baffled.

"I'm on my lunch break so I can't stay long," Percy explained. "Just wanted to stop by and say sorry about earlier. . . . I shouldn't have put you on the spot like that."

"Oh . . . it's okay," I stuttered.

"Soon as you left, my mother jumped on my case like she always does. I didn't mean to make you feel uncomfortable."

"It's nothing," I said. "I did what I did back then . . . I can't deny that."

"Yeah, you were a wild child, for real!"

"It's embarrassing."

"But you shouldn't be embarrassed," said Percy. "Look at you now, volunteering . . . doing your thing."

I flashed an awkward smile.

"So what's your *real* name?"

"Kate."

"Pretty name."

"Thanks." I beamed.

Percy stared at me deeply with his clear light-brown eyes before saying, "This is my first time seeing you so up-close. Your skin is flawless. You look like a perfect ebony doll."

I looked down at the grass, blushing. Although Percy's words seemed like they were lifted straight from a romance novel, I was reading into it big-time, and loving every minute of it. The fact that Percy could appreciate my dark skin tone really made me feel good. I'm saying, turn on any commercial, movie, or music video, and you're never going to see a thick, dark-skinned girl like me being considered the object of beauty. Point-blank. Period.

Percy touched my hand. "So how can I make it up to you?"

I looked up into Percy's eyes, so beautiful and intense, burning straight through me. "Make what up?" I asked, in a daze.

"For putting you on blast," he explained, taking his hand away. "I feel really bad about that."

I was still so taken aback by Percy's magical appearance, I just didn't know what to say.

Percy tapped my leg, breaking me out of my trance. "Well, what are you doing later?"

"Oh, um, meeting my friend at the African Street Festival."

"Can I come with you?"

What? Could he come? My face lit up like a thousand suns. Of course he could come! Imagine me showing up at the festival with a hottie like Percy on my arm. No more pitiful third-wheeling. I'd be rolling with a serious dime by my side.

"If you want to," I said, hoping Percy couldn't hear the excitement bubbling in my stomach like gas.

"Cool," Percy began. "Let me get your math so we can coordinate."

"Oh, um, I don't have a cell phone."

Percy frowned. "Okay, I'll pick you up around four. Can you wait for me right here?"

"Yeah, I can wait," I said in my calmest tone. But oh man, I couldn't wait. I was too excited for words. The day couldn't move quickly enough. I wished I had a time machine so I could press fast-forward. Things were finally looking up for me, and it was about dang time.

When two o'clock rolled around, I was ready to strangle Mr. King. He was on my last nerve, asking me to do every freaking thing when he had other volunteers chilling like villains in front of his silly-looking face. I could no longer take him in my ear, yelling, "Kate, do this! Kate, do that!" True, I'm young. But I ain't dumb. I don't let *nobody* take advantage of me. And if it wasn't for Percy's promise to come get me at four o'clock, I would've *been* told Mr. King to buzz off. Volunteering is one thing. Slavery is another.

So when I spotted Mr. King scurrying toward me carrying a large empty trash bag, I said to myself, nope, not trying to be his garbage girl. I ducked him by pretending I had to use the bathroom. After that, I dipped and dodged the terrible tyrant until a quarter to four. When Mr. King zipped one way, I zipped the other. Maybe I was wrong for deserting my duty; maybe he was wrong for treating me like a greasy slave. Whatever the case, I was too busy thinking about my date with Percy to really care at this point.

I still couldn't believe I had a guy like Percy checking for me. Shoot, I wondered if he would even show up. But my fears were laid to rest when Percy appeared by the front gate at four o'clock on the dot. I hurried up to the gate and slipped out real slick before Mr. King could ask me for another freaking thing.

"Hey," said Percy.

"Hey," I said, slightly out of breath.

"You ready?"

"For sure." I grinned to myself. I couldn't wait for Felicia to feast her eyes on Percy.

"I'm parked across the street," said Percy, gently touching my back.

We walked halfway down the block, when suddenly a loud cherry bomb blew up. My whole body jerked in surprise. Percy laughed and put his arm around my shoulder. "Don't worry, I got you."

With his arm still around my shoulder, he led me to a sparkling fire-engine red Dodge Avenger sitting on twenty-two-inch dubs. Windows tinted silver, so you couldn't see inside. I climbed into the car, feeling like a grown woman. I was riding shotgun, like what?

Percy gunned the engine, then he pumped some booming beats and we sped down the block in stunner style. I wanted to roll down my window to show off, but Percy had the air conditioner blasting, so I couldn't. I wanted to sit back and enjoy the ride, but Percy was speeding like a madman, so I couldn't. Thank goodness we made it to the festival in one piece.

From outside of the tall silver gates, I could see red-and-white striped tents and swarms of people spread out all over a huge field.

"What you wanna do first?" asked Percy, grabbing my hand.

Since it was close to five o'clock, I pointed to the large stage across the field. As we snaked in and out of people I spotted Marlon and Felicia standing on the sidelines, hugged up as usual.

Felicia was so easy to spot with her tall, brown, slim self. She wore a short green and gold African-print tank dress, and gold-studded flip-flops. Her shoulder-length hair was pushed back into the usual ponytail. Marlon, also tall, brown, but not so slim, wore an African-print green and gold short set, his hair in a simple fade. They must've planned to look like twins. How cute of them.

"My friends are over there," I told Percy, trying to hide the excitement in my voice. "Felicia!" I yelled.

Felicia caught sight of me, broke out into a grin, and came running toward us. She took one look at me, then at Percy, and I could tell she was mad curious. Meanwhile, all I could think was: Finally, a foursome!

"You made it," Felicia exclaimed.

"Hey, Kate, thanks for coming," said Marlon, grinning wide, showing the gap between his front teeth. They both looked over at Percy, expecting me to make introductions. Oops, I forgot. I'm new at this, okay?

Percy introduced himself, and then gave Marlon the homeboy handshake.

"So, is the show starting soon?" I asked.

"They're having technical problems right now," said Marlon. "We just have to wait a bit."

So we stood around small talking. Percy's beautiful smile was on flash the whole time. He was so friendly, and I was impressed. I hoped Felicia was impressed, too.

But then our conversation started running out. The sun was relentlessly shining down on us. We all started complaining about the heat, and the technical difficulties. We didn't want to "stand by" much longer.

Finally, Marlon and Felicia were summoned by an announcer on-stage. Felicia turned to me in mock exasperation. "OMG, all of this hard work for my boo!"

"But he's worth it," I said, with a chuckle.

Felicia smiled. Then she snuck a glance at Percy, opened her eyes wide, and raised her eyebrows at me. This was her secret signal that she couldn't wait to get the full scoop on Percy. Shoot, I couldn't wait to tell her!

"Okay, girlie, be back in a minute," Felicia called over her back.

After Felicia and Marlon were out of sight, Percy turned to me and said, "Your friends are nice."

"True," I replied, but suddenly thought I should've said "thanks" instead. Your friends are a reflection of you. So he was actually giving me a compliment, too.

Ten minutes passed. Finally, three men in orange African costumes carried drums and chairs onstage to set things off. Then, *boom*, the trio started pounding the skin out of those drums. A group of small kids in similar orange African prints came running out doing flips and tricks all across the stage. The drummers were going hard. I turned to Percy, smiling. He was standing with his arms folded across his sexy chest, nodding his head to the beat. He saw me looking up at him, so he bent down to my ear and said, "This is really cool. I'm glad I came."

I looked up at him and smiled.

When the drumming died down, Marlon strutted onstage, carrying a huge wooden cane. He planted it on the stage and started spittin' poetry, contrasting Africa and the streets. "From glocks and hard knocks, I rise above it. Respect my homeland, Africa, I love it . . ." His flow was tight. I was surprised he could even spit like this, living in the ritzy part of Park Slope, and having absolutely no swagger. . . . But he treated my homegirl like gold and that's all that really mattered.

After Marlon's performance, we gathered back together again.

"My dude, you did really good," said Percy, patting Marlon on the back.

"That was *fire*," I joined in.

"See, Kate," Felicia exclaimed, "I'm so glad you finally got to see Marlon do his thing!" She squeezed my arm.

"No doubt," I said. "So what's next?"

"Three more performances," said Felicia.

"But do you still have to help backstage?" I asked.

"Yep, after this break, I have to go back."

"Oh, okay," I said, not hiding my dissatisfaction. Shoot, instead of her helping backstage, she needed to be hearing the backstory on Percy.

"But trust me, the next performances will be awesome," said Felicia. "Outstanding costumes, the works! And then later on, we can head to the after party in Clinton Hill." Felicia did a goofy dance, shaking her shoulders, trying to drop it like it's hot. We all busted out laughing at her. She could be mad silly at times. That's why I love her so much.

In the middle of us cracking up, Percy grabbed my hand, gave the tip of my fingers a quick squeeze, bent down to my ear, and whispered, "I'm sorry, but the sun is really getting to me . . . I don't feel up to standing in one spot to watch another show. I'd rather walk around."

I was disappointed, but not about to complain. Percy was the one who had brought me here, and I wanted things to jump off on the good foot. Our potential relationship was like a pair of fresh white sneakers—not to be stepped on.

"So, are you guys staying for the show?" asked Felicia, staring at me expectantly with her big brown eyes.

"Percy wants to walk around," I said.

"Oh . . . okay," said Felicia, looking disappointed.

Marlon was the first to hug me good-bye, followed by Felicia.

Percy waved good-bye to them.

Just as we were about to walk away, Felicia came running back up to me. "I forgot to tell you, my parents planned a last-minute trip to Martha's Vineyard. We're leaving tomorrow morning. I won't be back till Friday."

"Oh," I said, feeling even more let down. Now I'd have to wait a whole freaking week to express my excitement over Percy. I was really looking forward to hearing Felicia's thoughts on him, too. Oh well.

"But I'll call you first thing on Saturday," Felicia exclaimed. "I promise."

"Okay, cool," I said, hoping I'd be able to use the phone in peace that day.

After Felicia ran to catch up with Marlon, Percy turned to me. "You ready to see the sights?"

"For sure," I said, brightening up a bit.

He grabbed my hand and we walked straight into the crowd. The festival was alive and popping. People, people everywhere, selling colorful African jewelry, beautiful artwork, hot wings and hot dogs, candles and candies—everything you could imagine was in sight. I quickly got over my disappointment about not having a foursome. I was having so much fun with Percy, a romantic twosome. He held my hand firm the whole time, like he was claiming me to be his. I felt so proud to be with him. Shoot, I noticed a few girls openly drooling over him. I couldn't blame them. I was drooling, too.

Percy stopped short in front of a tent full of aromatic candles and bath products. "Want something from here?"

I looked around and shrugged. Stuff looked expensive.

"Pick anything you want," he said, noticing my hesitation.

Word? Just throw it in the bag?

I wasn't used to being treated to gifts. Most I ever got from a guy was a Twinkie. So what should I choose? Bringing candles into the group home would be a no-no. I could see crazy Tracy setting fire to my bed. And taking a bubble bath in our dingy tub would be impossible. I could hear Makeba knocking on the door every two seconds just to spite me. Finally, I chose a bottle of coconut lemongrass body lotion. Smelled fabulous!

"That's all you want?"

"Yes, thanks," I said, thinking it's better to be grateful than greedy.

Percy shrugged, bought the fifteen-dollar lotion, and handed me the small lavender gift bag it came in.

After another half hour of aimless walking, and not much talking, Percy said, "I just thought of something else we can do."

"Okay," I said, ready for the next chapter.

Percy locked hands with mine and led me to his car.

Chapter 8

The sun was still shining high in the sky when Percy cruised into a neighborhood called DUMBO. I had never heard of the place, so I felt like a dumbo. How could I be reppin' Brooklyn all day without knowing *all* its parts? I foolishly shared my ignorance with Percy.

"You never heard of *DUMBO?*" he repeated with raised eyebrows.

"No, I haven't."

"You don't get out much, do you?"

"No, not really," I replied with a shrug, trying to appear nonchalant instead of naïve.

"Well . . . we'll have to change all that." Percy smiled at me.

"So where are we going now?" I ventured to ask.

"You'll see," replied Percy mysteriously.

After a half hour of driving around, Percy finally pulled into a parking spot close to the Brooklyn Bridge's huge caissons. He walked around to let me out of the car like a perfect gentleman. Then he grabbed my hand like he was my man. Hmm, I could get used to this, I told myself, and then I wanted to pinch myself to make sure I wasn't dreaming.

As we walked over cobblestone streets, and passed rich houses and restaurants, Percy kept quiet. I wished he would talk to me some more. I wanted to know more about him without me having to give away all my business first. For instance, back in the car, Percy had asked me how old I am. I told him straight out. But when I asked him, he chuckled, and said, "Older than you." I didn't let the mystery of his age bother me that much though. We weren't in too deep . . . just yet.

As we passed by a pier, a wedding photo shoot was taking place. "Wow, she's so pretty," I blurted, at the sight of the beautiful bride decked in a flowing white lacy dress.

Percy finally opened his mouth again and said, "I can see you in that dress, one day. I know you'll make a gorgeous bride."

Awww.

In a flash, I pictured Percy as my handsome groom, Felicia as my maid of honor, Ted walking me down the aisle . . . okay, let me stop.

"You're a really pretty girl," said Percy, staring down at me. "You know that, right?"

"Thanks," I said, beaming.

Feeling giddy by Percy's words and this totally surreal day, I practically floated down the block. But when Percy halted in front of a tan six-story apartment building, I descended back down to the pavement.

"Hey, are you okay?" he asked.

"Yeah, I'm good," I lied. I didn't know where Percy was taking me, didn't know what he was expecting. If he thought he was getting sex *this* quick, he thought dead wrong. A girl has to take her time when it comes to the bump and grind. Rushing things be busting things, feel me?

I could only comfort myself with the fact that I knew Percy's mother. And Felicia knew who I was with right now. Percy couldn't be *that* bold to do anything crazy to me. Besides, up until now, he had been nothing but a gentleman.

I followed Percy inside the crystal-clean building, and we rode the elevator up to the sixth floor in silence. He pulled out a ring of keys and walked up to the first door on the right. "My dad's spot," he finally explained. "He's away for the summer."

We stepped inside the apartment and my bottom lip hit the floor. The place was baaaddd. Plush shaggy beige carpet covered the living room floor, a glass entertainment center sparkled like a jewel, a giant flat-screen television took up a whole living room wall, and floor-to-ceiling windows provided a dazzling view of the ocean. Like I said, the place was baaaddd.

Percy motioned for me to sit on the butter-soft beige leather couch, and he plopped down beside me. I was still looking around the room with my mouth wide open. All I could say was, "Wow, this is tight."

"Thanks," Percy replied. "When I need to get away from my mom, I come here . . . cool getaway, right?"

I nodded, in awe.

"See, if it was up to my mother, my dad wouldn't have all this. He does a lot of traveling as a business consultant, and he makes mad money doing it. My mom didn't want him out of her sight when they were married, so of course they got divorced. Now she's trying to pull the same mess with me. But I'm nineteen years old. A grown damn man. I go where I please, when I please."

Awkward.

This sudden outpouring of info was the most Percy had shared with me the whole day, and I didn't know how to respond. But at least I knew his age now. A bit too old for me. But then again, we weren't sexing or anything, just getting to know each other. No harm in that.

"My mother won't even give my dad his last name back," Percy continued, as if talking to himself. "She doesn't *deserve* his last name."

He looked so frustrated. Luckily, he soon changed the subject. "You hungry?"

I nodded.

"Okay, I'll order pizza . . . you like buffalo wings too?"

"My favorite," I said.

"Then I got you!" Percy laughed.

He jumped up from the couch, ordered our food, and then slid back beside me. He threw his arm around my shoulder and clicked on the television.

"What you wanna watch?"

"Oh, I think there's a Street Ball marathon on," I said eagerly.

"Nah, I'm not in the mood to watch basketball," said Percy as he clicked through the stations and landed on the nature channel.

So why ask me what I want to watch then? I wondered. And oh my gosh: Who the heck wants to see a deer get torn to pieces right before a meal?

"Um . . . I might lose my appetite watching this," I said coyly, hoping Percy wouldn't be offended. I wasn't used to being in a date-like situation with a new guy. Charles was my one and only boy-friend (if you could call him that) and we were free and easy with one another most of the time. I told Charles what I wanted straight up, and he did the same for me.

I didn't have that same vibe with Percy; then again, we were still brand-new.

Fortunately, Percy wasn't offended at all. He clicked off the TV, turned to me, and stared into my eyes. All I could do was stare back. Then he lifted my chin to raise my face with his pointer finger, and lightly touched the space between my right eyelid and eyebrow. *Oh brother, my scar.*

"How'd you get that?" he asked, frowning.

I really don't like bringing up my gangster past. But since Percy had already witnessed a part of it, I figured I might as well tell him the end of it. "Remember the gang I used to run with?"

"How could I forget?" Percy snorted.

"Well, when I got jumped out of the gang . . . Icy cut me."

"Oh man, that's terrible," he replied with knitted eyebrows.

"But I'm good," I said. "Other girls don't get to leave so easy."

"I always knew you didn't belong with those girls," said Percy. "And I always hoped you'd get out."

Percy's comment really touched me. Right then and there, I felt genuine concern for my well-being exuding from his pores. I can't even explain it . . . I felt such a powerful connection between us, like there was a magnetic force drawing us closer and closer together.

"And I promise you this," Percy continued, lightly tracing his finger over my scar. "I would *never* hurt you."

With these words, I suddenly thought back to how I had literally hurt him back in the day. Choked by guilt, I paused, and then spoke. "Well . . . I'm sorry for kicking you . . . you know where."

Percy chuckled. "Baby, you don't have to apologize to me. That was *years* ago. I'm fully healed. See?"

He grabbed my hand and acted like he was guiding me "there," but then he quickly switched it up (thank goodness) and guided my hand to his chest. "Can you feel my heart?" he asked. I nodded as I felt his heartbeat pounding rapidly through his shirt. "See? My heart's not broken. I'm good." He laughed at his own joke. I giggled, relieved that he didn't try to make me touch his stuff, and that he had accepted my apology so easily.

As nice as Percy was treating me, I couldn't help but feel bad, thinking back to how I had treated him and his mother. Even his arrogant mother didn't deserve the terror I used to set off in her store. Shoot, if Mrs. Thomas could give birth to a fine specimen like Percy, she couldn't be all *that* bad.

After a moment of silence, Percy's gaze flickered over my face, then my breasts, then my whole body. He started rubbing my neck, blowing his warm breath in my ear, turning me on like hot popcorn. I quickly relaxed under his spell. He slipped his tongue inside my mouth and kissed me so hard and passionately, like he was hungry for me, starving. His tongue was so delicious, so skilled, like a grown experienced man getting it *in*. Percy took complete control of my mouth.

"Mm, sweetheart," he moaned. "You feel so good."

Percy gently laid me down on the couch, and I sank into the leather. My body dissolved underneath him.

He hiked up my shirt, but the buzzer stopped him cold flat.

Pizza delivery saved me from some serious temptation.

When we finished eating, Percy tried me again. Kissing me all over, and feeling me up. This time, he went for my panties. "No," I said, and pushed his hand away.

Surprisingly, I only had to say it once.

"Okay, I can respect that," said Percy. He got up from on top of me and went into the bathroom. I fixed my clothes and thanked goodness he understood. A lot of guys think you being in the crib gives them the green light to get it. I felt so much admiration for Percy because he had actually respected my wishes without burying me in guilt. Now I was digging him more than before, if that was even possible.

We watched television for an hour, hugged up like a cute little couple. Then Percy turned to me and asked, "Are you having a good time?"

"For sure," I said. Shucks, I was cuddled next to a fine dude, far away from my group home. My guard was down and my spirits were up. Life was good.

Percy chuckled. "You said 'for sure' like a valley girl. It's supposed to be 'fo' sho.'" Are you sure you from Brooklyn? I'm saying, with a name like Kate, who you trying to fool?"

Ha, ha, very funny. People always got jokes about my plain-Jane name; but I've come to love my name, plain, and simple, because it's *mine.*

Oh, and by the way, wasn't Percy the one telling me how *pretty* my name was earlier? Now all of a sudden he was clowning on me?

I'd been trying to act extra mature around Percy, so I'd been holding back my playful side. But cracking back was long overdue. He had jokes? Shoot, I had jokes too. "Well, I never heard of a dude from *my* hood, or this *century*, named Percy!"

Percy's face grew serious. "I was named after my father. Please don't disrespect my father's name."

"Oh, sorry," I said.

Awkward.

Percy sat in silence for a couple of minutes. I felt like I wasn't sitting next to him. Like he was light years away. Finally, Percy came back down to earth and said, "I have a surprise for you. Let's go."

He jumped up from the couch, grabbed my hand, his keys, and we left the apartment. We headed down the brightly lit hallway and entered a dark stairwell. He led me up one flight of stairs, pushed open a heavy metal door, and boom, we were on the rooftop. There was a group of white people already up there, standing around talking with drinks in their hands. A few Asians, too. This was my first time being in an apartment building shared by other races. I felt worlds away from what I was used to. Percy didn't seem to know anyone, so he took me to a spot in the cut, away from everybody else. He guided me to the roof's ledge and stood behind me, hugging me. His arms felt so good wrapped tightly around me. I felt so wanted, so *needed.*

We had a clear view of the East River. Stars were sparkling in the sky. This was such a magical moment for me.

I didn't figure out that we were waiting for Macy's fireworks until the first burst of red, white, and blue pyrotechnics lit up the sky. "Wow," I exclaimed. "I've never seen fireworks up this close!" I looked up in awe at the breathtaking explosives crackling and popping over the ocean.

"See, baby, I can show you a whole lot if you let me," said Percy, hugging me. His hug was like a vise grip, so tight and intense, like he never wanted to let me go.

We watched the fireworks, hugging and kissing at intervals. Dazzling rainbows of light lit up the sky and my spirits, making me feel so alive inside. I had never experienced anything close to this magical moment.

This was a night wrapped in romance, Percy's lips so soft, gentle, and warm on my neck. I was overwhelmed. I didn't want the bliss to end.

But then I glanced at my watch. Ten o'clock curfew was looming over my head. Even though my group home was mad lax, I didn't want to take advantage of that. I turned to Percy and said, "Um, I have to go."

He looked disappointed. "Why?"

"I have to be back by ten," I said, and left it at that. I wasn't looking forward to explaining my foster care status.

"Where do you live?" asked Percy.

"Gravesend."

"Sounds depressing."

"Yeah, and you don't know the half," I blurted. That was all I planned to say.

"Well, let me clean up first; then I'll take you home."

I helped Percy clean up our earlier food mess, and then he grabbed the keys to the Avenger. While sitting in his car, I was busy thinking of an excuse for Percy to drop me off without seeing where I lived. I wasn't ready to let him fully inside my complicated life. The only guy I'd ever felt comfortable with knowing my personal business was Charles, because Charles had shared his own personal family drama with me many times before. . . . And speaking of Charles, oops; I had left my boy hanging!

As soon as I climbed into Percy's car, I turned to him and asked, "Can I use your phone for a quick second?"

"Sure," said Percy. He was about to hand me his BlackBerry, but when I whipped out the pamphlet from my pocket and started searching for Charles's scrawled number, Percy held on to his phone. He looked at me curiously. "I thought you were calling home." He jutted his chin toward the pamphlet. "You don't remember your own phone number?"

"No, I need to call my homeboy . . . I was supposed to braid his hair today."

Percy chuckled. "Oh, so you trying to call the *next* man on my phone? You got a lot of heart, shawty."

"He's just my homeboy," I repeated, not sure if Percy was kidding or not.

"Yeah, that's what they *all* say," said Percy, his head thrown back, laughter booming at his own joke. I still couldn't tell if Percy was seriously doubting my word, because he was laughing the whole time. But when the joke was over, and the laughter died down, he still didn't offer his phone. Maybe he forgot, I reasoned. So I just left it alone. Hopefully, Charles would understand.

Chapter **9**

T he closer we got to the group home, the more anxious I became.

"Can you drop me off at the corner of my block?" I suddenly thought to ask.

"But I want to see you safe inside," Percy protested.

"You can't," I said, shifting uncomfortably in my seat.

"Why?" he asked, with knitted eyebrows.

"Because."

"Because, why?"

It was dim inside the car, but I sensed confusion written all over Percy's face.

"What's wrong?" he asked, with concern in his voice.

Well, I wasn't about to lie about strict parents just to get him off my case. So boom. I caved in. Spilled my foster care story as if he had forced truth serum down my throat. Even sadder, I didn't stop there. I gushed about all my problems at the group home. My enemies, the dirty house, no privacy, no peace. When I finished blubbering, Percy reached for my hand and held it for a long time. "Sweetheart, nobody should have to go through all that," he said, wearing a sad expression.

I loved the way he called me "sweetheart," and I really appreciated his concern. I just stared at him with hope in my eyes, holding back my tears.

Percy finally let go of my hand and said, "So if the crib is strict like that, how can I stay in touch with you?"

I shrugged, dunno.

He leaned back in his seat, and said, "I'll figure something out." Then he reached for my hand again and rubbed it caringly.

I glanced at my watch. "I really have to go," I said, reluctantly.

"Well, when can I see you again?"

I wanted to ask if he was free tomorrow, but no, that would be too thirsty. "Is Wednesday good for you?"

"Wednesday is perfect," said Percy. "That's usually my day off."

"Where should we meet?"

"Give me a second to think." Percy caressed my arm with his warm, strong hands.

We sat in silent mode for five minutes straight. I know, because I kept peeking at my watch, feeling antsy about being late for curfew.

"Okay, I just thought of the perfect day for us," Percy exclaimed. "Do you know where the Atlantic Avenue Terminal is?"

"Yep."

"Can you meet me at the Starbucks inside the terminal at eleven AM?"

"Sure."

"Cool, then it's on," said Percy. "I'm going to show you a good time." He squeezed my hand tightly.

"Okay," I said, excited as ever. I had a second date with the man of my dreams. It couldn't get any better than this.

"All right, you better go now," said Percy. "Don't want you getting in trouble."

"True," I said, grabbing my gift bag from the backseat.

At the corner of my block, I jumped out of Percy's car, and waved good-bye, thinking he would peel off down the street. But Percy slowed his car to a crawl and tailed me to the group home's front door. At first, I felt apprehension, but the feeling quickly dissolved into appreciation. Percy cared. He really cared.

I swung open the front door, looked back at him and waved. Percy beeped twice, and the Avenger roared down the block.

Wow, the perfect gentleman, I marveled.

I walked—no, floated—into the house. I was hanging on cloud nine with Percy heavy on my mind. But as soon as I signed myself in, and went upstairs to my bedroom, I crashed right back down to earth.

Chapter 10

Oh. No. She. Didn't.

I stood frozen in my bedroom's doorway, staring at a disturbing sight: A new girl was sitting cozy on *my* bed with her back leaned up against *my* wall. She was a tall girl. Even sitting down, I could tell she had some height to her. She wore a tight yellow tank top and a light-blue mini jean skirt that barely covered her thighs. A smattering of red pimples covered her tan skin, and honey-brown hair flowed down her back. Her turquoise and pink Pastry sneakers hung over my bed, almost touching my doggone sheets. Pretty girl. But pretty bold. Her silly butt stretched all up in my spot, for what?

I glanced over at Tracy, who was sitting on her own bed, paying my presence no mind. Then I peeped a random twin bed squeezed into the far corner of our bedroom. I wondered why New Girl couldn't park her behind *there*, where it belonged. But then I quickly told myself: Kate, calm down, get a grip. I had no reason to trip. Technically, my bed was not *my* bed. Nothing is really your own in foster care. I been in this game long enough to know how it goes down: We run out of room. We get moved around and squeezed together like a can of freaking sardines. Tracy was already a problem. Now I simply had another one.

New Girl stared at me waiting for me to say something. But my tongue was stuck to the roof of my mouth.

"Kate, you can come in now," she finally said in a hoarse voice.

I hesitated.

"I don't bite," she added, wearing a smirk.

Since she knew me by name, I could already imagine what mess Tracy and crew been spittin' about me. Shoot, I was surprised New Girl even bothered to greet me in the first place.

"Hey," I said, awkwardly stepping inside the bedroom.

"I'm Jeselle," she offered, finally jumping up from my bed.

Tracy didn't say a word to me. At least she was keeping it real.

"Night staff is out like a light," said Jeselle. "We about to go out on the back porch and get twisted. You coming?"

Tracy sucked her teeth, swung her burgundy weave, and leaped from her bed. "I'mma be outside," she squeaked to Jeselle and bounced out the room.

"A'ight, ma," said Jeselle. Then she turned to me and asked, "So what you did for the Fourth? You got a man?" She jutted her chin toward my gift bag.

"I volunteered for a community garden," I said, wanting to add, "but I *might* have a man soon."

"Volunteering on a holiday?" Jeselle jerked her head back. "The hell made you do *that*?"

"My homegirl gave me the idea."

"Shoot, couldn't be me working for free . . . but good for you." Jeselle knitted her eyebrows and started shaking her head. "I didn't get to do anything today. Too busy getting kicked out my momma's house and moving here. My voice is mad froggy from yelling at her. She act so freakin' stupid sometimes . . . hitting me for no damn reason. She didn't think I'd hit her back this time. Well, she thought dead wrong."

I wasn't shocked by Jeselle's random confession; in foster care, you get used to the same sad stories volunteered out of nowhere.

Some girls don't care who they tell their stories to; they just want to get it out of their system, out into the open.

But since I didn't know Jeselle like that, I kept my mouth closed.

Jeselle unzipped the large black tote bag sitting beside her. "See, that's why I'm 'bout to sip me some Henny and get real relaxed. You coming?"

"Nah," I said, quickly leaving out the part about me being public enemy number one at the group home. I also left out the part that I don't drink anymore; somehow it always sounds like I'm trying to be high-and-mighty when it ain't even like that. It's like this: I get stupid when I drink, and I don't find vomiting and hangovers enjoyable, so I don't care what people think. I don't drink. Period.

But Jeselle seemed anxious to include me. "Aw see, I'm trying to toast to my new roomies." She jumped up and started singing, "Party, party, party, let's all get wasted!" Then she plopped back down on the bed, smiling at me, waiting for me to give in.

I wasn't about to. Instead, I decided to share a snippet of my situation. "Real talk, I don't get along with nobody up in here, so I'm not trying to get in where I *don't* fit in. Feel me?"

"Girl, don't let these crazy chicks intimidate you," said Jeselle, waving her hand in the air. She unearthed a big bottle of Hennessy from her bag. "Are you really gonna let them make you miss out on the good stuff, ma?" She put the bottle to her lips and pretended to sip. "Mm, mm, good!"

I cracked a smile, and then quickly grew serious. "Nah, I'm just not in the mood for nobody's bull right now."

"Now *that's* some bull," Jeselle teased.

"Nah, for real," I countered. "I already know what time it is. In my old group homes, I barely gave new girls a chance, either . . . now I'm getting it all back. . . . Karma ain't no joke."

Jeselle chuckled. "Yeah, I been in plenty group homes, too . . . used to boss them broads around like they was on my payroll. Girl, pimping wasn't easy!" She fanned her face and pretended to wipe invisible sweat from her forehead. I busted out laughing over her dramatics. Jeselle joined in at the sight of me cracking up.

Once our laughter died down, I thought, *Wow*, I don't even make friends this easy. In less than ten minutes, Jeselle had managed to defrost the icy wall I usually put up with new girls. Don't get me wrong: We weren't official homegirls yet, but there was something about her, something so real and upfront about her. I was impressed and cautious at the same time . . . you never know what folks are really up to. Only time would tell.

"Karma can't catch me here," said Jeselle, out of the blue.

"Yeah, I can see that," I replied. "You got Tracy on your team mad quick."

"Please, girl, Tracy and her goons knew they couldn't start none with me. I don't play that. Soon as I walked through the door they already knew. But they was talking mad smack about you, especially Tracy. I told them chicks straight to their face: I'm not trying to pick sides. I'm just here to do my time with no drama. I got enough drama at home."

"I feel you."

Jeselle held up her pointer finger and added, "If I don't work things out with my mother, then I only got one more year in the system. When I turn eighteen, I'm out of here . . . but hopefully, my mother will take me back."

"Why would you go back?" I wanted to ask. A mother physically fighting with her daughter is not a good look. But minding my own business, I simply said, "Five more years for me . . . and I don't have any family to go back to."

"Wow, that's tough," said Jeselle, as she dug in her bag again and unearthed a stack of plastic cups, followed by an empty orange knapsack. She stuffed the Henny bottle and the cups inside of the sack, hopped up from her bed, and headed toward the door. Before leaving, she stood at the doorway and said, "If you change your mind, come outside and get twisted with us."

"Okay," I replied. But *yeah right*, no, I wasn't.

I was already drunk with thoughts of Percy. He was still heavy on my mind. Had me floating on cloud nine. All I wanted to do was repeat the details of our romantic night in my head and then hit Replay all the way until the next day. Percy was so remarkably fine *and* kind. He made my night . . . maybe one day, my whole life.

Man, I was so hot for him. I needed to cool myself off with a shower. But no showers were allowed past ten. So I washed up real quick, threw on the pretty pink cotton nightgown Lynn bought me, climbed into bed, and pulled the sheets up to my neck. I drifted to sleep dreaming of Percy. I couldn't wait to see him again.

On Wednesday, at eleven o'clock on the dot, I stepped inside of Starbucks, anxious and excited. Percy was already sitting at a table near the window, caught up in his BlackBerry. He didn't see me. So I decided to try my hand at flirting, since I was so brand-new at it. I snuck up behind him, and wrapped my arms around his neck. Bold of me, but hey, I wanted to step my girly game up.

Caught by surprise, Percy swiveled around in his chair, looked up at me, and his face broke out into a smile. He stuffed the BlackBerry in his back pocket. "Hey, baby," he said, then brushed my cheek with his soft lips, grabbed my hand, and we headed for the number 3 train. I walked tall with my handsome hottie by my side, proud as I could be.

While standing on the sweltering station's platform, Percy turned to me and said, "Sorry I couldn't pick you up in style, but parking in Manhattan is a pain, especially on a weekday."

"Oh, I don't mind," I replied, really meaning it. Shoot, I was just happy to be out and about with Percy, grateful that he was actually willing to rock me out in the streets. Most guys don't try to date you, they're too busy trying to *do* you; from day one, their main agenda is to get you to the crib and get the skins.

Percy was racking up so many points with me. And when we boarded the number 3 train, he racked up even more by asking, "So tell me, Kate, what's your favorite thing to do?"

Wow, what a guy, I thought. Percy was showing so much interest in getting to know me. Such a rare situation. My goodness! How could I not be impressed?

"Well, let's see. . . . I love basketball," I began, "and writing, and reading, and bugging out with my best friend, Felicia—"

"Whoa now," exclaimed Percy, in between chuckles. "I only asked for *one* thing."

I smiled, and thought to ask him the same question. It can't be all about me all the time.

Percy put his finger to his chin as if in deep thought and said, "Well, my favorite thing to do is . . . being with you."

"Aw," I said, beaming, "that was cute."

We got off the train at Chambers Street, and then waited for the number 1 to South Ferry. When the train finally came, Percy and I got on board, grinning up in each other's face. We continued grinning all the way until South Ferry, the last stop. Holding hands, we walked up what felt like a hundred flights of stairs, and made it out into the open air. The sun was shining, the weather was warm— what more could a girl ask for?

We walked toward a huge terminal where a bunch of people were flowing out.

"I hope there's not a long line," said Percy. "Don't want us to miss the next boat."

"Boat?" My eyes lit up. I hadn't even bothered to think about where Percy was taking me. I was just so happy to be with him. But now I was ecstatic. We were about to ride a boat! See the city sights! This was the kind of touristy thing Felicia and I used to do all the time—before Marlon came along.

We stepped inside the terminal. The line was perfectly short.

Five minutes later, we boarded a big white boat. Percy guided me to the railing, and stood behind me, holding my waist, as we sailed away from the pier.

"Ever heard of Governors Island?" he asked.

"Nope."

"It used to be a Coast Guard military base. Now it's like a public park."

"Wow," I said, feeling amped and giddy. I always wanted to do a date in the park. Now I was finally getting my chance.

"I was supposed to join the Marines last year," Percy suddenly volunteered. "But my mother needed help with the store." His face clouded over.

Oh no, here we go. His mother, again.

I always felt so torn when people complained about their parents. A part of me wanted to cuss them out for complaining, thinking at least they weren't discarded at birth the way my drug-addicted parents did me. The other part of me knew the sad truth: not every parent is meant to be. And sometimes you're better off *not* knowing who you come from. Blood ain't always thicker than water. Shoot, I'd take Ted, Lynn, Felicia, Tisha as my family any day; immerse myself in their *real* love instead of crying over fake blood.

In any case, who was I to judge? If Percy had to vent, let him vent. You never know what someone is going through until you're actually walking in their shoes. Percy looked so sad right now. It was amazing how the mere mention of his mother affected his mood so easily.

In an attempt to comfort him, I gently touched his arm, looked up into his beautiful light brown eyes, and said, "But if you had joined the Marines, I probably would have never had the chance to see you again."

A smile crept over Percy's lips. Instead of responding, he just gave me a hug, a big warm hug, and it felt so good. I loved how affectionate he was toward me. Percy didn't know how much I needed his affection right now. And I wasn't about to tell him. I was learning to keep some things to myself. Sometimes, boys use your confessions against you when thing go wrong. Percy didn't seem like the type to go sour on me, sweet as he was . . . but hey, you never know.

"Can you ride a bike?" asked Percy.

"Yeah . . . but I never owned one."

"Well, guess what we're about to do."

"Ride bikes?" I exclaimed. "Oh, that's what's up! I haven't ridden a bike in a minute." I was feeling so excited and antsy, like a five-year-old child.

As soon as we got off the boat, Percy made a beeline for a parking lot filled with a bunch of shiny blue and gold bikes. I was about to pick my own, but Percy said no, and pointed to a two-seater bike with a canopy on top. Oh, how cute.

"We can ride together," he explained. "I want you sitting right next to me." He winked at me. Like a shy doofus, I glanced downward, feeling all coy and girly. I swear, I wasn't used to this.

Percy paid for our two-seater, and off we went! The island was so picturesque; even with its abandoned brick buildings and occasional rocky pavement, there were so many hilly green lawns to admire throughout, so much history to learn about. We circled the whole perimeter of the island, taking our sweet time, talking, laughing, and pedaling away.

When we returned the bikes, our stomachs were audibly growling. We cracked up laughing, and started searching for food. Found a Jamaican lady selling good-smelling grub from her truck, which was parked on the grass.

Percy bought us a huge plate of rice, beans, baked chicken, and fried plantains. I couldn't wait to dig in. We went hunting for a spot to eat. Found a perfect picnic table under a perfect tree. Instead of sitting opposite me, Percy squeezed in right beside me, making sure our legs touched. He reminded me of Charles when he did that. But that's where the comparison ended. Percy was a perfect gentleman; Charles, a perfect player.

Percy handed me my fork, and we ate our food from the same plate. Such a romantic situation. I was self-conscious about my eating, though. Didn't want to be talking with my mouth full. Couldn't have any food stuck between my teeth. Everything Percy did was smooth and refined. I wanted to impress him, show him I had some class, too.

After lunch, we walked around the entire island. We stopped at a colonial house that had been turned into a museum, and admired all of the colorful artwork inside. Once outside, we sat down on a random bench, and Percy grabbed both of my hands and held them for a long time. "I'm having such a good time with you."

"Same here," I replied, staring into his magnetic light-brown eyes.

When it was time to leave, I didn't want to go. I wanted the boat to leave us behind, so we could be left alone on this beautiful island. This was the best day I had ever experienced in my whole entire life. And that's real talk.

"Thanks for taking me here," I said.

"Thanks for appreciating it."

Once on the boat, we stood in the same position as before, me leaning against the rails, Percy standing behind me, holding me close. I dissolved into his arms.

And when we rode the number 1 train, same idea, different position. His strong arms around my shoulders as I leaned up against his sexy chest.

When we were about to part ways, Percy asked, "Are you sure I can't call you at the group home?"

"Yeah, I'm sure."

It wasn't the staff or the bogus rules I was worried about. It was Makeba and her motley crew who would be blocking me from my potential boo.

Percy touched my shoulder and massaged it while saying, "But I need to stay in touch with you, sweetheart."

"I know," I replied, "I really wish things were different."

Percy paused in deep thought, heaved a big sigh, and then said, "Listen, stop by the store tomorrow at six o'clock. Wait for me across the street because I don't want my mom in my business. Can you do that for me?"

"Yes, I can," I said, feeling alive inside. Percy was really gunning to see me again. And the feeling was so mutual.

Percy leaned in and gave me a soft sensuous kiss on my awaiting lips. "I'm looking forward to next time."

"Me, too."

He grinned at me and said, "Yeah, I can see myself with you for a long, long time."

I timidly looked down at the sidewalk, stunned by the intensity Percy radiated inside my soul. He bent down to kiss me again. His kiss lingered on my lips all night long.

Chapter 12

As I waited for Percy across the street from his store, the powerful July sun beat down on me. I was hot as blazes, sweating through my t-shirt, feeling smothered by the humidity in the air.

I was a half hour early because I didn't want to be late, but I couldn't take the choking temperature much longer. I impatiently eyed the Fulton Street Market, wanting to run inside to escape the heat, but not while his batty mother was in the building.

Thankfully, at six o'clock on the dot, Percy emerged from the store. He was wearing a fresh white button-down short-sleeved shirt, beige linen shorts, and tan grown-man sandals. I didn't dig the sandals, but he looked really nice otherwise. Meanwhile, I was rocking a plain white T-shirt, baggy blue shorts, and my dollar-store flip-flops. Oh well.

Percy came across the street to greet me. He smiled slightly, hugged me tightly, and led me around the corner, away from his mother's line of sight.

Dead in the middle of the block, he stopped short, and started tonguing me down, taking me way off guard. He had given me no chance to even pop a mint! I hoped my breath wasn't kicking.

Guessed my breath was acceptable because Percy moved me up against the brick wall of an apartment building, and started getting at me again. Percy and I were acting out a love scene on the sidewalk. I melted into his strong arms, feeling so wanted, so needed, so happy to be with him. I was starving for his affection. A whole year of no hugs and kisses had me feeling deprived.

Now I was completely revived.

Percy finally released my waist and said, "I missed you."

I smiled at him, shyly. I didn't want to say "Missed you, too." This sounded too sappy for me. I needed some time getting used to this lovey-dovey stuff. Everything was happening so fast. But can I tell you? I was loving every minute of it.

Percy grabbed my hand and steered me farther down the block to his car. Once inside the Avenger, Percy pumped the air conditioner. The cold air felt so good blowing on my skin.

Percy turned to me and said, "I was hoping you'd wear something sexy. I wanted to take you out somewhere really nice today."

"Then why not let a girl know?" I *wanted* to say. But instead, I simply said, "Oh, I'm sorry."

Shucks, the concept of getting all dressed up to go on a date was straight-up foreign to me. Besides, I didn't think I needed to dress up. Percy was feeling me the last time he saw me in my simple-as-can-be outfit, so I assumed he'd be feeling me in a similar getup. My bad.

Percy was still looking disappointed when he said, "Anyway, I have something for you." He leaned over to open the glove compartment, and pulled out a shiny pink BlackBerry Pearl.

My eyes lit up like Christmas. "For me?" I asked, surprised out of my mind. "Are you sure?"

"It's nothing, sweetheart," said Percy, placing the phone in my hand. "My ex-girl's phone. All I had to do was turn it back on. She didn't appreciate it . . . but I know you will."

"Wow, thanks," I said, smiling so hard my cheeks hurt. I didn't think I'd own a celly till I turned eighteen. Percy was going hard for your girl, Kate!

Even though I'd already been warned that it's not good to accept early gifts from guys, I wasn't trying to give this phone back for nothing in the world. Call me stupid, call me crazy, but at least you could *call* me on my own phone for a change!

"Anytime you need me, I'm just a phone call away," said Percy. *Holla!*

I happily toyed with the buttons of my new phone; it felt like gold in my hands. I couldn't wait to call Felicia with it. Now I would be able to talk to my homegirl outside of the group home without having some silly chicks breathing down my back. Shoot, I could dial my girl's number till my fingers turned black and blue.

"There's no data plan on the phone yet," Percy explained, "but if you behave, I'll add it for you later."

"So how do you make calls?" I asked.

Percy looked at me like I was an alien, took the phone, and showed me the basics. When I finally got a clue, he gave me back the phone. Then he gripped the steering wheel and gunned the engine. "Which train is better for you to get home?"

Hm, I had to think about that. The F train was better for me, but its closest station was miles away, in Downtown Brooklyn. I didn't expect Percy to drive me all the way downtown, so I told him the A train at Utica was fine.

"The A train goes to Gravesend?" he asked, with raised eyebrows.

"No, but I can transfer to the F train at Jay Street."

"Sweetheart, I asked which train is *better* for you," said Percy.

"The F . . . but that's way downtown," I explained. "I don't want to take you out of your way."

Percy chuckled. "You're sweet, but hardheaded. Did I *ask* you all that?"

"No."

"Okay then," he said, a bit abruptly.

"I was just trying to be helpful."

"And I appreciate that. As a matter of fact, I would've taken you all the way home if I could, but I just remembered I have to go handle some business." Percy paused for a moment, and then added, "But the next time I ask you a question, just give me a simple answer, okay?" Now, a bit of bass in his voice.

I was taken aback. There was no need for him to be getting snappy. Normally, if somebody snaps on me for no reason, I'm snapping back in under sixty seconds. But I didn't want the hard-core part of me to scare Percy away. I had already shown him how "Rocky" gets down, kicking him in the family jewels and whatnot. No doubt he *felt* the power of what I could do. So I wanted Percy to feel my softer side, the loving side of Kate. I finally had a man in my life who seemed to really care about me, so why should I ruin things over a silly misunderstanding?

"You catch the F at Jay Street, right?" asked Percy.

"Jay Street is perfect," I said.

Percy clicked on the radio. I sat in silence, looking out my window, a little pissed, but fighting the feeling.

As we cruised by Fulton Park, I spotted Charles posted up on the corner with his boys. I wanted to jump out the car to tell him sorry about Saturday, but I had a feeling Percy wouldn't like that. So I turned my head, and stared dead ahead.

When we pulled up in front of the Jay Street station, Percy boldly double-parked beside a police car. He jumped out the car, walked around it to open my door, and pulled me up out of my seat. Then he leaned me up against the back car door and wrapped me up into his arms. With his soft juicy lips, he planted a long juicy kiss. "Call me as soon as you get home," said Percy. "And don't let anybody see your new phone."

"I won't," I replied. I was way ahead of Percy in that regard, already planning a place to hide it. I trusted no one. Not even Jeselle. Been robbed in too many group homes to be letting my valuables hang loose.

As soon as I got home, I made a beeline for the bathroom. There was a cleaning cabinet, clearly not in use, with a bunch of stale cleaning products, buckets, and rags stuffed inside. Cool. I planned to stash my Blackberry there. Keep my phone in quiet mode, use a plastic soap storage box as a protective case, and then I'd wrap up the case in one of the rags. This tacky arrangement would have to do until I figured something else out.

Later that night, I checked my phone to see if Percy had called. Turned out, he had texted me three hours earlier. He must have hit me up as soon as he dropped me off at the train station. How very sweet and attentive of him, I thought.

I MISS YOU ALREADY.

MISS YOU TOO.

I WROTE YOU HOURS AGO. :(

SORRY. JUST GOT YOUR MESSAGE.

I WAS WORRIED ABOUT YOU. I TOLD YOU TO CALL ME.

SORRY, I DIDN'T GET THE CHANCE. BUT I'M OK. HOME SAFE.

GLAD YOU'RE OK. CAN'T WAIT TO SEE YOU AGAIN!

SAME HERE.

GNIGHT, BABY.

GNIGHT.

Chapter 13

On Friday evening, I was locked up in the bathroom, checking my phone. A text from Percy was waiting for me.

CAN I SEE YOU TOMORROW AT FIVE?
YES.
LOOK FLY FOR ME, BABY.
OKAY.

But, oh no! How could I look fly? I had no fly gear in my closet. Maybe some flies, but not any fly gear. What was a broke broad to do?

I flew out of the bathroom, and headed to my bedroom, gearing up to hunt for an outfit. But I stopped short at the sight of Mrs. Cooper, perched on the edge of my bed. My first thought was: Why is she still here? Her old butt should've *been* gone for the day.

"Kate, I need to see you in my office," she said.

My heart dropped down to my feet.

As I sat inside of Mrs. Cooper's cluttered office, wringing my hands, mad nervous, I wondered what the heck she wanted. The radio was pumping religious music. The fan sitting on her desk blew dusty air all over the place. I wished Mrs. Cooper would open the freaking window. Instead, she closed the door behind her. "Don't look so worried," she said with a raspy chuckle.

I flashed a nervous smile, nervous because random office visits never meant good news.

"Kate, I want you to know I've been thinking about your situation ever since you arrived," began Mrs. Cooper, holding a pencil to her mouth.

And?

"I understand you're on the fast track to success, while the girls here are . . . well, they could still use some guidance. The only reason you were placed here is because of a shortage of beds at another facility better suited for you."

My ears perked up. When, oh when, could I pack my bags?

"I just wanted you to know that you're at the top of the Green Hills' waiting list. They're expecting a free bed by September."

My high hopes dropped down to zero. Oh, come on now. Why would Mrs. Cooper call me into the office making grand announcements if the situation wasn't even set in stone yet? She must've read the extreme disappointment in my face because she added, "I see that you're having trouble fitting in with the other girls here. I just wanted to give you some good news to look forward to."

"Thanks," I muttered.

"In the meantime, is there anything I can do to make things better between you and the girls?"

"Yeah, kick everybody out the house," I wanted to suggest. Instead, I said, "That's okay. I'm good." Besides, Jeselle's presence was actually making things easier on me. Since all the girls were riding her bra strap, I could breeze by without beef because Jeselle had my back.

"Kate, you can't get through this alone," said Mrs. Cooper, fiddling with her lopsided Afro. She stared at me with sadness in her eyes.

Whatever.

It wasn't even that serious. My new thought process: Born alone.

Die alone. So what if the chicks here hated my guts? I've been through much worse. I could hold my own.

"I'm worried about you," said Mrs. Cooper, shaking her head.

"No need to." I shrugged. "But thanks, anyway."

Mrs. Cooper pointed the pencil at me and said, "Well, Green Hills is one of the best facilities in New York City. They'll help you with your independent living goals, and all of the girls there are on the same page as you, so it's a teamlike atmosphere. I'd be excited if I were you."

Well, you're not me.

Excitement refused to register on my face, because I'd learned a long time ago not to count on anything in foster care. Plans always change, and rarely for the better. No need for me to be doing cartwheels just yet.

Mrs. Cooper babbled on and on about a few more "great" Green Hills details. But by this time, I was watching her mouth move without listening to a word she said.

I nodded at intervals with fake interest; all the while, I was thinking of my upcoming date with Percy, itching to bounce from the musty old office so I could head for my closet to hunt for something decent to wear.

Mrs. Cooper tapped the desk with her pencil and said, "Do you mean to tell me I stayed after office hours to tell you the good news, and all I get is a blank stare?"

"I'm sorry," I replied. "I do appreciate you letting me know." I hoped this would be enough to zip the lady's lips. No disrespect, but she didn't know when to leave things alone.

Mrs. Cooper sighed at my response, and finally told me I could go. I thanked her, hopped out the chair, and flew out the door.

I stepped inside an empty bedroom, thanking goodness for some alone time. I started raiding my side of the closet for Operation Percy, only to resign myself to a plain shapeless white summer dress. It would have to do. Oh well.

After picking out my outfit, I had a whole hour to be by myself and bask in it. I really liked Jeselle, but she talked too dang much. And Tracy . . . well, you already know.

Unfortunately my peace was shattered at eight o'clock on the dot. Jesselle came busting inside the bedroom looking pissed to the tenth power. "Girl, you need to handle your business," she shouted. "Tracy trying to play you for a chump!"

"Huh, what?"

Jesselle plopped her butt on my bed, and shook her head. "All I'm saying, if I were you, I'd stomp Tracy out. Don't let her disrespect you no more. Stomp that girl out!"

Chapter 14

After Jesselle told me what had happened, stomping out Tracy didn't sound like such a bad idea. Apparently, earlier in the day, when I had gone to the store to buy me a pack of sunflower seeds, Tracy went shopping inside my knapsack. She had found my silver bracelet, threw it on her wrist, and rocked it right out the house. Jeselle saw the whole thing go down.

I hadn't noticed my bracelet was missing, because aside from my store run, I had stayed in the house all day. No reason to put it on.

"Wow," was all I could say, shaking with anger.

It was almost too hard to believe that Tracy could be that bold. Taking my bracelet in front of a witness? Really? A part of me was tempted to double-check my knapsack. But double-checking would be an insult to Jeselle. I had to believe her. And why would she lie?

Jeselle took off her sneakers and said, "Word to my mother, I wanted to wipe that stupid smirk off Tracy's face before she left the house. Reason I ain't do nothing is because I want *you* to do something. You too quiet around here and you gonna keep getting played for a punk if you don't stand up for yourself."

"Oh, I'm far from a punk," I said. "Trust."

"Well, that's not what I heard."

"I don't care what you heard," is what I wanted to say. But I didn't dare get smart with the only girl in the house who seemed to like me.

So I just sat still, quietly plotting on how to go about things in my head. Jeselle's only solution was a straight-up beat down. But nah; there had to be a better way. I turned to Jeselle and said, "See, I'm not trying to go backward for no silly broad. I came too far to go back there."

"Listen, if *you* can't handle her, *I* will," exclaimed Jesselle, still upset, as if the bracelet were hers.

"But I don't want you in some beef over me, because—"

"Listen," she interrupted, "if you can't handle her, I will."

"Nah, I'm good with my hands. I'm just trying not to go there—"

"Whatever," cut in Jeselle, clapping her hands with force. "I swear, I'm stepping to Tracy if you don't. Can't stand a thief. Wait until that girl gets home. Watch what I do."

Well, I didn't have to watch Jeselle do anything, because *I* did all the doing. It was time to show and prove that I could hold my own. And this is how it all went down.

I had calmly taken a seat on Jeselle's bed, peereing out the window every five minutes. Jeselle was sitting next to me, busy chattering away about nothing.

After the third time of Jeselle witnessing me peek outside, she finally thought to ask, "Why are you staking out our block?"

"You'll find out," I replied, with my forehead pressed against the windowpane.

Fifteen minutes later, I finally peeped Tracy walking up the street, alone.

"Guess it's time to put a chick in check," I said, jumping up from the bed. I raced down the steps two at a time. Jeselle was close at my heels. Night staff was nowhere to be found, and the other girls were missing in action. The perfect setting.

I flung open the front door with force.

Before Tracy could step over the threshold, I cut her off at the pass. Jeselle closed the door behind us. We stood on the porch, glaring at Tracy. "See what I'm saying?" Jeselle pointed to Tracy's arm.

Sure enough, Tracy had my beautiful silver bracelet on her wrist. I wondered if she was planning to rock it straight to my face, or was she planning to hide it before she stepped inside? Whatever the case, the sight of her brazenly wearing my property raised my temperature to boiling.

Tracy swung her weave bangs out of her face and said, " 'Scuse me. Why y'all blocking me?"

"You real funny," I began. "Are you serious right now?" I wanted to hit her so bad my hands were shaking.

"What's the problem?" asked Tracy, like she really didn't know.

Real talk, the old me would've punched Tracy dead in the throat and yanked the bracelet off her wrist. The new me was trying to be civil about it.

"Take off my bracelet," I demanded, holding out my hand.

Tracy leaned her head to the side and said, "I'm saying, you be using up my perfume and stuff, but now I can't borrow your bracelet?"

"You didn't *ask* to borrow it," I snapped. "And you know full well I don't be using your stuff."

"*I* used your stuff," Jesselle piped in angrily. "Now what?"

Tracy stood her ground, not budging on the bracelet. So I got a little closer to intimidate her, although I was still determined to keep things nonviolent. My fighting days were supposed to be over.

"You better back up off me," said Tracy through gritted teeth.

"Then take off my bracelet . . . or do I have to take it off for you?"

Tracy looked over at Jesselle, and then at me.

"We not trying to jump you," blurted Jesselle. "I'm a fair fighter. So go 'head, Kate. Get it in!"

"Nah, I'm not trying to fight this broad," I explained. "She's not worth it. I just want my bracelet back."

My words must've sounded weak and spineless to Tracy because all of a sudden she got bold, raised her pointer finger to my face, and said, "I don't have time for this." Then she nudged me hard in the forehead. To top off her nerve, she turned her back on me, thinking I was too much of a punk to check her. I lost it then and there.

"You must be out your mind, trick!" I grabbed a handful of her weave, wrapped her hair around my wrist, and yanked her head straight back. While my left hand gripped the hair, my right hand balled into a fist and connected with her face, full force. Tracy almost dropped from the blow. But I held her up by her hair and was about to pound the girl to death.

"I'll kill you," she yelled, crying and spinning her arms at the empty air in front of her.

I let go of her hair and effortlessly tripped her to the ground. My fists were cocked and ready to launch. I wanted to stomp Tracy out. But something inside me stopped me cold flat. I was overdoing it. In actuality, all I wanted was my bracelet back. So I sat on her stomach, grabbed her right arm, and yanked my prized possession off her chubby wrist.

"We could've done this the easy way," I said, out of breath.

Jeselle stood behind me laughing her head off. "Dang, Kate, that was quick. I didn't know you could get down like *that*!"

The next day, everybody but the staff knew how I got down. Jeselle had bragged about my fighting skills all day, like a proud parent. Now the girls were steering clear of me. They knew what I could do, and they didn't want to get *done*.

Tracy avoided eye contact with me the whole time at the breakfast table. I felt so bad seeing the nasty bruise splotched on her dark brown skin, looking like permanent purple Magic Marker. It was easy to see that she had gotten clocked in the face; nothing else could explain the damage. But the no-snitching rule held mad weight in our house. So Tracy blamed the bruise on a fight during her home visit. Then she bounced from the crib immediately after breakfast, scared straight, I guessed.

Although I didn't get punished for my actions, I still felt troubled. Troubled because when you have the kind of life I have, it's so easy to get sucked back into violent mode. I couldn't believe that I had risked everything over a bracelet that could be replaced. Tracy's life couldn't be replaced if I killed her from a freak accident, a fatal punch gone wrong—you never know. And as angry as I was last night, that's what I could've done.

The longer I thought about it, the sicker to my stomach I felt. I replayed the fight over and over in my head, so mad at myself for not handling things differently.

But soon, enough was enough. I did what I did, and hopefully I wouldn't have to do it again. I pushed the incident way in the back of my mind, and forced myself to push pleasant thoughts in the forefront, namely thoughts about Percy. I thought about his sexy lips, his sensuous kiss. Thoughts of him easily relaxed my mind.

Then it suddenly hit me. I *shouldn't* be so relaxed when it came to my appearance; Percy was too special for a shapeless summer dress. What in the world was I thinking? What was I going to wear? Saturday was less than twenty-four hours away!

I tore up my side of the closet again, hunting for something decent. Nothing. I had absolutely nothing. I badgered my brain trying to think of a solution. Couldn't think of a doggone thing. Our allowance was so sorry; a few dollars a week couldn't buy me *jack*. And none of these broads would let me borrow their clothes. Please, I wasn't foolish enough to ask any of them. Then again, Jeselle was crazy cool and would most definitely hook me up. Too bad she was taller than a tree; nothing of hers would fit me—

See . . . that's why I wished things were different around the house. Tracy is a shorty like me, in fact, my *exact* body type. Why couldn't we be were more like sisters instead of stone-cold enemies, fighting and beefing over nonsense? Imagine how dope it would be if we could share one another's clothes and secrets, getting along with each other like one big happy family. That's all I ever wanted was a family : . . but anyway. No need to get off track. I had to bring my mind back to Percy.

I had disappointed my dream boy once already, looking like a straight-up cornball last time I saw him. There was no way on Earth I was going to disappoint him again.

Chapter 15

Early Saturday morning, I jumped out of bed with a single hopeful thought swirling through my head: Felicia. Felicia might be able to save my day!

Back in June, Felicia had mentioned a yellow stretch dress she had bought for one of her countless dates with Marlon, but ended up not wearing it.

"OMG, the lycra emphasizes my lanky bones," Felicia had complained. "I don't look sexy. I look anorexic!"

"Aww, poor anorexic baby," I replied, forcing a laugh. At the time, I was depressed about leaving the Johnsons and trying to hide it behind a jokey façade.

"One size fits all, my behind!" Felicia continued.

"What behind?" I teased. "I thought you didn't have one."

"Well, you definitely have the curves to do this dress justice," explained Felicia. "You can come get it whenever you want."

At that time, I was too busy moping to be thinking about a dress. So I told her I would come, but never did. I had no reason to.

Fast-forward to today. Now, I had a purpose. A hot, hot date, and I couldn't wait! I hoped Felicia hadn't given my dress away.

I took my shower, hopped into any old thing, and ran out the house with my BlackBerry stuffed inside the pocket of my jeans. I walked two blocks to a small park, sat on a bench, and dialed Felicia with anxious fingers.

"Hey, Fee, welcome back, sorry for calling you so early, but I need a big favor."

"Wow, you said a mouthful," exclaimed Felicia. "What's up?"

"Do you still have that yellow dress you wanted to give me?"

"Yep. It's still in a bag waiting for you."

"Oh man, thank you so much!" I sighed with relief. "What's the earliest I can come through?"

"Anytime you want. I have to get ready soon anyway. Marlon's been whining about missing me all week, so he's coming over for breakfast. My mom is making us a serious spread . . . of course you're welcome to join us."

"Oh, no thanks," I said quickly.

I couldn't stand Felicia's parents, both big-time lawyers who held their noses too high, not a down-to-earth bone in their bodies. In the projects is where Felicia's parents first met, but they were steady trying to forget, acting all stiff and superior over others. I could tell they didn't really approve of my friendship with Felicia. And the only reason they tolerated me was because I rocked good grades and was the first *real* friend Felicia ever had.

"What number are you calling me from by the way?" asked Felicia.

"It's a surprise," I replied. "Anyway, I'll be there around eleven," I added, hoping they'd be done with breakfast by then.

"Okay, and don't think I forgot, Ms. Thing," began Felicia. "I *will* be grilling you about your new man!"

I giggled, feeling all girlish and giddy. I couldn't wait to be grilled.

At eleven o'clock on the dot, I landed on Felicia's spic-and-span front porch, and rang her bell. Her house was the best on the block, a flawless brownstone painted peach on top and dark brown at the bottom, a shiny black gate, not a crumbling step or chipped stone in sight. Even her garbage cans sat there all prim and proper.

Felicia flung open the door, and greeted me with a big hug. "What took you so long?" she asked, playfully.

"Shoot, I ran all the way here," I joked.

As soon as I walked through the front door, the delicious aroma of bacon, waffles, and coffee wafted in the air. The kitchen was miles away from their brightly lit hallway, but the smell of good food was overpowering me. "Dang, Kate, you be tripping," said my stomach, resenting my foolish pride.

"Come say hi to everybody." Felicia led me into the kitchen.

I reluctantly followed.

Felicia's kitchen was all glossy wood and tiles shining, and in it sat Felicia's beefy, bespectacled father, her skinny serious-faced mother, and Marlon. Their oak kitchen table was huge, but Marlon was sitting right up under Mrs. Coldwell, already looking like part of the family. Felicia's father sat opposite them, with *The New York Times* raised up to his face. I got a quick hello from everyone.

Then Marlon continued where he had left off. "My mom may be a chef, but she can certainly take lessons from you, Mrs. Coldwell."

Oh, what a brown nose, I thought; but I wasn't mad at Marlon. You gotta do what you gotta do to get in good with the parents!

Mrs. Coldwell gave a fake, restrained laugh, and she patted Marlon's shoulder. "You're too sweet."

Felicia beamed at the scene.

"So, how are things with you, Kate?" asked Mrs. Coldwell.

I put on my proper voice and replied, "Everything is fine, thank you."

By now, I was fidgeting. I wanted to get my dress and be out. So I turned to Felicia and said, "Sorry, but I really can't stay long."

I was glad Felicia got the hint. She told everyone, "Be right back," and led me up the polished wooden steps into her colossal bedroom. This year, her walls were painted lavender, a new plush purple comforter covered her canopy bed, and lacy cream curtains adorned the room's huge windows. Before stepping fully inside, I slipped off my sneakers. Then I plopped down on her bed and ran my feet through her lavish cream carpet.

Felicia plopped down next to me and exclaimed, "OMG! So tell me more about Percy. Where'd you meet him? How old is he? Why haven't you mentioned him to me before the festival?"

"Whoa, slow down," I said, laughing. "You got twenty-one questions!"

"Can't help myself," exclaimed Felicia, giggling. "Percy is definitely a cutie-pie!"

"I know, right?" I beamed. "He's really feeling me, too. He can't keep his hands off me—"

Just as I was about to give Felicia the full scoop, my cell phone rang. This was such a proud moment. I coolly whipped out my pink BlackBerry Pearl from my pocket, all smooth and cool. Yes, your girl, Kate, was flossing with her Pearl. I checked Felicia's reaction from the corner of my eye, but I couldn't tell what she was thinking.

"Hey, baby," said Percy in his sexy deep voice. "How you doing?"

"I'm good," I replied, smiling.

"Where are you?" he asked.

"Felicia's house."

"Who, Miss Africa?" Percy laughed. I chortled, uncomfortably. Felicia was sitting right next to me and could probably hear him. So I got up and walked over to the window, pretending to look outside.

"Listen, change of plans for today," Percy began. "One of our customers sold me last-minute tickets for a Broadway play called *King of Pride*. We have to be in Manhattan by two o'clock. Can you be ready in time?"

"Sure," I exclaimed. Wow, this would be my first Broadway play ever. Percy was really going hard for me!

"Right now I'm downtown running errands for my mother," explained Percy. "So can you meet me in front of Macy's by one o'clock?"

"No problem," I said, without thinking about all I had to get done, namely my hair. My cornbraids were mad frizzy, and I didn't have time to go all the way back to the group home to fix it. But even that fact couldn't lessen my excitement.

"I can't wait to see you, sweetheart," said Percy.

"Same here," I replied.

I hung up the phone, grinning, my heart fluttering. So many times I had to overhear Marlon talking sweet nothings to Felicia, while I had nothing. Now I had *something*, a real relationship. I was finally someone else's sweetheart, and I was going to see a Broadway play with that someone, a special someone I never dreamed I could get.

Before I could turn from the window, I felt Felicia's breath on my neck.

"Wow, cool phone," she said, her eyes mad wide.

"Thanks." I beamed. "Percy gave it to me."

Felicia's eyebrows twitched, and she paused before saying, "Oh . . . that's nice."

"What's wrong?" I asked.

"Nothing," said Felicia, averting her eyes.

"But your whole attitude just changed," I insisted.

"I said nothing's wrong."

I twisted my lips to the side, which was my yeah-right look. "Felicia, come on now. How long have I known you? Why are you fronting? Tell me why your whole face just changed. What's the matter?"

Real talk, Felicia was ruining my moment. My agenda was supposed to be: give her the scoop about my two magical dates with Percy, get my dress, thank her profusely, and be out.

But now this.

I refused to leave Felicia's crib without making sure she was okay. Point-blank, period, I had to know what was up.

"Do I ever hold back on you?" I asked, growing frustrated.

"Kate, please don't press me," Felicia pleaded. "Nothing is wrong. I swear."

Whatever.

When you're really tight with someone, they can lie with all their might, and you can still see right through them.

"Spill it, Felicia," I insisted. "Don't have all day."

Felicia heaved a big sigh and said, "Okay, since you asked for it." She couldn't even look at me when she began to explain. "I don't mean any harm . . . but isn't it too soon for Percy to be giving you a phone . . . an expensive phone at that?"

Oh, is that all?

"It's not a new phone," I quickly explained. I walked over to Felicia's bed and plopped down to put my sneakers back on. I was gearing up to go, even though I could tell Felicia had some more nonsense to say.

"Kate, don't you think it's too soon to be giving out phones, period? I mean, Percy seems like a really nice guy, but you've only known him for what . . . a week or two?"

"Hi, hater," I said, half-jokingly.

"I'm not hating," Felicia objected. "Just concerned."

"Concerned about what?" I asked, cocking my head to the side.

"Well, the only reason I know a guy to give a girl a phone so soon is to keep track of her . . . I mean, you *just* met the guy."

"Not true," I corrected. "Percy and I have known each other for years. Besides, like I said, it's not even a new phone. So please relax." I chuckled, trying to keep the mood light.

"Okay, let me mind my business. . . . It's just that . . . well, you know my mom is a prosecutor . . . and I hear a lot of stories."

"Yeah, okay, I feel you," I said.

I had to admit, Percy *was* spending money on me mad quick. But he was holding down a job, his parents were paid, so I knew he wasn't hurting for cash. Shoot, at least I didn't have to sleep with him to get mine.

And how *else* was Percy supposed to stay in touch with me if he didn't give me this BlackBerry? Felicia knew the group home drama I had going on, so why was she acting brand-new?

Besides, Tisha was the main one forever lecturing me about knowing that I deserve the best in life. So why should I question all this good stuff I was finally getting? Why not appreciate the gift-giving while it lasted?

"Just be careful," said Felicia. "That's all I'm saying."

"Yeah, yeah, I feel you," I said, growing antsy. I had no time for lectures. I had things to do.

I *been* ready to bounce. But then I suddenly remembered: my dress. So I kept my butt planted on the bed, regreting that I had to depend on someone else for my gear; it was the same sad story last year. My ex-friend Naleejah had treated me like a straight-up charity case, and had reminded me about my sorry hand-me-down existence to a whole audience's face. Although Felicia would never do me like *that*, my clothing dependency was still whack. Right then and there, I vowed to start earlier on my summer job hunt next year, so I would have some real paper in my pocket to buy my own dang clothes for a change.

"Well, Percy definitely is a cutie-pie," said Felicia, as an after-thought. Probably trying to make me feel better.

"Isn't he, though?" I said. "So um, can I get my dress now?"

"Where are you guys headed?" she asked, still forcing an uncon-cerned air.

"Um, Percy says it's a surprise," I fibbed. If Felicia was already questioning my phone, why would I fix my mouth to tell her about a Broadway play?

Felicia moseyed over to her walk-in closet and pulled out a small red shopping bag. I took the bag and said, "You really saved me, girl. Good looking out . . ."

Then my voice trailed off. I suddenly realized I needed shoes, too. Couldn't rock my raggedy sneakers with a banging stretch dress.

Felicia's feet are way bigger than mine so I couldn't borrow her boats. The only other choice was to ask for a loan, something I had never in my life done before; my pride had never let me . . . until now. "Um, Felicia, can you lend me a twenty until Friday?"

Felicia opened her brown eyes wide, clearly shocked. As many times as she tried to push cash on me, even in my neediest times, I've always said no . . . so I could see why she was stunned.

"Is everything okay, Kate?"

"Everything's fine," I said. "I just forgot my money at home, and I need to pick up a few things. Don't worry, I promise to pay you back on Friday."

Felicia tapped my arm. "Stop playing, you know I trust you. I just can't believe you're finally asking. How many times have I told you that you never have to go without as long as you have me?"

"Aw, thanks girl," I said.

Felicia walked over to her shiny cherrywood desk, and pulled out her wallet from the top drawer. She handed me the twenty. But I felt like she still had some unexpressed Percy questions. So it was time to make my exit. Quick.

"Well . . . Marlon is probably missing you," I said.

"Oh . . . okay."

Felicia's demeanor was still funny-style. I couldn't believe she was still concerned over a silly phone. Because really? It wasn't that serious. And honestly, I couldn't care less what she thought. I was ecstatic about my new phone and my new man, and I didn't want anybody bringing me down.

Felicia followed me downstairs. I poked my head into the kitchen and said my good-byes. Once outside, Felicia leaned against her door's frame and said, "Have a nice time."

"Thanks, girl," I called over my shoulder. "I will!"

I ran all the way to the Utica Avenue train station, and was still catching my breath when the A train pulled in.

On the train, I plotted my action plan. First, I was going to run to the beauty store to buy some gel and a cheap scarf to press down the frizz in my cornbraids real quick. Then I was going to find some decent-looking sandals for under fifteen dollars.

However, as soon as I made it out of the Jay Street train station, I ended up stumbling upon a random discount-shoe store. I bought a pair of average black open-toe sandals. Planned to buy gel and scarf next. But then I checked my Blackberry and discovered it was fifteen minutes to one.

Oops, no time for that! I flew inside Macy's third-floor bathroom, slipped into my sexy dress, my sandals, and then, with horror, stared into the mirror at my fuzzy head of hair. I already knew it was bad, but the bright light emphasized the fright. Nothing I could do, though. There was no time. In a panic, I rushed outside to meet Percy.

I dashed up to my post in front of Macy's, and waited for Percy. At one o'clock on the dot, he strolled up to me, looking gorgeous. His hair was cut close to his perfectly shaped head, and his edges were lined up with precision. He wore a navy-blue short-sleeved polo shirt, baggy beige shorts, and tan grown-man sandals. His vanilla-almond skin glistened in the sun. First thing he said to me, "Wow, sweetheart, you look really good . . . but why didn't you fix your hair?"

"Yeah, I know," I stuttered, "but you didn't give me enough time to get ready."

"Oh, so it's my fault?" Percy asked with raised eyebrows.

"No, no, I'm not saying that—"

"Forget it," interrupted Percy.

Without grabbing my hand like he usually did, Percy started walking down the block and expected me to follow. Meanwhile, dudes on all sides of me had their tongues wagging out their mouths at the sight of my curvaceous body sheathed in yellow stretch material— fuzzy hair and all. Maybe Percy suddenly realized this, because halfway down the block, he finally reached for my hand. When we got to his car, he held the car door open for me.

Back to being a gentleman, thank you very much.

During the ride to Manhattan, Percy was quiet. The radio was pumping loud bass-driven beats. I just sat back in my seat, enjoying the view of the busy streets, and then the Brooklyn Bridge, vowing to one day walk over it, hopefully with Percy.

We made it to the theater in record time. I stared up at the brightly lit marquee for the *King of Pride*, and started getting excited. When we got inside the theater, I was bowled over by everything. I stared in awe at the huge glittering crystal chandeliers, hundreds of red seats in neat rows, and fancy-looking folks mixed in with casually dressed people.

"I lucked up getting these tickets," said Percy, out of the blue.

"I'm glad you did," I exclaimed. "This is my first Broadway play."

"Yeah, I can tell," said Percy.

The usher showed us to our seats and handed us our playbills. I already planned to put my playbill straight into my Lifebook's inner fold. This was such an exquisite experience, I needed to preserve it.

We sat in the middle row, close enough to see the full stage. My mouth dropped open as soon as the curtains parted, revealing a breathtaking backdrop painted bright red, orange, and cobalt blue. Tribal beats filled the theater and huge puppets and people in masks began running across the stage, dancing and singing all over the place. One magical scene flowed into the next. By the time the show was over, I was close to tears. It was such an amazing experience. I wanted to yell out, "Encore, I want more!" But I didn't dare. Percy would probably not approve.

Once outside of the theater, he turned to me and asked, "Enjoyed the show?"

"Big-time," I exclaimed. "Thanks for taking me . . . wow."

"You hungry?"

"For sure," I said.

We were walking down Forty-second Street and Percy stopped short in front of McDonald's. "I would take you somewhere much nicer to eat, but I have to rush back to the store. My mother's doing inventory today, of all days." Now he looked pissed.

"I'm not mad at McDonald's," I said, trying to cheer him up. "Love me some French fries!"

We stepped inside McDonald's, and I had to double-check the double arches on the cashiers' shirts because I had never been in such a clean and fancy fast-food restaurant in my life. I was surrounded by nice brick walls and dim lighting and computers lined up to my right. "This is the baddest Mickey D's I've ever been in," I exclaimed.

"Please, this is nothing," he replied. "I'll show you a *real* fancy restaurant . . . one day."

Without asking me what I wanted, Percy placed two orders of McNuggets and fries. I asked him to add a hot chocolate to the order. "Hot chocolate in the summer time?" he exclaimed.

"I have a taste for it. Love me some hot chocolate," I said, giggling.

But I stopped giggling when he ordered me fruit punch instead.

No reason to beef about it, especially not after my beautiful Broadway treat, so I ate my food, and drank my punch with a smile.

Percy finished eating before me. He pushed back his chair and got up before I was through eating my last few fries; I gobbled them down and got up, too.

His car was parked on Fortieth Street, close to Bryant Park.

"It's a nice day, let's sit in the park for a few minutes," said Percy.

He grabbed my hand and led me across the street. There was a huge fountain in front of us spewing water. People sat all around us, reading newspapers, lying out to get some sun, and just plain old chilling. Percy pushed two green chairs together and made us a bootleg loveseat. We faced the huge lawn and he wrapped his arm around me, stroking my shoulder with his warm hand. No words were exchanged, but it was such a romantic moment, a moment that unfortunately had to end way too quick.

"I have to head back," Percy said with a sigh.

"Well, I had a really nice time."

"Me, too, sweetheart," said Percy. "I love being around you. You make me happy."

I went to bed dreaming of Percy; and woke up in the middle of the night scared to death. First, I heard Jeselle's voice. Then I opened my eyes to the sight of someone climbing through our window. I sat up in bed with a jolt.

My eyes adjusted to the darkness. I realized it was just Tracy.

"We forgot to tell you," whispered Jeselle, "got us a new system. If you want to stay out overnight with your man, just let us know and we got you."

Jeselle explained the system, the fake body in the bed, and the window tap. Tracy and I still weren't on full speaking terms, but having one another's back in sneaky situations was customary in most group homes. It's usually "us" against "staff," so we had to look out for each other no matter what.

I almost busted out laughing when Tracy uncovered the two large plastic bags full of clothes that was supposed to be her body. I had never seen this brand of trickery before. Reminded me of a jail-break plot.

Later that day, I said to Jeselle. "Shoot, as long as Belinda and Gerald work here, it seems like we don't even have to go through all that body-bag stuff. We can just walk straight through the front door any time of day. They don't care."

Jeselle waved her hand to dismiss my comment. "Nah, girl, we can't be doing things straight to their face. That would be disrespectful."

"But batty Belinda barely makes the rounds for head counts," I joked. "Does she even have a brain inside her head?"

"Yeah, but the body-bag trick is better than nothing," Jeselle insisted.

Meanwhile, I was thinking how I might be needing a body bag soon. Percy had hinted that he wanted me to spend the night with him. This is something I would have never considered if Common Grounds was a normal group home. But since staff was such a big joke here, why not go for broke in order to please my man?

Chapter 17

I WANT TO SEE YOU, BABY. I MISS YOU.

I MISS YOU TOO.

CAN YOU COME OVER MY FATHER'S HOUSE TODAY?

YES.

COOL. MEET ME AT JAY STREET. SAME SPOT. SIX O'CLOCK.

OKAY.

My Friday was all set. First, I had to pay Felicia back her money as promised. Then, I had to see my baby. Since Felicia and Marlon already had movie plans at the Court Street Theater, I would be able to kill two birds with one stone. The theater was only a few blocks from where I had to meet Percy. So first stop, the theater.

Felicia and Marlon were standing outside waiting for me, dressed like twins again: identical purple T-shirts, and blue jean shorts. So corny and cute of them. "Y'all are too much," I laughed, handing Felicia a crispy twenty-dollar bill.

"Oh goody," she exclaimed. "Now we can get some extra popcorn, Marlon!"

I chuckled at how Felicia loved to play off her wealth. Homegirl could buy a hundred bags of popcorn if she really wanted to. But no one would ever guess from the raggedy way she dressed. I admired her humbleness, though. So many kids in the hood be dressing too good with no money in the bank. I'd rather be rich and raggedy than fly and faking it. Who do I need to impress? Well, maybe Percy. . . .

"Kate, you should come with us," said Marlon.

I smirked at the idea. I knew he wasn't joking because I'd been invited to go to the movies with them in the past. But now that I had Percy in my life, I didn't feel so pitiful over his suggestion this time.

"I would love to join y'all," I began, "but I'm meeting Percy in a few."

As soon as I said this, my BlackBerry buzzed in my pocket. Amazing, I thought, just look at how strongly I was connected to my baby!

"Hey, sweetheart," Percy began, "I'm here earlier than expected. Where are you?"

"Court Street."

"Court Street?" he repeated. "How far away from Jay Street?"

"A few blocks away . . . I'm in front of the movie theater."

Guessing it was Percy, Marlon tapped me on the shoulder. "You guys should join us. Ask him!"

"Who's that?" asked Percy, with sudden bass in his voice.

"Marlon," I said, taken aback by Percy's tone.

"Who?"

"Marlon," I repeated. "Um . . . you remember. . . . You met him at the African Festival . . . Felicia's boyfriend . . . and she's here, too."

"But why are you there with them, when you're supposed to be meeting me?"

"Because I didn't expect you to be ready until six."

Percy paused and then said, "Well, I'm ready now. Are you?"

"Yes, I'm ready," I said. "I only had to drop something off real quick," I added, defensively. I wanted to snap on Percy for snapping on me, but I couldn't; I had an audience.

"Well, I'm coming to pick you up," said Percy. "Wait for me there."

"Okay," I said, feeling funny, and hoping it didn't show in my face.

I glanced at Felicia. Her face looked just as funny. Knowing my homegirl, I already felt her "concern." The fact that I had to explain myself to Percy clearly didn't sit right with her.

Marlon was either playing it off, or didn't have a clue, because he said, "We should really do the double-date thing soon, though. So let's make it happen, Kate!"

I forced a chuckle. Then Felicia had the nerve to say, "I doubt that she can."

"You doubt *what?*" I asked, with an attitude.

Felicia had nothing to say.

Yeah, you better zip it, chick.

There was no need for Felicia to be a smart aleck about my relationship in front of Marlon. This was exactly why I had avoided calling her smart-alecky-butt all week. I knew if I spoke to her too soon, I'd end up slipping about the Broadway play, and she'd end up lecturing me about "early" gifts. I didn't need her in my ear flapping her gums about nothing.

Don't get me wrong. I appreciated Felicia's concern—whether valid or not—but she was really overdoing it right now, eyebrows raised, all dramatic for no reason.

Marlon checked his watch and told Felicia, "Listen, if you want to get popcorn, we better go."

"True," said Felicia. "Talk to you later, Kate." She gave me a stiff hug good-bye. Then Marlon hugged me, too, and they went inside the theater arm in arm. Five minutes later, Percy pulled up to the curb. I hopped inside his car.

"So where's your friends?" he asked, in a suspicious tone.

"They had to leave." I fidgeted in my seat.

"So soon?"

"Their movie was about to start," I explained. Honestly, I didn't appreciate Percy's line of questioning, but I wanted to keep an open mind about it. Come to think of it, If I called Percy and heard a fe-male's voice in the background, I'd probably be tripping, too.

"I can call Felicia if you like," I volunteered, hoping he'd say no.

"But did I *ask* you to call her?"

"No."

"Okay then."

Percy peeled down Court Street. He hopped onto Atlantic Ave-nue, and started driving like a madman.

By the time we got to his father's house, I was not in the best of moods. So when he laid me on the couch, trying to go for my draw-ers, I told him no with so much firmness in my voice.

"Why?" he asked, still tugging at the elastic of my thong.

"I'm not ready," I said.

"But if two people are feeling each other, the natural thing to do is to make love."

"Yeah, I hear you, but fall back," I wanted to say. Instead, I just lay there quietly, pushing his hand away every time he tried me. This was such a drag. Maybe we needed to do more outdoorsy ac-tivities. Oh well, I thought, what a letdown.

Percy finally sat up on the couch, clearly pissed. He wouldn't talk to me. And I'm no dentist; I wasn't about to pull teeth. Besides, what happened to the guy who told me he respected my wishes when he had tried me last time? This was a different Percy; I wanted the other one back.

"Maybe I should go home," I said, sadly.

"Yeah, maybe you should." Percy jumped up from the couch, grabbed his car keys, and drove me to the F train instead of all the way home. Not a problem for me. It was only eight o'clock, a nice warm summer night, and during my walk home from the train station, I had some time to think. Told my Lifebook all about my thoughts.

My relationship with Percy is starting to feel like a roller-coaster ride. My stomach dips and flips at the thought of disappointing him. Why was he so huffy over me not wanting to have sex with him yet? He claimed he can see himself with me for a long time, so what's his rush? If Percy expects to get my treasure, then he needs to start treating me like gold, all of the time, not just some of the time. I may be new at this relationship stuff, but I have to stay true to myself, no matter what.

Chapter 18

CAN I SEE YOU TODAY?

I read Percy's text, scowling. I was still upset about yesterday. I sat on the tub's edge, glaring at the screen of my phone.

Then he texted me again, a split second later.

I WANT TO TAKE YOU OUT SOMEWHERE SPECIAL, BABY. PLEASE?

Baby?

Please.

Percy was still getting no answer from me. I couldn't believe his utter flipping nerve. He had practically kicked me out of his father's house for not giving him any sex, making me feel like a defected object he could no longer use, and yet, here he was, texting me like nothing happened? True, I was the one who had suggested me leaving, but he didn't have to jump at the chance to show me the dang door.

I'M REALLY SORRY ABOUT YESTERDAY.

Okay, finally, a "sorry." At least now he was showing me some accountability. However, hold up. Sorry or not, I was still wondering if I should even respond to Percy.

But before I could make up my mind, my phone vibrated in my hand. Percy's name lit up in lights. I answered in a lackluster voice.

"Hello?"

"Hey, sweetheart, did you get my texts?"

"Yes, all three of them," I said, sarcastically. I couldn't help myself. Nobody craps on Kate without repercussions.

"Well . . . I wanted to say this to you over the phone, instead of a text. . . . I'm sorry for the way I treated you, okay?"

Percy's ears were met with silence.

"Hello, Kate?"

I had the right to remain silent. I wanted to take in his words, detect signs of sincerity in his voice. I wasn't about to take him back, just like that.

"Helllooo?"

"Yes, I'm here."

"I said I'm sorry. . . . I'm really, really sorry for the way I treated you. . . . I lost my temper, and I'm sorry about that, okay, sweetheart?"

Percy's shaky voice softened my resolve like Silly Putty. He was sounding so pitiful and sorry right now that I had no other choice but to lower my defenses.

"I accept your apology," I finally said. "It's over and done with."

"So, can I see you today?"

I paused in thought. It was a quiet day. Nothing to do. What the heck. "Yes, I'm free."

"Cool," exclaimed Percy. "I have a special day planned for us. So wear something really nice for me. Okay, sweetheart?"

"Okay, I will," I said. Meanwhile I was thinking, Oh boy, here we go again. What to wear? What to wear?

"I can't wait to see you, baby," said Percy.

For some reason, I didn't respond. I just got the meet-up details, hung up the phone, and immediately started fretting over what to throw over my body.

As soon as I tucked my phone away in its hiding place, it vibrated. I opened the cabinet door back up, pulled out my celly, only to discover a text from Felicia, which raised my blood pressure.

JUST WANT TO LET U KNOW, IT'S NOT OK FOR PERCY TO BE
QUESTIONING U LIKE THAT.
HE WASN'T QUESTIONING ME. WE WORKED IT OUT. NO NEED TO
WORRY.
IT'S TOO LATE. I'M WORRIED.
WELL, DON'T BE. TTYL.

What a knucklehead, I thought, putting my phone away. If I wasn't so concerned with preparing for my date, I would've called Felicia up to set her completely straight. I wanted to tell her that she had no right to talk down to me like I had no sense when it comes to men. Okay, I really don't have much sense when it comes to them, but she didn't have to be so freaking condescending about it! Who uses phrases like, "It's not ok," to their homegirls? Come on now, let's be for real.

Two seconds later, Felicia actually called me. I sent her butt straight to voice mail. Anyway, back to my date with Percy. I needed something to wear.

Of course *now* I couldn't turn to Felicia for help. So Jeselle ended up saving my day. She hooked me up by letting me borrow her large orange cotton V-neck shirt that was so long it could pass for a cute mini-dress, and her thick brown leather belt adorned my waist. Wasn't the best outfit, but my curvy shape brought the sexy back.

Jeselle flat-ironed my hair, however; it was too thick to get straight, so I wrapped her tan paisley silk scarf around my head, like a headband, and left the back of my hair flowing; I was Afro-puffing it like Foxy Kate, ya dig? Done with that, I slid my black open-toe sandals on my feet, and I was ready to bounce.

"Looking fly, ma," exclaimed Jeselle. "Just get your lip gloss poppin', and you're good to go!"

"Man, listen, you really came through for me," I said.

Jeselle flashed a cheesy grin. "Who got your back, homie?"

"You do." I smiled and reached out to hug her for the first time. Fortunately, Jeselle wasn't afraid to hug, like I used to be. And she had no idea how much our new friendship meant to me.

Because at the moment, it felt like I was about to lose my *best* friend over a silly situation. Of all things, a guy? I didn't want that to happen for nothing in the world. I just needed Felicia to mind her own business; I never stuck my nose in her and Marlon's affairs.

"Why you suddenly look so sad?" asked Jeselle, bringing me back to the present. "Flippin' moods like a light switch."

"Oh . . . it's nothing," I replied, turning away from her concerned stare. "Anyway, my man is waiting. Gotta run."

"Alright, ma, have fun!"

Yeah, I really hoped so. No complications with Percy this time around. No drama. No misunderstandings. This girl just wanted to have fun.

Chapter 19

Percy picked me up on Jay Street at seven o'clock sharp as planned. Before I hopped inside the car, I spotted a single red rose sitting on my seat. "Aw, thank you," I said, sticking my nose inside of the petals to get a good whiff. "Smells really good."

"You're welcome, love."

We drove to Brooklyn Heights, the ritzy part of Brooklyn. When I got out of the car, Percy looked me up and down. "Oh snap, you look like a pumpkin all dressed in orange" he said, chuckling, "but at least your hair looks decent this time."

His words were a lethal blow to my head. Shot down again. I had tried so hard to look good . . . I guessed orange wasn't my color. I just couldn't seem to measure up for him.

On the other hand, Percy looked utterly gorgeous. He wore a button-down crispy white shirt, baggy jeans hanging slightly off his sexy behind. The waves in his hair rippled wonderfully and his edge up was flawless. He was the picture of perfection. Wished he felt the same way about me.

"Let's go," said Percy, grabbing my hand. He led me to an extravagant restaurant situated on the corner of Montague Street. As soon as we stepped inside, a tall, blond hostess rushed up to us. "Table for two?"

She pulled back a red velvet curtain and led us into a plush fancy room full of dressed-up people. When we were seated in a quiet corner, I looked around admiringly at a large mural of Italy on the left wall; the rest of the place was all cream and gold. The tablecloth was cream, the silverware was actually gold. I felt like a queen for the day.

"Classy, right?" said Percy.

"Very," I replied, still looking around in awe. This was the fanciest restaurant I'd ever been in. Percy was right. McDonald's just couldn't compare.

The hostess handed us our menus. There was so much fancy food to choose from. Five minutes later a pretty, slim, light-skinned waitress wearing all black came up to our table. "My name is Bianca, I'll be your server for today."

"Pretty name," said Percy, flashing the same sexy smile he usually flashed me.

Um . . . okay. . . . Well, Bianca was very pretty, and Percy wasn't blind. No need to trip over this . . . I guessed.

"What can I start you off with?" she asked.

I was about to ask Bianca if the chicken Parmesan came with—

"Two glasses of water and the lasagna special, please," Percy, ordered before I could even open my mouth.

I placed the menu down, feeling like a mute fool.

Bianca took our menus and sashayed away. Percy looked after her, but I tried not to let it bother me. I felt so insecure, but I didn't want it showing up in my attitude. So I blurted any old thing to take my mind off the incident. "I've never seen a ceiling painted gold," I said, looking upward.

Percy grabbed my hands and held them for a long time. "Like I told you before, I can show you a whole lot of things. . . . I want to make you happy."

But I didn't feel so happy at the moment.

Out of the blue, Percy started snapping his fingers, rocking in his seat and singing, "I just love to be around you, oh baby. You been so good to me . . ."

"Lenny Williams," I interrupted, trying to stay upbeat. "I like that song, too."

Percy's eyes widened in surprise. "What you know about Lenny Williams, young' un?"

"My foster father used to play his old-school records 24/7," I explained, now smiling at the memory of Ted dancing around the house trying to imitate Lenny. "Oh, oh, oh, oh, I love you," he would croon to Lynn, sounding off-key but extremely sweet.

In all of the houses I had ever lived in, it was rare for me to see a husband crazy about his wife. Singing love songs to her. Showing her respect all day, every day. For instance, this past May, driving downtown with Ted to pick out a gift for Lynn on "Foster" Mother's Day. We were in Macy's, standing on a dumb long line, when a tall brown-skinned woman with ridiculous beauty and curves spun around to ask if she could step out of line real quick. She held up a red silk nightgown and pointed out the unwinding thread at the bottom of it. "No good," she explained.

"No problem, dear," replied Ted, wearing a friendly grin.

The woman must have been encouraged by the word "dear," so when she got back in line, she started forcing small talk on us, batting her eyelashes and smiling the whole time. True, Ted's probably handsome for his age, but dang, have some pride, lady! She was acting so thirsty, I was embarrassed for her. Ted called everybody "dear," even his male boss, just as a running joke.

But the woman pressed on, not catching the hint. "Is that your daughter?" she asked, flashing me a fake smile.

"Sure is," said Ted, without hesitation, making me feel good inside. I felt even better when Ted showed the lady no love, even when she found out he was a mechanic and asked for his business card, clearly trying to get his digits on the slick.

Click.

Ted hung up on her request by simply saying, "Sorry, I ran out of cards." Then he told the thirsty broad to have a nice day. When we left the store, I jokingly said, "Wow, Lynn has you trained!"

"No," he corrected. "Lynn has my heart."

"Okay, player," I said, patting him on the back. "That was a smooth line you just laid on me."

"It's not a line," said Ted, his face turning serious. "It's the truth. And when you're old enough to date, make sure you command the same respect from your guy. Make sure you have his whole heart. Never settle for less."

Never settle for less.

Was I settling for less now? I wondered. I wished Percy would hold me down like Ted did for Lynn. Then again, maybe Ted's discipline came with his age.

But that thought didn't hold weight for long. What about Marlon, even younger than Percy, and holding Felicia down all day, every day? His eyes never strayed to the next chick as far as I could see. As a matter of fact, Marlon was the *first* guy ever to pay my big boobies no mind when I first met him; he kept his pupils trained on Felicia the whole entire time.

"I'm glad you came out with me, baby," said Percy, breaking into my thoughts.

"Me, too," I muttered.

"What's wrong?"

"Nothing," I said, looking down at my lap. Percy reached for my hand across the table and stroked it. "Baby, what's wrong?"

"Nothing," I repeated, forcing a bogus smile. "I'm good," I added.

To make my words match my mood, I tried to think of the bright side. I looked around the elegant restaurant that Percy was nice enough to take me to. This was more than any guy had ever done for me. Might as well be grateful and make the best of my night.

Our food came, smoking off the plate. I was about to dig in, but Percy grabbed the white cloth napkin from the table and told me to put it on my lap. "Oops, my bad," I said, trying to play it off like I knew. If I wasn't mistaken, Percy even shook his head at me.

Well, I wasn't about to embarrass him anymore tonight, so as hungry as I was, I took small, dainty bites of the lasagna. It was delicious, but still, small, dainty bites . . . while Percy wolfed down his food.

Bianca came back to our table. "Is everything okay?" she asked Percy.

"Everything is fine," said Percy. When he said "fine" he emphasized the word, as if he was referring to her. And when Bianca placed the check on our table, she flashed Percy one last googly-eyed smile, and said good-bye to him, barely acknowledging me.

Percy paid. We got up and headed for the exit. I spotted Bianca standing in the corner of the room. Before leaving, I flashed her my famous eye roll, and then sashayed behind Percy, holding my head high.

Once outside, Percy turned to me and said, "Let's take a walk to the Promenade. Ever been there before?"

"No."

"See?" began Percy, "there's always a first time when you're with me."

As we walked down a quiet, cobblestone, tree-lined street, Percy asked, "So did you really enjoy dinner, or were you just gassing my head up?"

"No, it was really good," I said. "Wish I could make lasagna."

"I know how to make lasagna. It's easy."

"You can cook?" I asked, incredulous. I never met a guy who admitted being able to cook. I was impressed.

"Please . . . my mother had me in the kitchen as soon as I was tall enough to reach the stove." Percy's face darkened when he said this.

"Oh," I said, feeling awkward. His mother, again. At least this time, he quickly recovered, thank goodness. And if he could recover so quickly, so could I. I pushed Bianca way in the back of my mind. Maybe I was being too sensitive anyway.

"Matter of fact, I can teach you how to make lasagna," said Percy.

"Wow, really?" I had always wanted to play house with a guy I really liked: him cooking beside me, me washing dishes, him drying. I had all of these romantic scenes in my head and they were finally about to play out with Percy.

We sat on a bench facing the inky-black water, watching the small boats and big ships sail by. The Brooklyn Bridge loomed in the distance. The night summer breeze felt good on my skin. I was feeling so warm and fuzzy in the company of my man. Percy kept grabbing my hand and kissing it, telling me how much he was enjoying himself. I was in seventh heaven. I didn't want the night to end. But as always . . . here comes the curfew countdown.

"Well, I have to go," I said reluctantly.

Percy sighed, got up, and we walked to his car.

Once inside the car, Percy immediately went for my lips. We were parked on a quiet street, so no one was around to see us getting down. Percy was going hard, feeling me up all over, and making me feel so good, like he was yearning for me.

Then he stopped his lips short and told me to climb in the backseat. As I climbed, he reached out and tapped my behind. "Man, baby, you got it going *on*."

Percy settled in beside me and we started going at it hot and heavy again. But when he started sucking ferociously on my neck, as good as it felt, I told him to stop.

"Why?" he asked, panting heavily.

"I don't want a hickey," I said, pushing his lips away.

Percy jerked his head back. "Black as you are?" he exclaimed. "Nobody's going to see it." He busted into chuckles, but then he noticed I wasn't even cracking a smile.

"Honey, what's wrong?" he asked. "You can't take a joke?"

I didn't say anything. I didn't want to argue. I just looked away from Percy and stared out the window deep in thought.

For as long as I could remember, I had a complex about my dark skin, about not being model thin. "You're pretty for a dark-skinned girl" was all I heard growing up. And just when I started saying to myself, "Bump the color-conscious clowns, I'm black and I'm beautiful," now I had my doubts again.

Percy grabbed the bottom of my chin. "Why won't you look at me?"

I had nothing to say.

"So you're going to stay mad at me?"

"I'm not mad," I lied.

When I wouldn't budge on my brooding, Percy huffed, and climbed into the driver's seat. I stayed seated in the back. So he drove me home like a cab driver. And when he tried to kiss me good-bye, I gave him my cheek instead of my lips. I left my rose inside his car on purpose.

YOU LEFT YOUR ROSE.

SORRY. I FORGOT IT.

SO IT DIDN'T MEAN ANYTHING TO YOU?

LIKE I SAID, I FORGOT IT. SAVE IT FOR ME.

IT'S ALREADY DEAD.

Percy didn't contact me for three days. I didn't bother reaching out to him, either. I was still upset, and it's never good to communicate when you're upset. I wasn't so sure if Percy's words were reason enough to *end* our relationship, but I knew I was surely hurt by them.

As disappointed as I was, I had to admit: I missed Percy. Three whole days without him had dragged by like a year. I had gotten so used to Percy's daily texts, checking up on his "baby." I had gotten so used to Percy period, the first real boyfriend in my life.

So when Percy texted me three days later, I can't even front, the butterflies revived inside my stomach; and his foul "hickey" comment flew right out the window like an annoying fly swatted far away from my mind.

Percy asked me if I could come over to his father's apartment to learn how to make lasagna. Of course, I could, was my reply. So Percy ran down the meet-up plan. And I flew out the house anxious to see my man.

I was picked up at the Jay Street station. Percy passionately kissed me hello like we hadn't seen each other in years. His usual intensity overpowered me so much, I leaned my head back in exhaustion after the kiss.

We drove to Pathmark to buy the lasagna ingredients. On the

way, Trey Songz singing "You Belong to Me," was pumping through the speakers, and Percy kept reaching over to caress my hand, while he steered his wheel with the other.

I felt so loved and adored.

When we stepped inside the brightly lit supermarket, my ecstatic feelings continued. We walked up and down the aisle searching for ingredients, giggling with each other, comparing prices; it felt like we were an old married couple. Shucks, I even pictured a baby girl riding inside of our shopping cart. I noticed women shooting wistful glances at us. I couldn't blame them. We looked mad cute together.

Percy paid for everything, and kissed me on the cheek in front of the cashier. I felt so special. I can't even begin to explain how special I felt.

We hopped back inside the car. Then Percy drove to DUMBO at breakneck speed. My heart was in my throat the whole time.

As soon as we walked inside Percy's father's apartment, he set down the bags and pressed me against the hallway wall. He tongued me down for ten minutes straight. His feverish need for me was so incredible. The way he held me in his arms so tightly, like he never wanted to let me go. I swear, it felt like any minute, he could get *it*. We shared so much earth-shaking passion between us; our chemistry was off the Richter scale. It was taking all of my might not to give in.

"Okay, baby," said Percy, pulling himself together. "Let's get it popping in the kitchen."

"No doubt," I replied, all giggly. "Show me the oven!"

First, Percy handed me a knife, an onion, and instructed me on how to chop it into shreds. My eyes were burning and watering like mad, so I said, "Cutting onions is not a game!"

"Yeah, that's why I have you doing it." Percy laughed.

"Aww, that's not right," I joked. "Why do *I* have to do all the dirty work?"

"Because you're the woman of the house," said Percy, smiling. "That's what you're supposed to do."

I chuckled slightly, but my eyes were not amused. I wiped a tear away.

Finally, I got through with the tortuous onions. Then Percy poured the chopped onions and ground beef into a pan. He boiled a box of noodles and when they were done, he showed me how to peel them off of each other by running cold water over them.

Everything was coming along nicely. The meat was simmering and smelling good. My stomach growled.

"Sounds like you got a rabid dog inside your tummy," said Percy.

"I know, right?" I giggled.

Percy stood behind me as I followed his instructions, adding layers on top of layers of ricotta and mozzarella cheese. I was having so much fun.

Done with my duty, Percy grinned at me and said, "I see you're a pro at this."

"Oh, yes, I am." I laughed and hugged him, feeling myself opening up to him even more. "Thanks for teaching me."

"You're welcome, Baby." Percy kissed me, and then patted my behind.

The lasagna was lip-smacking delicious. I wanted seconds, but the other day Percy had made a comment about my weight. So I wasn't about to reload my plate.

After we washed and dried the dishes, we lounged arm and arm on the couch.

"That was so good," I said, "I can't believe I just made lasagna." I leaned my head against Percy's chest.

"*We* just made lasagna," corrected Percy. "We're a team, remember?"

"True," I said. "And now that I can actually cook, I'll be one step ahead when I get to Green Hills."

"What's Green Hills?" he asked.

I explained the whole independent-living program and Percy looked so sad after I gave him the explanation.

He softly caressed my face and said, "Kate, if *we* work out, you won't have to be moving to another facility. We could get our own place together."

I thought Percy was joking, so I smirked.

"Wipe that silly look off your face. I'm serious. What? You don't see us being together?"

"I do . . . but—"

"But what?" Percy interjected. "Don't you know how much I love you?"

I just stared at him, dumbfounded.

"I love you," repeated Percy, looking deeply into my eyes. This was my first time ever hearing these three words from a guy on the serious tip. I felt overwhelmed. Too overwhelmed to say the words back.

"Don't you love me?" asked Percy.

I nodded, feeling rushed off my feet.

"I don't read sign language, sweetheart. Do you love me?"

"Yes."

"Then tell me you love me."

"I love you."

Boom. I said it. Now it was official.

Percy caressed my face. "I'm giving you all that I have . . . so please don't play me." His eyes were blazing with full concentration on me.

"I won't play you," I said. He squeezed my hand tightly, and stared at me deeply.

Percy's intensity was almost ruining this beautiful moment.

"Kate, I don't think you understand how much I care about you," Percy pressed on.

"I do understand."

"Then act like you know, sweetheart. Don't look so afraid about what I'm saying to you."

Percy grabbed my chin and brought my face close to his. First, he he kissed me gently on my mouth, suckled my bottom lip, and then he kissed with so much force and passion, I melted into him. My body drifted away from my mind. I was burning inside. I matched his tongue movements stroke for stroke, even threw my arms around his neck and held on to him mad tight.

"So, when can I make love to you?" Percy whispered in my ear.

My arms dropped away from his neck. Here we go again.

"I don't know . . . soon," I said.

"How soon?"

Obviously, he wasn't going to stop questioning me about it, so I had to think of a bulletproof excuse. "Percy . . . trust me . . . I want you, too . . . but you already know it's illegal for us to have sex . . . because of our age difference—"

"And?" he interrupted.

"And I don't want you going to jail over me."

Percy jerked his head back. "You plan on telling somebody?"

"No."

"Okay, then, what are you saying?"

"Percy . . . please don't take this personal. . . . I'm just not ready. . . . It has nothing to do with you."

"Listen, just forget it," he snapped.

And just like before, Percy looked mad disappointed. Without a word, he got up and went into the bedroom. He stayed in there for a while. And then he took a trip to the bathroom. Then he went into the kitchen, walking around aimlessly, opening cabinets and closing them with a bang.

He had left me on the couch, sitting there like, duh? What just happened? But I wasn't about to follow him around like a lost little puppy. I knew in my heart I was in the right. He was in the wrong. *Real* love waits for sex, point-blank period.

I sat in my spot self-righteously until Percy returned to me. When he finally came back, he clicked on the television, and pulled me up into his lap, like nothing had happened.

I blinked. A brand-new Percy. Just like that.

He started massaging my back. Then he reached down and removed my sandals and began rubbing my stubby unpolished toes; even more confirmation that he had to love me. I'm saying, who does that?

"Feels nice," I said, in ecstasy.

"I can make you feel even better . . . if you let me."

Just then, my phone rang in my pocket. I was about to ignore the call, but Percy told me to answer it. Before answering, I was about to get up from Percy's lap, but he pulled me back down. So I answered from where I sat.

"Hey, Kate . . . I need to talk to you," blurted Felicia.

"Who's that?" Percy asked.

I was hoping Felicia didn't hear Percy. Apparently, she did because she said, "Oh, you're with *him* now."

"Yeah," I said. Then I took the phone away from my mouth and whispered to Percy, "It's Felicia."

"Tell her you're with your man right now."

When I got back on the phone, I told Felicia I had to go.

"Oh," she said. I could tell she was holding back words.

Click.

Just in case she tried to call me again, I secretly pushed the "off" button on my Pearl; I had to do it slick. Didn't want Percy getting suspicious over why I had to turn off my phone.

After that fiasco, nine o'clock rolled around. I told Percy I had to go.

"Damn, Kate, I really wish you could stay with me all night."

"Me, too," I said.

"I mean, we don't have to have sex. I just want to hold you in my arms all night."

"Yeah, that would be nice."

"So then, let's make it happen."

"Okay, I'll try."

"You'll try?" asked Percy. "That doesn't sound so convincing."

"Okay, I will," I stated firmly. I didn't want to upset Percy again.

"When?"

"Soon," I said, vaguely. "I promise . . . real soon."

Luckily, I really had to go, so he didn't press me further.

Chapter 21

Bright and early in the morning, Belinda called for me from downstairs. "You have a visitor," she announced.

Oh really? I thought. Who could it be? I knew Percy wouldn't risk getting me into trouble. I was mystified. When I got downstairs, Belinda nodded her head toward the door, which was cracked halfway open. I hesitantly made my way to the threshold, and *boom*, there was Felicia, standing on the porch, looking nervous and fidgety. She wore a bright yellow T-shirt, black yoga pants, her favorite busted yellow sneakers, and she was holding a manila envelope close to her chest.

"Sorry I came unannounced," she began, "but you refuse to return my calls."

I paused, still taken aback by her presence. "Um, I been real busy," I finally managed to say, feeling bad for dodging my best friend all this time.

"Well, I just came to give you this," she said, handing me the envelope. "My mother is parked a few cars down. So I can't stay long."

Dang, she even had her mother bring her here? I scanned the street and sure enough, three cars down, I spotted Felicia's mother sitting in their shiny black SL550 Benz.

"What is this about?" I asked, apprehensively staring at the envelope.

"You'll see," said Felicia. "Just don't open it until I leave, please."

My goofy, loveable homegirl was now acting so cold and businesslike toward me; it was hard to take.

"Well, alrighty then," I began, slowly. "So, um, can I call you later?"

"Of course you can," said Felicia. "That's why I'm here. I need to talk to you."

"Okay, but really . . . I meant to call you back. . . . I just been mad busy."

"Okay, Kate," said Felicia. "Whatever you say."

Felicia's mother tapped the horn twice. Felicia's cue to go. Good, because I felt the tension thickening in the air between us.

Felicia gave me a stiff hug good-bye and reminded me to call her.

"I will," I promised.

But once I was locked safely inside the bathroom, and ripped open the envelope, I wasn't sure *when* I'd be calling that fool.

I sat on the tub's edge, and muttered, "Is she serious right now?" as I laid eyes on an Abuse Facts Sheet, five pages long. I couldn't believe Felicia had really taken it there. But like a car wreck you can't look away from, my eyes gravitated toward some of the warning signs, including: frequent check-ins on a mate's whereabouts, bursts of bad temper, name calling and put-downs, controlling the way one dresses, eats, talks. . . . I couldn't read any further. None of these warning signs *really* applied to Percy. But then again . . .

I blocked the words out my head. I ripped the sheets to shreds, balled up the scraps, and made a three-point shot into the bathroom's garbage can.

Relationships can be so confusing. When you're in a shaky situation your mind starts leaving out the bad parts of your guy, and concentrates on the good, painting pretty little pictures in your head. I know there's a bad side to Percy, but the good in him outweighs the bad. I feel happy and loved whenever I'm around Percy. Never in my life have I felt this way before. I want to be happy, just like Felicia is with Marlon. Nobody's perfect. Everybody gets mad in their own way. Too bad Felicia doesn't understand. It's best to avoid her right now. She has too many questions I have no answers for.

Chapter 22

Five o'clock on a Saturday morning, Jeselle rapped hard on our window. I was the first to wake up, groggy as ever, and pulled the window open for her. She struggled over the sill to get her long limbs inside. Even in the darkness of the room, I could see her eyes were watery.

"What's wrong?" I asked, still half-dazed, but alert enough to be concerned.

"My mother has a new boyfriend. She kicked me out. Can't visit her anymore . . . ever."

"Wow."

"Yeah, it's a wrap." Jeselle sniffed.

"Let's go in the bathroom to talk," I suggested. I didn't want to wake up Tracy. I didn't want her in the conversation. This was a delicate matter.

I turned on the bathroom's nightlight instead of the bright light, and Jeselle and I sat on the edge of the tub next to each other. It was so hurtful to see big and bad Jeselle reduced to a puddle of tears.

I scooted closer to her and wrapped my arm around her shoulder. "Keep your head up, ma. It's going to be okay." I repeated this over and over again.

Keeping my head up was the only way I knew how to cope with

my own parentless condition. Shucks, at least Jeselle's mother had tried and failed instead of not trying at all. My own parents abandoned me before I could even walk.

And if you ask me, Jeselle was better off without a mother who fought her like a stranger in the street. Just because a woman has a child doesn't make her a real mother.

However, Jeselle *didn't* ask me for my opinion, so I didn't dare offer one. Folks get mighty touchy when you jump on their loved ones, even if their loved ones are already jumping on them.

"You good?" I asked, before leaving the bathroom.

"Yeah, I'm okay," Jeselle finally said.

But later that day, she moped around the house and all of the girls were asking her what was wrong. To take Jeselle's mind off of things, I asked if she wanted to cash in on an earlier promise to cornbraid her hair. "Yeah, that's cool," she said. "But I don't want to be in this house. Let's go out on the back porch. I need some air."

"No problem," I said. The backyard wasn't so bad now that Gerald's lazy butt had finally cut the grass. The only downside was that we had a clearer view of the cemetery.

I grabbed my comb and brush, Jeselle grabbed a folding chair, and we carried ourselves out to the back porch. I didn't expect to see the rest of the crew already outside passing a fat blunt around. Two were sitting on the railing, and three on the steps. I placed the chair six feet away from them, trying to avoid the smoke.

As soon as Jeselle sat down, Tracy got up, passed Jeselle the blunt, and said, "Burn it down, chick."

Jeselle took her puff and passed it up to me. "Nah, I'm good," I said.

"You square as hell." Jeselle laughed.

Instead of taking offense, I joked back, "You don't want me braiding your hair while I'm high, do you?"

Jeselle chuckled at this. I even thought I heard Tracy chuckle, too.

Then I got to work on Jeselle's hair. This was my first time work-ing with such long hair; it wasn't as easy as I thought. But I was de-termined to hook her up, especially with her feeling so down and all. I parted her hair carefully, and concentrated all my efforts to tighten every braid.

The girls were busy getting nice with their weed, so they weren't loud and distracting me, thank goodness.

In the middle of braiding, I had to stop to use the bathroom. While in there, I pulled my phone out from the cleaning cabinet to check for messages.

I had a missed call from Felicia. Ignored that. And then there was Percy's text:

CALL ME AS SOON AS YOU GET THIS.

CAN I CALL YOU LATER?

I NEED TO SPEAK WITH YOU RIGHT NOW.

Normally, I tried not to make phone calls in the bathroom. I didn't want the girls thinking I was crazy and talking to myself. But since Percy said "right now," I called him immediately.

"Baby, why are you whispering?" he asked.

"I'm in the bathroom," I explained. "Can't talk loud."

"What you doing right now? Can I see you?"

I paused, thinking of Jeselle's half-done head and her jacked-up spirits. Nah, I couldn't leave my girl hanging like that. "Um . . . is tomorrow okay?"

"But I want to see you today."

"My friend needs me right now."

"What friend?"

"Jeselle."

"But what does Jeselle have over me?"

"Nothing," I said, exasperated. "I'm just doing her hair."

"You're always doing somebody's hair," Percy complained.

Now that was a boldfaced lie, but I didn't bother to address it.

"Please, baby? I want to see you. I really miss you," pleaded Percy.

I almost gave in to him, but the image of Jeselle's watery eyes caught my soul. "I'm sorry, my friend needs me."

"But *I* need you," said Percy.

"She's going through something," I tried to explain. And it was none of Percy's business what Jeselle was going through, so I finally grew some guts, lied, and said someone was knocking on the door. I had to go.

Percy hung up on me without even saying good-bye.

I went back outside, walked through the cloud of blunt smoke, and asked Jeselle to hand me the comb. My mood was mighty low.

"Dang, what took you so long?" asked Jeselle. "I thought you got flushed down the toilet." The girls busted out laughing. I chuckled, wanting to be a good sport.

"You okay?" asked Jeselle.

"Yeah, I'm good," I lied, and resumed working on Jeselle's head. My braids were coming out dumb fly. Ciara thought so, too. She stood over Jeselle's head and said, "You do hair better than those African braiders."

I looked up into her eyes that were bloodshot from weed. "Thanks," I said, shaking Percy out of my mind.

Then Tracy rolled up behind Jeselle's head and said, "Your parting skills are mad precise." The friendly tone in her voice surprised the heck out of me.

"Thanks," I said, flashing a grin. It was such a relief to finally be cool with my roommate—not best buddies—but at least cool.

Venus rushed up to me and asked, "Can you do me next?"

"Yeah, no problem."

"How much you charging?" she asked.

"It's okay, I got you," I said. "They barely give us pocket change up in here, so I don't expect you to pay me."

Venus clapped her hands twice and said, "Chick, please, I can afford it. I don't depend on no allowance. That's what boyfriends are for."

Well, I wasn't about to beg her *not* to pay me, so I said, "Okay, thirty dollars." I needed the money anyway.

I braided the last braid in Jeselle's hair, and stood back to admire my work. As soon as Jeselle got up to go check her hair, Venus bum rushed the seat, yelling, "I got next!"

Then Jeselle came back outside smiling from ear to ear. She hugged me mad tight, and said, "You just hooked a sister up!"

"You know I got you, homie," I replied, reaching up to smooth down the top of her fresh long braids.

"So every week you got me?" Jeselle joked.

"Shoot, if I had bomb hair like yours, I'd never put it in braids. My hair would be flowing with the wind all day, every day."

"Whatever," Jeselle said, flipping her hand in the air. "People always think they want what they don't have. Shoot, I'm ready to cut my hair bald."

"Are you crazy," I exclaimed. "You better not!"

Venus tapped me and said, "Um, when are you planning on getting started? I'm a paying customer!"

Jeselle laughed. "My bad, let me leave Kate alone. Go 'head and do your thing, ma." She stepped aside.

I started in on Venus's thick head of hair.

Out of the blue, I said to Jeselle, "Percy says he prefers longer hair."

"Oh yeah?" said Jeselle, raising her eyebrows. "Well, tell *Percy* to buy you a damn weave then." She cracked up at her own joke. I chuckled, but for some reason, I suddenly felt sad.

I DON'T UNDERSTAND WHY YOU COULDN'T MAKE TIME FOR
    ME TODAY.

MY FRIEND NEEDED ME.

BUT I NEEDED YOU. AND I'M MORE THAN YOUR FRIEND. I'M
    SUPPOSED TO BE YOUR MAN.

I KNOW.

CAN I SEE YOU TOMORROW?

YES, I CAN SEE YOU.

MEET ME AT JAY STREET. THREE O'CLOCK. MAYBE WE CAN
   GO TO PROSPECT PARK.

SOUNDS GOOD.

CALL ME LATER TONIGHT. I WANT TO HEAR YOUR VOICE
   BEFORE I GO TO SLEEP.

OK.

I called Percy at eleven o'clock that night. Nobody was downstairs guarding the phone, so I had taken a chance with the landline. When Percy answered, he sounded so happy to hear from me. He asked me how I was feeling. I told him I was fine. He said he was fine, too. Our conversation was going along just fine until he broke the spell by asking, "So what was wrong with your homegirl?"

Here we go again.

I had already promised myself that Jeselle's business was none of his, but Percy wasn't the type to leave things alone. He always pressed and pressed until he got the answers he felt he deserved. Well, I was not in the mood to be pressed tonight, so I gave him a snippet of what happened, and ended with, "Jeselle got slapped by her own mother in front of this new loser boyfriend."

"Oh man, Jeselle is crying over a little slap?" asked Percy in disbelief. "Please, that's nothing. My mother broke a broomstick over my head once just for spilling Kool-Aid on the carpet."

"Your mother beat you with a broomstick?" I stuttered in shock. I knew Mrs. Thomas was a witch, but I didn't think she was a *violent* one.

"Broomsticks, belts, extension cords . . . whatever she could grab."

Wow, I said to myself, shaking my head in disgust. My heart went out to Percy. I mean, I had been beaten by many foster parents before, but never by my own flesh and blood—wherever they might be.

Percy suddenly added, "Don't get it twisted, sweetheart; you said 'beats' as in present tense. I'm talking about back when I was young. My mother knows better than to try that mess with me now."

Awkward silence fell over the phone.

Then I heard footsteps creaking on the stairs.

"Someone's coming," I whispered. "I gotta go."

"I'm looking forward to tomorrow, sweetheart," said Percy. "I can't wait to hold you in my arms again."

First thing in the morning, I peered out of my bedroom window. Storm clouds wrapped a huge gray blanket over Brooklyn. Oh well, I thought, Prospect Park was clearly out. This was a day to be inside with your boo. Sure enough, my boo was thinking the same thing, too. I received his text at twelve o'clock on the dot.

WEATHER SUCKS, BUT I STILL WANT TO SEE YOU.
SAME HERE.
CHINESE FOOD AND A MOVIE?
SOUNDS GREAT.

I met Percy at Jay Street at three o'clock. Then he drove us to a giant video store. We stepped inside the joint holding hands like an adorable couple. I witnessed lonesome people staring blankly at the huge movie selection, and sassy couples bickering about which movie to pick.

I didn't go through the trouble of bickering with Percy about movies. I just let my man take control; I doubted he would let me do the picking anyway.

In less than ten minutes, Percy snatched up two new releases. I didn't bother to look, or ask, for the titles. What mattered most to me was the upcoming opportunity to be snuggled up on the couch with my baby. Oh yeah.

We stood on a long line waiting to check out our movies, still holding hands, Percy bending down to kiss me on the cheek every few minutes. When our turn finally came, we were served by a tall, bucktoothed cashier. He greeted us in a loud, lively voice. "Great day for a movie, isn't it?"

Since Percy didn't say anything, I piped in, "For sure."

The cashier held up one of our movies and said, "I don't want to ruin it for you, but the butler did it."

The cashier was so corny, but he was older, and reminded me of Ted with his dry jokes, so I was chuckling at everything he said.

I didn't realize that Percy had a problem with this, until we got inside his car. Before he cranked the engine, he turned to me and said, "So you like attention, huh?"

"What?" I asked, jerking my head back in confusion.

"Why were you flirting with that guy so hard?"

"What guy?" I asked, because he surely couldn't be referring to the doofy cashier. If I'm going to flirt with someone, *at least* he's going to be a dime. Doofy dude was a penny; I wasn't attracted to his old butt at all.

"So you think it's cute to disrespect me out in public?" demanded Percy.

I was truly stunned by this accusation. All I could do was sit in silence as Percy yelled at me, asking the same stupid question over and over again.

"I wasn't flirting," I said, hopefully for the last time.

"Yes, you were."

"No, I wasn't."

"Yes, you were!"

I turned from him to stare out the window, disappointed and confused.

"I don't know why you feel the need to lie to me," said Percy. "I was standing right there. I saw you flirting with him!"

Okay, I had enough. I didn't have to put up with this bull, especially because I was completely innocent. "Listen, if you're not going to believe me, can you please take me to the train station? I want to go home." Now I was close to tears.

"I'm not going anywhere until you answer my question."

"If you can't take me, then I'm leaving." I grabbed the car door handle as a threat. I had never seen Percy this angry before. He was starting to scare me.

"You're leaving me because you're guilty," spat Percy, his light brown eyes blazing with anger.

I yanked the door open, got out, and slammed it shut behind me. Percy yelled out his car window, "Don't be slamming my doors, stupid!"

"You're the one who's stupid," I yelled back, surprised that I was actually cracking back on him. I had been holding in a whole lot since being with Percy.

I started walking down the block, my head bent down low, bewilderment coursing through my brain. Did that really just happen? Out of nowhere? Wow.

The fiery red Avenger trailed me, its crazy owner still shouting at me. "If you need attention that bad, you don't need to be with a guy like me. My woman has to show me respect. You hear me? Respect!"

I just couldn't wrap my mind around the sudden turn of events. This couldn't be the same guy who had done so many sweet and thoughtful things for me.

I didn't recognize Percy anymore.

Just then, I felt a raindrop fall on my eyelid. How appropriate, because I was already starting to cry. This was supposed to be a nice, simple day: Chinese food, a movie, and me and my man cuddled on the couch. But now, I was about to get stormed on. I needed my umbrella, which was still inside Percy's car. Damn.

Percy still had his head stuck out the window, shouting out craziness and trailing me, so I asked in the nicest tone possible, "Can I just get my umbrella please?"

He fixed me with a mean stare and yelled "You should have thought about that before you disrespected me."

Beeeppp! Beeeppp! Cars were now honking at Percy who was holding up traffic. So he peeled off down the street, leaving me in the dust . . . or should I say the rain. Lightning lit up the sky, and then came the snap, crackle, and pop. Drops began to fall in sheets, drenching me instantly. I was a wet, cold mess.

I walked with my head down being pummeled by the rain. Six long blocks to go. When I finally made it inside the train station, I was soaking wet and crying.

During my long train ride home, I shivered with cold and hurt over what had just happened. . . . It was supposed to be a nice, simple day.

Later that night, I received a text from Percy:

DID YOU MAKE IT HOME OKAY?

I left his question dangling in the air.

Chapter 24

I'M SORRY FOR GOING OFF ON YOU, BABY. PLEASE DON'T BE
   MAD AT ME.

I GO CRAZY WHEN I THINK OF YOU BEING WITH SOMEONE
   ELSE.

KATE, I NEED YOU IN MY LIFE, BABY. PLEASE DON'T DO THIS
   TO ME.

PLEASE CALL ME, SWEETHEART. I PROMISE IT WON'T HAP-
   PEN AGAIN.

WHY WON'T YOU WRITE ME BACK?

LET ME MAKE IT UP TO YOU, BABY. TEXT ME WHEN YOU GET
   A CHANCE.

Yeah, fat chance. In less than twenty-four hours, Percy was actually
expecting me to give him a clean slate? Hell no! I ignored all of
Percy's texts. I was too upset, and like I said, it's never good to communicate when you're upset. I needed a moment. Matter of fact, more
than a moment. Making me walk in the pouring rain was something
only a cruel person could do. So should I break up with Percy? Or
give him another chance? My mind was split in two.

   A part of me wanted it to be over, but the other part was holding out hope, remembering the good times, so many good times. I needed to sort this whole thing out in my head.

Problem was, Percy wouldn't give me a chance to clear my brain. He texted me twenty more apologetic messages, no exaggeration, before I finally decided to give in and text him back.

I JUST WISHED YOU BELIEVED ME. THAT'S ALL.

I DO BELIEVE YOU NOW.

AND I PROMISE NOT TO GO OFF ON YOU LIKE THAT AGAIN, OK, BABY?

OK.

Now don't get me wrong. My "OK" meant, yes, I hear you, now please fall back from texting me, and give me some freaking space.

But Percy texted me ten more times, begging me back into his life.

Lucky for me, I had gotten sick from being drenched in the rain, so it was easy for me to put down my phone and stay away from Percy. I was glued to my bed for three whole days with the covers pulled up over my head. Chicken soup, hot tea, and Jeselle made me feel better.

When I fully recuperated, and checked my phone, no lie, I had about fifty texts from Percy apologizing fifty different ways.

I went through all of his "sorry" messages, pressing the Delete button, and shaking my head in disbelief. He was so extra. Borderline obnoxious.

Then suddenly, one text caught my attention. It said the following:

AUGUST 4TH OUR ONE-MONTH ANNIVERSARY. I WANT US TO DO SOMETHING SPECIAL. I REALLY MISS U.

First, I was surprised that Percy actually remembered our special day, because I had forgotten it. Second, I started thinking that Percy must really care about me to be so persistent to the point of pitiful. Super fly guys like him are usually not willing to lose their pride, sending a million texts, begging some girl for forgiveness when they have so many other prettier girls to choose from. In all of my years, no boy has ever fought so hard to keep me in his life.

So maybe Percy truly loved me, I told myself. Maybe he was only having a bad day that day, and maybe, just maybe, I *did* disrespect him for being too friendly to the cashier, and maybe we all lose control at times . . . the truth is, nobody's perfect. Besides, as out of control as *I* used to be, who was I to judge Percy? Where would I be if Tisha had given up on me?

With these thoughts running through my brain, I finally caved in and texted Percy back. I told him that I missed him, too, which was so very true. A split second later, Percy popped the question:

CAN YOU COME TO DUMBO AND SPEND THE NIGHT WITH
ME TOMORROW?

It didn't take me long to text back: YES.

I missed Percy. Really missed him. I wanted to be wrapped up in his beautiful strong arms again. I couldn't wait to feel his warm sensuous lips against my skin.

Operation DUMBO was about to be in full effect.

As far as the group home was concerned, I wasn't worried about a spend-the-night strategy. By now, everybody at Common Grounds was doing the same overnight thing; so just add a sister to the mix. My only concern was Percy's expectations. He promised that our night didn't have to be about sex if I didn't want it to be. Well, I didn't want it to be. I was determined to hold down my get-to-know-me-first rule. Abstaining from sex was the only power I had over Percy. And I wasn't about to lose my power just yet.

"I need you to take a cab to my father's apartment," Percy explained, when I had snuck a call to him later that night. "Be at the crib by eight o'clock."

Percy gave me his father's exact address. Meanwhile, I was thinking, Who has money for a cab?

Luckily, Percy read my mind and further explained, "Call me when you're close by, and I'll come downstairs to pay."

"Okay."

The plan was tightly set.

Time to pack my bag.

Jeselle sat on my bed watching me fumble through my dresser drawer looking for some overnight gear. "Girl, you better pull out some sexy lingerie," she exclaimed.

"Nah, it's not about sex tonight," I said with a chuckle.

"Homegirl, you better get your mind right and let Percy hit it before he finds somebody else."

Jeselle's words rang in my head like a warning bell.

But then the memory of Tisha's advice bing-bonged even louder: "Kate, don't give up your treasure to just any old body. Make sure the guy is worth it first. If he loves you, he will wait."

Now that's what's up.

With this comforting thought in mind, I threw my overnight bag on the bed, and began packing.

But Jeselle broke into my thoughts again by saying, "If Percy fine as you say, best believe he's getting skins from someone else."

"Well, Percy already told me he can wait," I firmly stated. Jeselle was about to get on my last nerves if she didn't zip it. Loved her, but she really needed to zip it. She didn't know what she was talking about. Besides, girls and guys be jumping between thighs without bothering to get themselves, or their partners, checked. I wanted to take a trip to the clinic with Percy before I gave him my treasure.

Show him I am clean; and let him do the same. Only problem was, I doubted he'd be game.

Anyway.

I purposely packed my big-girl panties and sports bra, figuring no need to be tempting a brother with lacy lingerie. If Percy peeped me in droopy granny panties, he probably wouldn't be wanting me too tough.

Jeselle cracked up hard at the sight of my underwear, though. "Are those curtains?" she asked between guffaws. "Or a pillowcase? Girl, you got some big old drawers!"

"Whatever, I'm all set," I said, grinning, my bag over my shoulder, my feet pointing toward the doorway.

"Well, have fun tonight," said Jeselle, giggling mischievously.

"Don't worry, I will." I smiled, feeling elated. I couldn't wait to be back in my baby's arms again.

Chapter 25

At first, everything was going according to plan. Mrs. Cooper was long gone. Belinda and Gerald, missing in action as usual. At fifteen minutes after seven, I took flight from the group home, thinking my estimated time of arrival to DUMBO would be on point.

But when I hit the streets, I couldn't find a cab for nothing. Avenue U, empty. Stillwell Avenue, plenty of cars but no cabs.

I nervously checked my BlackBerry. There was only one battery bar left. Now I had to turn my phone off to save power. Not a good look, since I wouldn't be able to call Percy and tell him I couldn't catch a cab to save my life.

Gravesend was a ghost town. No exaggeration, I had to walk thirteen blocks before I finally hit a busy intersection. Sadly enough, three cabs passed me by on purpose; I know because they looked dead at me as I waved for them to stop.

Then, finally, a shiny silver cab raced up to the curb like a victorious chariot, ready to save my night. I hopped inside, told the cabby where to go, and he whisked me away.

"Excuse me, sir, what time is it?" I asked, as we cruised down a dark stretch of road.

The cabby needlessly swiveled all the way around and said, "A little after eight o'clock, honey. You late for a date?"

I didn't answer him. I was too busy fretting. I was indeed late. I had tried my best not to disappoint Percy. But it seemed like everything I did led to his disappointment.

When we finally headed down Percy's father's block, I pulled out my phone, which was hanging on to its last bar.

"Yeah?" Percy answered in a monotone voice.

"I'm downstairs."

Click.

The phone went dead. I wasn't sure if we had a bad connection, or did Percy just hang up on me? For some reason, my hands were shaking.

As soon as I caught sight of Percy, I knew he was upset. His body language was stiff and his face mad rigid. He didn't look my way once when he came up to the cab, holding a billfold. "Here you go, my man," he said, peeling off the cab fare. He must have given a nice tip because the cabby exclaimed, "Thanks, and have a wonderful time, lovebirds!"

Well, this bird wanted to fly away because Percy was showing me no love. My heart felt like a stone sinking inside my stomach, as Percy ignored the mess out of me.

He was quiet as I followed him up the stairwell. But as soon as we were behind closed doors, he got up in my face and said, "What took you so long?"

"I had a hard time finding a cab," I stuttered. Percy backed me up close to the wall, and slammed his hand against it. I jerked my shoulders up in shock.

"I told you to get here at eight o'clock," Percy shouted. "You couldn't make a simple phone call to tell me you were running late?"

"I'm sorry," I said. "My battery was running low."

Percy walked away from me, shaking his head. I followed behind him into the living room.

The living room was dark, lit by candles sitting in ceramic holders on each side table. I smelled strawberry incense floating in the air. Percy had tried to set moods, and the mood was now ruined. I plopped down heavily on the couch, and placed my overnight bag beside me to keep me company.

Percy was pacing around the living room, with his hands behind his back. "Couldn't even make a simple phone call," he said, more to himself than me. I cast my eyes down to the carpet to avoid his angry glare.

Then out of nowhere, Percy swooped down and snatched my overnight bag from the couch. He stormed into the nearby kitchen, and flipped on the light. I could see him from the overpass, digging furiously through my bag.

"I gave you this phone to keep in touch with you," Percy shouted. "You're supposed to have it on 24/7." He fumbled through my bag, yanked out my BlackBerry, and said, "So let's see who you been calling."

He had a right to be mad at me, but now he was overdoing it. I didn't say anything, though. I was too scared; he was too angry.

After Percy finished checking my BlackBerry's call log, of course he found nothing.

I thought my proven innocence would calm him down. But I thought dead wrong. The next thing I knew, Percy's arm pitched back like he was playing baseball, and a split second later, the Blackberry came hurtling toward my head. I ducked in the nick of time. The phone just missed the glass coffee table and landed with a thud on the plush beige carpet. I curled up on the couch into a fetal position, shocked as hell and frightened to death.

Percy stormed into the living room and stood over me. "I had everything planned out for us, trying to make our night special, and you messed it all up."

"I'm sorry," I said, shielding my face.

"Put your hand down," he snapped. "I'm not going to hit you."

I unshielded my eyes.

"How could you do this to me, Kate?" he asked, his voice a bit calmer, "Look at everything I tried to do for you."

Percy grabbed my hand, lifted me from the couch, and took me on a tour of ruined romance. First, he led me into the kitchen, lifted the lid of the garbage can, and showed me a glob of uneaten mashed potatoes, corn on the cob, and fried chicken mixed with potato peels. A part of me thought this extreme of him, throwing away good food that could have simply been warmed up. But the other part of me was touched; he had cooked us a delicious dinner for our anniversary, all for nothing.

Then Percy led me inside the bathroom. Two candles sat on either side of the tub. Red and white rose petals were scattered all over the tub's edge and the white tiled floor. The bathroom even smelled like roses. The tub was filled up to the brim, with a few bubbles still floating lifelessly around. A fluffy white towel and a brand-new red robe sat atop the wicker hamper situated in the corner. "I remember you complaining about having no hot water at your house," Percy began, "so I ran a hot bath for you . . . but now look." He dipped his hand in the water. "Ice cold." He flicked the water at me. "I should make you get in it," he added.

I was almost tempted to hop in the cold water just to show him how sorry I was. I mean . . . look at everything he tried to do for me, and all I had to do was simply keep my phone charged. Nobody had ever done anything this special for me. Romance was for people in the movies before I met Percy. My first *real* boyfriend had tried to treat me like a lady, and I had acted like an irresponsible little girl. I looked down at the floor. I felt so bad. "I'm really sorry," I said. "I just wasn't thinking."

Percy must have sensed my sorrow, because he finally calmed all the way down.

"I'm tired," he rasped, in a hoarse voice. "Let's go to bed."

———

"Baby?"

"Yes?"

"I'm sorry for throwing the phone at you." We lay in the big soft bed, our bodies intertwined like a pretzel.

I didn't know what to say.

If I said, "It's okay," that would make Percy think he could throw phones at me again, but if I told him that it *better not* happen again, that would make us get into an argument. So I said nothing. Absolutely nothing.

"Did you hear me?" asked Percy, rubbing my arm with his warm hands.

"Yes, I heard you."

"And I promise it won't happen again, okay, baby? It's just that I was trying to do something nice for you and you made me upset. Do you forgive me?"

I nodded in the dark.

Percy rubbed my leg. I could tell he was going to try me again. But I was fortified down there. Wide awake, mad alert, determined to keep Percy out of my panties. I brushed his groping hand from the side of my grannies, from the top, front and back. Finally, he gave up the struggle and left me alone. I think he would've pressed me further if he hadn't already played baseball with my phone.

"Don't you love me, baby?" Percy whispered feverishly.

"Yes."

"Then tell me you love me."

"I love you," I said.

"Then *make* love to me."

"I'm just not ready." How many times did I have to tell him, I wondered.

Percy kept quiet. He just waited for a while, and then went for my panties again. Growing agitated, I pushed his hand away. Then Percy puffed heavily and turned his back to me.

I felt so bad. Rejected. Dejected. I really wanted to please Percy—just not in that way. So I reached over to hold him in my arms, trying to show him I cared, but he pushed my arm away with force and said, "Now you see how I feel."

Chapter 26

I didn't hear from Percy for a few days, and I didn't bother reaching out to him, either. Seemed like this was an ongoing pattern between us. He does something foul; I catch an attitude. Then he reels me back in with the bait of his romantic words. Fortunately, Jeselle and I were starting to get closer, so I didn't miss Percy as much this time around.

Percy ended up texting me on Wednesday, asking me to call him when I could. Since I already had a taste of his persistence, without delay I made sure the coast was clear, shut myself inside the bathroom, and called him, just to get it over with. The first thing he said was, "Hey, baby, I know it's hump day, but that doesn't mean we have to hump."

"Huh?" I asked, perplexed. I was sitting on the edge of the bathtub, trying to make this call quick and painless. I had no time for riddles.

"Hump day is considered Wednesday," Percy explained, "because it's the middle of the week. So I'm saying, even though it's Wednesday, I already got over the hump . . . get it?"

"Oh," I said, not amused. All joking aside, I still had some lingering problems with Percy and there was literally no rug in this bathroom to brush them under. I had to let him have it.

"Percy, I didn't appreciate the way you treated me at your father's house," I blurted. "Yelling at me . . . pressuring me for sex . . . I thought you said you loved me."

"I *do* love you," insisted Percy.

"But sometimes it doesn't feel like it."

"Listen, baby, I'm sorry, okay? I lost control."

"Yeah . . . tell me about it."

"Please don't be sarcastic with me," said Percy. I could tell he was monitoring the bass in his voice. Because real talk, if he started yelling at me again, I was ready to hang up on his crazy behind. And he knew it.

"Everybody loses control every once in a while," he explained. "And no disrespect, sweetheart, but you really need to start learning how to forgive people."

"But I have forgiven you," I snapped. "More than once!"

"Seems like you're not in the mood to talk," said Percy, sadly.

Between me and you, I wasn't in the mood. Percy had a way of twisting things around, always trying to make me feel like I was the one at fault. I missed him, yes, but I was getting tired of his mess. Percy was putting me through so much nonsense in such a short period of time. I wasn't sure what to think. If this was how relationships worked, maybe I needed to be single.

One thing was for sure though: I needed to get off this phone. *Now.*

Jeselle and I were about to take a walk around the neighborhood park. I was trying to show her simple pleasures, the same way Felicia had shown me.

"Anyway, I have to go now. Me and my homegirl are about to head out."

"Head out where?"

"The park," I said firmly, daring Percy to interrogate me.

He dramatically heaved a sigh and said, "Okay . . . once again, your friend comes first. . . . I already know the drill."

But Percy *didn't* know I had built up enough courage to show him how the dial tone feels. *Click.*

Percy called me right back.

At first, I wasn't about to answer. But I knew he was the type to keep on calling until I picked up the phone. So I answered the phone, eyes rolled to the ceiling.

"Yes?" I said with an attitude.

"Listen, Kate, let's not do this," Percy began, his voice mad humble now that he knew I meant business. "There was no need to hang up on me."

"Okay, sorry for hanging up, but I already told you I have to go."

"Can we please stop fighting?"

"I don't want to fight, either."

"Then can I see you again?"

"I don't know."

"Oh, so you *don't* want to see me?" Percy asked in a pitiful voice. "Are you determined to stay mad at me?"

"No . . . it's not that."

"Then what is it?"

"Well . . . if I see you again . . . it has to be outdoors."

"What? You don't trust me anymore?"

"I didn't say all that," I countered. "I'm just saying, why tempt ourselves? I'm not ready to have sex yet, and you can't seem to accept that. So it's better that we see each other outdoors."

Percy paused, and then spoke. "Okay . . . so if I promise not to try again, are you willing to come over? We can watch TV, or play cards, whatever you want to do . . . and I promise not to lay a hand on you."

"I don't think that would be a good idea."

"Okay," Percy said in a low voice. "I can respect that."

"Thanks for understanding."

"Anyway, I better let you get back to your little friend. Bye."

When I hung up the phone, my heart sank. I wasn't happy with the way things were going between us. I wasn't about to call Percy back, though. Maybe we needed some time apart. But to my surprise, two hours later, Percy texted me, asking me to call him.

I had just gotten back from my walk, and was feeling free and easy, but as I stood in the bathroom, staring at Percy's text, I felt like the walls were closing in on me.

I took a deep breath, and made the call.

"Hey, baby," Percy exclaimed. His voice sounded mad happy, like nothing had happened, like la-di-da!

"Hey," I said, in a lackluster voice.

"I just found out there's going to be a free concert at Boys and Girls tomorrow."

"Oh," I replied, still taken aback that he was calling me so soon.

"And guess who's performing."

"Who?"

"Fabolous!"

Now my ears perked up. I was feeling Fabolous. And his concert was free? Oh yeah, best believe I would be there. But really? A part of me wished I was going with my girls instead.

Chapter 27

The concert was set to begin at three o'clock, but I was out of the house before twelve. I was not trying to be late. No mistakes allowed. I wanted no reason for Percy to pop off on me, because, hey, you never know, I might just pop back.

I arrived in Bed-Stuy at 1:30 PM. Cobalt-blue sky. Sun beaming down on Brooklyn. It was a very beautiful day.

I was supposed to meet Percy in front of the Boys and Girls entrance at two thirty. So I had mad time to kill. First things first; I needed something to eat.

I headed to the pattie place located near the Utica Avenue train station. Once inside, I stared hungrily at the yellow cakes and bread pudding sitting behind thick glass. The line of people was dumb long. My stomach rumbled every two seconds; Jamaican music was blasting so no one could hear how hungry I was. As the line inched forward, I shifted from foot to foot, impatient as ever.

I was next in line to order, when I felt a tap on my shoulder. I swiveled around to face Charles, who was grinning from ear to ear. "Yo, shawty, you owe me a pattie," he said.

"Hey, Charles," I replied, smiling. "What brings you here?" I was so happy to see him, but playing it off, as usual.

"I spotted you as I was passing by. I swear, I could be anywhere in the world and I can always spot my girl, Kate."

"Okay, that's sweet. But fall back for a minute, please? I'm starving!" I turned to the lady behind the counter. "Miss, may I have one chicken pattie, please?"

"Aww, so well-mannered," joked Charles. "Too bad you're uncivilized when it comes to your homeboy. Tell me why you left a brother hanging on the Fourth?"

After paying for the pattie, I addressed Charles's remark, feeling guilty as ever. "My bad," I began, "things got really hectic that day."

"And my feelings got really hurt," Charles replied. "You had me stuck in the crib for no good reason."

"I'm really sorry. My bad." I looked down at the floor.

Charles patted my shoulder. "I'm only messing with you. I accept your apology. Nobody told me to wait inside the house, anyway. I had choices." Charles smiled and extended his fist for a pound. We pounded. We cool. Simple as that.

"Can you keep me company while I eat?" I asked, brightening up, as we walked out the store. It felt so good being next to Charles. I felt so relaxed, so *myself* with him.

"Where are we headed?" asked Charles.

"Fulton Park."

"So I'm guessing you're around the way for the Fabolous concert?"

"No doubt!"

"Meeting up with Felicia?"

"Nah," I said, not bothering to mention Percy. I was enjoying Charles too much right now. For some reason, I didn't even want to think about Percy.

Charles and I sat on a park bench under the shade and I dogged my pattie like a savage while Charles watched me. I didn't feel self-conscious at all. When I was done, Charles laughed at me and said, "You wolfed it, son!"

"Yeah, a sister was starving." I laughed.

Charles grabbed my paper bag, fished out a napkin, and caringly wiped the crumbs away from my mouth. "Thanks," I said, as my stomach took a quick dip into butterfly land. Oh man. Charles was starting to get to me again. My homeboy seemed to have a permanent spot in my heart.

"So you lookin' nice," said Charles, looking me up and down, at my plain old outfit.

"Thanks, you, too," I said, admiring his fresh white tee and criss-cross cornrows, wondering what broad fixed it for him, and growing resentful at the mere thought. I stared at his head for a minute before saying, "So you found one of your many girls to braid your hair, huh?" I didn't mean to sound jealous, but hey, I was.

"Not a girl," Charles corrected. "A grown woman from the African hair-braiding shop on Throop. How many times do I have to tell you there are *no* other girls right now? I'm still trying to get with *you*."

"Yeah, right." I smirked.

"Kate, I already told you I've slowed down a whole lot."

Slowed down. These words reminded me about our last conversation in front of the Garden. He had mentioned "slowing down" and "Naleejah" in the same sentence. I reminded him about needing to spill the gossip. "Still not a good time," he explained.

"Oh hell naw!" I protested, grabbing his arm. "You promised to tell me."

Charles suddenly grew very serious. He paused, and then spoke. "Well . . . how can I put this . . . Naleejah has a *House In Virginia*."

"She has a house?" I repeated in disbelief. "Wow, she must be tricking big-time! Who bought it for her?"

"Oh . . . I guess you never heard that term before."

"What term?" I asked, exasperated. "Quit with the riddles and tell me what's up."

Charles paused again, and then blurted, "Naleejah has HIV."

My bottom lip hit the floor. My hand flew to my mouth. As much as I couldn't stand the girl, my heart suddenly went out to her. "Oh my gosh. How'd you find out?" I asked in horror.

"Divine told me . . . he got a call from the clinic telling him he needs to get tested."

"Wow," was all I could say.

"I feel so messed up for my boy because he hit Naleejah *raw*."

"Oh my gosh." Tears started welling in my eyes.

"Yeah, and he didn't take the test yet. . . . He doesn't want to know."

"So, what if he unknowingly gives it to the next chick?"

"I know, right? See, that's why I *always* use condoms with girls like that," said Charles, shaking his head.

"Not just with girls like that . . . with everybody," I muttered. Charles needed to get his facts straight. "Nobody is immune to AIDS, no matter how innocent or fine. Everybody's status is suspect. Trust."

"I feel you," Charles replied. "But I'm careful. I got tested. I'm good."

"Well, I'm glad," I said.

"I still see Naleejah around the way," continued Charles. "She still looks the same. Same weight. Hair done. Wardrobe always on point. You can't even tell she has the virus . . . and that's the scary part."

I stared at the ground, still blinking back tears. Poor Naleejah with her low self-esteem, and neglectful parents . . . sleeping around to find love. The girl already had so many problems. And now she had a *deadly* one.

Charles lifted my chin and stared at me with concern. "Are you okay?"

I nodded, but I was lying.

"See, I told you this wasn't a good time to tell you."

"Yeah . . . I should've believed you."

A part of me wanted to reach out and call Naleejah. But her number was in last year's trash. And I didn't feel comfortable making a pop-up visit to her house. Face to face, what could I say to make things okay? All I could do was wish the best for her.

Charles, seeing I was really shaken, reached over and pulled me close to him. I put my head on his chest and rested for a while. I don't know how much time passed before he pulled me away and said, "Okay, now I need you to cheer up. Let's head to Boys and Girls. My homeboys will be there, but I'll tell them I'm chilling with you."

Oh, no. Percy.

I checked my watch. Twenty minutes to spare. I breathed a huge sigh of relief.

Charles was up on his feet, but I stayed put. "Why you sitting there like a statue? You rolling with me, or what?"

"Um, I have to wait for somebody," I said.

"Here?"

"Yeah," I lied. Even in his absence, Percy had me shook.

"Well, I'm not going to let you sit here by yourself."

"It's broad daylight," I said testily. "I'm good."

Shoo, Fly Boy, Shoo!

Charles paused and stared at me for a minute. Then he said, "All right yo, I'm out."

Finally.

I watched Charles walk toward Malcolm X Boulevard. Then I made my move. I looked both ways and ran across the street to stand at the entrance of Boys and Girls High. I was fifteen minutes early—just in case. Just to be safe.

But ten minutes later, my safety net was torn up from the floor up. Charles and a troupe of his boys came walking up the block, headed straight toward me. I wanted to sink inside the sidewalk.

I hoped with all my heart that Charles would just wave at me and keep it moving. But nope, he stopped dead in front of me, and kept his boys moving. "I'll get back up with y'all on the inside," he called after them.

Charles turned to me and said, "So we meet again." But before he could say anything else, a pretty cinnamon-brown girl rocking wavy *real* hair and a killer pink minidress rolled up on Charles from behind, showing all her teeth. "Hey, Charles," she said in a flirty voice.

"Hey, what's up, Rosa," said Charles, barely looking her way.

"Did you see Melanie go inside yet?"

"Naw, I just got here," he said, distractedly.

"So are y'all gonna be in the back, or the front?"

"Not sure yet," Charles replied with a shrug.

Rosa was acting thirsty, but Charles didn't seem interested in quenching. A spark of jealousy ran through me, but at the same time, I wanted Rosa to win her flirty game. Then maybe she could lure Charles away from my vicinity before Percy showed up.

The next thing I knew, Charles said, "Yo, Rosa, I'll catch you on the inside, okay? I'm talking to my shorty right now."

Rosa and I wore the same shocked face at Charles's words: "My shorty."

Really?

As flattered as I was, I wasn't grinning. My mind was totally fixed on Percy's reaction if he caught me standing with Charles. So the minute Rosa sashayed away, I got busy trying to think of a way to get rid of Charles. I was as nervous as ever and he sensed it. "What's wrong, Kate?"

"Still thinking about Naleejah," I quickly said. This was half true. I was really sad about my ex-homegirl, but more panicky about Percy.

"Try not to think about it," said Charles. Taking me off guard, he reached out and wrapped me up into a big bear hug.

Then *boom.*

As if some force of nature was playing a bad joke on me, tell me why Charles chose to embrace me the split second Percy rolled up in his car?

There was a parking spot two cars away from where we stood. In a snap, Percy whipped the Avenger into the spot, hopped out of the car, and slowly approached us. He didn't look happy at all.

Percy's lips were set into a thin firm line. He didn't say a word.

"Hey, Percy," I stuttered.

He ignored my greeting, looked over at Charles, then looked at me and said, "Can I talk to you for a second?" Without waiting for a reply, Percy grabbed my hand and pulled me away from the front gate that I had been trembling up against.

"Kate, are you okay?" Charles asked, following after us.

"Yeah, yeah, I'm fine," I said, not wanting Charles to get involved. This was my battle. I got myself into it. Now I had to get myself out.

Charles lightly touched my arm. "Are you sure? Everything cool?"

"Yeah, yeah, it's cool," I insisted.

Percy put on a friendly mask and said, "My man, I just need to talk to my girl in private, a'ight?"

Charles ignored Percy and fixed me with a serious stare. "If you need me, holler at me, okay?"

"Oh stop, I'm good," I said, faking a laugh.

Charles finally walked away. I didn't dare look after him, fearing what Percy would say. The evil jealousy in his eyes was frightening.

We crossed Fulton Street, away from the concert. I was bewildered beyond words. Percy's hand squeezed my arm so hard, it felt like he was taking my blood pressure. He walked me down Stuyvesant

Avenue, stopped short at the corner, and then hemmed me up against a mailbox.

I was scared to death. Bad as I am, I can't beat a man.

"So you messing with that punk clown, aren't you?" demanded Percy. The vein in his forehead suddenly popped out.

"No, I'm not," I stuttered. "Charles is just a friend."

"You think I'm stupid, huh? I bet he's the one smashing it . . . that's why you won't give me any."

"No, he's not," I said, now close to crying. "Why are you yelling at me? I'm telling you the truth!"

Percy grabbed me by my top and said, "You're lying, Kate. I know you're lying. That's the same punk you were hugging up on like a slut at the Garden."

Whoa.

Two blows hit me at once. First, Percy had just fixed his mouth to call me a slut. Second, that he had been watching me the whole time I was with Charles at the Garden on the Fourth of July. Who does that? How creepy.

I stared at the vein in Percy's forehead, at the red splotches on his cheeks, and the crazy look in his eyes. Any love I had for Percy vanished at that moment. This was not the same man I had fallen in love with. This was a crazy man who I had to get away from. Fast.

I made a move to leave. Percy yanked me back like a rag doll. "Don't walk away from me when I'm talking to you."

"Get off me, please," I said, calmly.

"Where you think you're going?" he demanded. "I'm not finished talking to you!"

"But you're yelling at me . . . and you don't believe anything I say. What do you want from me?" I blubbered.

I swear, this whirlwind love affair was turning into a freaking nightmare.

Tears welled up in my eyes. Why? Why did I trust this man with my heart when he couldn't even trust *me*? I never flirted with anybody in front of him. In fact, *he* was the one flirting with the waitress, and who knows who else? I decided to hit him with this fact. I was so hurt, I had to fight back. "Percy, did I say anything to you when you disrespected me?"

"When did I disrespect you?" he demanded.

"Flirting with that waitress."

"Say what?" Percy boomed. "You lucky I didn't drop your little black behind to be with her!" he shouted. "She looks way better than you. I can be with anybody I want. But here I am wasting my time with a loser like you."

Wow. Really? What a low blow.

Something inside me flipped, like a courage switch. Percy's words were so hurtful, so dead wrong; I had no choice but to find my own voice. "So, if I'm such a loser, why are you stressing me then? Calling me off the hook, and begging me to be with you? If you can have anybody you want, then go be with them. Stop stressing me!"

"Please, B—, nobody is stressing you," said Percy with a dismissive wave. "Who are you to stress? Nobody wants you anyway."

"Then leave me alone!" I shouted.

Better yet, let me leave *him* alone, I thought. Why was I standing here taking all of this crap from Percy when I had two feet and my own mind to walk away? Percy had no right to detain me. Bump that. I had come all the way to Bed-Stuy to see a Fabolous concert, and a Fabolous concert I would see.

Reviving the courage that had almost died inside of me, I took one last look at Percy and mentally broke free. "I'm *out*," I said, tasting freedom on the tip of my tongue.

I spun on my heels and headed back to Boys and Girls. Held my head high with every step down the block. It felt so good to leave the crazy man right where he stood. But when I made it to the corner of Fulton Street, I looked to my right.

There was Percy.

In the flesh.

Leaning against the STOP sign across the street, his sinister stare aimed dead at me.

Chapter 29

I had to make a sudden change of plans. If I allowed Percy to follow me inside Boys and Girls High, I'd be feeding him to a vicious pack of lions. Man, listen: If Charles witnessed Percy disrespecting me, he would fly Percy's head, not to mention his boys carried weapons. Since jail time over me was out of the question, I had to steer clear of the school.

I hurried down Fulton Street, every few seconds glancing over my shoulder. Percy kept ten feet behind me, probably playing innocent in case I screamed for help. But I wasn't about to scream. I didn't want to bring any attention to myself. This was *my* battle that I had to fight. I got myself into this mess; I had to get myself out.

Finally. Utica Avenue train station.

I raced down the steps. Out of nowhere, Percy rushed up from behind, grabbed my upper arm, and spun me around. We stood on the middle of the staircase, mean-grilling each other.

"Why won't you talk to me?" he demanded.

I just stared at him like he was stupid, because he was.

"What do you expect me to say?"

"You know I love you," he suddenly cooed. "So why are you doing this to me?"

"Doing *what* to you?" I demanded, shaking with anger.

"Why can't you be honest with me? Tell me what's going on between—"

I yanked my arm away from him. He was obviously nuts. I had already told him once, Charles is just my friend. Enough was enough.

I dug in my pocket for my Metrocard, and made a move toward the turnstile. But Percy grabbed my arm again and said, "Why do you keep walking away from me?"

"Can you let go of my arm, please? I'm done talking to you."

"Oh, it's like that?"

"Yeah, it's like that," I said calmly. "I'm too ugly for you anyway . . . so go ask Bianca for her number."

"I already did," Percy spat.

"Then call her," I said.

"I will," he replied. "So, matter of fact . . . give me back my phone, slut."

"Wow, so I'm a slut now?"

"A sloppy black slut," said Percy, emphasizing every word. "I can't believe I even wasted my time with someone like you."

Wounded by Percy's words, but determined to hide it, I furiously dug up the BlackBerry from my pocket, tempted to throw it at him. Then again, nah, I had my dignity.

I planned to hand the phone back like a lady, but Percy snatched it savagely from me. "Now you can't call the punk you been cheating on me with."

"Nobody's cheating on you," I snapped. "So go ahead and take your little *tracking device* back. I don't care."

I was about to step away when Percy lifted his right arm, hauled back, and slapped the living mess out of me. I saw stars and lights flash before my eyes. My hand flew up to my cheek; it burned like hell. It felt like Percy's handprint was actually branded on my face. No one was around to ask, "Did that just happen?" I couldn't believe it.

"See what you made me do?" Percy yelled.

I pressed my hand against my cheek, staring at Percy in disbelief. He had the craziest look in his eyes. This was one of the scariest moments in my life. I had been through hell and back throughout my time in foster care, but I never had someone who claimed to love me, put their hands on me to hurt me. I was shaken to my core.

"See, if you didn't make me so mad that wouldn't have happened." Percy grabbed my arm again and held it like a vice grip. I was too afraid to move. "Why are you acting this way, huh? Don't you know how much I love you?"

Just then, an A train rumbled into the station. People started climbing up the stairs. Now that I had witnesses, I could finally leave Percy where he stood.

Adding to my confidence, I spotted a police officer walking toward us, like a savior fallen from heaven.

I twisted from Percy's grip and darted through the turnstile without looking back.

I sat in a quiet corner on the A train with my feet up on the seat, knees up under my chin. I held my head down so no one could see me crying. A woman tapped me on my shoulder and asked if I was okay, but I had no strength to look up to see who she was. At my stop, I dried my eyes with my T-shirt, but during my walk to Common Grounds, I was crying again.

I had to pull myself together before I stepped inside the group home. I didn't want anyone to know what had just happened to me. I was too embarrassed and ashamed. There was no one I could talk to but myself.

I can still feel Percy's handprint burning on my face. How could Percy do this to me? How could Percy tell me he loves me in one breath, and then hit me the next? I can no longer deny it; Percy is not the man for me. I need to put an end to this relationship, this abusive, unhappy relationship. My heart is finally telling me what my mind knew all along. Percy is just another piece of the sorry puzzle called My Life. All I ever want is love; all I ever get is hurt.

It was five o'clock in the morning, and I couldn't go to sleep for nothing. The memory of the previous day's events pounded in my skull like an unbearable headache. Writing about Percy in my journal didn't help shed any logical light on him. My mind was split in two confused pieces. Half of me was completely done with the madman. The other half missed the gentleman. Percy was the first guy I ever loved. This was the first *real* relationship I ever had. It wasn't going to be as easy to erase Percy completely from my heart. But I knew no matter what, I had to let him go.

I tossed and twisted in my bed, feeling restless and crazy confused. The terrible things Percy said to me kept revolving around in my brain. How could Percy fix his mouth to call me a sloppy black slut? I thought I was his ebony doll.

Did Percy love me, or did he not? Had this all been a bad dream? My mind was such a murky mess right now. I desperately needed to talk to someone. But who?

I couldn't talk to my closest friends. I was too embarrassed to admit that I had gotten myself hit. I could already hear Felicia saying, "I told you so," and I could already picture Jeselle, clapping her hands and yelling, "Stomp Percy out!"

Tisha was the only person I could talk to. But she was about to leave on her honeymoon. I wasn't sure of the exact date, but she was headed to Paris soon enough, and didn't need to be hearing any drama from me.

Still, I desperately needed to talk to someone. I battled myself on whether to call Tisha or not, and finally lost the battle. I had to call her ASAP, or I was about to lose my freaking mind.

Tisha usually turned her phone off after hours, so I planned to leave a message on her cell phone, marked *urgent*. I quietly crept downstairs to make the call before the whole house woke up.

I anticipated voice mail. So imagine my dismay when Tisha answered her phone in a groggy voice.

"Oh, my gosh, I'm so sorry," I stuttered. "I didn't mean to wake you."

"Kate? What's wrong?" Tisha asked in a worried tone.

"Well . . . you told me to call you if I ever needed your advice. I really need it now."

"Why? What happened?" she asked, now sounding more alert.

I gave her a brief summary of my relationship with Percy, saving the slap for last.

I could almost hear Tisha's bottom lip hit the floor. "Please tell me you're okay."

"Yeah, I'm okay," I said. "And don't worry . . . I'm not planning to go back to him. I'm just feeling a little confused right now. I can't understand how things went so wrong, so fast."

"Well, just be glad Percy showed you his true colors so soon. Some guys can hide their craziness for years."

"True."

"Do you love him?"

"I don't know . . . well, no . . . not anymore."

"Did you sleep with him?"

"No . . . but I was going to."

"Just be glad you didn't. You saved yourself from a complete loser. I can't believe he laid his hands on you."

I didn't want Tisha to get the idea that Percy was a *complete* loser, so I told her about all the nice things he had done for me. But Tisha wasn't having that. "Kate, I'm sorry to tell you, but abusers do nice things to *keep* you, not because they *love* you."

"Oh . . . okay . . . well, it's just that . . . I guess a small part of me is just wondering if this was a one-time thing . . . him hitting me, I mean . . . nobody's perfect, and—"

Tisha cut me off before I could complete my sentence. "Listen, a pigeon-toed guy isn't perfect, a guy who talks with his mouth full isn't perfect, but a guy who disrespects you and puts his hands on you is damaged goods. Send Percy back, without looking back. It never gets better, Kate. It only gets worse."

I remained silent, taking in the power of her words.

Tisha continued. "Listen, as much as I love my husband, if Greg hit me today, I'd be signing divorce papers tomorrow. Trust me, I don't play that. Greg would be straight out of luck. Do you hear me?"

How could I *not* hear her? Tisha was yelling in my ear now. And when I made the mistake of saying, "Feels like I'm always out of luck . . . I'm the original bad luck girl," Tisha started yelling even louder.

"Kate, bad luck has nothing to do with what happened to you! You *chose* to walk into this relationship with your eyes closed. You bumped your damn head, and now I'm knocking some sense into it. Don't ever let a man make you feel like you're nothing, like he's doing you a favor by being with you. How many times do I have to tell you, you're worth more than that?"

I was sniffling over the phone now. This was all so hard, so embarrassing.

"I don't understand you, Kate. Last year, you let some girl make you feel like you weren't good enough to be with her, and this year you got some guy doing the same thing? This isn't about luck; this is about your poor choices . . . your obvious lack of self-esteem. Understand me?"

I had nothing to say.

Tisha continued. "How many times do I have to tell you that you had no choice with your parents, but you can choose more wisely when it comes to your friends and your men?"

"But I didn't *choose* Percy," I objected. "He chose me . . . and I didn't *expect* to fall in love with Percy. It just happened."

"Well, don't be *falling* in love then," snapped Tisha. "Watch where you're going next time, or you'll end up hurting yourself again. No more falling. You need to *walk* into a relationship with your eyes wide open. And when you see warning signs, you need to get out fast. Understand me?"

"Yes," I said, still sniffling. "I understand."

Tisha finally calmed down and said, "I don't mean to be yelling at you, but I'm just so shocked and upset."

She sounded *really* upset, and I didn't even mean to upset her, or keep her on the phone this long. I wanted to hang up now.

"See, I wish you would've called me before you got in this deep," Tisha continued. "You and I are long overdue for a lunch date, but I'm flying to Paris today for my belated honeymoon."

Paris *today*? Of all the days to call Tisha, I had to pick the day of her honeymoon? Worst timing in the world strikes again. Way to go, Kate.

"I'm so sorry for calling you this early," I said. "I had no idea you were leaving today."

"Listen, I'm glad you called me," said Tisha. "I have a lot going on, but I want to be there for you when I can. You understand me?"

"Thanks, Tisha."

Before getting off the phone, Tisha made me promise to have a final exit strategy with Percy. She told me it was dangerous to leave him without a plan. "Be respectful to him, but firm," she told me. "Don't give him any reason to hope he still has a chance to get back with you." Then Tisha gave me important Web sites to look at and phone numbers I could call:

www.loveisrespect.org—1-866-331-9474
National Domestic Violence Hotline—1-800-799-SAFE (7233)
www.breakthecycle.org

Apparently, I wasn't the first girl to be going through this, because Tisha had all of the info at her fingertips. I felt so protected and relieved when I got off the phone with her.

I was not alone.

There was no doubt about it now. Percy did not love me. Percy was dangerous. I had to set him completely free. It would be hard, but I had to be strong. I owed it to myself to stand up for myself, or else, fall back into Percy's dark and twisted little world.

"Hi, Kate," said a stranger's voice. A squeaky little girl's voice.

"Who's *this?*" I asked, perplexed. The only female who ever called me at the group home was Felicia—back when we were talking. This was surely not Felicia. This girl sounded like a ten-year-old. I looked at Makeba, who had handed me the phone. Confusion was written all over my face. Makeba shrugged and walked away.

"Hello, Kate?" Now it was Percy on the line.

My bottom lip hit the floor. Really? I couldn't believe his everlasting nerve. My chest tightened and heaved up and down like it does when I'm about to have a fight. How dare Percy have some unfamiliar chick calling my crib, let alone calling me *period*, after all the dirt he had done to me? Did he really think letting a few days pass would erase my freaking memory?

"Why are you calling me?" I demanded. "And why are you getting other people involved?"

"Oh, that was just my little cousin Shante . . . I didn't want to get you in trouble."

"Oh, how nice of you," I said, rolling my eyes to the ceiling.

"Listen, baby, I'm sorry about what happened between us, okay? Let's just put it behind us. I'm really sorry."

"No you're not," I snapped. I was about to go off on him, but Venus was nearby, watching TV in the living room. I didn't want her in my business. I wanted to brush my big mistake safely under the dirty carpet.

Lowering my voice, I said, "Listen, please don't call here anymore, okay?"

"Can't we talk about this in person?"

"No, we can't."

"Why not?"

"Well, this sloppy black slut is incredibly busy right now."

"Sweetheart, you know I didn't mean that, right? I was just having a bad day. Don't you know how much I love you, Kate? Can we please try to work things out?"

"There's nothing to work out," I said. "You'll never change."

"But I need you in my life, Kate. . . . Please don't do this to me."

"Do *what* to you?" I snapped. "You're the one who did it to *me*. Don't try to turn things around like you always do."

It felt so good talking back to Percy with full force. But I was about to go against Tisha's advice and completely lose my temper with him. So this back-and-forth mess had to be cut short. Luckily, the excuse of my group home's fifteen-minute rule saved my day. But it didn't save my week. I got a call from the same strange little girl every single day, and each time I had to play it off like I knew her, talk to Percy, and try my best not to cause a scene.

My cover-up routine was so exhausting. But Percy wouldn't take no for an answer. He needed to speak with me in person, he explained. He *had* to speak to me in person. "One last time."

But I knew Percy was only trying to reel me back into his tangled, drama-filled web in order to feed me more promises he would never keep. Nothing Percy could say would bait me back. I deserved so much better than Percy; and he did not deserve me. Like waking up from a deep sleep, I had finally come to my senses once and for all.

"Baby, just give me one more chance," Percy pleaded.

"Percy, it's over," I firmly said, hopefully for the last time. "Seriously, don't call here again."

Click.

Chapter 32

Bright and early in the afternoon, Ciara called for me from downstairs. "You have a visitor," she announced.

Oh really? I thought. Was it Felicia again? It was going to be so uncomfortable facing her right now. Trust me, I was planning to call her, but not just yet. I was still too embarrassed. Too ashamed.

I climbed down the stairs with my heart stuck in my throat.

The front door was cracked halfway open. Apprehensively, I inched up to the threshold to find not Felicia, but a preteen in a ponytail staring at me with big hazel eyes.

"Hi, I'm Shante."

My bottom lip hit the floor.

"Percy wants to see you," she said. "He's waiting for you across the street."

Wow. This was some bull.

Percy's blind ambition was inescapable. This guy was absolutely nuts. Not nutty over me, just plain old nuts. I was far from flattered by his persistence. Percy's persistence had nothing to do with love. Percy didn't love me. I had to keep reminding myself of this simple fact, told myself to never, never look back. The good times we shared had been a fairy tale. Our relationship was over. The End. And apparently, I needed to tell this to Percy's face because he wasn't getting it. Bad idea, but what else could I do? Him showing up at my house, and bringing little girls into the situation was not a good look. The madness could not go on. I had to set Percy straight one last time.

I didn't want Shante to witness this. She was too young to be caught up in this dramatic mix. "Wait right here," I told her. Then I went back inside the house and got Ciara. I pretended that I needed to "get busy with my man real quick" and asked her to sneak Shante past Belinda's snoring face, straight to the back porch.

"Girl, go get your freak on!" said Ciara, wearing a mischievous smile. I wished I had a reason to smile back.

I took a deep breath, and bravely stepped outside into the warm afternoon air. Percy's Avenger was haphazardly parked in front of a fire hydrant, diagonally across the street from the group home. He was sitting inside the car, apparently waiting for me to hop inside. But please, homeboy, I'm not that stupid. I was planning to stand outside in full view.

Unfortunately, just as my awful timing would have it, I spotted Jeselle and Makeba coming up the block with grocery bags in their hands. So I quickly swung open the car door and ducked inside before they saw me. I didn't want them to have a clue about what was going on. Things could possibly get ugly.

As soon as I settled in my seat, Percy reached over to give me a hug. I flinched and ducked his arm. I didn't want him ever touching me again.

"Is something wrong, sweetheart?"

Come on now. What kind of dumb as dirt question was that? Seriously, I wondered if this dude had amnesia, or something. His forgetfulness was so convincing, I almost thought *I* was the one losing my mind.

"I got something for you." Percy reached into the backseat and handed me a lovely bouquet of red roses. Lovely as they were, I didn't take them. I just looked at the flowers as blooming lies. "These are for you, sweetheart," he explained, as if I was clueless.

"No, that's okay," I said, staring him dead in the face.

"Look, I'm really sorry for what happened," said Percy, putting the roses down. He stared at me for a long time. But the intensity in Percy's light brown eyes was no longer thrilling . . . quite chilling if you ask me.

"Percy, I accept your apology, okay?" I said, looking away from him. "But I can't get back with you. I'm sorry. I just can't."

"I don't understand," he began. "Why can't we try again? Every relationship has its problems."

"Not problems like *this*. You put your hands on me. And I'm sorry . . . but I'm not putting up with that."

"But why can't you forgive me?" asked Percy, sounding about ready to cry.

"I just told you. . . . You put your hands on me." I wore a determined look on my face.

"But I didn't mean to," whined Percy. "And I promise it won't ever happen again. . . . Please, baby, don't hold this against me. I need you in my life."

I already knew where this was headed; I was wasting my time and words on Percy. "Listen, I have to go." I reached for the door.

Without warning, Percy slapped my hand away from the handle.

"So you're really trying to leave me, huh?" he demanded, bass suddenly in his voice.

I was taken aback by Percy's sudden mood flip, but then again, why was I surprised? This was exactly why I needed to leave him. Dr. Jekyll could no longer hide.

"Look . . . I just need to be by myself right now," I said in a softer voice, trying to pacify this beast.

Percy quickly calmed down. His voice spun right back to sorry-mode, like magic. "Baby, I can't afford to lose you. Are you really going to leave me over a silly mistake I made? I didn't *mean* to slap you, okay? It was just a mistake."

"A mistake?" I repeated in disbelief, my anger rising again. "Stepping on my foot would be a mistake. *Slapping* me was deliberate as hell!"

"And you're going to hold that over my head, huh? Didn't I just say I was sorry?"

"Yes, and I accepted your apology. But I just can't be with you anymore. It's over."

Suddenly Percy's face darkened.

"So you want to be with that punk, don't you?" he shouted. "That's what this is all about, isn't it? Don't lie to me, that's what this is about, isn't it?"

I couldn't take it anymore. I made a move for the door. He slapped my hand away.

"So you're saying you don't want to be with me anymore?"

I had to get out of his car. Fast. I tried to open the door again, growing very, very afraid. A single blow has been known to kill, and Percy looked like he was ready to kill me. But every time I tried the door, Percy slapped my hand away.

"Please let me go," I said, my voice quivering.

Percy started pounding the steering wheel with clenched fists as he shouted, "You promised to never leave me. Now look at you. Running to the next man."

Since his hands were currently occupied beating up his steering wheel, I took this opportunity to make my escape. I shoved open the door, jumped out the car, and was about to run across the street. But Percy caught me by the arm in the middle of the road.

Fear and adrenaline pumped through me. I was about to make a run for it again, but Percy held my arm with a vise-like grip and snatched me up into a powerful bear hug.

"Get back in the car!"

"Get off me," I yelled. "It's over. Why can't you accept that?"

Percy fixed me with a look I'll never forget. "Get back in the car," he said between gritted teeth.

"No!"

We struggled for a few painful seconds, him wrenching my arm this way and that, hurting me, scaring me.

"Get off of me!" I shouted.

"Get in the car."

"No!"

"Okay," Percy began calmly, "if that's how you want it . . . if I can't have you, nobody can."

Before I could figure out what Percy meant by these words, he dragged me to the sidewalk, shoved me up against a gate, drew back his fist, and punched me dead in my stomach. I swallowed a mouthful of air, and doubled over in pain. Nobody had ever hit me so hard in my life. A scream caught in my throat. Before I could recover from the blow, Percy hit me again, and again, and again. . . . I tried to shield myself. But he grabbed my arms and pushed them away from my face, then began to pummel me like a punching bag.

I suddenly found my voice. I started screaming at the top of my lungs. "Stop!" I cried, "Please stop!" I hoped the neighbors would hear me. Somebody. Anybody. But Gravesend was a ghost town. Not a soul around. I soon realized I had to help myself.

My whimpering turned into a battle cry.

A black blur of rage came over me. I summoned all the strength I had and tried to fight him back. With every ounce of me, I tried to fight through the pain, block his blows. But I was no match for Percy. I threw punches and missed, so weak from the beating I was taking. Percy knocked me in my eyes, my mouth. It felt like he cracked one of my front teeth. He grabbed me by my shoulders and tripped me to the ground. Then all I saw was the white of his sneaker kicking the mess out of me. I covered my face, crying hysterically. "Please stop! Please—" My throat was hoarse from screaming.

The next thing I knew, I heard Jesselle's voice hollering, "Get off her!" and then I heard Makeba yelling, "Call the cops! Call the cops!" As their voices came closer, Percy pounded on me even harder. He banged my head against the sidewalk.

Then everything went black.

Chapter 33

I woke up in a hospital bed, shivering under a flimsy light-blue gown. I looked around the stark white room, confused and disoriented. Then it all came back to me. The beating, the shouts, the madness. How long have I been here? I wondered. My whole body throbbed in pain. An IV was hooked up to my arm. Gauze and tape covered my mouth. I couldn't talk; I could barely move. I lay stock-still like a frozen slab of meat.

The nearby window let in morning sunshine. But all I wanted to do was sleep. When I finally gathered the strength to hobble to the bathroom, I looked into the mirror and stared in disbelief at my black eye, my swollen face. I looked a hot mess, like a train wreck. Then again, a train wreck would've made much more sense. I couldn't believe that the man I once loved had done all this damage to me. This was my first time in the hospital since birth; and someone who claimed to love me had put me here. As bad as I looked, there was no way I wanted anybody I knew to see me like this.

So imagine my dismay when in walks Mrs. Cooper, the very next day; she had all six girls in tow, carrying a gang of "Get Well" helium balloons. I was half embarrassed, half touched because these girls had actually come to see me. Mrs. Cooper was the first to speak. "How are you feeling, honey? Are you okay?"

I nodded my head lightly because it hurt like hell. I reached over and grabbed the pen and pad a nurse had supplied me with earlier. "I'm okay," I wrote. There was no need to stir up pity going into detail about the excruciating pain I was in.

"We can't stay long, honey," said Mrs. Cooper. "All of us aren't supposed to be up here at one time."

Jeselle stepped forward. "Please, Mrs. Cooper, they mad lax up in this hospital. They ain't even make us sign in." Jeselle plopped down on my bed. "Shoot, I'm staying with my girl for as long as I want."

If I could have moved my mouth, I would've smiled at Jeselle. If I could have moved my body without so much pain, I would've hugged her, too. I wrote, "Thanks for coming," and held it up for all to see. Everybody was quiet. Just staring at me with pity in their eyes.

Jesselle broke the ice by saying, "Well, at least the bastard is in jail where he belongs. I hope *he* catch hella beat downs while he's there."

Percy, in jail?

The words "jail" and "hospital" just didn't go with the word "love." It was so hard to believe that our relationship had started out so beautifully only to end up like this.

But then again, I was still alive, so I made it out easy compared to some. The day before the attack, I had decided to do some research on abusive relationships. I read crazy stories. Scary stories. I learned some girls have to leave their relationships in a body bag. I left that library stunned out of my mind.

I almost lost my life for love.

I was so hurt and confused by this whole sad turn of events. But the Common Grounds crew really cheered me up. I looked at my balloons, and felt so cared about, so special. As much as we misunderstood and couldn't stand each other, the group home girls were my family. When I got back, I vowed to get along with each and every one of them even better, even if I had to try that much harder.

"All right ladies, Kate needs her rest," said Mrs. Cooper, though she looked like she needed it more. Her eyes were red, but I couldn't tell if she was tired or about to cry for me.

"Hold it down, Kate!" shouted out Jeselle.

The rest of the girls smiled and waved good-bye.

After everybody left, my thoughts turned to Felicia. I wasn't planning to tell her what happened until much later. If I told her now, she'd be hassling me about getting restraining orders.

I wasn't ready for aftermath arrangements. For now, Percy was in jail and that was more than enough to comfort me . . . for now.

Later in the day, I lay in bed with my eyes closed. Then I heard voices. "I think she's sleeping," someone whispered. I opened my eyes and that someone turned out to be Felicia, standing over me with Marlon and Charles by her side. Their presence was completely horrifying.

See, my group homegirls I had quickly gotten over; we'd all seen our share of traumatic times in the system. Felicia? Well, I could even handle her company; after all, she's my best friend, the one person in the world who knows almost everything about me. But Charles and Marlon? Oh man, I was mortified. Members of the opposite sex, witnessing what one of their own had done to me. I felt sick to the pit of my stomach, as they inched up closer to my bed. I wanted to pull the covers over my head and play dead.

"Hey, Kate," the boys said in unison.

The genuine look of concern fixed on both of their faces instantly stopped me from tripping. I quickly came to my senses, realizing that Charles and Marlon had nothing to do with Percy's horrible actions. They were visiting me because they cared. They were good guys. Percy could never compare.

"Hey, girl," said Felicia, in the saddest voice I ever heard.

Felicia was holding a giant card, Marlon a bouquet of sunflowers, and Charles an adorable pink and white "Get Well" teddy bear.

I slowly sat up. A streak of incredible pain shot through my back like a bullet. I struggled to reach for my pad. Charles could tell I was struggling, so he handed it to me.

"Thank you for coming," I wrote.

All three of my friends looked at me with so much sympathy in their eyes. I tried to ignore their compassionate stares. Awkward silence filled the room. Felicia was the first to speak up. "Well, Kate, you can't deny our connection now. Something told me to call the group home to check up on you . . . and Jeselle told me everything." Charles sat down at the foot of my bed, removed his iPod earbuds, and said, "I'm so sorry this happened to you." He shook his head. "Percy is such a sorry excuse for a man."

"For real," added Marlon. "A sorry excuse."

"You deserve so much better, Kate," said Felicia.

Charles continued his train of thought. "The day I saw you with him, I *felt* something was wrong, but you played it off so well, I tried to be chill. I wish I would've stepped to him then. Trust me, though, I got mad peoples on the inside, from Rikers to San Quentin. Fly one kite and Percy is a dead man. Believe that."

I wrote, "Please, don't. He's not worth it."

"Man, listen, I'm so sorry this happened to you," said Charles, shaking his head. "I don't know what to do."

The mood in the room was getting too melodramatic. So I drew a smiley face and pointed to it. Charles forced a chuckle and touched my leg over the sheet. "You better keep your head up, you hear me?"

"Her birthday is coming up, too . . . sweet sixteen," said Felicia, trying to force a cheerful topic in the mix.

"Yeah, I remember," said Charles. "My girl is getting old."

"We all need to do something together," said Marlon.

"No doubt, I'm down," Charles replied.

Wow, I thought, Charles was so cool. Felicia and Marlon are far from his type of hangout partners, but he was still willing to hang with them—unlike Percy, the loner, who had no friends of his own and had tried to isolate me from everybody. What was I thinking getting involved with a guy like Percy? Well, I *wasn't* thinking, that was the problem. Never repeating this mess again, that was my solution.

I had too much to live for to be getting sucked into another abusive relationship. Surviving Percy was like falling off a cliff and living to tell about it. Wished I didn't have to learn the hard way, all bandaged up and in so much aching pain; but at least I had learned. Relationships are hard, but they're not supposed to hurt. I can't even picture another guy trying to control me, push me around, talk down to me. Please, I'll kick his behind to the curb and ask questions later. Felicia and Tisha were right: I deserved so much better than Percy.

And at least I now understood what a good relationship looks like: Felicia and Marlon, Ted and Lynn. No disrespect and drama in their world, just petty little arguments every now and then. So if I couldn't have the real thing, I'd rather be alone.

"I can't wait for your stitches to come out," said Charles. "I want to see that pretty smile of yours."

Charles got up and walked toward the head of my bed. He clicked on his iPod, gently placed one earbud in my ear, and the other one in his. "So Beautiful" by Musiq Soulchild was playing. Charles was looking at me with so much concern in his sparkling dark brown eyes. In an instant, a magical atmosphere flowed throughout my hospital room. Felicia and Marlon seemed to disappear.

"Want you to know . . . so beautiful," Charles sang.

"My favorite song," I wrote.

"See, you and Felicia aren't the only ones with a connection." Charles winked at me.

Charles seemed so different these days, like a changed man. So much more chill and mature. Not so thirsty for booty like before. Shucks, the old Charles would've been bumping "Birthday Sex" in my ear.

A short, burly nurse came into the room, and told my friends visiting hours were over. I needed my bandages changed.

"Get well soon, so we can hang out," said Charles. He kissed my forehead.

Felicia kissed me on the cheek. "Stay strong, we've got things to do!"

"I say we go bowling," said Marlon.

"I never bowled in my life," piped in Charles, "but I'm down!"

"Thanks for stopping by," I wrote. "I can't wait to hang with y'all."

But when I got out of the hospital, I didn't hang with anybody right away. I needed some time to myself, time to figure out why I kept getting involved with the wrong people. I had to ask myself this question, and actually answer it this time, before I repeated the same mistake.

Obviously my self-esteem wasn't where it should have been; so I needed to raise it higher, out of reach from haters and abusers. I needed to be around people who made me feel good about myself, namely people like Felicia, my eternal homegirl, who always believed in me and never put me down.

But even Felicia had a life outside of me, traveling with her parents, hanging with the Stuck-up-Duo, and of course, there was Marlon.

I had to get my own life, too.

So when school started, the first thing I did was sign up to be a math tutor; I rocked math equations like it was nothing, so might as well get in where I fit in. Then I made an appointment with Children's Services to see about becoming a mentor for a younger girl in foster care. Tisha used to continuously remind me, "There's always someone out there who has it worse than you." So why shouldn't I help another young girl make it through?

I had already helped my girls at Common Grounds. After seeing me laid up in the hospital, every single one of them vowed to keep their eyes wide open when it comes to boys and abuse. We even made a pact to reach out to each other if any one of us got trapped in an abusive relationship. "There's nothing to be ashamed of," I had told them.

Reaching out is the right thing to do. But staying quiet and hiding behind dark glasses is dead wrong, and not the way to cope with the pain. In fact, days after I had gotten out of the hospital, I still looked like a one-eyed raccoon, with a black half-moon underneath my right eye taking forever to heal. I didn't try to hide it. No sunglasses on my face.

One day, I overheard Ciara explaining my black eye to a homegirl that she had snuck into the home. The girl had stared at me longer than necessary when we were introduced. Guessed she was curious; I couldn't blame her.

I was about to come out onto the back porch where they sat, when I heard the girl say, "Oh hell no! That could never be me. Let some guy try to put his hands on me. She's stupid."

Stupid? Excuse me?

Part of me was pissed that Ciara was actually spreading my personal business; the other part was determined to set the record straight. And this was the part that had me boldly stepping outside the door with a mouthful to say. "Oh, yes, it could be you," I blurted, while pointing to my eye with no shame. "Nobody is immune from abuse. Tough girls, smart girls, pretty girls, rich girls, white girls, black girls . . . even grown women get abused. Depending on where your self-esteem is on any given day, *anybody* can fall prey. So please don't get it twisted, okay?"

The girl's eyes were big with shock, maybe from my words, or maybe because I had busted through the door out of nowhere. Whatever the case, I really hoped she understood. You never know how you'll deal with a situation until you're actually in the situation. Never thought this could happen to me. Now I knew.

When it was time to leave Common Grounds, I was actually sad to go. Dirty house and all, I had mad love for all the girls I was leaving behind. We had more bad times than good in a short period of time, but these girls had my back during my darkest hour, and I would never forget them for that. Jeselle cried the hardest when my bags were officially packed.

"Girl, you act like I'm headed to Siberia," I joked, trying to keep the mood light. "The Bronx isn't that far."

"Shut up, silly," Jeselle said, between sniffles. She hugged me so long and so tight, like she wanted to come with me. I wished I could take her, but she wasn't ready for Green Hills. Their rules were off the hook. Strict curfew, maintaining grades, actual chores—what? Jeselle would be ready to choke a chick if she had to live there.

Green Hills was everything Mrs. Cooper had promised, to my relief. Big clean home in a beautiful section of the Bronx. Nice and friendly staff, and crazy cool girls who were on the same page as me, all about their school grind. It was going to take some time for me to get used to their routine, but I was looking forward to knowing them, to growing with them. This year was all about growing and learning, and never looking back.

I'm a survivor. Always have been. Always will be.

Chapter **34**

It wasn't until the middle of September that I felt ready to return to familiar faces. It started out with a phone call from Felicia on a sun-drenched Saturday afternoon.

"Hey, Kate!" Felicia exclaimed.

"Hey, girl, what's up?"

"Marlon and I bumped into Charles on the A train yesterday. He begged me to tell you to call him. I told him that I was busy begging you to call me, too. I mean . . . we don't hang out anymore. I miss you."

I chuckled at the animation in her voice. "Well, my homework is done, chores are straight. Are you free today?"

"Totally free, but . . . Marlon is with me. . . . Is that okay?"

"Um . . . well, I—"

Before I could cop a plea, Felicia thought to say, "Why not call Charles right now? I could get him on the three-way. Maybe he can come!"

"A'ight," I said, trying to hide the excitement in my voice. I missed my homeboy, too. I hoped Mr. Fly Boy was available.

Charles answered on the first ring. Surprisingly, he was ready to drop everything and come hang with us. Felicia assured him that she'd find something for us to do on the quick tip; Google was her best friend—after me.

Sure enough, twenty minutes later, Felicia called Charles and me back via three-way, her voice mad amped like a speaker. "OMG! Jazmine Sullivan is performing at Central Park. We have to go, you guys!"

"That's what's up," I exclaimed. "What time do we have to be there? A sister is way up in the Bronx."

"Show starts at three," said Felicia. "But we should be there by at least two o'clock so we can get a good spot."

Felicia laid out the logistics like a perfect event planner. And thanks to her, we all managed to meet up at Central Park, on time, with no problems.

The day was hot and beautiful. And so was Charles. First, I was surprised to see he had cut off all his hair. His short waves were back, smooth and precise. He wore a blue and white jersey top with baggy khakis hanging off his behind just right, and he rocked super clean white K-Swiss sneakers. His dark-brown chocolate skin glistened in the sunshine.

Wow, he looked mad good, felt mad good, smelled mad good when I hugged him hello. No words were exchanged. We just stared at each other like mad. Our chemistry was crazy intense.

To deflect my feelings, I jokingly asked, "Why'd you cut off your lovely locks?"

Charles smirked. "Shoot, if I waited for *you* to braid my hair, I would've gone bald from old age!"

Suddenly feeling awful and completely embarrassed, I looked down at the ground and said, "I'm really sorry for that. My bad."

Charles touched my shoulder. "Why are you tripping, Kate? You know I'm only joking."

Flashbacks of Percy.

After all the guilt games Percy had played on me, it was hard to take a joke. But instead of explaining myself, I quickly pulled myself together, and turned my attention to my other homies. Felicia and Marlon were keeping it simple in plain white tees and baggy shorts. "Good to see y'all," I exclaimed, giving them both big hugs.

We hopped on the long, snaking line that slithered forward at a slow pace. "Man, when they gonna let a brother in?" asked Charles.

As we waited and waited, the sunbeams were starting to get to me. I looked up at the sky and said, "I really don't need to be in this sun . . . black as I am." Then I laughed at my own joke—by myself. No one else found my comment funny.

Charles cocked his head to the side and said, "I don't know what you're talking about . . . the blacker the Kate, the *sweeter* to me."

I playfully hit Charles and said, "You so silly."

But really? He was so sweet, trying to uplift me, upgrade me.

Evidently, Percy was not completely out of my system. My black eye was gone, my ribs were healed, but it would take much more time for me to fully recover from Percy's mental abuse.

Finally, the line started moving into the arena. In single file, my group trooped into a row of seats five levels high. Not bad. Kinda cool. We had a clear view of the stage. When Charles plopped down next to me, our legs touched. Electricity shot through my body like lightning. I wondered if he felt it, too.

"This is so exciting," said Felicia, sitting on the other side of me.

"I know, right!" I replied.

We had to sit through a few cool acts before Jazmine finally busted onto the stage, reppin' hard in her fabulous royal-blue outfit, glossy hair flowing in the wind. She got the crowd hype, and then started hitting them jazzy notes, rocking us from side to side. When she sung my favorite song, "I Need You Bad," Charles bent down to my ear and sung with her. "If I had you back in my land, I would prove that I could be a better man."

"Those are not the words!" I said, laughing.

"Those are *my* words I'm singing to you," Charles replied.

I smiled at him and shook my head in awe. He was so dang irresistible.

Charles peered over at Felicia and Marlon who were now leaning up against each other, holding hands. So Charles reached for my hand. But I pulled it away. Our intensity . . . it was too much for me to handle right now. I wanted Charles as bad as I needed the air I breathed, and I could feel deep in my heart that he wanted me, too; but still, I needed time. I'm not on that: on to the next one, hopping from boy to boy.

I needed to be alone for a while.

So when Felicia tried to sell me Charles as we stood on a long bathroom line after the concert was over, I had to tell her, "Fall back, Ms. Matchmaker!"

"But Charles is so in love with you!" she insisted.

"Well, if he is, then he's not going anywhere," I replied.

"Seems like he's really changing for the better, too," Felicia added. "I don't see him around the way with every girl in the world anymore."

"Time will tell," I said. "So give a sister some time, will ya?" I playfully tapped Felicia's arm.

"Okay, but don't wait too long. I'm just saying, somebody will snatch that fine boy up quick!"

I suddenly thought about Tisha and Greg, their love story twenty years in the making. "Nah, Felicia, as corny as it sounds . . . if it's meant to be, it will be."

"Okay, whatever you say," she replied with a shrug.

We joined Marlon and Charles, who were leaning up against the front gate, talking like old friends.

"So what's next?" asked Marlon, staring at Felicia with his usual lovey-dovey look.

No one had any suggestions, so I piped in. "Suddenly, I'm in the mood for hot chocolate." Maybe because Charles was so dang hot and chocolate.

"Odd choice, but I'm down," replied Charles with a chuckle. "So let's go get you some hot chocolate."

"I could use a Mocha Frappe," said Marlon, grabbing Felicia by the hand.

"Me, too," said Felicia. They walked way ahead of us down a rocky pathway. Charles slowed down to a stroll. Then he tried to hold my hand again. I let him this time.

Out of the blue, he looked over at me and said, "I just want you to know, I love being around you, Kate."

"I love being around you, too," I said, "but you already know what I've *just* been through. So please . . ."

My voice trailed off. I didn't want to start crying out of nowhere.

"Listen, Kate, I understand all of that. But please don't let Percy cheat you out of a relationship with me. We'd be so good together."

I slowly looked up at Charles. I didn't want to bring up the way he had hurt me in the past, but then again, I had to keep it real with myself and real with him, too. "Well, you weren't exactly faithful to me the first time around. Remember? Because it seems like you keep forgetting."

Charles paused and then spoke. "Okay . . . I'm not going to lie, most people *don't* change. But a few people do, and I'm one of the few. I don't run loose anymore, collecting girls' numbers for no rea- son—" He broke off his litany, whipped out his cell phone, and showed me his address book. A bunch of male names popped up as he scrolled through the list.

"See?" he said, staring at me, his eyes so serious. "Females get deleted quick these days. I don't have time for their games anymore. It's getting real old."

"Aw, that's probably just your *business* phone," I joked, keeping my defenses up.

Charles looked at me for a long minute. Then he put two fingers in his mouth and whistled to get Felicia and Marlon's attention. "Hey y'all, go ahead of us," he shouted. "We'll link back up at the entrance of the park."

"Not a problem," Felicia called back, grinning from ear to ear, clearly thinking something juicy was about to go down. Well, she was thinking dead wrong. No matter what Charles said to me, I was not about to rush into anything with him. I would stay in touch with him, watch his behavior over time, and then I'd make an informed decision based on what I saw. In other words, I would be walking into this relationship with my eyes wide open. No more bumping my head; it hurts too much.

We were standing under a tall oak tree when Charles gave my hand a gentle squeeze, and said, "Well, I hope you give me a chance someday."

A half smile touched my lips. I liked the sound of someday.

"So does that smile mean I have a chance?" asked Charles, flashing his boyish grin.

"A very good chance," I said, grinning back.

Charles, emboldened by my words, cupped my face in his warm hands, and said, "So how can I make our chances *great*?"

"By you being you, and letting me be me."

"Oh, I can definitely do that," said Charles.

I pursed my lips into a playful air kiss. Charles pretended to catch it. Then I removed his hands from my face and said, "Now that we're straight on the subject, let's go get our hot chocolate on!"

"No doubt." Charles smiled, grabbed my hand, and held it gently as we walked through the park. I snuck a glance at him and imagined his face as it would be in ten years, twenty years, thirty years. . . . I couldn't wait to grow with him, flow with him. Deep down in my heart, I knew that Charles was The One for me. The way he looked at me with so much love in his eyes could not be mistaken for anything but a strong and true connection between us. Our *someday* would most definitely come soon, but for now I had to focus on me.